THE PACKAGE

A Morghana Hamilton Novel

James Rozhon

Gotham Books
30 N Gould St.
Ste. 20820, Sheridan, WY 82801
https://gothambooksinc.com/

Phone: 1 (307) 464-7800

© 2022 James Rozhon. All rights reserved.

No part of this book may be reproduced, stored in a retrieval system, or transmitted by any means without the written permission of the author.

Published by Gotham Books (December 30, 2022)

ISBN: 979-8-88775-172-6 (sc)
ISBN: 979-8-88775-173-3 (e)

Because of the dynamic nature of the Internet, any web addresses or links contained in this book may have changed since publication and may no longer be valid.

The views expressed in this work are solely those of the author and do not necessarily reflect the views of the publisher, and the publisher hereby disclaims any responsibility for them.

Table of Contents

Prologue 7
Chapter One 13
Chapter Two 27
Chapter Three 41
Chapter Four 57
Chapter Five 73
Chapter Six 87
Chapter Seven 103
Chapter Eight 118
Chapter Nine 136
Chapter Ten 150
Chapter Eleven 166
Chapter Twelve 181
Chapter Thirteen 197
Chapter Fourteen 213
Chapter Fifteen 229
Chapter Sixteen 243
Chapter Seventeen 259
Chapter Eighteen 273
Chapter Nineteen 295
Chapter Twenty 310
Chapter Twenty-Two 329
Chapter Twenty-three 345
Chapter Twenty-four 359
Chapter Twenty-five 375
Chapter Twenty-six 387
Chapter Twenty-seven 403

Prologue

It seemed the perfect place to put an end to it. Morgahna's office. Evan Hamilton knew despair in all of its finest details and had for years. Who said it? We live lives of quiet desperation? Henry David Thoreau? That seemed correct and appropriate at the same time.

Her office. His wife's office behind their home.

Savannah.

He grew up there, knew the city and the way it worked. Morgahna knew it, too, but he doubted she knew it quite like he did. He knew the gritty parts, knew the various reasons for the dirt, knew the people who lived there, knew that they had little choice in their lives. A small smile spread like an oil slick across his face as he saw the ultimate irony. She was a reporter for the local newspaper, the Savannah Morning News. Much more than a mere job, it was a passion that she pursued with an orderly flair. Her office? Nothing was out of place, out of sync, outside her immediate control. The working assumption of her life and her profession was to know the city and how it worked. That was her job. A reporter reports on what she knows and Morgahna knew the city of Savannah, Georgia. Evan was a lawyer, a criminal lawyer, and knew far more of the insidiousness of the city than Morgahna could ever know. The pity was that he loved his wife and always had. It was, however, never enough. In some small way, she was too controlled but not controlling. That was a fallacy of perception, of people thinking long before the brain had a chance to catch up to their mouth. It was people, it was life and it was the way the world worked in all its subsumed glory.

The gun was heavy in his hand.

Another small irony was the blood that would splatter the area around where he sat. Part of him sought ways to minimize the mess she would face, but that part of him stopped caring long ago.

Morgahna was perfect, absolutely perfect and lived her life to that expectation. Her planner was furiously full and she meticulously charted the progress of her life against that book. She was a charging twenty-seven-years-old and he was not quite two years her elder. In the

Prologue

beginning, her strict forward course through her own life pushed him along in her wake and he found himself sloughing off the unnecessary baggage that his mind insisted on keeping aboard. Unfortunately, she had such little creativity, such a scarce amount of curiosity that he wondered about her job and what her superiors thought of her. How could she function? How could she see the curves in the road, see the people for what they wanted instead of for what they said?

Children.

She did not want children and that was something of a plus. They did not fit into her view of the world. Children were a distraction from her chart, from the way she had her life planned out. "Evan?" she said to him once. "Before I'm thirty, I want to own a home worth half a million dollars and have a quarter of that available in liquid assets."

Evan.

She had no warm nickname for him. He called her, "My minx." It bestowed upon her attributes she did not have and did not seek. Morgahna was never precocious and never seductive. To her, sex was a bother that men, that he, inflicted upon her. Her sexiest piece of lingerie was a vanilla white bra from Sears.

Was that it, though? Sex?

No, it was far more than that. Despite his love for her, he wanted an intangible, something that he could not quite see, nor quite grasp. His own goal included a visit to The Pyramids in Egypt, a thing that would never happen, not now, not before now either. A vacation, an extended one would include at least two weeks away from chasing the brass ring of Success. She had no hobbies except work, no friends away from the job except Debbie Jenson, a girl with some enthusiasm for life that exasperated Morgahna endlessly for being "frivolous". He liked Debbie and always had.

She worked seven days a week, never resting, sometimes simply crashing and sleeping for twelve hours only to awake in a full sprint toward the horizon that she chased with a relentlessness that seemed born of impatience. That lack of creativity he saw in her was replaced by a conscious and logical pursuit of stories and angles designed to make an impact on her boss and her career. Never dishonest, never crass or cruel, she dismissed as worse than unnecessary but as entirely pointless, the southern preconception with race. The new rainbow was made from Profit, from the endless machinations of scores of Capitalists who always tried to undercut the bottom line by gouging anyone in their sights. A very close second was terrorism and the veiled threat it held for everyone. Evan saw no dangers at all, saw only the fear that the unknown held for people. Morgahna capitalized on that fear by writing about it and chiding people for their stupidity.

The day was warm and humid, a spring day that hinted at endless summer. The room could be a garage, a place for him but was an office for her. There were times when he paced restlessly around the house because he wanted her, not sex, just wanted a piece of her time. Morgahna had the ability to drive him to a franticness that was almost despairing. She could slide her brown hair behind her left ear, smile coyly at him as though it was a conscious act and that image would tear at him with a ruthless energy that she never contemplated at all. She was five-seven, just tall enough for him. Once when they went to Charleston for a short weekend – from Saturday afternoon to Sunday evening – he chided her for not buying a pair of burgundy heels that would have highlighted her outfit perfectly. Her tallest shoes were two-inch stubbies that did nothing for her at all.

She had great legs.

He sighed and held the gun in his lap. It was the perfect answer for his pain and for what he'd done. He knew she would find out one day and then realize why this was necessary.

Would it hurt?

That was no inhibition for him. His life was pain and this last one would be insignificant.

The only remaining question was easy.

Would he miss her, miss Morgahna Hamilton?

The answer was always yes. He loved her and would miss her. The sheer amount of energy she had to point at the world was phenomenal. She seldom slept for more than six hours and never seemed to tire except during those binge sleeps she did infrequently. Even being a lawyer and having a heavy workload, he couldn't match her pace. Her

Prologue

freakish control of her life given that pace was mesmerizing, extremely so. So, yes, he would miss her and would never get that answer. Would she ever stop and see the details of life? Would she ever become curious as to why he could no longer endure the life he was leading?

That left only this, his last answer.

His life, that of a lawyer was in finding answers for his clients, legal ones. His partner, Tom Underwood, would know why he did this but he doubted Tommy would tell her. Call it the ultimate answer in client privilege. He began a slow smile as he saw his wife hounding Tommy for The Answer. "Why, Tommy?" she would ask with persistent clarity. "Why did he do this?" Tom was as secretive as any lawyer he ever met but Evan was glad the man was his partner. Nothing escaped him and few tried to fool him. Those that did were turned away empty and wiser. He knew, however, that Morgahna was far more insistent and far more capable of prying answers from a wall than anyone he knew. If anyone could find out, it was his wife.

There were no tears of regret. His sin was too heavy and not one he wanted to inflict on her.

In the end, it was the only way he could see. To continue past this point was to know endless frustrations and pointless agony. People said he was a dreamer but he totally disagreed. He liked the broken continuity of life, the way lines never went as straight as Morgahna wanted. He liked the variables and inconsistent pace, the variations in color, the way blue was not always blue, the way circles were sometimes ellipses. He liked bookstores and prowling through them with the thoroughness of a burglar. He loved museums and the way they provided a unique window on the past, the way he one day would be one of those windows. He loved rainy days and puddles, loved kittens and the promise they bestowed on those who held them, loved Morgahna's face and the way she smiled when she was content.

He closed his eyes and saw her dimples, the same ones that she saw as childish, the same ones he saw as being dynamic and adding something to her personality that she desperately wanted to hide as being beneath her dignity.

Another irony.

Maybe this would remove those dimples once and for all.

Maybe this would cause her to stop smiling.

No.

If he changed his mind and didn't do this, he would ruin her perceptions and reasons to get up in the morning. It was not proper to inflict his failures on her.

He would miss the way her hair curled gently to her shoulders.

The way she was light on her feet.

Her voice.

The way her lipstick tasted.

The way his arm could curl around her waist.

The way her nose wrinkled when she laughed.

Her voice and the way it flowed like the river beyond the wharves.

Her energy.

Her ass under a skirt.

He put the gun in his mouth and pulled the trigger before he could change his mind and ruin her life as well as his own.

The blood splattered the wall behind him, splattered their marriage certificate that Morgahna hung where she could see it.

It was over for him.

And just starting for her.

There were things even lawyers did not foresee.

Chapter One

I was screaming at Tommy, my voice to that level where merely understanding the words I spoke was almost impossible. I was being vile, vocal and profane. The house was a mess, my work largely unfinished and woefully inadequate. My boss was screaming at me in the same manner I was screaming at Tommy. I hadn't combed my hair in three days and my breath smelled like a sewer only because I'd gotten drunk last night and had yet another hangover. "Fuck you, Tommy! Get out! You have no right to be here! Get out!"

Tommy Underwood was my husband's partner and I hated him with the full fury of a grieving widow. In any other condition, in any other time, I'd call him handsome, look twice and go about my work.

Work.

That's all I've ever done.

My name is Morgahna Hamilton and I killed my husband.

That was six weeks ago and I still see his body in my mind. It was late in the day, nearly eleven o'clock in the evening. Taylor Street in Savannah was quiet; the sky was cloudy and I still had more work to do. This is why I never wanted children. They simply would have gotten in the way of my fucking precious schedule and goals I kept for myself. I dropped my purse next to the coffee pot, made a fresh pot and flexed my shoulders as I waited for it to perk. Those five minutes were all the break time I ever allowed myself. My mental clock was ticking like it always had, like I always assumed it would. I was scheduled to do a series of articles on the Port of Savannah and I needed to do some background work for it. Another sixteen-hour day. For me, that was normal. A hundred hours a week and two forced weeks of vacation every year, weeks I took sparingly, a day at a time.

That cup of coffee was going to be my bulwark until two in the morning when I would sleep until eight and then rush back to work where I'd huddle with Dave Woods about our port story. Then, I'd run off to a staff meeting, work on my story about gangs in the city and then get the first look at my story about River Street and the plans for the next St.

Chapter One

Patrick's Day Parade. Juggling that cup of coffee and my purse, I hurried out into the courtyard and headed to my office that fronted Jones Street behind the house.

I've never been an intellect despite my degree in journalism. I have, however, always been competent. Deathly, so. If given an assignment, I will run it down, hogtie it and completely suffocate it with my enthusiasm if not my skill. That night? I never even noticed the lights were on inside the office. I just skipped down the steps sipping at my coffee, hunching my right shoulder in order to keep my purse on it and walked into something worse than Dante's Inferno because my soul started burning and has yet to stop.

State of mind. Mine.

I lost it and have no idea, no memory at all of my initial reaction. If pressed, I would admit to stark and total fear that this *thing* was all too real. Actually, if pressed hard enough, I would admit to being legally dead for several long empty minutes. Coherency was not something I could admit to, not then. In fact, as a cement for that feeling, I saw a murder scene and not what it was. I may have even screamed that word, "Murder!" It would take another two weeks before I could even speak that word, speak the word "suicide". The way I saw it, that made me guilty of killing him, of being the thing that drove him off that cliff of deep despair and wild depression.

Ever since that night, I have drifted farther and farther from the shores of mental clarity and lucidity. Tommy was losing patience with me as I screeched at him. I had no notion of what I was doing, saying or why any of this was happening *to me*.

I never sought counseling.

I never sought out a friend.

I never visited Evan's grave.

I didn't throw away his clothes.

In fact, a part of me absolutely refused to believe this was real. Psychosis? Well, thy name is Morgahna Jayne Hamilton. Evidence? That night, the night Tommy came by to see if I was coping any better, I was wearing the same dirty clothes that he'd seen me in three days before and couldn't care less if I ever changed them again. I was sitting in the middle of my bed, *our* bed, and looking at pictures I had of Evan, ones where he was smiling and happy. I remember talking to him and expecting an answer. Not getting one would send me off into hysterics that had been ongoing ever since his funeral.

Tommy finally managed to get his arms around me and just held me as he said, "Jaynie, baby? I miss him, too. Life goes on, though. You can't keep doing this. Come on. Let's take a walk down to Forsyth Park and stroll around the fountain." To him, I was Jaynie, not Morgahna. That seemed too imperious to him, so he adopted a nickname for me. Jaynie. I hated that name. It sounded artificial and brazen, like a creation of Hollywood.

"Let me go, Tommy," I said defiantly.

"Get a shower and come with me, okay? We can walk and talk. You can get your life back together."

I have never been anything but a girl and I mean that in the purest sense. I know nothing about self-defense and have never contemplated learning it. I don't carry a gun, don't own one and can never foresee the need for one, not even in self-defense. Where Evan got that gun, I will never know. The police said it was his, registered to him. That small fact, that gun, blossomed inside my mind and began to dominate everything I thought I knew about my husband, Evan Hunter Hamilton. Perception versus reality seeped into my life in uneven quantities after that. For example, that gun. Why did he need it? Why? To take himself away from me. I drove him to it. I never saw that gun for what its intended purpose was. Self-defense.

"I don't want my life back together, you imbecile. I want to sulk and be miserable. Leave me alone, damn you."

Swearing is not easy for me. Well, it was or used to be. Now? I can roll off a line of cursing so strong that longshoremen down at the port would blush.

"Jaynie? Please. This is killing me."

Well, an idea surfaced and I calmed myself, just let my muscles go limp and I actually gave him a small smile. "Tommy? Really. I'm

Chapter One

okay. I was going to the shower when you came in. I'm tired of living this way. I need to get back to work."

That was about as far from the truth as New York is from Honolulu. I was erratically emotional and my mind kept insisting I killed my husband though I couldn't see the mechanism of it at all. My nerves were frayed, my mind was a jumble of conflicting self-hatreds and this well-meaning man was only trying to help me.

So, naturally, I lied to my husband's best friend.

Tommy has hair that is real handy on St. Patrick's Day, it's as red as any Irishman you will ever meet. One year, he dressed up in drag with the help of a girlfriend that taught him how to walk in regally tall heels. Then I asked *him* to teach me how to walk in them only because the arches on my feet always scream whenever I try to wear anything four inches or higher. Thus, I don't own any and those lessons only resulted in sore feet. Now? I wish I was wearing a pair of good spikes because I'd stomp his insole and get him off of me.

"You sure, Jaynie?"

I smiled and tried to make it look demure. "Yeah. Really."

"You want to take that walk?"

Well, actually, I'd rather he pulled out my teeth one at a time with a pair of pliers. "Tommy? Look at this place," I said. "I need to clean it up some. I'll pass, okay?"

"You sure?"

"Yeah," I said and tried to force a blush. Men always like that stuff. I can't say I've never blushed but never around Tommy Underwood either. Starting now was not an option, though I tried.

"You okay, Jaynie?"

Another smile and this a time I gave him a minor threat. "You keep calling me 'Jaynie' and I'm going to pretend I'm fishing and gut you like a catfish."

"Atta girl," he said. "Can I stop by in the morning?"

"Whatever, Tommy."

"I'll be here."

I live at 301 West Taylor Street in Savannah. It's on the corner of Taylor and Jefferson, not far from the civil rights museum and Interstate 16. That park Tommy talked about? Forsyth Park? Well, that's four blocks away over on Gaston Street and has a huge and very photogenic fountain in it. It is, without doubt, the most photographed fountain in the city and the city has lots of photogenic places. Living in Historic Savannah bestows a certain gentility on me that I have always cultivated like a rare flower. I wear easy shoes and wouldn't wear heels even if they didn't hurt my feet. I have no desire to look like a streetwalker. And yes, I have been known to wrap a sweater around my shoulders as I work and play. I love the casual image even if I am not casual at all. I have always been a high maintenance broad. Well, woman. I hate being called a broad. It's disrespectful and I apologize for my own slip. Tommy hugged me and I tolerated it. I hate being hugged by people that aren't married to me.

As soon as the door closed, I said hotly to it, "And fuck you, too, Tommy. You didn't kill Evan. I did."

My plan was simple. I was going to get stinking drunk.

Again.

I love scotch and love it sparingly. Getting drunk on it, however, makes all that pain go away and as soon as I saw Tommy's new T-Bird pull away from the curb down by the stairs, I went to the cupboard where the Dewar's bottle was less than half full. My plan was simple: I was going to talk to Evan and keep talking to him until I heard him answer me. Why did you do this? What did I do to force this on you? What pain was so deep that this was your only answer? Mostly, though, I had one question that addled my mind every time I thought of it. Why couldn't you talk to me? That first shot always goes down hot and hard. My eyes watered and, baby, I was on my way.

Then, the phone rang.

Well, Yankees and tar and feather, too.

It was just after ten o'clock in the evening and the only person that could be calling me that late was my editor, Harley Hood. Without even checking the Caller ID screen on the phone, I answered it and said with impatient irritation, "What is it?"

Chapter One

My bedroom, *our* bedroom, was always my room, never his. It is entirely a room that belongs to a girl, a female, a woman. It is not a man's room at all. Evan just hung his clothes here in a closet beyond my view. That office outside and beyond the garden? It could be a garage, a woodshop, could hold a pool table, anything but my office. You know? I have an office upstairs that I never use. Why? Because Evan could too easily interrupt my work inside the house. Putting *another* office outside was doubly cruel and I wondered now why I ever did that to him.

As I sat there cross-legged on the bed, sat there amid all of his pictures and all of his memories, that voice turned *black,* negro. It spoke with hesitancy, briefly, spoke quietly as though afraid. "Missus Hamilton?" it asked in a soft drawl that angered me a little. Why did it anger me? Look, I don't know. That voice was Old South, full of black deference to a white master. That's how and what it felt like. Missus Hamilton. It beckoned legions of slaves to seek the shelter of the white mistress of the manner. I felt, always felt, that America was past all that stuff, all that racism. The sixties died over forty years ago and the problems with it.

"Yes?" I said. "Who is this?"

The voice belonged to a squeaky female, a mouse that nervously stuck its head from its hole. "Um, Evan…" and she hung up the phone, the mouse retreating in the face of a snapping and snarling cat that would corner it.

Maybe it is true that women understand telephones in a way that eludes men altogether. Maybe. Personally, given that Evan was a lawyer and Tommy was his best friend, I think that's nonsense. More evidence? Well, Caller ID works both ways and I know that, know that because I have used that device so many times over the past few years that when I paused and stared at that phone for *several minutes,* I was dumbfounded later on when I thought about it. Had I merely redialed the phone as soon as she hung up, things might have been different. Again, maybe. Being a reporter for a newspaper, I don't hang much heat on that word. Maybe the Yankees swept the Red Sox in the 2004 ALCS. Maybe they did. Well, they didn't. Maybe the Braves haven't a division championship in thirteen years. Well, they've won their division in each of those past thirteen years, so you can see what I think of that word. Maybe stinks. So, since I didn't call that number as soon as she hung up, I got a deep voice that said, "Sugarplums."

"Sugarplums?" I said. "River Street?"

"Yeah," the voice said as though I was a bit *deficient*.

"I just a got a call from this number. A girl."

"Lots of girls here. Which one you want?"

Sugarplums was a bar-*cum*-restaurant down there that catered to the upscale crowd. The bartenders were muscular and the waitresses were tiny. One looked like they needed the other. Women loved the place. "The one that called me. Is this a public or a private phone?"

"Neither. It's my phone."

"Who are you?"

"Tony. Who are you?"

"Morgahna."

"Cool name. You looking for a job?"

I'm not much for impulse shopping. Oh, I love to shop and Evan always said he liked shopping with me, but now I wonder. However, my reporter's brain was screaming with the force of a foghorn out on Tybee Island where the lighthouse stands. I have learned to listen to that voice because when I ignore it or simply fail to heed its warning, I usually suffer. Well, professionally, maybe. There was something, however, inside me, something that was telling me this girl, my husband and that bar meant more than a mere late-night phone call. Exactly what it meant, I didn't know but desperately wanted to find out.

So...

I said, "Yeah. I need a job."

"How tall are you?"

"Five-seven."

"Fatty?"

"No," I said. "I work out."

Chapter One

"Muscular."

"Feminine."

"Can you be here in an hour?"

"Yeah."

"You know where it is?"

"Yeah."

"See ya," and *he* hung up.

I put the glass of Dewar's on the nightstand and ran to the bathroom and the shower in particular. I peeled off all my clothes and jumped into the shower for the first time in three days. Fortunately, taking a shower, for me anyway, is brainless. I wash myself in the same way every time I get into it, do the same things in the same sequence and have done them that way since I was eight. As I showered, my mind kept pushing at that small voice, that black and very faintly feminine voice that asked about my husband. Who was she and did Evan know her? Was I jealous? Jeez, no. He was lawyer, a criminal lawyer, and as such could very easily have known her that way. Evan knew a lot of people that I would never allow into my home. More than once, I said, "No, Evan. We have valuables here." How many people did I miss because the things of my life were more important than the people in it?

So, why did I want to do this? Well, that was easy. Who would call me at ten o'clock at night and use his first name? That was a mystery, a question, to which I needed an answer. Clients would call him Mr. Hamilton and defer to him that way, not by using his familiar name.

Since it was a family place, I dressed conservatively and that is something I've done a lot of in my life. I actually wore a sweater to my senior prom. A sweater. At least it wasn't wrapped around my shoulders. I remember three-inch heels and feet that screamed like a Marine drill instructor. Evan once asked me to dress up for him and I didn't have anything that fit his criteria for the erotic. I promised to buy something and never did. Being sexy for him, for anyone, was *never* a priority. All that meant was that applying for a job at a conservative family restaurant was something I could dress for. Thank god for small favors.

I am, also, a Republican. Democrats have always seemed rather reckless to me.

I wore very loose dark brown slacks, a high-button white cotton blouse and a very modest gold chain necklace that was mostly buried under the folds of my collar. To top off my outfit, I slid a headband across my head and pulled my hair back in the best imitation of Betty Crocker I could manage.

And flats.

I was ready for a new job.

Well, I was ready to see where this went. I have a job even if Harley is a bit pissed at me right now. He lost his wife to breast cancer four years ago and he has no sympathy for me. Oh, he tries to act kindly only because he's a southern gentleman and that role requires a submissiveness in the women around him. Submissive? I once shined his shoes in his office at a staff meeting. Honest-to-fucking-God. Spit-shined them. Technically, I am on a paid administrative leave which *probably* means I'll be fired when I go back to work on Wednesday next week. That was actually one of the reasons I was drinking because I love my job. Being a reporter is all I ever wanted to do or be. I actually wrote stories when I was twelve and pretended to publish them in a newspaper that I drew longhand on legal-sized paper. The Daily Morgahna News. That's what I called it. In it, I wrote about everything my family was doing and why I thought my brother, Mark, was a deviant life form from the planet Xephon. This, however, was Thursday night and I was going undercover, a thing I always found romantically fascinating but practically useless, practically speaking.

As soon as I was out the door and down the stairs, my tenant, Albert Daniels, came outside and said, "Hey, Morgahna. How are you?"

Tenant.

Okay, I probably need to explain that one to you Yankees.

The home is *technically* a three-story townhouse. I live on what you would call the second and third stories while the first story is a rental. Albert shares that level with a lady named Shannon. He's husky and muscular and she's tall and stupid. Okay. Translated, that means she has bigger boobs than I do. It doesn't help that she's blond and a student at

Chapter One

the Savannah College of Art and Design. Jesus, she looks like she could be a madam in a whorehouse or a true Southern Belle. She actually talks like she's *from* Savannah although I know she's from Decatur, Illinois.

"Okay, Al," I said. "I figured it was time to stop sulking."

He smiled and it looked good. Albert Daniels is a very handsome specimen. You know? I never noticed? I mean, seriously. He's the kind of man on whose face you want to sit and squirm. Lord Almighty, didn't *that* make my compassionate conservatism stand on its hind legs and beg for mercy.

"That's good, Mrs. Hamilton," he said. "Evan was a good man, but life needs to be lived."

"How's Shannon?"

"Good. She's good."

One of the reasons I rented to them was privacy. I didn't want to become a *landlord*. I wanted a tenant that could and would be as self-sufficient as possible. The reason should be self-evident. I was always working and being a landlord required certain obligations that I just didn't want to meet. So, I rented to the first people that met that criteria. Albert and Shannon made enough money to afford the rent and they never bothered me, so they were perfect.

"Al?" I said. "Gotta go. Got a date down at Sugarplums."

"A date?" he said with a secret smile.

Well, damn. I am nothing but a southern conservative with conservative values and I always vote Republican.

So.

I *had* to stop and clarify what I meant. Dating, for me, was out. Completely out for *at least* a year. That was me, my values, and I couldn't allow them to become muddled with misleading innuendos. "Oh, I got a weird phone call from Sugarplums and I'm going to find out who made it and why. Nothing worse than that."

Al just smiled and said, "Being a reporter again, huh?"

That made me blush. "Well, I guess so," I said because it felt that way. I hadn't felt like a reporter in six weeks, not since I walked into that horribly disgusting scene and began to blame myself for what happened to my husband.

My own identity was always wrapped around my profession, the one I wanted ever since my eighth birthday. It got me through college, through high school and its attendant inanities. It excluded me from a lot of childhood friendships because kids my age saw me as a snitch and many of them refused to befriend me. It has always been my own personal monomania. I have, however, learned to live with it. That meant stopping occasionally and explaining what my latest explosion meant and that it was entirely harmless. A date? Oh, no, no, no. I seldom even dated Evan, my monomania was that overwhelming.

We were married for five years and in that time, I can't honestly say we had a blazing romance going. Yes, I loved him. Period. Seeing him like that, seeing what I drove him to do was still killing me and if that voice, that girl, knew anything, I had to know. Did she know him? If not, then why was she asking about him? If she did, then why call me from a place like Sugarplums?

Al said, "Well, that's good, Mrs. Hamilton. You need to do stuff, you know? You need to start living again."

"Thanks, Albert. I'm trying."

I drive a black BMW Z3 coupe and somehow that seemed a bit much for any job I could get at a place like a restaurant that doubled as a bar. It was too far to walk and make my appointment at the time I told Tony I would be there. It meant driving down toward River Street and parking several blocks away. If pressed, I would say I took a bus. Admitting to driving a Z3 was not going to get me in there.

It was a humid night, another one in Savannah. The few stars that were visible blinked in and out from behind passing clouds. Mostly, though, the city lights obscured them. Me? I *never* looked at the stars. My feet were always on the ground and that's exactly where I always wanted them. For that matter, it could have been raining and I wouldn't have cared much. What mattered to me was a direction and the proper direction was always the one I was following.

Chapter One

The lights along the river were always bright. As a tourist haven, it was almost perfect. Most of the shops along the street catered to them and the few serious bars were obvious. Most of River Street, the current version anyway, has been fashioned from old cotton warehouses. Some of the stores and bars used to be hotels and office buildings. The city has done a commendable job in converting a mess into an attraction.

Sugarplum's is right up Drayton Street. Just follow it to the end, go to River Street and you're there. Of course, I had to do it a bit different than that. I drove downstream a bit, just followed the Savannah River a few blocks over, parked in a lot and walked the remaining few blocks to the restaurant. River Street never closes and that doesn't really surprise me. There are places along the street, along the river that are a lot like me, always going. I found the place and entered it as though entirely sheepish and withdrawn. What would it take here? Would shy and reserved win or would brash and outlandish? The place, or at least the restaurant end of the business, was closed. The bar was open for another two hours. I walked up to a huge bartender and said, "Tony?"

"Doug."

"I'm here to see Tony for an interview." The place was almost empty; a few people were here and there, none of them tourists. A old juke box played something from ZZ Top, something about legs. I hate that group. Weirdoes and zombies. I swear, music gets stranger and weirder as time goes by.

"I'll get him," he said. "Wait here."

That was no problem. I slid onto a barstool and realized I hadn't done much of that in my life. Lately, my benders have been done at home in my bed. That's me, a conservative drunk. I won't get drunk anywhere except where I can pass out safely. I played with my fingers because I still saw Evan, still saw that blood splattered across the wall where he lay slumped back in that chair. I don't think that image will ever go away, not entirely. I sighed and was faced with a big man, another one.

"I'm Tony Slayton," he said, his head bald and perfect. *Another* man on whose face I would love to sit and squirm. His neck was as thick as his arms and his voice was deep and rugged. He reached across the bar and said, "Morgahna?"

"Yes, sir," I said standing and taking his hand. "Morgahna Hamilton."

His smile was friendly and he nodded toward the restaurant end of the business. "Let's go on back to my office back there. That okay?"

There were a few other people in the bar, those few plus him and the bartender whose name I knew only as Doug. Tony walked ahead of me as we entered into a sea of empty tables. He stopped, turned on a bank of lights that converted the whole place into one expectant of customers and life. He stood aside, his bulk formidable but his smile still friendly. He nodded toward a doorway beyond the cash register and said, "My office? We can sit in there and talk. Is that acceptable?"

"Certainly," I said easily and looked at the tables, the place settings and wondered if I could really be a waitress. It seemed easy enough and I had the energy for it. The way I saw it, I had enough energy to power a nuclear generating station.

There was an area behind the grill that was probably saved for clocking in and out. Beyond that was a door that was his office. He was behind me as I walked through the empty kitchen and passed the small storage areas on the way to his office. He leaned forward, opened the door and gestured me inside. The room was utilitarian and that meant basically empty. His desk had a flat screen on it, a keyboard in front of that. There was a thick ledger next to a pencil holder that was full of a mixture of both pens and pencils; a protractor stuck up between them like a radar mast. He gestured again, this time to a chair and said, "Have a seat and let's get started."

I sat easily and decided I was going to ace this interview.

He drew a pad of paper from his desk, a yellow legal pad and made himself ready to take notes. "Your name?"

"Morgahna Hamilton, sir."

He smiled. "I'm just Tony," he said easily, lightly.

"Okay, Tony."

He was about to ask another question when he stopped, held up his index finger and said, "Oh, excuse me. I forgot something." He punched a button on his desk phone and said cheerfully, "Hey, Doug? Can you come down here for a minute? I forgot your paycheck."

"Sure," Doug said. "Be there in just a second."

Tony looked a bit flustered. "See what being shorthanded does to you?"

"I'll bet," I said.

"Any experience?" he asked with a warm smile. I liked Tony.

"No," I said. "Is that bad?"

He grinned and said, "Not necessarily."

The door opened and it was Doug. He smiled at Tony, then at me and approached the desk. I turned back to Tony as Doug walked up behind me. As I was looking at him, a hand went over my face, a rag went over my mouth and nose and he lifted me from the chair with an easy motion. The smell was faintly sweet and I tried to hold my breath and fight back. The problem was I was a girl, had always been a girl and they had no trouble subduing me.

I looked up at Tony and he smiled. "Just breathe deeply, lady. It will over soon."

I began to lose consciousness, then I blacked out entirely.

My life as I knew it had changed entirely and abruptly.

It was worse than a u-turn.

It was a crash into a cement wall going eighty miles per hour.

I'd say it hurt, but that's probably redundant.

Chapter Two

Wherever I was, I was groggy and slightly wobbly. Each time I was almost fully awake and cognizant, something went back over my mouth and nose and I slowly faded like an old dream. Then, after a while, the blackness lifted again and I felt myself being held down by powerful hands. As the fog slowly lifted, I realized I was being held face-first in a man's crotch. My hands were free but they did me little good. Whoever was holding me was far stronger than me and my best efforts to free myself. Also, we were driving over very uneven ground. My guess was we were in the country somewhere. The vehicle stopped and the passenger door opened into a thickly wooded world that could have been anywhere from north Florida to eastern Alabama. I screamed a call for help.

Then I got punched and felt my lip split.

Blood splattered down my chin and I moaned painfully, the entire left side of my face little more than agony covered by bloody flesh. Someone had me by my right wrist and was literally dragging me through the underbrush. Branches, twigs, tree stumps, all manner of obstructions hit and batted at me until a tall canopy of leaves and branches shadowed a narrow tree trunk and that was all I saw. Hard hands pushed me up to the trunk and stronger hands tied mine behind it with wire that was twisted around my wrists until I felt it cut through the skin as blood began to seep down onto my hands.

It was Tony and Doug, the two men from the Sugarplum's.

One of them put a flashlight directly in my face and I saw nothing, had to squint to keep from going blind. I begged them, "Why are you doing this?" I was confused and disoriented. I tried to raise my hand to wipe away the blood that was rolling down my chin but that wire was firm and the blood dripped onto my chest.

Something long and hard, a long metal tube of some sort I think, crushed the cheekbones in my left cheek and came very near to knocking me unconscious. Then another shot to my left chest cracked something and I could barely breathe. Each breath returned wracking pain and then

Chapter Two

that metal tube or rod hit my stomach with full force and I lost the ability to breathe at all. The last thing I remember was something cracking hard on the left side of my head, bright lights, a sizzling in my ears and then nothing.

Before all this happened, I was no more than ordinary. Maybe a little more energetic than most people, but I cannot believe I was anything but ordinary. I was pursuing a career that many people before me pursued with the same energy that I applied to it. Even my marriage was no more than ordinary. Had Evan lived to a ripe old age, it is very possible we might have divorced somewhere along the line. In all, however, I was attacking my ordinary life with extraordinary energy and courage. No one and nothing got in my way, no one made a dent in my own timetable for success. I was chasing that brass ring with unparalleled enthusiasm and not bothering to look to either side and certainly not behind me. I was focused and uncommonly so.

All that, however, was in my distant past, my very distant past.

As the buzzing faded from my ears, I awoke to intense pain all over my body and something like that brings you awake immediately. I could barely see and what light I saw was fuzzy. Everything was indistinct and only my hearing worked and even that was precarious as the buzzing was still audible in both ears.

Someone spoke.

"Lady? You been busted up badly. My name is Billy. Don't try to talk 'cause you'll loosen them teeth even more. Kin ya nod?"

Nod? Was he kidding? I started screaming and didn't stop until I felt hands patting mine gently and a voice saying, "Ma'am? You'll be right safe here. Don't gotta worry. You say and I'll call a cop and they'll take you home and all."

I was panting voraciously and began to cry because I was in such pain. Even holding my hand caused pain up and down my right arm. I vaguely felt a line of drool escape my mouth and rough skin touched my lip and gently wiped it away.

"Lady? I'm gonna put a straw to your mouth. It's water mixed with a lot of aspirin that will help the pain and the swelling. It ain't nuthin' more than that. Just sip and try to finish it. It ain't all that much."

I felt that long straw against my lips and involuntarily sipped the mixture. It tasted bitter like my memory said it would. I sipped just a bit because swallowing was hard. Breathing was harder because my chest felt as though someone was sitting on it. "Breathe," I moaned. "Can't breathe good."

Just saying that brought intensely horrific pain throughout my chest.

"Lady?" that voice said again. "I figure you got at least two broken ribs. Yer face is shattered and swollen along your left cheekbone. You need mor'n I kin give you, but I figure if I take ya back now and the guy that did this finds out yer alive, then mebbe he'll finish it."

"Who…are…you?" I croaked.

"My name is Billy Ray Simpson. You don' gotta tell me yers for a while. You got worse trouble than telling me yer name."

"My…legs…hurt….my head…too."

I heard a long sigh and then, "Lady? You got a concussion, I figgur. I shaved away some hair along the left side of yer head and dabbed around a tad bit, but only time will tell if you got damage, you know neurologically speaking. I removed some bone chips from yer scalp and that ain't good. Yer legs? Both of them are broken but I splinted them and they should be okay given some time."

Neurologically speaking? What sort of language was that for Jethro Bodine? "Neu…"

His voice lightened and he said, "I was a Marine Corp medic in Iraq. Saw a lot worse than this here, lady." His voice settled a bit and then that straw was pressed back to my lips. "Just drink this stuff, ma'am. After a while, the pain will lessen and some of the swellin' will abate, too."

Sipping was still painful but I did.

I heard a young voice, another deeply southern one. "That lady got right nice titties, Uncle Billy Ray."

What followed was emphatic. I heard the sound of a chair creaking and then the unmistakable sound of a solid punch followed by

Chapter Two

a body hitting the floor. The nephew was down for the count, I guessed. Like I cared, you know?

The chair creaked again and he said, "I do apologize for Silas. He's a young buck and yours is the first female anatomy he's ever seen. That ain't right, still."

"My…eyes?"

"Don't rightly know, ma'am. Yer cheeks is swollen pretty badly and that's the reason you ain't seein' much. The swellin' is up past yer eyes and my opinion is that you'll need some sort of plastic surgery to make yerself look like you used to."

"What…day…is…" and I lost the ability to finish a simple sentence. I was exhausted, in deep pain and the effort to ask that simple question was beyond me.

"Monday, ma'am. You been here since I found you last Thursday. You kin probably press charges agin me but I feel that keepin' you here was keepin' you alive."

Fours days? Was that possible? I moaned from a combination of pain and depression. I tried to move and that just made everything hurt more. I could turn my head to either side and that was about all I could manage. My vision was blurry, so badly so that I just closed them and wondered what to do. I was still scared and that had little to do with Bill Ray Simpson. Truthfully? I don't remember the pain or the beating, though it must have been savage to leave me this way. I remember with stark clarity the fear and horror I felt as those men dragged me through the woods and bound me to that tree. Without even a word of explanation, they beat me and left me to die. Why wasn't even a question I could ask yet. Why was still in the future beyond all this pain that each slight movement gave me. Even breathing was precarious.

Squinting, I opened my eyes and tried to see this man that seemingly saved my life. A blurry face that could have been anyone was all I was able to see. "Closer…please?" I said with an agonized effort merely to talk to him.

"My face?" he asked gently.

"Yes," I answered with deep pain rolling and stabbing me across my chest. The more it hurt, the more agitated I got until I felt his hand in mine.

"Ma'am? Please. Settle yerself. Ain't no one gonna hurt you here. Getting all worked up is just gonna cause more pain and that can wear you down worse than anythin'."

He leaned close over my face as he spoke, close enough to see a man that looked worried and grim. Was that grimness about me or was he always that way? He looked fit and wore an old Braves baseball hat. Well, he could have been the Hunchback himself and with the way my eyes returned things to me, I'd never know. I closed them and just felt the bed, the room and my life. Nothing fit and I wanted to get up and run away. Bending my legs was impossible, so I asked through a haze of pain, "My legs?"

"Busted yer thigh bones, ma'am. They're big bones and they should heal right nicely. You should be thankful they didn't bust up yer ankles or you might never walk again."

"Ribs?"

"Got Sylvia coming from the base. She's gonna check out yer worse injuries. The one I'm worried about is that concussion. Yer face? God knows, ma'am. You got a family? Someone worried about you?"

Family. My family was Evan and my memory kicked in with evil efficiency that reminded me that he was dead. I hadn't even seen my brother, Mark, other than the funeral in almost four years. My parents? They were alive and living in Florida. I hadn't seen them much either. Personally, I think my family saw me as too much of a handful and were silently glad that I got married when I did. Mark lives in New Orleans and drives a truck. Real blue collar. My father is a carpenter and my mother is an administrative assistant to a real estate developer. My father and my brother get along real well. Me? Well, not even my mother calls me. "No," I said. "No family." Then, "Debbie."

"Who's that?"

"Friend." Then, I asked, "Sylvia?"

"Ma sister. She's Silas' momma."

Chapter Two

"He hurt?"

"Better be. He ain't, I'm gonna smack him agin."

I let it go because breathing was difficult and I felt dizzy. I wasn't a sickly child. Being sick was never much fun because I was always in a hurry and having to stay home to recuperate was taking too much time out of my day. This, though, was like hanging over a canyon as a stranger held my feet. Could I trust him? Could I trust Billy Ray Simpson? Did I have a choice?

I must have drifted off to sleep because I woke or became conscious during the night and grew scared of the wind, of the shadows, of everything that moved around me. I saw those faces, those two placidly evil faces as they beat me with those metal pipes. I cried out in the night and heard a sound from the next room. Billy Ray came in. There was no one else it could have been. I saw him move easily across the floor after the door opened. "You okay, ma'am?" he asked sleepily. Even in the dark, I could see him in more vivid contrast than the last time I'd seen him. His face was young and hard, his chin firm and his mouth all too easily set against the people who would try to hurt him. A champion? "Fuck you," I moaned. "You're like your nephew."

He did a strange thing. He sat in a chair and smiled. "Ma'am? Yer probably right. Silas got a lot of me in him. I'm his uncle, you know? He spends a lot time out here huntin' with me. His momma and me go out sometimes. There's deer out here. You ever hunted?"

"No," I said. I reached out blindly in the night and found his hand. "Sorry…Billy. Scared. You know?" I held it tightly and he allowed it.

"Sylvia asked me some stuff about you. She asked if yer confused. You know, like mental."

I tried to smile but nothing happened except endless pain. "Always…been…mental."

"Told her you was lucid, right properly lucid."

"Billy?" I asked. "Who…are...you? Where…am…I?"

He reached up to touch my face and I flinched and screamed fearfully. I squeezed my eyes shut and just screamed because my mind insisted he was going to beat me, was going to be those men who did this.

Nothing happened and I felt his hand retract, sliding from mine. "Ma'am? I ain't gonna hurt you. You wanna go to a hospital? You say and I'll do it."

"Yes!" I spat eagerly. "Get me home! Get me to a hospital!"

Your emotions have never been a concern for me. Whoever you are. People are obstacles and roadblocks. That's why I don't have more friends besides Debbie. That's why my husband committed suicide rather than confront me with his own pain. Before last Thursday, I can't see how I would have listened to him at all. That's how shallow I am or have been. My life, my goals, my timetable have always been the most important things in my life. Nothing Evan ever wanted, even a mildly wicked night on high heels, could I find it in myself to give him. I gave him long nights spent alone, gave him attention only when the coffee pot was perking, and sex was a distraction I didn't need.

In every respect, Billy Ray Simpson was just another person who was in my way. There was no profit in it to have him around or even in the shadows of my life. The problem I was facing, however, was seriously compromising my life. So far, he'd done nothing to me at all other than be helpful and insightful. He was probably right about saving my life by keeping me in his home rather than calling the police. Me, little miss compassionate conservative, was a huge supporter of law and order as applied by the police. I never, *ever*, considered self-defense as an option because the Savannah Police Department are paid to do that, to protect me.

There are, and have been, times in my life when I have actually slowed to a stop and thought about my life and where I wanted it to go. Within those times were a whole host of assumptions and suppositions. Just one of them, a small one at that, was the police and how I saw their job vis-à-vis me. I *always* assumed they would protect me and never really gave it much thought beyond that. For me, society has always been orderly, a thing to be navigated faster than the guy or girl next to you. A conservative will always see society as static and not fluid. You would think that a reporter, that someone in my position, would see the city, the country and the world with slightly grittier eyes than I have heretofore. You remember I mentioned Dave Woods? Dave is a bit older than me and sometimes forgets to comb his hair. I honestly don't think he's ever voted

Chapter Two

and doesn't care about what people say, just what they do. Neither conservative nor liberal, he's the ultimate in practicality. He sees the city for what it is and not what the chamber of commerce wants you to believe. Well, I miss him now, miss Dave and the way his life is neither too cluttered nor too hectic, the way mine was.

Billy Ray just smiled and said, "I kin understand that, ma'am. I'll make that call right quick and get you to a hospital."

He offered no argument, no delays and made no move to talk me out of it. Just before he exited the dark room, I said, "Wait…Billy." My vision, though clearer, was still partially obscured in my left eye and I had to close it in order to see him properly. He was just standing in the doorway waiting for a decision. "Why…Billy? Why are you…doing this?"

Motivation. Almost every story I ever filed contained that information. Who did what and why. Motivation, therefore, was something I understood intimately and before I could leave here, I needed to know his. Yes, I was in pain, every single breath bringing small agonies with it. While that pain clouded my mind a bit, I have never been without the crisp and incisive ability to think. Did this represent a clear mind, a clear thought, something done with coherency or was this simply pain speaking? Why. I had to know why.

"Iraq, ma'am," he said. "It ain't no more simple than that."

I was breathing harder because I was getting an answer, but not one I understood. My mind, the one I always took to work, was in the way. "Never…been…to Iraq. What's…that mean?"

When you start out in a career as a reporter, you get the crappiest assignments. I got city hall and council meetings for eighteen months. Somewhere along the line, the job got excruciatingly boring and I needed something to do. No, not another job, but a different way to see the same one. I found myself reacting to them, to the people I met there and talked to, as though everything they said was exactly what they meant. I used that same chamber of commerce idea for the first time during that span of my life. According to them, Savannah is clean, cultured and a magnet for people of all types and ages.

Well, crap.

Until that moment in that bed in that small but sterile room, I never saw it for how it was. Oh, I gave myself high marks, and so did Harley, for how I began to handle that assignment. I can't say I became cynical because I'm not. Cynicism doesn't exist in an orderly world. In my world where everything was logical and Step B always followed Step A in the same sequential order, cynicism was a liberal disease and committed by chaotic minds. Yeah. You had to commit to being cynical.

Those stories I filed began to get noticed by Harley. I will never admit to approaching a city hall meeting with cynicism because my response was never in that tone or in those conditions. I simply began to ask questions that no one ever thought to ask before. I almost had to force myself to stop listening to their words and hear questions they never even asked. Most of them spoke in such generalities that their answers were worse than useless. My idea, and one that propelled me out of the city council chambers and into a better job with the newspaper was to ask questions as though they were follow-up to ones they never asked. It confused some and made others wary of me because I was asking hard questions and demanding more completely honest answers.

His answer? Billy's? It contained more kernels of truth than most answers I ever got in a council meeting but didn't go nearly far enough. My reply was designed to get him to talk about Iraq. I supported that war and supported it completely. I believed with the fervor of the newly converted that freedom really was on the march. It took Dave and an offhand question to make me think. "Really, Morgahna? You can force people to be free? Wow. That's a novel approach."

I call that a freeze-dry moment. You know? You hear something, a question maybe, and when you start to form an answer, your brain just freezes and you realize there is no answer you can give that fully explains the question. I realized what we were doing in Iraq was classic despotism. Okay, I'm not an intellect but I'm not stupid either. Words are what I do, have always done. So, when I requested a clarification from Billy Ray Simpson, I got one.

"Ma'am? I got real tired of being the one. That's all, just the one. I served in Baghdad and Fallujah. I saw pieces of flesh that were no longer recognizable as people. I saw that on both sides. You ever seen a man after he steps on a booby trap? Well, the first thing that gets you is the

Chapter Two

smell. You smell death before you see it. Then I saw our people, my friends and colleagues, saw them dead. Then I saw the others, the Iraqis. Ma'am? I am a soldier at heart but I find choosing my battles is easier on me. You? I found you bound to a tree about five miles from Fort Stewart in thick woods. I could hear animals around, ones that were getting ready to start feasting on you. Ma'am? You really need a mirror right now."

"Why?" I asked even though I felt I knew the answer.

"To see what they did. It's been several days since I found you and you look better now than you did then. But I kept wondering who put you there and why. I see things that many don't. I saw people who would come back and make sure you were dead. I saw a pity in my mind. My heart went out to you and my anger to those that did this. Mostly, I saw someone who would want to come back and finish it. I kin do that, what you ask. I kin call 911 and get people to pick you up and take you to a hospital. But you'd be steppin' on a bear trap, ma'am. You'd be doin' exactly the wrong thing. That's my opinion but I'm done bein' the police for people."

"You…gonna…hurt me?"

"No, ma'am."

"Silas?"

"No, ma'am."

"Sylvia?"

"She's an army doctor, ma'am. She's bit older than me but she's good people, a good troop."

"Anyone else?"

"No, ma'am."

"Kids talk."

"He does and I'll break his fat neck."

I tried to smile but it hurt too much. "Sylvia…be…mad."

The darkness hid his smile. "Yeah. She get over it, though."

"Am I ugly?" I asked as pain continued to crowd my world.

"As a day-old baby, ma'am."

He walked back to the bed, sat down in that chair and placed his first two fingers of his right hand to my lips. "Feel that?"

"Swollen."

"Hard ta talk?"

"Yes."

"Yer whole face is swollen, ma'am. Yer arms ain't broke but you got black and blue marks all over them, the rest of yer body, too. Those'll fade over time, but yer face is different. Will be anyway. You took an awful beatin', ma'am. Awful."

There existed between us something entirely unspoken and hidden. He knew it and so did I. He was being patient and had the time to be that way. Even if I never regained my former strength and stamina, it would take time for that to happen, time and lots of rehab. Evan always said I had good legs, nice ones that he liked watching move as I walked. Now? Would anyone ever watch again? And my face? How ugly was I?

He moved his hand around my cheek and pain followed. "These bones is all busted up. They'll basically reshape your face. Mebbe you'll be as ugly as sin. Mebbe not. You got any money to have an operation?"

"Can I see?"

He swallowed hard and I took that as a yes, a very, very qualified yes. "I'll be right back, ma'am."

It's impossible to be female and not wonder about your looks, about how men see you, about your self-image and whether you can attract a mate. As soon as I knew Evan was attracted to me and that he was a lawyer, I got interested real fast and convinced myself that I was in love with him. We had more sex before than after our marriage. It was a realization and not a pleasant one. Evan? I'm sorry. You will never know how so. That divorce I mentioned had he lived? Possibly, very possible that was true. That pain I felt with every breath? That was my penance and I was going to accept it. I might even fight fixing it if it would keep my head straight from now.

Chapter Two

Billy Ray came back in carrying a mirror that looked like it came off a wall somewhere. He turned on the lights in the room, sat and held it facedown in his lap. "You sure?"

I closed my eyes, swallowed hard and said, "Yeah."

"Ma'am?" he said as he continued to hold that mirror facedown. "You gotta realize that a lot of what you'll see will fade away as the bruises fade and the swelling goes down. You gotta see that."

"Let me see."

He sighed and held that mirror up so I could see myself.

No.

No, that wasn't me.

Oh, my good god, no.

What I saw brought tears to my eyes and I wanted to be as dead as Evan. My face was hideously lumpy and misshapen. Moving my hand to touch my face was painful in more ways than I ever imagined. I used to see pain as a spectrum of emotions and not as a pinpoint thing that could cause troubling and annoying stops in my life, stops that were momentary and not ongoing. My lips were purple and swollen things through which I was barely able to breathe. There was a mark on my neck. "This?"

"Tracheotomy, ma'am. When I found you, you were struggling to breathe and became unable to do it. I did it right there at the base of that tree. It's the best I could do. Sorry. Otherwise, you'd be dead."

It was a gash at least four inches long that was slowly turning into a long ragged scar right at my throat. My face held more bruises, more dark purple splotches than clear white skin. My hair, my head, everything looked different. My cheeks were so badly broken up that I literally did not recognize the face in that mirror. I put it down, turned my face to the wall and began to cry.

We are all destined to die one day. All of us. The rich, the poor, the idle, the infirm, the strong, the weak, all of us. Before I held that mirror to my face, I had a good idea of where my life was going, Evan notwithstanding. I was going to be a senior editor and would be toasted throughout the southeast, Savannah in particular. They would name a street after me, build a park in my name, dedicate a ship to me. No, I can't honestly say I looked forward to those, just that in my world, such things accompanied greatness and I was going to be great. I had a daily planner, a monthly one, a yearly one and I *regularly* referred to them to see how true I was being to my own goals. That included money as well.

Perhaps I should throw this in for good measure. My income did not drive our little family. Evan's did. He was a devoted husband who only wanted to see his wife wear high heels *just once.* As a goal, it was modest and not something I was unable to do. Okay, they made my feet hurt. Once he even joked that I could wear them to bed where they wouldn't hurt and I thought he was joking. I can remember him telling me that I drove him crazy. Me? No, not me. I don't try, Evan. That's what I told him. Anything to avoid that sexual frenzy that did little for my goals. Sex took time and time was worse than money, it was money *and* goals at once.

Now? Who would care?

But, we are all destined to die because we are all human, people. We are totally unable to escape our fate. The best we can do is postpone it as long as possible. We can join groups, jog, workout, do any of a number of things to improve our chances of life, but in the end we all wind up feeling the way I did on that bed. Life was altogether unfair, arbitrary and uneven. Worse, it was *democratic.*

I wanted to die rather than look like this.

That's when Billy Ray Simpson made a difference in my life.

Did you ever see that HBO miniseries *Angels In America?* I thought it was dreadful, simply dreadful. I actually said that to Evan after I watched the whole series. Dreadful. I actually used that word to describe a cinematic masterpiece. That film, that series, upset my nice and ordered life. It wasn't complicated at all. It simply upset how I viewed the world. I saw it as a chain of events that all happened sequentially. Men loved women and women loved men. Angels protected the world and kept it orderly.

When Billy Ray crawled into the bed and reached out for me, I was terrified for a second. He was in his underwear and an old army t-

Chapter Two

shirt, nothing more. When he lifted the covers and rolled me onto my side and held me, I was convinced he was going to extract his price right then and there. I stiffened, tried to scream and he just said, "Please, lady. I saw so much bad stuff over there. So much stuff. You seem nice and I miss nice people. Please, just be still and let me try to calm you a bit."

Evan always smelled like cologne. It was never the same twice. He had an eclectic taste. Eclectic. Another word meaning he was bored with me.

Billy smelled like the woods around us.

I held onto him and cried for what seemed like hours.

A woman's tears meant nothing to him. He'd seen far too many and simply wanted me to be okay.

As morning broke, I was calm but still ugly.

I was going to learn about ugly, that it was a state of mind.

The concept of liberals and conservatives was going to drop away completely and be replaced with something far more basic that those two simple terms. I was going to find out what it meant to be a human being. I was going to learn what motivates people and why some of us become targets.

I was still a target, though. This target was going to fight back, however, because it was in her nature.

She had a good teacher.

Chapter Three

I noticed the humidity first. My entire body was dripping with sweat. I must have smelled like a football player. It was afternoon from what I could gather. The day was neither new nor old. Even though I was still in pain, it wasn't as bad as before. A better sign was my impatience. I wanted, *needed*, to get out of bed and go back to work. That pain and those casts reminded me of my condition and what had happened to me. I sighed and noticed that everything worked except my knees and legs. The splints on both of them went to my mid-calves and would keep me from walking until they were either removed or I got crutches.

My own impatience pushed me to slide my legs off the mattress. That was a big mistake. I cried out as more pain than I'd felt all night hit me.

The door blew open and Billy Ray rushed into the room. "Good Lord, lady. Please. You need to rest."

A woman followed him in and she calmly introduced herself as, "Doctor Morris, US Army."

Billy got me back into the bed and I had to wait for several long and agonizing minutes as the pain subsided. She stood there patiently waiting for me to become able once more to talk coherently. When that happened, she said, "The wheel chair I stole from the base will help you, ma'am.

As more sweat poured from my forehead, I looked up and said with painfully stabbing breaths, "Sylvia?"

She inclined her head. "At your service."

She was shorter than her brother and far more slender. Her hair was short and black, her complexion hinted at being outside more than inside. She had no fingernails, at least none that a woman would envy. Hers were short, blunt and probably sterile. The uniform, that distinctly army green one, fit loosely and made a closer inspection of her dubious

Chapter Three

at best. Yes, I am woman. Hear me roar at other women. As I saw it, she was a roadblock, just one of many in my life.

"Silas is a punk," I said gritting my teeth.

"Agreed. My little brother will make a man of him where I have failed," she said as she moved to my bedside and began picking through short strands of hair as she looked at that wound on my left temple. She touched it gingerly and said, "That hurts."

"Like you wouldn't believe."

My hair hurt. As much as it did, it was no worse than the rest of my body. Given the fact that the pain I was in was not as overwhelming as it was yesterday, maybe you have an idea of how bad my head hurt.

"Oh, I believe it," she said. "Billy Ray says you should stay here and rehabilitate. My opinion is that you could be in danger of a hemorrhage that could kill you."

"I'll stay," I said.

"Take two aspirins and have Billy call me in the morning."

"That's your professional opinion?"

"Lady? I'm an army doctor. I've seen soldiers get up and fight with more serious injuries than you've got."

"Your soldiers wear helmets and flak jackets."

"I can get you a helmet."

"Gee, thanks."

"Billy? Get that wheel chair."

"Sure," he said and left the room.

She had a manly face, one that wouldn't attract attention. Well, that was my professional feminine opinion but then I don't think Pamela Anderson is pretty either. I said that once to Dave and he just smiled and said, "Don't matter how pretty a woman is, Morgahna. You get a man worked up enough and she'll fit any ideal of beauty you can name."

"Then he wakes up, huh?"

"Yep. We all do sooner or later."

Dr. Morris might have been a stone vixen for all I cared. I wanted relief from the pain, from her and wanted it sooner rather than later. When she sat in the chair next to the bed, I figured I was going to get a lecture. I was right.

"Your ribs will hurt for several weeks, at least as long as your legs heal. I'll be back in the morning to properly set them. If I assume you'll be patient and give them time to heal, you'll be running laps around the house and that will cause permanent damage. You need to be on your back if you want everything to straighten out in its own time. Did Billy Ray explain this to me properly? You were beaten savagely and left tied to a tree?"

"Yes."

She slumped back in the chair and that was her first attempt at civility and a bedside manner that wasn't out of "Swimming With The Sharks". "Call a cop," she said with what sounded like genuine empathy. "Then go see a doctor."

Well, I said it. Frowning and holding back tears, I said, "My husband committed suicide." Those words sounded awful and saying them made them feel worse because that was the first time I had. Why did I say that to her? Why after that statement? Why at all? My eyes grew misty and I had to look away, had to look at that wall that bordered the bed to my left.

The room fell absolutely silent for a moment as I stared at that wall and she did whatever flippant doctors do. Slowly, she said, "Tell me about that wall."

"Go to hell," I said with less anger than I felt.

"Come on, lady. Tell me about it. What's there that is so fascinating?"

I am the product of blue collar parents. I am the product of people that never had a higher or more insightful thought than, "What is Spock's middle name?" My father knew how to hang doors and make buildings stand straight. My mother knew more about Microsoft Office than Bill Gates. My brother? Well, he once tore apart a carburetor blindfolded. That's my family. I believe that is the genesis of my claim not to be an intellect. It requires nothing higher than firm morals to be a Republican

Chapter Three

and those require nothing sturdier than strong knees, ones that stay stubbornly together when faced with men even if they are your own husband.

Doctor Morris had more intellect than me but she wasn't the first such Poindexter I ever faced. She was, however, the first one that knew every movement I was making was painful and completely so. She had, in other words, an edge over me that I never conceded to anyone before. Combine that edge with her experience, her battlefield experience, and she could pretty much do with me whatever she wanted. I was hurting, missed my husband, was depressed over my appearance and she wanted to know what I found so fascinating in that wall.

"What?" I said sneering at her.

"Well, that's a classic retreat. You get faced with something that's packed solid with emotions like that and you retreat into tears. I've seen that reaction on men who have lost a limb or three. I've seen it on faces of men who were blinded by the flash of a nearby explosive. It's as though they needed to retreat in order to regroup. You? How long ago did this happen?"

Being a girl's girl, I have never been in a fight, not even one where pillows were the weapons of choice. Yes, I have had a few vicious cat fights where spitting and hissing were all I did. I have never slapped anyone, scratched anyone, spit on anyone or ever touched anyone in anger. However, with that rather placid past, I wanted to splatter that woman all over the room but my limiting factor was experience. So, fear kept my hands in my lap as I said, "Why?"

"Curious. You look like the type that keeps it inside. Right? You probably get drunk a lot, or at least have gotten drunk a lot since it happened. You don't ask for advice either. You chase people away. How close am I?"

Well, the cat in me escaped to say, "Oh, fuck you, lady."

"At least a month," she said critically. "Maybe two."

"Why don't you…"

"A real bitch, aren't you?" she said coolly, said without so much as a disturbed eyebrow.

I swallowed hard and that had nothing to do with that emergency tracheotomy. I swallowed hard because my memories hurt so bad. Was I that transparent? Was I willing to chase away people that were only trying to help me? You don't have to be an intellect to see pain. I found myself looking at the wall for a long moment and then heard her comment about the wall being so interesting. I tried to sigh but it hurt just to breathe. It was getting more and more frustrating, too. I itched to get up and do something but was effectively pinned to that bed.

Billy Ray came back into the room pushing a wheel chair. I closed my bad eye and looked at him with what I hoped was a bit of jaundice. He was taller than everyone in the room and moved easily and gracefully. Slowly, I began to grow suspicious of them, especially of the doctor.

She turned her head just a bit and said to him while looking at me through the corner of her eye, "Billy Ray? We have here a damsel in distress. Help her. Without a good man, she'll turn into a little girl and the world will spit her out."

"Knock it off, Sylvia," he said with a growl that was meant to be final.

The doctor stood, grabbed a pillow from the bed and I thought she was going to smother me. Okay, I'm a paranoid American. That makes me normal. When she saw me blanch, she smirked, "Oh, for heaven's sakes." She handed the pillow to me and said, "Hold it against your chest and breathe deeply ten minutes on every hour. It will help the pain and lessen the chances of pneumonia." Then she looked at her brother and said, "Aspirin?"

"Broken up in water. She's got some damage to her teeth."

"Loose?"

"Yeah."

"Prognosis?"

"They'll heal. How long? Don't know without x-rays and what are the chances of that happening?"

"Which ribs, Billy?"

"Third and fourth. She got lucky."

Chapter Three

"Easy for you to say," I barked only because they still hurt.

"Billy's right, lady," the doctor said with an air of great patience about her. "Damage to the first two ribs might involve damage to the major blood vessels that carry blood to your heart. Damage to any lower ones might accompany damage to your liver and spleen. He's right. Despite the pain, you got lucky. Still, despite the luck, do those breathing exercises because otherwise you might damage your heart."

I swallowed hard because the evidence – and as a reporter, I was big on evidence – was beginning to confirm that Tony and Doug wanted to kill me and failed only by the slimmest of margins. My mind began to insist on a replay of that attack. I've never been called brave by anyone and I certainly didn't think I was being brave in that room. My life depended on them, on strangers, and I have a Republican's typical mistrust of strangers. I didn't trick or treat until I was twelve and only then with three other friends. That scene, however, was going to take some small dose of bravado for me to deal with it like my mind was asking me to. For example, my memory was telling me I was tied to a tree in the deepest woods. If Billy Ray Simpson wasn't part of it, then how did he happen upon me like he claims. So, I asked. "Where am I? How did you find me because my mind insists that I was left alone in the woods?"

"Wheel chair, William," she said.

He smacked her arm. "Don't call me that," he threatened her. It was the first real anger I'd seen him exhibit. It was more than brother-sister silliness, it was deep and lasting. Something in there was hurting and being called that name was a reminder.

Doctor Sylvia Morris had been as cold as a northern glacier up to that time. She reeked competence and showed a lot of evidence of dealing with soldiers who were short on patience and long on the ability to inflict themselves on other people. She showed an immediate softer side when she hugged him and said, "Sorry, little brother. It was a slip. Won't happen again."

Simpson looked at me and said, "To answer yer question, I gotta take you outside. You feel up to it, ma'am?"

Smiling was painful but I managed a small one. "Oh, yeah. I'm ready."

"I gotta touch ya, ma'am. I ain't gonna do anything, just lift you from the bed and put you in the wheel chair. That okay?"

"Yeah," I said. "Go ahead. Get me out of this bed."

I'm not afraid of people despite my apparent demeanor. Oh, I'm quite aware of men and how they look at me, quite aware that Evan tended to stare at my butt sometimes. The cruelest things I ever did? I caught him staring wistfully at me that way. I was standing on a step stool in the kitchen reaching for something on a high shelf and he came in the doorway and stared at me. Irritated because I was running late on *something*, I just snapped, "Oh, for God's sakes, Evan. Grow up." His face fell a bit and he'd had serious criminals say much worse things to him than that. Coming from his wife, however, seemed to deflate a piece of him and now I wondered if that little scene wasn't at least a small reason why he did what he did.

When Bill Ray reached under me, I reached over his shoulder and hooked my arm around his neck. With God as my witness, the pain that made me scream quite involuntarily was worse than my memory of that night, the night all this happened. He dropped me immediately back onto the bed and said, "We don't have to go outside, ma'am."

Every nerve in my body was screaming incessantly. *Every* nerve. I was breathing hard and that just exacerbated the problem because my ribs began to scream and that made breathing harder. Doctor Morris knelt next to me and put that pillow on my chest. "Deep breath, girl. Deep breath." I listened but obeying was harder. Slowly and painfully, I wrapped my arms around that pillow and breathed hard and deep against it. The pain radiated outward and sharply in all directions from my chest.

"Relax your muscles, girl," she said quickly. "Just relax them. It will lessen the pain."

That was a lot easier said than done but I gritted my teeth – and I mean that literally – and slowly forced myself to relax. I went as limp as circumstances would allow and the pain became bearable. "Okay, Billy Ray," I said. "I'm ready." That wasn't the biggest lie I'd ever told but certainly the most recent. It hurt, everything did, not just my chest

Chapter Three

although that seemed to be the worst of it. My headache took a long backseat to my ribs.

"We don't have to," he said with his own pain in evidence.

I almost snapped at him. The *only* reason I didn't was Evan and that look I remember so vividly when I told him to grow up. He was attracted to me and my behavior suggested I wish he hadn't been. Did I love him? I always thought I did. Now, I wonder. I managed to catch my anger before it flew off on its own and said through those same gritted teeth, "Oh, yes, sir. I do. I need to get off my butt and see what you want me to see."

"I could just tell you."

"I'd rather see for myself."

Sylvia knelt next to me and said, "We'll get you to a sitting position and then pick you up together." She looked at her brother and said, "Ready?"

"No. I don't think we should. She's in too much pain."

I looked up at him and said, "Billy? I have to pee."

His forehead wrinkled and he said, "Yer wearin' Depends, lady. Piss all you want."

Oh, my, god. I blushed. Why? Well, that little revelation meant that he knew more about me than he'd let on. *He'd been changing me for five days.* After the blush faded, the rest of the blood in my face drained away and I think I was in shock for a few seconds. I dropped my hands to my lap and was able to confirm his allegation. Yep. I was wearing diapers. "Um..."

"I'm a friggin' medic, lady," he snapped angrily. "I've seen everything from ten-inch wangs to the nicest pussies you ever saw. Yers ain't nuthin' special."

That caused a sputter of laughter from Sylvia and she said, "Your bedside manner leaves a lot to be desired, Billy Ray."

"I just think she should stay where she is."

My brother Mark fought me with a lot when we were kids. My standard for brother-sister relations was a brother that sneered, smacked my arm and called me "dirtbag". That was the nicest thing he ever called me. After he had a reference for the female anatomy, he started calling me, "Taco breath". *That* took some years and cultural reference points to understand. Once I did and my own reference points were up to speed, I retaliated by calling him "a worm" with just the right amount of emphasis. Then I'd finish with "a tiny worm".

Well, Sylvia just put her hand on his arm and said, "I know, Billy Ray." I thought she was agreeing with him but it became obvious her remark had nothing at all to do with me. She was referring to something personal, something painful, something that he wasn't finished with yet. "I agree with her, though. Getting her out and around is the first step toward a successful rehab. It's going to hurt, Billy. You know that."

Billy Ray Simpson has an interesting face. It ripples with life. He lifted his ever-present Braves hat, ran his hand through his brown hair and stared at me like I wasn't there. I've interviewed a lot of people in the last two years. I've interviewed a few criminals and saw their expressions when they talked about their crimes. I've talked with politicians and saw that same look when they talked about their accomplishments. The look Billy Ray Simpson was giving me was something I was not familiar with in any format. He was reaching back into his past and looking at something of which I was only a reminder. "I know," he said as he stared at me. "I know, Syl."

"Then, let's help the lady."

"I can't," he said.

A young voice from the doorway said, "I'll help." He was maybe ten, maybe twelve. Just young enough to know that girls are somehow elegantly different from boys and that I was an unqualified *girl*. Silas Morris was a younger version of his uncle. Tall and straight, a growing ramrod.

Billy Ray turned and stalked from the room. Sylvia sighed, a small measure of defeat on her face and asked, "You up to this, lady?"

"Yes. He gonna grope me or anything?"

"No, ma'am," he said. "I'm powerful sorry about before."

Chapter Three

He had a bruise on his chin.

"Then get me off this damn bed," I groused.

The doctor got me to a sitting position by being patient to my grunts and moans as they moved me. Taking nearly ten minutes just to get me to the edge of the bed, they knelt on either side of me and slid their arms under my butt. I gave Silas my best evil eye and he did nothing but grasp his mother's hands. They strained and I bit into my lower lip and held my breath because it was still an agonizing experience. I put my head on her shoulder, on Sylvia's, because I didn't trust the boy. My breath caught several times as deep, sharp pains lanced across my chest. My legs threw in their own objections as they slowly put me into the chair. I gripped the handholds on it tightly as the spasms slowly passed. Sylvia didn't lift my legs onto the outstretched leg wells until I nodded. Even that was painful. She placed that pillow in my lap and said gently, "Don't leave home without it."

"Thanks," I said grimacing. I picked it up after a few long minutes of gasping for breath and began those exercises again. As much as it hurt, I had to admit that it helped in the end.

Sylvia hugged her son and said, "You did good, Silas."

"Thanks, mom," he said to her proudly. "Is she gonna be okay, mom?"

"I think so. Rehab always hurts."

"I kin push her, okay?" he said.

"Carefully, son. You hit her legs against something and she's gonna hurt a whole powerful lot."

"I'll be careful, mom."

I've never known a hermit before. Billy Ray was my first. His home, the one his sister condemned her son into staying, was nothing more than a small two-bedroom house that was totally devoid of any domestic touches, ones that a woman would put there. There was a Harley Davidson logo on the wall behind a TV with *rabbit ears* but there was nothing more than that one picture in the entire room. I'd say the sofa was second-hand but I'd be lying by at least two generations. There was another door off to my left and a smaller one to its left, a second bedroom and a toilet. The kitchen was just another area of the room and it held an old refrigerator that sat behind a rickety table and four chairs. A book by Carl Sagan sat on the smallest coffee table I'd ever seen.

Silas was pushing me with all due caution and doing it slower than a melting snow pack. The entrance was covered with a screen door that opened out onto a porch that was covered by a slanting roof. The humidity was intense and suffocating. A few flies and fewer mosquitoes buzzed about randomly.

We were in the middle of nowhere.

Cypress trees grew everywhere and that meant water was nearby. I may be a Republican but I know about trees and Georgia. There were a few maples and gumtrees in the mix but that wall of trees was pretty thick and adamant. "He lives out here?" I asked through a grimace of pain.

"Yes, he does," Sylvia said somewhat sadly. She pointed and said, "Fort Stewart is that way, Ten miles give or take a few." She turned and pointed, "And Savannah is maybe thirty miles over there. My little brother has quite effectively hidden himself from the world out here."

A deep green Range Rover sat on a dirt driveway behind a black Ford pickup. The SUV was clean; the pickup was not. A kayak lay in the bed of the truck surrounded by the flotsam of the sport. There was no gun rack in the window of the truck and that was a singular lack out here. "Why?" I asked. "Why does he live out here?"

A figure, Billy Ray, came out of the trees and said hotly, "That's none of yer business, lady. I like it here and that's all you need to know." Then, to his sister, he said, "Go back to the damn base, Sylvia. Leave me be. I kin take care of her. Take yer brat with you."

She nodded and said, "Okay, Billy. I'll be back in the morning to properly set her legs. You take care of her or I'll take care of you."

"I ain't goin'," Silas said stubbornly.

"It's up to you, Billy Ray," his sister said matter-of-factly.

The boy said it again. "I ain't goin'."

And he ran off into the woods.

Great, I thought. The family circus, Georgia style.

Chapter Three

As stupid as that scene was, I realized that Billy Ray Simpson saved my life despite the turmoil in his own. For that alone, I was grateful to him. His sister looked competent but weary of the fights. Billy looked stubborn and ready to argue inch-for-inch with her. As much as I wanted to add my point to the argument, I wanted to breathe even more and each breath was still painful. I closed my eyes and that old insistent friendly voice that echoed inside my head made me remember that coming out here, coming outside at all, was his idea. What changed his mind? What happened in that room to set him off, to make him surly and defensive? What had we been talking about? *Pain. We were talking about pain. Mine. He knew it was going to hurt and it did.* Well, it still did so what did all that mean? Why would my pain make him run off like that? "It's peaceful here," I said as the two siblings stood facing each other.

Sylvia just hugged him. "I'll go look for Silas. You take care, Billy."

He sighed and said, "Nah, leave him. He'll come back later. Always does."

"You sure?"

"Yeah," he said and nothing more.

"You take care, Billy. I'll see you in the morning."

"Yeah," he said again almost stubbornly.

"Girl?" she asked me as she descended the two pitiful steps to the dirt that spread around the house like an oil slick. "You got a name other than Morgahna Jayne Hamilton of Taylor Street in Savannah?"

It struck me hard that she knew me and I can't say quite why that was. How was that possible? "How...How do you know me?"

She smiled and said, "Your name is all over the television and newspapers back in Savannah. A lot of people are looking for you. A lot more think you're already dead. There's a report of your car, a cute little BMW, being found in a parking lot. You're a reporter, right?"

It was a shock. *They think I'm dead.* I have never been at a loss for words. I am verbal and intensely so. I've been known to bore people to sleep. Harley Hood? My boss? I actually put him to sleep in the interview where I was hired and that ability impressed him so much that he hired me on that basis and no other. I've been called a pain in the ass because of my ability to talk, but this actually silenced me entirely and it had nothing to do with two broken ribs.

While I was busy being dumbfounded, Sylvia looked at her brother and said, "Billy Ray? That lady has enough trouble of her own. Don't inflict yours on her. You hear me?"

"Yeah," he said as he stared at me.

"You be good, little brother."

"Yeah," he said again, still staring at me.

She got in the Range Rover, backed out and drove away through the woods. Billy Ray watched her leave and only then did he approach the porch where I sat in pain clutching that pillow to my chest. "Is that true?" he asked.

"Which part?"

"Yer a reporter?"

Well, jeez. Was I? My guess was that Harley was going to fire me even if I did show up to that meeting that was going to be held…tomorrow? I was losing track of the days. "I was," I said a bit painfully.

"Was?"

"I have personal issues," I said.

"Did those issues get you tied to a tree?"

Did they? I honestly couldn't see how. No matter what I did or how I presented that question to myself, I just didn't see it. I clutched that pillow tight, took a deep ragged breath and said, "I don't know. That's the best answer I've got." If that was true, if I got tied to that tree and beaten within an inch of my life, then Evan was involved in it somewhere. Was that possible? If it was, then what was it?

"What do you want to do, lady?"

And that became the million dollar question. He seemed willing to help me and that was a plus I hadn't counted upon. Did I want his help? If not, then I had to go back to Savannah and trust my training and my

Chapter Three

political orientation. If I went back, I would be trusting my life to the police. Would they protect me? I wanted desperately to say yes but if that was true, then where were they last Thursday night? If I committed myself to this course, then I was committing to it alone. Right? "You didn't call an ambulance, Mr. Simpson. You say it was for my benefit. What are you committing yourself to here?"

"Rehab, lady. Nothing more than that. It'll hurt and you'll call me vile names, ones I've already heard a million times. After that? Yer on yer own."

"How long?"

"As long as it takes to get you healthy."

"My face?" I said.

He shrugged. "Mebbe you'll have to get used to seeing a different face."

"Will the pain go away?"

"Depends," He said looking at me directly. "Depends on which pain yer talkin' about."

I smiled and it hurt. "Depends, huh?"

He blushed. "Sorry, ma'am."

The situation could simmer for a while. I had time and no friends. Well, Debbie. She was a friend but I couldn't take the chance and call her. She tended to be a blabbermouth and I didn't need that right now. I needed to heal and think about my marriage and what it had been and what it may have done to me. Were you involved in this, Evan? Did you know those men? Did you somehow conspire with them? If so, why? Like I said. I had time to think while my body healed.

My trainer was perfect.

He thought I was hideous and had his own problems that he didn't share with me.

Silas came back that evening with catfish. He cleaned them and we had a quiet dinner until I mentioned the bathroom. The boy's head came up from his place and said with a thick drawl, "I'll hep 'er."

Billy Ray jumped up and pushed the boy to the wall behind where he sat. He doubled his fist and was going to punch him again. I picked up the table knife from my place setting and threw it at his back where it landed flat against his shoulders. He turned, saw the knife where it landed on the floor and only then did I say, "Learn another way to deal with him, Simpson. I thought he was cute."

"Then I kin hep 'er?" he said with a bright face.

"No!" we both hollered.

It was going to be a long summer.

Chapter Four

I am an impatient person. Period. I do not walk when I can easily run. While I have never been in a physical altercation, I've been involved in some serious cat fights. I once called a woman who cut into line ahead of me at a store where I was shopping for a sweater, "A hopelessly misshapen cretin who is a descendant of Satan's own pawns". Unquote. She did not move until my stare melted her into the linoleum.

I called Billy Ray Simpson a "moldy backwater jerk with delusions of stupidity" as he held my ankles. I was doing sit-ups and my chest hurt so bad that tears rolled down my face. He frowned, stood and began to leave. Silas jumped in, held my ankles and that caused Billy to push him aside and continue to let me berate him as he refastened his massive hands to my ankles. The way I saw it, at least he didn't punch the boy.

"Just continue, lady," he growled.

Sit-ups are difficult to do with broken ribs. Although they were healing because they no longer hurt when I breathed, the strain of doing thirty of them just added to the sensitive areas under my breasts. Hence my remark about backwater jerks.

The hardest part of my rehabilitation was my face. I didn't look like Morgahna Hamilton anymore. My nose had been broken and not reset. I looked like a bad boxer. Billy just grunted and said it added character to my face. Silas touched it and asked if it hurt. As bad as having someone else's nose in the middle of my face, my crushed cheekbones healed in such a way that my entire face was different. Only my chin was the same.

The casts came off my legs after seven long and frustrating weeks. The various pains ebbed away and that left me closer to going home. I have to admit that there were times I thought Billy Ray was going to throw me out. Yeah, times. Plural. I was very nearly hyperactive and those casts on my legs irritated the hell out of me. Had Silas not been around to watch and leer at me in a very juvenile way, I may have gone crazy. I may have driven them crazy. Once when I was doing simple

Chapter Four

calisthenics, Silas stared at the way my shirt rippled as I stretched. I knew that look and knew it all too well. He was checking out my rack even though he might not have known that's what men call it. I turned my back to him and he left the room. Yes, I was grumpy with both of them. I was, however, ambulatory and that was far more than half the battle. As my health returned, I began to see a need for skills I never had.

So, I cornered Silas. "You know anything about hand-to-hand combat?"

"Um, sure," he said as his Adam's apple bobbed like a cork on a fishing line.

That meant no. To him, I was still a girl and, thus, to be feared and wanted at the same time. I sighed and *that* was a mistake. He swallowed and I heard it across the room.

Billy Ray stepped between us and said, "Why do you want to know?"

"When I leave? I'm going to have to know how to take care of myself better than I did before. If that happens again? I'll need to know how to respond to it. That's why."

"Ask me. He's a kid with a peckerful of problems around you."

"Okay, then," I said. "Turn around."

"Why?"

"I'm going to show you what they did to me and how I was caught. I need to know how to get out of that situation should it happen again."

He turned around and I was facing his broad back and shoulders. He was taller than me, huskier and stronger. Was this a fair test? I reached up a bit, wrapped my left arm around his neck and placed my right hand over his nose and mouth. "It was like this. They had a cloth or something in their hand and I passed out after a few seconds."

"So, no matter what happens or might yet, you have only a few moments to respond?"

"Yes."

"Is this how it happened? You were standing?"

"No. I was sitting in a chair."

"Let's do that, then," he said as he slid easily from my grasp. He pulled one of those rickety chairs from the table and sat down in it, his back to me. "Like this?"

"Yeah."

I laid my hand on his shoulder and paused. It felt good, felt good feeling a man like that. He had muscles but not ones that were overdone. I picked my hand up off his shoulder, put it down again and he snapped cruelly, "You done fondlin' me, lady?"

Truthfully? No. It felt nice was all, felt good to touch a man and he was the only one available. Still, I understood his remark, his impatience and his demeanor. We were there to learn and heal, not fiddle around inside childish fantasies. I slid my right hand tightly over his nose and mouth and said with some superior defiance, "Yes."

His palms exploded against my ears and my entire head rang like a bell. I fell to my knees, my hands over my ears crying and fuming. "Damn, that hurt!" I whined finally.

Naturally, Silas bellowed, "That was cool, Uncle Billy."

Billy knelt next to me and lifted my chin so he could see my face. He was watching my eyes. He pointed at the ceiling and said, "Follow my fingertip."

"Why?" I asked nastily.

"Just do it, dammit."

I followed that fingertip as the pain slowly subsided. Okay, he was worried about that concussion I'd had. I tracked his finger easily and that seemed to satisfy him. He helped me to my feet and said, "Did you understand that?"

"Do I get a chance now?"

"Sure," he said as I sat in the chair.

His left arm went around my neck and his right covered my mouth and nose. As soon as it settled into place, I made tiny fists and thrust them upward at his head as angrily as I could. Before they got halfway to their

Chapter Four

target, he twisted my head to the right, I fell off the chair and I was on my stomach, his hand still covering my face. I was still dead. Then he released me and stepped away. "Look, lady," he said. "A gun is a whole lot easier."

"You don't carry one."

"I'm a lot bigger than you are."

"With enough training, I could defense those moves a lot easier than I did."

"I don't have that much time."

That was an interesting remark. I'd been in his home for nine weeks and he hadn't gone anywhere the whole time except to the store for food, groceries and other supplies as I needed them. Even then, he made sure Silas was with me when he left. A couple of times, Sylvia came by and she was much better company than a twelve-year-old whose interest always seemed to be just below the level of my chin and above my waist. I actually stopped him a few times by fuming, "I'm up here, stupid." I did, however, refrain from telling Billy Ray about it. The kid was basically harmless and those infrequent stares were the product of rampaging hormones.

Those nine weeks, however, were interesting in that he seemed to have no job. Rather than not having enough time to teach me the basics of hand-to-hand fighting, he seemed to have a huge surplus of it. Also, despite the fact he knew my name was Morgahna, he hadn't used it one single time in all those nine weeks. I was always referred to vaguely as "lady", "ma'am" or "lookee here". I was never Morgahna despite the fact that the boy was always Silas.

"Okay," I said with a vague sense of dissatisfaction lingering about me.

I was willing to let it go only because I was so impatient. I can't say that being that way has ever gotten me into trouble – not before this anyway – so being impatient to go home and pick up my life where it left off was a powerful urge.

We hadn't talked about what was going to happen when that day came either. Billy Ray seemed wholly focused on my recovery. He seemed, however, detached and a bit too professional. You remember I said I was sweaty and that it got worse? The next morning just before his sister got there, he came in ready to give me a sponge bath. Well, no. I objected and Sylvia did it with the door locked. It felt wonderful and I felt a bit refreshed after she finished. Then she took off the splints and gave me two very solid and very professional casts that immediately began to itch if only subliminally. She rolled me into kitchen where Billy was waiting with a bottle of shampoo. Without waiting for permission, he put my head in the sink and washed my hair. That was as close to orgasmic as I got for a long time. That man knows how to wash hair.

Sylvia touched and inspected my head wound and gave it a satisfactory rating. I was healing and things got better over the next two weeks. Most of the pain went away. I still got occasional stabbing, blinding pain from that head wound and Sylvia was consistent in her opinion that I needed an x-ray and a specialist. Billy objected firmly, categorically and I did not get that specialist. Sylvia never pushed it as long as my progress was good. About two weeks into my stay with him, she came in with a walker. You know, those old people contraptions that allows them to get up and around? Well, I did and the first thing Sylvia said to her brother was, "Hug her."

"Hey," I said because I just didn't want him to touch me.

"Relax, ice queen," she said with a smile. "It's therapeutic. I want him, a larger person, to hug you and then tell me if it hurts."

"Oh."

I know he's a big man and that when he slid his arms around me it was "therapeutic". However, it still felt nice and I didn't even notice the small twinges of pain as he did. I laid my head against his chest and imagined he was Evan. God help my soul, but that helped. I imagined he was here and that this was a rather frightening dream but nothing more disturbing than that. I may have sighed but I can't swear to that.

"Well?" she said when it was over.

With God as my witness, it was like falling off a cliff. I was being held in a very similar way that I always allowed Evan to do and it felt ungodly wonderful. I stammered because I was flustered. "Oh, okay. Not much pain. A little but compared to the way it was, it's nothing."

Chapter Four

"Do it again," she ordered. "This time make it be really therapeutic."

I looked up at Billy Ray and his face was severely neutral, savagely neutral. He hugged me, then made it a bit tighter and then a bit tighter yet. It was no better or no worse than before. He released me and Sylvia asked, "And?"

"The same," I said staring up at him.

His face was blank, expressionless. What lingered there? They put me back into the wheel chair and gave me something to think about. With another check of my head wound and then the facial bruises, she stood and said, "Morgahna? You need to make a decision about the condition of your face."

"What's that mean?" I asked as a small streak of panic rose like a bottle rocket.

"I've seen your photograph on TV, Morgahna. You don't look like her anymore."

No, I didn't. I knew that much. It is impossible I think, quite impossible, for something like this to happen to a woman and her not feel deeply vulnerable. Walking around with someone else's face was difficult to accept in the first few days and weeks. As the bruising faded and I was left with a new reality, mirrors made me uncomfortable. I am, however, nothing if not aggressive. So, I took that mirror he gave me on the first full day and stared at myself ceaselessly for hours. I needed to see this new face and wonder what to do with it. My cheekbones were much different and my nose was slightly bent. Personally, I thought those two men left me hideous and ugly. Worse, my cheekbones didn't even match anymore. It left me with only a chin that I recognized as belonging to me. Yes, I cried. And, no, no one held me as I did. Well, Silas would have but I didn't want fingerprints all over me. It left me, that new face did, more alone than ever.

It was hard not to be depressed and I might have fallen completely toward apathy had Billy Ray not been there. No, he was almost no help emotionally but the way he handled me and helped my therapy along was the difference, *the* difference. For the first few days when everything was painful, he fed me. Those damn Depends were the worst thing to ever happen to me and I never did learn how to take a dump in them. I insisted on being helped to the bathroom. Urinating was interesting because I did many times in them. I cleaned and pushed myself harder in order to gain access to the bathroom whenever I needed it. Motivation, I guess, comes in all forms.

The casts came off after five weeks and I had to learn how to walk all over again. Despite the few slips I had, times when a piece of soft flesh met a firm hand, nothing remotely emotional happened. He remained stubbornly remote and removed from me. He smiled when necessary but kept to himself otherwise.

Silas helped, too.

He learned how to wash my hair but it never felt as good as when Billy Ray did it.

It all came down to now, came down to leaving because I felt ready. I could dance and we did a few times. He has some interesting *records* that we played one night. Silas was home with his mother and it was just us. It was dancing where you didn't touch and that made it okay for both of us. We just wiggled – well I did – and it felt so close to normal. It felt almost as though I was visiting a friend instead of dancing with a man who was still remotely mysterious but who just happened to save my life.

It was Friday night, late.

The moon was above the cypress trees and I was restless after my abortive attempt at hand-to-hand training. I walked out onto the small porch and headed toward the trees.

"Where are you going? It's dangerous out there."

"I need to get out, Billy. I want to go home tomorrow."

He stared at me for a long time and then nodded slightly. "Okay. Tomorrow morning?"

"That would be wonderful."

For all of those nine weeks, Evan was always on my mind. While never being introspective, there is nothing quite like two leg casts to make you be that way. So, I began to dissect my marriage and I kept coming up

Chapter Four

short. I could remember – and I even wondered why *these* thoughts kept announcing themselves – many times, many, many times when Evan woke *ready*. Please don't make me embarrass myself even more by asking, "Ready for what?" He was *ready*. Okay? The worst part was that in every single case, I couldn't have cared less. I saw it as a grand distraction but nothing more than that. I never rolled on top of him, rolled him on top of me or attempted *any* of the various things a man and a woman can do in bed.

And he was my husband.

One that I claimed to love.

One that I claimed to honor and to show devotion.

One that went to work *many* times without getting a chance to do more than peck his wife on the cheek.

A peck. A lousy fucking *peck*.

Oh, we enjoyed conjugal bliss. And isn't that a sterile term for love? I put aside time in my planner for it and marked it "personal". I couldn't even call it love. It was simply "personal" like having my nails done or buying a new pair of shoes.

That night? That Friday night? I was considering going home to the one place that was going to push me closer to the edge of complete hysteria. For the record, Billy Ray didn't have to comfort me that way, not once. I made rehabilitation a goal and I have always been a goal-oriented person. I pushed myself until my chest ached, my headaches caused me to see in bright sparkles in the corners of my eyes, until my legs screamed for relief and went to bed a few times in tears because I hurt so much. As all those small pains began to fade, I began to realize home was getting closer.

So, I left the house and just walked around its perimeter. The woods were dark and the moon was full. It was portentous but nothing happened. I walked and began to feel more and more alone. No one knew I was alive and that was a report from Sylvia. I asked her about the news every time she came to the house. Slowly, my name faded from TV and I became nothing more than another missing person. The problem, and one that I saw intimately, was that if those men came back to that tree and found me gone, then they would always wonder where I was and if I was dead. They would, in other words, do it again.

I went back to the house and stood against a tree, my back to its harsh bark as I stared up at it. In all those nine weeks, no one had visited except his sister and her son. No one. I knew vaguely where I was and Billy Ray acted as though he didn't care if the rest of the world existed.

The animals out in the woods made their presence known and had been doing it for all of those nine weeks. God, I almost wished I smoked. That scene, that night, would have been perfect. I could have smoked a long cigarette while I stared at that house and the man inside it. Who was my benefactor? The problem as I saw it, was that I was taking *him* for granted just like I'd taken Evan. I was always willing to be married to him, but it was *always* on my terms and never on his. When we had sex? I almost never got anything out of it because my mind was always on my daily planner and my precious goals. I know that Evan got off but never really found out if it was even a little enjoyable. To me, life was endless work and when he died, he took all those answers with him. Not even a note. Not even a goodbye.

Evan? I will never *know* if you loved me. Me? I know that I lost a chance to have a great love affair with a man I at least admired. You gave me a good life and allowed me to work toward what I saw as an important life. Now that you are gone, I see what I missed and cannot get it back. You are gone and I am sliding toward the belief that everything that happened those four months ago was my fault.

So. I flicked that invisible cigarette into the night and walked back to the house. Billy Ray was washing dishes and I just slid in next to him and started drying them. Neither of us said a word until I asked, "William? What's wrong with that name?"

I had two basic inconsistencies where he was concerned. The first was that very first night when he actually crawled in bed with me. The first emotionally charged thing he ever said to me referred to Iraq and the many bad things he saw there. Almost as though I reminded him of battlefield wounded, he reached out to comfort me, not to fuck me. That had never happened one single time in all those weeks. I wasn't interested in sex, not with him, not with anyone. To me, that left surface issues and I was always very good with them. I could mingle in a crowd, at a party,

Chapter Four

at any social gathering like you never saw. I was grooming myself to be mistress of the manor, a social butterfly that was all fluff and no stuff.

That first night was almost as though he cared for my injuries far more than he cared for me. My mind was scattered across several counties and I was terrified that this guy was going to finish what Tony and Doug had only started. Looking back, I reacted to his words and not to my fear. Why? Not that I'm frigid, but why would I snuggle with a complete stranger like that? Why would I make that assumption? Part of the answer lay in the way I was taken to that tree and merely trussed up as though I was nothing more than a target. I can still feel that thin wire as it was wrapped around my wrists, still feel the absence of care and that I was one of them, a person. To them, I was nothing at all and then they began to prove it. Snuggling with *anyone* after that was easy and I did. I imagine you can put that under "any port in a storm".

The second was that name, William. He reacted badly to it when Sylvia called him that. Why? Wasn't Billy a corruption of William? His entire manner changed after Sylvia called him that. It took an apology to get him back into character. Again, why? Maybe I've been a reporter for too long. Maybe. Maybe I'm just pushing anything in front of me in order to keep from thinking about tomorrow, the day I go home.

When I asked him that question, his reaction was total and immediate.

Before I can describe what it was, I need you to understand that he hadn't given me any reason to be frightened of him during all those nine weeks. In fact, he did everything I asked of him and a lot of what I asked him to do could be classified as busy work. For example, my clothes. Other than what I'd been wearing that night, I had nothing at all. I asked for such things as underwear, pants, shorts, bras, blouses, shirts, shoes, makeup, hair care products, more makeup, boots, feminine products and other stuff that simply escapes me. He made a list of everything I wanted and even returned a few things that I couldn't use for any number of reasons. He also bought stuff I hadn't asked for, stuff like various mascaras, nylons, books, tennis shoes, snacks of all sorts and never even smiled when he presented them to me. I wasn't afraid of him and that was only because of his actions and not because of his words.

That night in his kitchen after I asked him about his name? He grew ugly immediately and dropped a metal plate into the sink where it clattered to a noisy stop. With his hands free, he reached up with his left hand and pinned me to the wall next to the sink by grabbing my neck and pushing me straight backward. It startled me and, yes, I was frightened for a moment.

"God*damn* you! Don't call me that name! You hear me!"

His grip around my neck was tight and could be as permanent as he wanted to make it. Against him, I was physically helpless and he could do whatever he wanted against me. I had to force myself to be calm because nothing he'd done to that point was threatening in any way at all. Okay, the subject upset him and this was how he exhibited that rage or whatever this represented. His hand was clamped heavily around my neck and his voice was likewise threatening. So, I did the only thing I could ever do. I talked. "So, you nurse me back to health only to mess me up again because I asked you a *question*?" I twisted my face into something that looked both confused and exasperated.

When I saw his right hand form into a fist, I winced, closed my eyes and said, "Really, Billy Ray? This is what you do after nine weeks? Really? You mess me up again and make it easier to go home?"

He growled like a wild animal and stalked out into the night. I panted heavily because the mere idea of him going off on me like that was harrowing. I slid to my butt on the floor, my hands shaking all the way. I expected him to come back after a few minutes and when that didn't materialize, I got shakily to my feet and went back to my bedroom. No matter what happened now, I was going home in the morning. If he wouldn't take me, I ask Sylvia to do it the first time I saw her. If not her, then Debbie. If not her, then my thumb. Either way, no matter what, I was going home for a number of reasons and he really wasn't one of them despite what he'd just done. Other than threaten me, he hadn't done anything at all.

I dropped out my clothes and got into a nightgown that he'd bought for me as a surprise some weeks ago. It was another small reminder that he was helping me and had indeed saved my life.

The surrounding woods were always alive at night. In the daytime, you tend not to hear those noises and sounds. In all those nine weeks, I

Chapter Four

hadn't been afraid of anything I'd heard because, in truth, I knew what a lot of them were. A variety of birds including owls and not a few larger animals, black bears especially. In all those nights, however, he was always there and that gave me a sense of security. I am, like I have maintained, a girl's girl. That night, it was spooky and the moonbeams slanting in through the single window in my room held shadows that moved around ominously. It was as though the room itself was alive. I didn't sleep much at all.

I turned the bedside light on for a while and that just made things worse because I lost sight of everything outside that small circle of light. The unknown simply got worse. I switched it off again and tried to sleep but the night was alive and I was still recuperating from savagely inflicted injuries. I heard crickets and knew frogs and toads couldn't be far behind, knew that some coyotes and a few wolves prowled the area as well as skunks, raccoons and possums. None of those animals ever pressed himself on me before like they did that night. I interpreted every nudge, creak and crack in the night as an animal entering the house and searching for me alone.

And one came in.

It was nearly two in the morning when I heard the screen door open, then close and the sound of soft footsteps in the night as they crossed the floor to my room. It was a person and the only one I knew out there that also knew about this house was Billy Ray Simpson and it was him. He came to the bedroom door, opened it and stood there in the night. I cringed to the wall behind me and waited for what I assumed was going to be the rest of his explosion. Instead, I heard the unmistakable sound of tears as he said, "You got a small face just like she did. I almost didn't help you, Morgahna. I almost left you there because your face is small like hers was. So soft and delicate. I shoulda know'd she would die like that. I shoulda know'd better. I don't hate you, okay? Please don't think that. I'd never hurt you and I'll take you home in the mornin'."

Then he turned and walked back to his own room.

I flopped my legs down in front of me because they had been curled up around my face as I hid behind them. After he walked out, I was angry at myself for not seeing this as it happened. Twenty-twenty hindsight is great but I am a college graduate and I knew I couldn't have seen this without some input from his end.

Well, this was it.

Despite some small nagging pains that still inflicted themselves in me, I crawled out of bed and heard his sobs before I was halfway to his bedroom door. I knocked gently on the open door and said, "Can I come in?"

"I'd rather you didn't, ma'am," he said as he retreated behind that wall again.

I took a deep breath and a big chance, not only with him but with myself as well. "Evan was a good man, Billy Ray. It's very possible that I didn't deserve him. I made his life difficult if not downright impossible. I've been trying to convince myself that he didn't commit suicide because of me and have mostly failed. Maybe if we'd been better friends, he might have been able to talk to me and then maybe this wouldn't have happened." I shuffled my feet, dropped my face toward the floor and tried hard not to cry and failed entirely. "I'd rather you said yes, William." I exhaled a trunk full of tears and stood wracking with sobs.

"C'mon in," he said as he sat on his bed alone, his hands between his knees and his head down.

With god as my witness, I suddenly felt nervous, like a girl getting ready for the prom. Was I attracted to him? No. Emphatically no. As I thought back, it was very possible I wasn't attracted to Evan either and I wasn't about to compound one mistake by making another one just like it.

His room is Masculine Definitive without the dirty clothes scattered about. That Sagan book, Pale Blue Dot, was on his nightstand and a bookmark showed that he was nearly two-thirds done with it. "You like his work?" I asked nodding toward the book.

"The man was a fucking genius and we make fun of him. Yeah, I like his work."

"Contact?"

"Interesting book. Shitty movie."

Chapter Four

I reached up to wipe tears from his face and he flinched. I grabbed his chin and said, "Hold still." He wouldn't look at me as I wiped away those stray tears that hung from his eyes like daggers from his heart. The heart always messes us up. Always. We think we know what we want, think that it's lucid, calm and focused and then the damn heart interferes. With Evan? No. I can say that now. My heart never intruded on me from the time I first saw him to the last time I did in that coffin. To him, I always cold and distant. I can't see how he wanted to be with me.

Billy's face is rugged but maybe that's just the way he forced himself to live. Maybe it's as gentle and kind as his heart. I know his heart better than I know his face because he's shown it to me so many times over all these weeks.

"You ain't her," he said as I wiped those last few tears.

"No, I'm not."

"Morgahna?" he said.

"Yes, Billy Ray?"

"I can't."

"Me neither," I said. "What killed her, Billy Ray? You know about me and what happened."

"Childbirth killed her and took my son with her."

"Her name?"

"Aileen."

"And you treat her memory like it's forbidden? Bill Ray? Did you love her?"

"So much that it still hurts."

"How long has it been?"

"Eleven months, thirteen days and a few hours. I used to know minutes, too."

"Can I hug you?"

"Ma'am? I'd really rather you didn't."

I did anyway and we cried together.

My biggest goal as we cried was no more than allowing someone else's emotions to be become as important as my own. I was always the one running toward the horizon at full speed. While that might get things done, a lot of people drop off along the way for any number of reasons. Among them is the problem that people present, or can. People are far more important than things. Trust me on this one. My home is full of things but not the man whose voice I still needed to hear. The things will always be there, but people tend to be transient. They tend to die. The things they leave behind are not them and will never speak with their voice. I needed a friend and Billy Ray seemed like a logical candidate.

Hmm.

Logic.

An and old very unreliable friend.

Chapter Five

I was nervous as, well, that whore that keeps going to church. You'd think she would know better, but she keeps going anyway. Maybe I should have left well enough alone, but my life had been taken away from me and I wanted it back. The problem was I didn't know what that meant. So I asked Billy if I could ask him some blunt questions about what had happened.

"Only as long as I can give you the same blunt answers," he said with his face immobile.

"Sure," I said smiling. "I wouldn't have it any other way."

"Then, shoot."

"Should I be nervous about going home? I am. I know who did this. If they find out I'm alive, then they'll do it again. Maybe next time they will succeed. Should I go to the police?"

We were standing on his porch just watching the woods beyond the perimeter of his property. He slid his hands into his pockets and said, "You know about the Iraq prison scandal." It wasn't a question. It was a reaffirmation that he knew my background as a reporter.

"Yeah," I said watching him because despite his manner of few words, I know him to an intelligent man.

"They pinned a few charges on a few stupid fools who went to prison for a while and the public was satisfied."

That was it. Nothing more.

"And?" I said expectantly.

"There is no and," he said calmly, unemotionally. "The public was happy."

I slid my arm inside his and said, "Just say it, Billy Ray. What is it?"

"You know anything about prisons?"

"Nope," I said smiling at him.

Chapter Five

"Well, the guards are only one aspect of the prison. Nothing happens by accident in one of those places. Nothing. The prisoners are under the face of a gun and they can't do anything but time. Period. If abuse happens on a scale like that, then someone above the level of prison guard not only approved it but got away with it. You can go to the police and tell them what you know. They'll arrest those two guys if they can find them. What are the chances, though, based on what you've said, that those two men acted alone and without any direction from someone else?"

Well, basically, nonexistent. As I held his arm under mine, I looked into his eyes because I was getting close to being able to read through their placidity. There was more there, more lurking just below the surface. "They're muscle for someone else?" I asked.

"You described yourself once, Morgahna, as a girl's girl. That true?"

"You could rape me and I would do nothing but scream."

His mouth quivered toward a smile. "You know I'd never do that."

"So," I said with a smile. "We both know who I am. Why?"

"You need someone to help you."

"Debbie?"

"She any good?"

"I don't think it is humanly possible to rape her. She'd enjoy it too much and call it the beginning of a relationship."

"So, no?"

"Um, no."

"So?"

"I don't know, Billy. You know anyone that good?"

"Yeah," he said.

"Anyone I know?"

He sighed, shook his head and said to my surprise, "No."

"No?" I said with genuine surprise.

It was his turn to smile. "You don't really know me."

"Booger," I said smacking his arm. "You volunteering to help me?"

That's when it got serious for the first time. I believe that one of the reasons I have had both success and catastrophic failure in my young life is that I lurch from crisis to crisis. The ultimate in tunnel vision, I see what is in front of me and give that issue my full concentration. As the Saturday morning heat began to gather and make itself felt in the form of sweaty armpits, I watched as his face went from mildly playful to as serious as I'd seen it. "They tried to kill you, Morgahna. If you do this, if you stay out of the public eye, then you're inviting more trouble just like you had." Then he turned his face on me and gave me the full impact of what lay beneath that mask. "You ready to be tied to a tree again? You ready to let them do whatever they want?"

"I'm willing to let them try, Billy Ray. Besides, even if I go to the police and let them handle this, they know they failed and they'll try again. Answer the question, William. Are you volunteering to help me?"

"You need help, Morgahna. You need it badly."

"Answer the damn question, Billy Ray."

He shuffled nervously. "You gonna try to kiss me or anything?"

"No," I said adamantly.

He nodded as his gaze rested on the woods. "Okay. Let's go home."

The Billy Ray Simpson I'd met and befriended was quiet and unassuming. The one that rode back to Savannah with me was far different. Like me, he squirmed ceaselessly until I asked, "Okay, dammit. What's wrong?"

He looked away from me and said, "You're cute."

There must be a better way of responding to something like than a laugh that appears quite unbidden between you. Cute? Teddy bears are cute. Three-year-girls are cute. Me? I was a lumpy misshapen hag whose

Chapter Five

best days were left at the foot of a gum tree back in that swamp. "Oh, stop," I said laughing loudly. "My ribs hurt."

"Sorry," he said sulking.

"Billy Ray..."

"I won't say it again," he said sulking. "Ever. Okay?"

"What are we going to do first?' I said. "I was always big on planning things."

"The first thing we do is make sure your cute face stays that way."

"Billy..."

"That's first. Second, we make a list of everyone that you can tell about this. Everyone. No one goes on the list unless you're positive they can keep a secret."

"For how long?" I said only because it seemed reasonable.

"Indefinitely," he said.

"Okay, that makes the list somewhat shorter."

"Start."

"Debbie Jenson, Dave Woods, Harley Hood. That's it."

"You trust them?"

"With my life, Billy."

"That's the truth," he said. Then he added as though the result of deep thought. "Yer still cuter than a bug in January."

"Stop it," I said as I began to pout. I even crossed my arms defiantly in my lap.

Normally, I'd be fretting over how to get into my house because I had no keys and nothing to identify myself to the police and/or the neighbors should I try to ask anyone to let me in. Billy just passed it off with a wave of his hand when he said, "It ain't no problem."

"Really?"

"Really."

"My front door is on a deadbolt."

"S'okay," he said confidently.

"I have an alarm."

He patted my arm. "S'okay, cutie. Don't worry about it."

"Goddammit, Billy," I said as I lost my temper. "Stop it."

"Ya gotta make me, Morgahna. I think it's the truth and there's some guy out there that will agree with me."

"Yeah? And you? You're a big handsome man. Why hasn't some girl come along before now?"

"I'm waitin' fer a year."

We got closer to home and our conversation lapsed entirely. I was both fuming and pouting because *no one* was going to look at my face and see a "cutie" no matter how hard they looked. I was falling into a depression when he said, "Beauty's in the eye of the beholder."

"Dave Woods said that. He was full of shit, too."

"He sweet on you?"

I snickered. "Dave's sweet on the Falcons. He lives for football, the Georgia Bulldogs on Saturday and the Atlanta Falcons on Sunday."

"Monday through Friday?"

"He works."

"Uh huh."

My home is just a few blocks south of city hall. Yeah, that was another plan, or part of my master one. That home was going to be a problem for several reasons, not the least of which was the fact I couldn't afford it based on my salary. Oh, Evan thought of the money and what I would need should he die. Even dying the way he did, he left me quite able to afford it. Before I dropped off the end of the world, I was debating the merits of paying off my mortgage with the proceeds of his life insurance policies. He was going to be twenty-nine in July, a date that was gone now. He held those policies long enough to make the suicide clause moot. They paid off and it was like Las Vegas or Atlantic City all rolled up into one big payday. Yeah, that's the way I saw it, his death. It was a lucrative investment on *my* future. I'd like to say I had twinges of conscience when those policies cashed, but the truth is I didn't. Logic told me that *he* owed it to *me* for what he'd done. Kind of harsh, huh?

Before we went home, though, we went to the parking lot on River Street where I'd left my car and found that it was gone, just gone. I wasn't surprised, just a bit disappointed because with my new face, I could foresee all sorts of trouble proving to people that I was Morgahna Jayne Hamilton. The police probably had it in an impound lot and I could foresee all sorts of trouble identifying myself with that name. I didn't look like her anymore and the one way I could prove it was through fingerprints and DNA.

We were in Billy Ray's pickup as we drove back toward my home on Taylor Street. I love the historic area of Savannah. It's the way a city should look, at least in my own estimation. There are twenty-four squares scattered throughout the historic section of Savannah where I live, the closest being Chatham Square. There hasn't been any serious objection to their maintenance or creation either. Add in the old the buildings and their preservation and the city is perfect. My favorite buildings are the Victorian ones. There are other styles, but I love the way the buildings that are built in that style impress themselves on me. They scream luxury and gentility. I hope, pray even, that whatever happens to my life from here on, that the city never loses its charms on me. It seems to exude a welcome to anyone who comes here. Indeed, the story that has passed down through the generations of people who live here and call Savannah home is that as William Tecumseh Sherman drove through the south ripping and shredding every piece of our lives and heritages, that Savannah impressed itself on him to such a degree that he refused to burn it down. Maybe it's true. I'm not a historian, but a once-newspaperwoman.

We parked on Taylor Street by the stairs that led up to the second, and main floor, of the house. Billy stood back and looked up at the building as though surveying it for potential trouble. Me? Well, I can't say I saw trouble, but I saw questions. Albert Daniels, my downstairs tenant, was gone. The window that looked out onto Taylor Street from inside his own floor betrayed an empty room. As Billy headed for the stairs, I put my hand on his arm and said, "There should be a curtain in that window, Billy." I peered in through it and saw nothing inside at all, just an empty room that Albert used as a living room.

"You rented to someone?"

The mere fact that he could ask that question meant he'd lived here before. Yes, there was a lot I didn't know about Billy Ray Simpson. For example, in homes like mine the first floor can be almost anything. We chose to rent it simply to make ends meet better. Well, if you choose to read that as salving my conscience because the house was way above what a reporter on my salary could afford, you have my permission. "Yeah," I said. "A couple, Albert and Shannon."

"They have a lease?"

"Yeah, but it didn't expire until January."

I could think of several good reasons why Al and Shannon would move out like that, but the one that was most obvious was my apparent murder. Why would someone want to stay in a place where the owners of the house were apparent suicide and murder victims?

The entrance to the first floor was directly under the stairway landing to the second story. Despite Billy Ray's apparent impatience to go upstairs, I walked over to the door and it opened quite easily, quite surprisingly. He shouldered me out of the way and entered the empty level as though the place was booby trapped. He was helping and I didn't mind the gentle reminder that someone *had* tried to kill me. The place was entirely empty, not a stick of furniture was left. Al and Shannon moved in their own stuff and were so quiet that it was easy to believe they weren't there.

It was troubling because I was beginning to suspect everyone that knew me might be responsible for the attack I suffered. Were Debbie, Dave and Harley above suspicion? Well, as much as I knew them I had to maintain that they were.

"Upstairs," I said finally as we looked through the one bedroom that was on that level.

"Okay. Leave me to it, Morgahna."

"Sure," I said only because I was preoccupied with names, just names. Who would want me dead? I still didn't see an answer to that one.

Chapter Five

We moved out and I just followed him out the door and around to the stairs. I was troubled by Al and Shannon's disappearance, was thinking about the couple and their relationship with me. The more I considered it, the more I realized I didn't have one with them, with either of them. Was that a problem? I didn't know as I watched Billy Ray climb the stairs to my level. He moved slowly and silently up the stairs. He had guns but none on him. It was broad daylight on a Saturday morning and weapons down here could get us into trouble very easily. That was our decision before we ever left his house out by Fort Stewart. Maybe that was short-sighted but that was how we figured it. Well, he did. Me? I don't have a gun and I could never imagine owning one before all this started.

As soon as I got onto that stairway, however, I saw a problem. I have curtains in the windows, nice ones that cost Evan a small fortune. They were gone; the window was empty. "Billy?" I whispered up the stairs to him. "There should be curtains in the windows. They're gone, too."

"Stay there," he said pointing back down at me.

I'd call myself brassy but not brave. In my world, that nicely logical one, people responded to logical questions logically. My biggest asset, I always thought, was no fear of involving myself with other people. No one ever got physical, no one ever got in my face except to scream. Ever since that night out in the woods, my perspective has changed radically. I hate to say this, but I expect violence from people I don't know now. Billy Ray was outside those considerations only because he'd already proven himself to me. Anyone else was dubious at best and the top of those stairs represented very dubious territory so I watched him climb to the top of the stairs, test the doorknob and find it open. I looked up at him and shrugged because I really had no idea what was happening.

He licked his lips, opened the door quickly and shot a quick look inside before standing free of the room against the wall outside the door. I pasted myself against the wall and became a spectator. He looked puzzled and I mouthed, "What?"

He crooked his finger at me and motioned me up to the top where he stood just outside the door. "Were you refurbishing this place when everything happened?" he whispered.

"Refurbish?" I said confused. I craned my head inside the front door and saw that my home had been completely gutted. The drywall had been removed and the original framing was exposed. The furniture, all of it, was gone just like downstairs. The difference, of course, was that the downstairs was still intact. That quick glimpse troubled me even more than the beating did because this was my home and nothing that had happened here was part of any larger problem. Right? I looked at Billy but was reluctant to say anything, do anything or even look back inside. Finally, I screwed my faced into a mask of confusion and just shrugged my shoulders.

Holding his left hand out to keep me behind him, he moved inside and I moved carefully with him. My home was worse than as if it was under construction. The room just inside that door was a parlor, a room full of signs of welcome and gentle comfort. There had been an upright piano in here, one that I played fitfully because I never wanted to take the time to learn to play well. There was a grandfather's clock just inside the front door, a knickknack shelf opposite it. Paintings, mostly landscapes, hung from walls in groupings by artist and style. This room represented many long loud tantrums from me, fits of impatience that Evan simply tolerated with nothing stronger than a loud sigh. This room was supposed to be perfect, the perfect place to introduce someone to my home, the style of living I preferred and was supposed to be a glimpse of my goals for the future. My future.

To the left was the living room and I could see the walls inside the entrance way and that they were in the same condition. None of the walls were spared. Every single piece of dry wall had been removed along with the all of the furnishings. Nothing was left. With no pretenses, no fears, no hesitations, I wandered through what was left of my home and was so shocked and shaken that had anyone been lying in wait for me, I would be dead. I wandered up the stairs and went to where our bedrooms were located. We had a very plush king-sized bed on which little ever happened besides sleep. Now, the room was as empty as a newly-built house. Even the carpeting had been removed. It was worse than upsetting; it was positively nightmarish. I was in deep shock at the state of my home as I wandered aimlessly through empty rooms and walls that were worse than naked. I looked in empty closets and wondered where all of my clothes were and why someone had taken them.

Chapter Five

Finally, I felt a hand on my shoulder. "Morgahna?"

Billy Ray was trying to pierce the emotional shield I had thrown up around myself. His left hand was on my right shoulder; I put my own left hand on his and fought back tears. "Yeah, Billy?"

"They're lookin' for somethin'. You see that, right?"

His eyes were entirely sympathetic but questioning. I sniffled, my chin quivered and I nodded. No. I hadn't seen that at all. My affirmation was as lame as my career. "What…what were they looking for, Billy?"

He hugged me and said, "I was kinda hopin' you knew." Then he said, "You got neighbors on one side. I can ask them what happened and who did it. Okay?"

"You want me to help you? I know them, you know?"

"I'd feel better if you were out of sight for a while, Morgahna. The fewer people that know you're alive, the better your chances are of staying that way."

"Okay," I said quietly, said with a voice that clearly troubled him.

"You okay?" he said putting his hands on the points of my shoulders and staring hard at me.

"Why are you doing this, Billy? I'm no one special."

Without a trace of a smile, he said, "Cause yer cute. I always help cute ladies."

"I'm as ugly as a Yankee souvenir hunter."

"No, Morgahna. You are one cute and beautiful woman. Maybe you don't see it that way because your face is different. But that's not what I see."

Well, damn. That was worse. I frowned at him and said, "So, the only reason you're here is because you like the way I look? My ass, too? My rack? My…"

And he kissed me.

It surprised me, offended me, baffled me, overwhelmed me and made want to stay in his arms forever. He pulled me close to him and I actually held my hands out from my sides because I didn't know how to react at first. I needed people, though, needed to know that someone cared whether I lived or died. Did he? To that moment, he was little more than a new friend, one that could easily slide either deeper into my life or out of it completely. Slowly, I put my arms around his shoulders and held him as tightly as he was holding me. I'd like to lie and say I confused him for Evan for a moment and that was why I did this horrid thing, but that would be a lie, a complete and total one. He kissed well and I didn't even care, didn't even consider the other women he may have kissed this way. It was totally absorbing, totally captivating and I was completely his.

When he stopped, I found my left leg wrapped around his right in an erotic embrace that embarrassed me because it was so completely wanton. I have *never* been wanton in my life. I was never looking for a "relationship". I was looking for an upwardly-mobile husband and Billy Ray Simpson was a *hillbilly*. I was breathing hard when it stopped and I said with a broken voice, "Don't ever do that again."

And he did.

And the same thing happened.

I got totally lost inside him and that had never happened to me before. I felt myself wrapping both legs around his waist as he kissed me and even found the space and time to chastise myself for doing it. This was not me; this was someone else entirely. This was craven, brazen and so completely satisfying that I didn't even bother to unwind myself from him when it was over.

And, god help me, he held me, just held me.

"Morgahna? I ain't goin' anywhere until you tell me to leave."

My mind was so erratically addled that I had no words to use and *that* had never happened to me before. I had lots of words. I was, if you remember, a girl's girl. I could talk on any subject endlessly even if it made no sense at all. Now? I merely squeaked and meant it as a chorus of delight. What did this mean to Evan? He was dead four months and I was kissing another man in the home he gave to me as a present, as a down payment on our future life together. It was wrong but I hung onto Billy as though he was a human life preserver. Finally, I said into his chest, "I…I don't think I want you to leave."

"Okay," he said and nothing more.

Chapter Five

Slowly, my basically permanent temperament oozed back into me and I said as I unwound from him, "I...I'm sorry for being that forward."

"You need help and I'm going to give it. Can we leave it at that?"

Well, double damn. He turned and walked toward the stairs and I said incredulously, "What? You kiss me *twice* and that's all I get?"

"You seemed to need it."

Well, triple damn. Southern girls slap when they're offended. I walked up to him ready to lower the boom and when I tried he deftly grabbed my hand and then the other one when I tried to use it. "Damn you, Billy Ray Simpson! You make a fool out of me and then that's your attitude? 'I seemed to need it?' That's it? I'm a fluffball for your amusement?"

He lowered his head and said, "I apologize, Morgahna. You seem to think you're worse than a wallflower and I see you as sunshine after a morning rain. Fluffball? Oh, no, ma'am. Can we make a deal?"

Well, *fourple* damn. My skin felt as though it was on fire so I stupidly said, "Deal? What kind of deal?" Who was this man that made me forget my own expectations? I wanted to slap him and make him see it as I saw it, as proper and decorous and entirely fitting for me. I felt my hands grow into nervous fists, ones that would never see anger and waited.

"I won't do that again if you stop calling yourself and referring to yourself as ugly 'cause you ain't."

I nervously held out my hand to him and said, "Deal."

I expected him to grab me again and found myself mildly disappointed when he didn't but merely took it and said, "Agreed."

My entire life was gone, just gone, and I was staring at him with the deepest puzzlement I ever felt. I should have retreated to those tears that I dredged up but could only wonder about him and what he'd just done to my soul. It was an act of defiant will to change my focus from him to my home. "You're right. You should talk to the neighbors. Maybe someone saw something."

"We also need to find you a place for tonight."

"I can call Debbie," I said.

He gave me his phone and said, "You do that now and I'll come back alone to talk to the neighbors."

Life was pushing me relentlessly and I was letting it. Those nine weeks? They were a mere interlude into a world that I'd never considered possible, not one single time. I was about to be exposed to liars, cheats and thieves, some of whom I called friends at one time.

I was about to find out where Debbie stood.

Friend or foe.

They were all going to choose sides now that I was back.

Chapter Six

The worst day of my entire life, before that truly horrid one nine weeks before, was the night I was certain Evan was going to propose to me. He told me he was going to take me to a restaurant off Forsyth Park. I was living in an apartment towards Richmond Hill and was planning my ascent up the corporate ladder. I was a very foolish twenty-two year old girl masquerading as a woman. I was chaste, demure and used the word "charmed" as often as possible. Everything was charming including Evan. I called him a "charming dear" that night. We ate dinner at a fashionable restaurant, Drake's, over on Broughton that was within sight of the county courthouse. He was cheerful but my stomach rumbled all night and when he didn't ask me to marry him, I cried until four o'clock in the morning and then went to work three hours later.

That night pretty well sums up my life to that point of it. I was cold, calculating and cunning. Maybe Evan wouldn't agree and maybe I'm being too hard on myself. Personally, I don't think so. I think I am describing myself perfectly. I remember wearing something that would show a hint of cleavage but nothing more than that. A hint was all I ever gave him. I can't say that I was as cold and as calculating as I want to paint myself because it did hurt. When you are convinced you're in love with a man who will not ask you to marry him, you become dejected and depressed. It's what the girl's girl does and I did.

My work then was still minor, still the city council meetings and an occasional flower show like the big one down at the fairgrounds on Montgomery Street. I was being competent and trustworthy, two things that always got me more work. That day, the next one, I hadn't eaten, was grumpier than usual, snapped at Harley and called him, "An old man whose biggest thrill is watching Dolly Parton walk." I threw my briefcase into my cubicle and sat hard and angry on the chair in front of my terminal. That day, I was anything but competent and trustworthy. Dave Woods was still in my future, so my biggest contact on the way up was still my boss and I'd just called him a lecher.

I left work that day as depressed as any single one I'd ever lived through and I was a college graduate that knew the pressure of finals. My

Chapter Six

apartment was on the second floor and I fairly stomped up those stairs to it. I unlocked the door and entered a wonderland of flowers and soft music. Evan was on his knee in the middle of the room and said quite unbidden, "Morgahna Parker? Will you marry me?" I'd forgotten I gave him a key.

That was me, Morgahna Jayne Parker.

Obviously, I said yes.

Well, as bad as that day had been, this day was easily far worse than that one. Then, whether or not Evan married me made no difference on whether or not I lived or died. Then, I was merely upset that my plan to marry Evan Hamilton seemed to be a gigantic miscalculation. Now? If Debbie Jenson was in on this, I could very easily wind up dead.

I was about to find out, or at least try.

I dialed her cell phone number and knew she could be anywhere at all on a Saturday morning. Debbie's a hairdresser and seems to be a good one because her rates are astonishing. It rang three times which meant she was looking at the number of the incoming call and trying to determine whether or not she should answer it. *C'mon, you blond bimbo. Answer the damn phone.* Finally, with a voice dripping with sterility, she said, "Hello? This is Debbie Jenson speaking." At least she wasn't driving.

"Debbie?" I said quickly. "Please don't scream. It's me, Morgahna."

We've been friends since elementary school. To be technical about it, she has maintained our friendship throughout all these years. She sends Christmas Cards that I hurry to answer, birthday cards, insists on "girl day" every few months and tries to tease me into wearing something trashy. The only time she ever succeeded was Halloween two years ago when I went as a "bar girl". The rotten bitch didn't bother to tell me that's what GI's called girls they bought over in Vietnam. I had the costume right, a tightly-slitted skirt, my highest two-inch heels and the most garish makeup this side of the annual St. Patrick's Day Parade.

She tends to get a bit emotional at times.

"Morgahna!" she shrieked. "Where the fuck are you! Where the fuck have you been!"

"Deb? Scream? Remember I asked that you not?"

"MORGAHNA HAMILTON? YOU TELL ME WHERE YOU ARE BECAUSE I'M COMING TO GET YOU!"

"Are you home?"

"MORGAHNA! WHERE ARE YOU! TELL ME, GODAMMIT!"

"My house. Be here in half an hour, okay?"

"TEN FUCKING MINUTES, YOU ROTTEN BITCH!"

And she hung up the phone.

Just for the record: We are friends, Debbie and I, only because she tries, not because I do. That's only if I haven't made it clear. I switched off the phone and handed it to Billy. "She's on her way."

"You feel safe around her?"

The place was beginning to make me feel as though I really had been raped. I wandered down the stairs and out into the kitchen. I was learning how to cook and Debbie was teaching me. The room was stripped just like all the other rooms were. There was an island in the middle of it and it had been taken apart down to its framework and resembled nothing more than a radar assembly on a warship in Charleston harbor.

Billy Ray stood in the doorway that separated the kitchen from the dining room and I shrugged. "Billy? I trusted you and then you kissed me."

"Twice," He said as though correcting me. "Do you? Do you trust her?"

I was about to shrug and say, "I don't know." I caught myself and tried to straighten my shattered concentration. I have always been able to concentrate. Always. Even as a child, I could eliminate most everything else from my mind and concentrate on any given subject. School was never very hard only because work has never scared me. This has, though.

Chapter Six

I feared sleeping alone, sleeping in a house without Billy Ray Simpson within reach, within easy reach. "Billy?" I said. "I have no choice. She's it, my only friend."

"The other two men you mentioned?"

"Work colleagues. One is my boss."

"So, if this girl, Debbie, turns out to be on their side, how are you going to face this?"

How? Was he kidding? It was going to be a train wreck. *Morgahna? Don't you fall apart. You deal with this because you always have.* I took a deep breath and said, "One day at a time, Billy. I think you should let me face her alone, though. You could be my ace in the hole."

"Meaning?"

"If she goes bad, you can save my pretty face again."

"Deal," he said sticking out his hand.

"Deal," I replied and we shook hands just as I heard Debbie's Miata slide to the curb and her harried footsteps on the stairs outside.

Billy went back to the kitchen and I watched for the door to open because I was certain she wasn't going to knock and she didn't.

I covered my face because that's how it hit me. She was the first of all the people I knew who were going to judge me one way or the other. She's the erratically emotional one of us, the one who cries at wedding and funerals, the one who talks out loud in movies, the one who demands service in restaurants, the one who shrieks involuntarily when surprised.

"Morgahna?" she said with shock and surprise holding her voice together. "Where have you been?" Then, as she obviously saw the condition of the house, she said wonderingly, "What have you done to the house, Morg?"

"Debbie?" I said as scared as I'd ever been and I had a few good reasons to be scared lately. "Does it sound like me? Does it, Deb? Do you still hear my voice?" I was still standing in the living room, still trying to keep myself together because despite the silliness between Billy Ray and me, I wasn't certain I could live with this new face. It didn't look like me and I wanted my old one back, now more than ever. Debbie didn't know this face and I imagined all sorts of screaming and wailing when I dropped my hands. That's why I didn't. I stood still, stood trying very hard not to cry.

She touches people, always has. I am merely energetic, not engaging. She's closer to both. I felt her hands on my wrists as she stood in front of me. "C'mon, girlfriend. Let's see what you did. Plastic surgery, huh? Nose job, new house, rip it all out and start fresh. That's what I'd do." She pried my hands free and I was terrified because of all the people I knew, she knew me best. If she couldn't accept this ugliness, then who could? Me? Well, maybe not.

"Ooh, cool nose," she said touching it lovingly. "Morgahna? You really did a good job here. Who's the doctor? I have to meet this guy." She was smiling and looking at me, my eyes, everything. She touched my cheeks, my forehead, touched everything and said, "Does it hurt still? This is radical, babe. How much did it cost?"

"You recognize me?" I asked.

"Not a bit, girlfriend. You look like a runway model now. Your voice gave you away." Then she smacked my arm and said, "Where have you been? The police are looking for you. Tommy's going nuts. Morg, baby? For someone that needed a change in her life, this really fits." Then she turned and looked at the room. "Morg? This place was always too stuffy for me. I'm glad you're starting from scratch."

"Deb?" I said as she looked around. "A doctor didn't do this to me."

She has a bright face, totally open and cheerful. She highlights it with ruby-red lipstick that contrasts her white teeth perfectly. Nothing is wrong with her face, her appearance or the way she presents herself to the world. It's her damn personality that irritates the hell out of me. I tried once to find other friends for her besides me in the vain hope that I could pawn her off on them and discovered that she really doesn't have a lot of close friends, just boyfriends that want and usually get the obvious from her. I'm it as friends go. So we maintain this rather tenuous friendship that stretches back nearly twenty years. I can go weeks on end without seeing her but she seems to have a pathological need to see me more frequently than that. I can just bet she was lonely for those nine weeks. I watched her face as she turned around after I made that statement and

Chapter Six

realized I'd missed her, too. I realized I like her and always have, that any objection I ever had to her was career oriented. She lives in a condo down on Skidaway Road near the university. That ten-minute drive to get here? She must have been eighty the whole way because that trip takes more than ten minutes.

"What?" she said as her whole face froze for a moment.

"Deb? I was attacked and beaten. A doctor didn't do this. A lead pipe did. I was taken out into the woods near Fort Stewart, tied to a tree and nearly beaten to death. That's why I look like this. The house? I didn't do this. Someone else did."

She's a bit shorter than me, but only by an inch or two. There are times, I have found, that human beings become singular and stand out from their surroundings. The crowd they are part of just melts away and they stand alone and weakened somehow. That's how I saw Debbie just then; she was weaken somehow by the news that I was taken against my will and beaten very nearly to death. "You need to call the police, Morg," she said, her face showing concern and rising panic.

"Why?" I asked.

Her eyes bulged and she squealed, "Why? Are you fucking serious! This is criminal!"

"You aren't interested in how I got untied from that tree? I was in the middle of nowhere, Deb. Literally. They couldn't have found a better place to do it. This house? They think I'm dead, Deb. If I go public, they'll know I'm not."

Time usually heals all wounds. My face? Maybe one day I can have a plastic surgeon put it back the way it used to be, but that isn't what I mean. Time usually gives a person time to think and the two pieces of input I'd had were Billy Ray Simpson and Debbie Jenson. Somewhere inside that combination of people and events, a switch turned and I asked myself, "Who has the legal right to do this if I'm dead?"

And the answer scared me to death.

No, It wasn't Debbie.

It was Tommy Underwood. He has power of attorney on my estate should I die. Even if I'm not dead, he has that power. This house was searched and ransacked only because Tommy Underwood allowed it to happen. That does not mean he was the person who arranged my kidnapping and attempted murder but it suddenly made him a person with whom I could not deal openly. I murmured his name, Tommy's name. "Tommy Underwood."

"Are you okay?" she asked quietly, her hand on my forearm.

"Yeah," I said troubled.

"You looked faraway, girl."

"I was." I backed her up to a wall and she fit right between the two-by-fours. "Tell me you didn't do this, Deb. Tell me. Tell me my face isn't the same because you helped." I had my hand under her chin and was doing this the same way I remember Billy Ray doing it to me.

Tommy Underwood fits nicely into the same category that Debbie does. He's an infrequent friend, but one I've only known since Evan and me got serious maybe six years ago. In that time, he's been a friend but not a confidant. Debbie is that to me. She is the one to whom I spill my desires. She's the one that knows I married Evan because he was going to be a wealthy lawyer just as much as that I loved him. Within that narrow definition of friendship was a troubling thought. *Debbie knows that I married Evan for two reasons and that if he'd met only one of my criteria, I would never have married him at all.* She knows, in other words, my secrets and she is friendly with men. I could see her being dined by Tommy Underwood and telling him things about me that I'd told her in confidence.

"Morg," she said like a little girl who was being accused of something simply *unchaste*. "You don't think I had anything to do with this?"

"How did I get free from that tree, Debbie?"

"I don't know?" she said squirming under my hand against that naked wall.

"Think about it."

"Someone found you?"

Chapter Six

"Yeah. Debbie. I'd been tied to a tree, beaten with a metal pipe, had two ribs broken, a concussion, two broken legs and my face was beaten so savagely that it turned purple and stayed that color for several weeks as the bruising faded. I should be dead but I'm not. I have help, Debbie. I have help that has proved himself way beyond what you've been able to do. Convince me, Deb."

Events tend to show us who we are, who we really are and how we respond to crises. Me? Ten weeks ago, I would never have done something like this. This was far more physical than I'd ever been with another human being. Could I kill her? No. I have no idea how much strength it takes to kill someone this way, how many muscles are necessary to strangle someone who would certainly fight back. So, no. I could not kill her but I'm certain Billy Ray could do it. Inviting him into the fray now would not give me an answer as to whether or not Debbie was on my side.

Debbie, though, simply straightened up against that bare wall, straightened her shoulders and tilted her head back a bit. "Either kill me, Morgahna, or look in my purse."

It was draped over her right shoulder, a pink thing with tan leather. It was hideous but matched her outfit. I took it from her and she remained where she was standing as I opened it. Inside her purse was a readily accessible can of mace and a stiletto knife that was easily accessible and useable from where it rested. I took them out and said, "Okay?"

"Morgahna?" she said. "Can I show you why? Can I give you proof?"

"Yes, Deb. I need to know."

She took one step forward, threw me over her hip where I landed heavily on my back, her knee against my throat. "This is why, Morg. I took self-defense lessons years ago and I keep in shape. If I wanted you dead, you would be. You're a girl."

I'd never seen that look in her eyes or on her face. She was serious, straightforward and deadly. Well, compared to me, she was. Me? She was right. I was a girl and always have been. Whatever this was, whatever mess I was involved in, was going to require a more deadly face to the world than the one I'd given it thus far. The first test of that tough face was when I saw Billy Ray in the doorway behind her. I could focus on him and not her and she would know someone was behind her. It took effort, great effort, to remain focused on her and not transfer my gaze to him, the man who would save me *again.* "You're saying what, Deb?" I said to her.

"That you aren't a threat, Morgahna. I can deal with you and always have been able. I'm not trying to hurt you. I'm only trying to demonstrate what I know and that you cannot have hurt me." She stood aside, reached down and held her hand out to me.

I took it, stood and faced her.

"So," she said as Billy Ray loomed behind her. "Who helped you? Some old coot out in the woods?"

"Yep," I said seriously. "An old coot out in the woods."

"He take you to a doctor?"

"Nope."

"Then..." she said shrugging.

"He was a medic in the army. He had experience with battlefield wounds and his sister is an army doctor."

"Ah, you got lucky," she said smiling, her old personality settling back in.

"Sure did. Debbie? Turn around and meet Billy Ray Simpson."

That damn woman has *always* irritated me because she gets *frisky* around men. Like a cat in heat, she senses them and gravitates to them like bees to honey. Me? When faced with a strange man, I get politely formal *immediately*. My hand goes out to shake his, I put on my most neutral smile and otherwise act like a mannequin. Debbie? She just leaned on one hip and said, "Billy *Ray* Simpson, huh? I am *terribly* pleased to meet you."

Billy's jaw moved, his facial muscles rippled and he said, "I kissed her." Naturally, he meant me.

Debbie has a stock line for something like that. "I do a lot more than kiss, Billy Ray."

Chapter Six

"I don't," he said bluntly.

You ever seen a cat in heat? I mean, a lot of people don't like cats and never notice. Like me. I don't like cats because they spray. Male cats. Ew. Icky. And female ones. They rub themselves all over you and when they go into heat, they screech, prance and turn into feline whores. Well, with god as my witness, that's what happened to Debbie as soon as she saw Billy. "Well, I'll just bet you do and leave it at that."

"You'd be wrong, lady."

"Been wrong lots of times in my life but never about men. I'm always right about men."

"Deb…"

"Morgahna," she said as she circled Billy and stared at him while she did.

"Stop it, Debbie."

She stopped, felt his left bicep, closed her eyes and said, "Mmm. Men. I love them."

What happened next happened so fast that I literally melted against the wall and watched the train wreck. Debbie tried to throw him, he defended against it, she countered, so did he and she wound up on her back, his knee to her chin. She folded her arms across her chest, smiled and said, "I love rugged men."

"Is she crazy, Morgahna?"

"I'm afraid so," I said helping her to her feet. "Exasperating, too."

She circled him again and said, "He's a goddamn yankee liar, too," she said with her southern drawl much more pronounced.

"Oh?" he said.

"You didn't kiss her. She didn't even kiss old Evan, god rest his soul."

"He did, Deb. Twice."

"You sleep with him?"

"Nope."

"Then, I got dibs."

"So, I'm meat?" he said.

"Yep," she said quickly. "Just meat for my grinder."

"This is a complication we don't need, Morgahna."

"We?" Debbie said. "As in you're her partner?"

"In this case, yes," he said as he watched her circle him.

"Debbie…"

"Who's this guy, Tommy?" he asked as he stopped her by hooking her elbow with his hand and forcing her to stop directly in front of him.

"Old Evan's partner," Debbie said, her face not six inches from his.

"A lawyer, then?"

"Yep," she said licking her lips in his face.

"Debbie…"

"Where's his office?"

"Over on Broughton near MLK," she said as she put her hands on her hips and leaned seductively even closer to him.

That was enough. I've don't have many seductive bones in my body and the ones I have called this slutty beyond belief. I pulled her away from him and said, "Dammit, Deb. He's on our side."

"Our?" Billy said. "She looks like she's on her own side."

"Give me a second, Billy," I said to him and then pulled Debbie into the kitchen. "Dammit, Deb. Stop it. He saved my life and his sister helped. He could have killed me and he didn't. He did a lot for me."

She leaned into my face and said hotly, "Someone tied you to a tree, beat you half to death and left you?"

"Yeah."

"Why?"

"I don't know."

Chapter Six

"Well, maybe he wants to find out and saving your flat ass was the only way to do it. Maybe he's on their side and the fact he so conveniently found you isn't such a coincidence at all. Have you ever thought about it that way?"

I've always considered Debbie a bit dim. You know. *Dim.* Scatterbrained. It is very possible that I was always too busy to stop and see the real person. What am I talking about? Well, her objections to Billy Ray were very well spoken and dealt with issues I hadn't even considered. Considering that Billy did indeed kiss me not once but twice only verified her objections. What better way to throw a new widow off balance than by kissing her? Well, he did and I was. Off balance, that is. I was way off balance because in my profession I am trained to be neutral, to see the larger picture and be impartial. Billy Ray Simpson, in my mind anyway, was anything but impartial. Granted, when someone saves your life you should be grateful and I was. I was not, however, impartial. I was very partial and those kisses were only half to blame. The rest was that minor part of how he saved my life. I should have dissected his motives for doing it beyond a sappy story about his wife and unborn child. Okay, I have a small face and that may have helped him because people seem to see me as vulnerable somehow. Maybe that's why, my small face. No, Debbie Jenson was being anything but *dim*.

I frowned, turned my back on her and walked the length of the kitchen and back to where she stood. "You once spurted out in a movie starring Brad Pitt, 'God, give me ten minutes in a locked room with that man'. Not exactly cogently coherent, Debbie. Now, you show up with tight logic, a tight ass and ask all the right questions at the right time. Maybe I should be suspicious of you?"

"I have a tight ass?"

"See? Scatterbrained as hell when someone tries to pin you down. Who are you, Debbie? Maybe I know you as well as I know him?"

"You gonna let me kiss you?"

"Nope. Him neither. Deb? I'm saying - and trying to say it as bluntly as I can – that I have to trust someone and I trust you. Why not him? Why can't saving my life be a plus and not a question mark?"

"Does he kiss good?"

"So well that I wrapped my legs around his waist. Now answer the damn question. Why, Deb?"

This time, *she* turned her back and walked to a window overlooking the sink, a window that looked out on the courtyard behind the house. She didn't turn around but stood stick still. "Morgahna? You don't like me much."

"Deb…"

She held out her hand but didn't turn around. "Morgahna? No one likes me. You tolerate me. Okay, I'm a pushy friend and I've always known that. I take boyfriends from women I know and tried to take Evan once, too."

Okay, *that* was a bit too sacrilegious for me. I turned her around and said, "Repeat that. You tried to take Evan from me?"

"Yes," she said defiantly.

"Why?"

"Why not? You didn't love him. Look at this place, Morgahna. Could you afford this without him?"

"That has nothing to do with whether or not I loved him, Debbie. Maybe we aren't friends."

"See, Morgahna? Do you? I want to be your friend more than anything only because I've known you for so long. To lose you now would be the last straw. Okay, it was a long time ago, before you were even married, but nothing happened because he loved you and said so. Morgahna? Hate me if you must, but without me, you would never know if he loved you or not." Her eyes misted with tears and it was obvious she had that secret on her mind for a long time, endless time to her. She kept her arms folded against her stomach, either hand on the opposite elbow as she waited for my verdict.

What should I do here? Logic, that old, old and very unreliable friend, was screaming to cut her loose. Logic also told me to go to Sugarplum's that night. Logic seemed to be no help here. This was equal parts logic and emotion and I was treading across that bumpy ground carelessly. I stepped back, turned my back to her and considered everything she'd said. Emotionally, I wanted her out and so did logic.

Chapter Six

Maybe two minuses really do equal a plus because I couldn't do it. I turned back around and she was crying but silently. "Billy Ray isn't my toy, Deb."

She wiped her eyes and asked, "What are you saying, Morgahna?"

"I won't fight you for him."

"And Evan?"

"Thank you for his redemption."

"And us?"

I hugged her and said, "One of us has to keep our feet on the ground, girlfriend. It may as well be me. I've got lots of practice."

She cried hard and heavy and it felt like a catharsis, a shedding of old skin and a growing of a new layer. "I'm sorry, Morg."

"Deb? I'm a widow. I don't have a boyfriend. It's okay."

"Right," she said laughing as she wiped away the last few stray tears.

"What's that mean?"

"Oh, Morgahna. He'll be just like Evan was. He'll politely turn me down and the next thing I know, he's looking at you with those same eyes Evan had."

"He had eyes for me?"

"Puppy-dog eyes, Morg. That man was a puppy dog around you. So is Billy Ray. Trust me. I know about men."

"So, what now?" I asked.

Billy Ray said from the doorway, "I don't know about you two, but I'm hungry. I'd say lunch."

Debbie smiled wanly and said, "Sure."

Me? I knew what he saying and just said, "River Street?"

"Sugarplum's."

It took Debbie a few minutes to unravel the story as I related it to her. When I was done retelling it, she smiled and said, "Oh, in that case a late lunch. You need a disguise before we go in there."

"That would help," Billy Ray said. "What do you have in mind?"

"Something, slow, sultry and evil."

"I like it," he said.

"Well, tell me," I said.

Debbie just smiled and said, "You ever wear a big floppy hat?"

"No."

"Well, you will now. We're going back to my place."

Before we left, I stopped her and said, "Nothing overtly sexy, wanton, brazen or anything that might get me arrested."

"Ooh," she said frowning. "Conditions like that make genius difficult, but agreed. Nothing that will be considered alluring or enticing." She hooked her arm inside mine and said hopefully, "Friends?"

"Yeah," I said smiling. "Friends."

That little compromise I made with myself was going to be tested. Friendships were almost never made on a logical basis. They were unions of emotion and faith. Sometimes tedium pastes them together and ennui keeps them going. The best friendships, I suppose, are ones built on firmer ground than that on which ours was built. One way or the other, we were going to test that friendship and see how firm it was. Either we were going to be endless friends or she was going to drop out of my life for very good reasons. Personally, I wanted to be her friend because my life seemed to be headed into uncharted waters and company was always welcome in those situations. You know? When you've circled the wagons and the Indians are screaming and shouting as they circle, a few extra guns on the inside are always welcome. Those guns have a tendency to get pointed at enemies whether presumed or not.

I was going to find out where all of them fit, not just Billy Ray and Debbie. All of them.

It was going somewhere but I didn't know exactly where.

Chapter Six

It was the ultimate rollercoaster ride, only the course was hidden, obscure and mostly invisible.

Not a good situation.

Not good at all.

And it was going to get worse.

Much, much worse.

Chapter Seven

God*dammit*, I hate high heels. I hate walking in them, hate the way they make my feet hurt, hate the way men look at me when I'm wearing them and hate the idea of my flat ass being on display like that. I also hate tight clothes in public. I wore electric blue spandex workout clothes around the house until maybe six months before Evan died and stopped only because of how Evan said they distracted him. It didn't matter *at all* that he professed to liking that distraction and liking it a lot. It was that word "distraction" and the way it made me feel queasy and out-of-sorts. Otherwise, I had no skirts that I believe Evan liked to see me wear, nothing that gave more than a hint of cleavage, not blouses, tank tops or sweaters. Sure, I had all those things, but nothing that showed *me*. Now? I was tottering on five-inch spikes with an inch platform and a skirt that I got from her, from Debbie.

Okay. I've already alluded to the fact I'm a bit taller than her. I'm also a bit fuller than her, too. All that means is that *anything* I got from her was going to be too tight for me in *ordinary* circumstances. *Ordinarily*, I would have refused to wear anything that tight in public. It was a nicely fitted peach-colored suit whose jacket flared over my butt like a fan and a skirt that put far too much stress on the material. Those shoes were the only peach-colored ones she had that also matched the floppy hat with the veil. I practiced walking around her apartment and got spitting mad when I saw Billy Ray squirm in his chair at the kitchen table. I whipped off the hat and screeched, "I am *not* wearing this stuff!"

Debbie was right next to him and she looked worse than me, but then she normally did anyway, so that's not saying much. "Billy Ray? Do something."

"Like what?"

"I dunno," she shrugged. "Kiss her, maybe."

He turned his head briefly and said, "Don't think that will work twice."

Chapter Seven

"Well, somethin'."

"Debbie?"

"Yep?"

"You what know what it means when men can't stand up?"

She snickered. "Yep."

"Well, then, that's how it is."

"Kinda like the way material moves, huh?"

"Kinda her and it together, you know?"

"Seen that effect hundreds of times."

"Hey!" I screamed at them. "Don't talk about me like I'm not here!"

Well, damnation. Despite his self-imposed admonition against standing up, he did. I actually wobbled backward a few steps and came up against the sink, my butt against it. He stoked my cheek and said, "Debbie's right. This is, evidently, so against your image that no one will believe it's you. Please, consider the outfit as a disguise, one you can always discard later."

Nothing happened in that room as I stared up at him, my hands fluttering like wounded birds looking for a perch. He stroked my cheek again with the back of his hand and I closed my eyes and said simply, "Okay."

Debbie whistled and said, "Holy fucking shit. I've been trying to get you to dress like this for ten years, he walks in, strokes your cheek and you say as quiet as a church mouse, 'okay'? What is it and how much do you sell it for, Billy?"

He looked down at me and said quietly, almost reverently, "It's not for sale, Miss Jenson."

Look, I *had* sit down because my knees were so weak and that is something that *never* happened to me before. I dropped that wide peach-colored hat on the table and sagged into the chair opposite from where he sat down. I sighed and did it again for two reasons. One, that damned skirt and blouse were so tight that I had no choice and two, well, should be obvious. I had the female equivalent of not being able to stand. "What now?" I asked nervously.

"Talk about this Underwood guy," Billy said.

"He was Evan's partner in their law firm."

"How old was your husband? How old was Underwood?"

Everything was wrong, just everything. He was asking me to remember something I desperately wanted to forget. I fidget and play with things when I'm nervous, always have. Usually it's pencils but I've fiddled with pens, telephones, water glasses, wine glasses, eye glasses, everything. My mind was trying to run off in an aimless direction as I tried to form an answer. If I kept kneading the brim of that hat, I wouldn't be able to wear it, so Debbie took it away from me and handed me an empty glass which I immediately began to roll between my palms. "Evan," I said and held my breath. I wanted to continue but I did not want to cry either, so I held my breath and made a Herculean effort to remain dry and focused. Bless them, because they waited for my wilder emotions to subside. When I was more ready, at least readier than I had been, I said, "Twenty-nine." I paused again and said heavily, "Evan was twenty-nine." I took several quick and very deep breaths and said, "Underwood is thirty-eight, I believe."

"How long were they partners?" he asked.

"Evan was a full partner for the last two years, an associate for four before that."

"What's that mean? What's the difference between being a full partner and an associate?" Billy asked.

I knew the answer but only as Evan explained it to me. I suppose, at least in retrospect, that I should have double-checked his answers. I stared hard at the tabletop directly in front of me as I stopped twirling the glass and gripped it fiercely. "A partner is not salaried. He shares directly in the profits of the firm. An associate is salaried."

"How many partners were there?" Billy asked again.

"Just him, Underwood. Why?"

Chapter Seven

"How did Evan become a partner and why?" he asked, his gaze still gentle and willing to yield at the first sign of emotional distress from me. He was being kind and in my state of mind, I needed it and him to be that way. Otherwise, I'd fall apart and become far worse than useless.

I held that glass tightly in my hand and said, "He worked hard, brought in a lot of business. It was in Underwood's best interest to make him a partner."

"Anything else?" he asked.

"I suppose. I don't know."

Debbie looked at me hard and asked, "What sort of partnership was it?" Yeah, *dim*. She knew money, I guess. She knew it and lawyers. Maybe it's genetic and all females get it. Still, I was beginning to doubt my opinion of her. *Dim*. I was beginning to doubt that description of her.

I shrugged because I didn't know. Then I said it, "I don't know." They seemed to be making Evan part of the problem and I had a very hard time with that. Looking at that glass, I asked, "What does this have to do with Tony Slayton and that other guy, Doug?"

"Good question," Billy said. "Let's go find out."

Every woman who ever lived put on some piece of clothing at some time in her life that was too tight, too revealing and suffered the attendant embarrassments from it. That wasn't my first tight skirt but it was the first one I'd worn whose intention did not include marriage. I had – and promptly threw away upon marriage – a few pieces that I termed my "lust outfits". This was worse than those and those embarrassed me to no end. I felt naked and on display for anyone who wanted to stare and Billy did. Oh, he didn't say anything crass, or even say anything at all. He noticed because women notice when men do. My butt felt as big as a 757 and that skirt felt as though I was showing pubic hair for anyone that wanted to look. Okay, it wasn't that bad but perception is reality in most cases and my perception was that anyone could see anything. Had I not been wearing a hat with a veil, I don't think I could have done it, walked out in public dressed like that.

The afternoon was more humid than hot. I rode with Debbie in her Miata while Billy drove his pickup. I hate looking like this. I hate looking someone's idea of dinner. Given my basic uneasiness over whatever was happening to me, I was in an ugly mood and desperately did not want to take it out on Debbie, so I kept my gaze out the window as we neared River Street.

"Nervous?" she asked innocently enough.

"Yeah," I said with some irritation in my voice.

"Mad at me?"

"These are you clothes, Debbie."

"You look good in them."

"I look like a whore."

"You saying I look like a whore?"

"Absolutely," I replied expecting a defensive torrent in return.

Instead, I got a thankful giggle, "That's the sweetest thing you ever said to me, Morgahna."

I took a deep breath, then sighed and just apologized. "Sorry, Deb. I just don't understand what's happening. Why would someone want me dead? And why do I have to dress like this? Wouldn't a less graphic disguise make more sense?"

"Maybe it would, Morg babe, but anyone who knows you, also knows that this is not you. If they're looking for dress-downs and casual people, then they won't look at you and wonder if you're her."

Maybe, but it was bullshit, too. "I guess," I said as I tried mightily and without much success to disguise my displeasure.

Debbie doesn't get sad or dejected easily. That much I know about her. She's always upbeat and ready for a show. Her face fell and she looked like someone who got dressed down for something they didn't do. "Morgahna? Okay. I know we're not really friends. We talk sometimes but you almost never call me. I call you because you're the only person I really know like this. You may not be my oldest friend but you are my longest contact and that has always meant a lot to me. I'll stay out of this if you want. The hick back there seems to like you and is making it obvious. You'd be better off with him anyway. Me? I'm a third wheel and I feel like it more and more."

Chapter Seven

I don't forgive easily, never have. As we pulled onto the cobblestones of River Street and neared the parking lot at the western end of it, I knew I had no more than a few scant minutes to make a decision about her. She was right, though. We aren't and haven't been good friends, maybe just casual ones. There are things about her that simply irritate me, stuff like her insistence that my appearance is more clunky than conservative. Okay, I like sweaters. Lots of people do including her. Is it wrong that I don't like them so tight that you can forecast the weather by whether or not you can see my nipples through them? We stopped for a light and I decided I knew her better than I knew Billy Ray Simpson. So, I said, "Deb? This can get dangerous."

"Trying to let me down easy?"

"Trying to find out if my best friend wants to opt out."

"Morgahna? I'm not…"

I sighed and took her right hand, leaned over the center console and said, "Debbie Jenson? If not you, then who? Okay. Maybe I haven't been the best friend to you, but you've always tried more than me. I have no choice here, none at all. Someone wants me dead and I have to find out who."

"You can always call the cops?"

"In that sense, Billy's right. If I do that, then I drive him or her underground. You see that?"

The light changed to green and she headed toward the lot. "Yeah, Morgahna. I see it. I want to help only because you need it and that man makes you stupid."

I smiled and blushed simultaneously. "You see? I need a friend who wants to sleep with him. It will keep my mind focused on my life and how to save it."

She smiled back. "So, me being perpetually horny is a plus?"

"In this case, yes."

"He kisses that well?"

"Better than merely well. It's incredible. He really does make me stupid."

"You falling for him?"

The lot was no more than half full as she eased into a parking space and set her brake. I squeezed her hand and said with pure seriousness, "I'm not falling for anyone, especially someone I don't know very well."

"Good."

Good? Coming from her that was outrageous. Still, I merely smiled as she pulled the parking brake.

We got out into the thick heat and waited as Billy Ray parked. Our idea was to enter separately but sit close enough to each other to lend help should it become necessary. None of this would work if any of us acknowledged the other in public. As a reporter, I knew enough to recognize that public performances tend to get either seen, recorded or both. Parking lots were a dead giveaway because cameras are everywhere in American life and parking lots are under surveillance more often than not. If we acknowledged each other, then we might find ourselves regretting it later.

It wasn't hard to cover our short wait for him with a rummage through a purse, in this case, Debbie through hers. Gesturing as though talking incessantly to me, she rummaged through her purse until both of us saw Billy put his truck into park. Only then did we leave the lot and headed toward Sugarplum's.

You remember I said no matter what happens, I hope nothing happens to my own perception of the city? Well, River Street has always had the feeling of home to me and it still did. The stores that were gift shops, restaurants, clubs and bars were all fashioned from older buildings. It made me proud to be from here, from a place that has the ability to change itself according to its needs. There was a time that River Street was a slum but now it's more of an oasis than anything else. I don't mean to make it sound as though River Street is a watering hole because it's not. I mean that in a kinder way than that. The river that borders the street is soothing and rolls like an old man. Okay, old man river seems alive in Savannah when I walk down this street. It's home in the friendliest way I can make that sound. It's home because it comforts me and makes me proud to be from here and not from somewhere else.

Chapter Seven

As we walked down the street toward the restaurant, I got looks from both sexes. The men because, well, they're men and from a few women who wanted to put me on a barbecue spit and stick me in a rotisserie. Uncomfortable? I felt as though a gigantic microscope was hovering just above my head. I'd like to say the only reason I was doing this was because that veil was hiding my face but that would be a lie. I was doing this because of that tree out in that forest. I still felt that wire around my wrists and that blunt shock to my head as Tony and Doug hammered me into submission. If you've never been assaulted like that, let me be the first to tell you that it's terrifying beyond what you can imagine, beyond what you *can* imagine. Nothing you can conjure up in your mind will ever come close to describing what helplessness really feels like.

I suppose the worst part was the memory that other than talking, other than asking them why they were doing this, I didn't fight back at all. I even made their job easier by *allowing* them to twist that wire around my wrists. That memory hurt more than *almost* any other facet. The actual beating was far worse than that but that memory of being taken out there and submitting to them was still akin to a rock in my shoe.

Yes, I submitted to them.

Every time I play that scene back in my mind, the mere idea of what they were doing was so anathema to me that I simply and willingly allowed them to beat me the way they did. In all my life, in all my previous experiences, I could not imagine being tied to a tree and being beaten like that. I *expected* them to be logical, to make a demand that I could honor or at least accomplish fearfully. To be beaten like that was so far beyond my expectations that I may well have been black. Does that bother you, that analogy? It should. I am a southern white girl, one of those *femmes* that southern white men fought and died for ever since the Civil War and even before that. My honor as one of them, as one of those sacrosanct white women is so powerful that being trussed up like that is beyond horrible, it's entirely against the culture in which I was raised. I am white, female and the *idea* that a white southern woman could be tied to a tree and beaten to death by *white* people was against everything I knew or was taught.

So, I put my hands behind that tree and *expected* them to become sensible as soon as they had me under their control. I expected something far less than what happened to me. I expected pain, expected them to hurt me in a female way, to inflict some sort of injury on me that would make me think twice about whatever they wanted. I *expected* this kind of crime to happen to blacks, not to me.

I was, in other words, culturally immune from that sort of attack.

Yes, I am quite aware of the statistics about crime. I do, or did anyway, work for a newspaper and those institutions are notorious for running with stories about crime. I even interviewed a few victims in my life. I know about the crimes that are committed over drugs, for drugs, about drugs, know about the crimes of passion involving people of all races, know about victimless crimes like prostitution and gambling, know about all of it. To that night nine weeks ago, none of it applied to me and I can't blame that on my parents. They did not raise me to those expectations. They raised me to fend for myself, to work hard, to be myself and then let me go into the world to do those things. Everything else I applied to myself like a good coat of neutral fingernail polish.

The moment Tony Slayton used that pipe or whatever he used against me that night, the way I viewed the world and not just my appearance, changed forever. I did not begin to struggle until he hit me for the first time and even then I expected that wire to come loose so that I could become logical in the face of their attack. Logic always won in the end. I remember struggling but not really screaming. I remembering objecting but not as forcefully as I could have.

Now? I wanted to fight back and was totally without weapons other than my wits. I am neither as cute, pretty nor sexual as Debbie is or can be. That left me with whiles I had never used and efforts I had never made, not even with Evan. Those expectations I had with him included comfort in front of a fireplace, mid-afternoon strolls in a wider garden than what existed on Taylor Street and the soft clinking of wine glasses over non-sexual romantic dinners. To me, romance was chocolate candies and roses, not anything as banal and as trite as mere intercourse. I was one of those puritanical people who felt there were people out there having fun and *must be stopped.*

Chapter Seven

Evan once tried to initiate *something* between us and I stopped him colder than a mid-January day in Green Bay, Wisconsin, at Lambeau Field. He caught me in the pantry, cupped my right breast, closed the folding door and kissed me. What did the southern belle in me do? Did she squeal and tease like Scarlet O'Hara? No, she acted like the spoiled brat she was and slapped her own husband. Evan went to sleep that night with his back to me. That was nearly two and half years ago. Funny how memory serves no useful purpose sometimes.

We entered Sugarplum's and it became a battlefield for me, a place to regain my honor. Debbie did the talking by prior agreement and arrangement. We asked for a table as near to the bar as possible and got one within its easy sight. The decorations were deep green and the purest and most chaste colors of white, the colors of grass and virgins. The hostess was slim and easily fit the image of the dainty southern miss. She smiled demurely and helped us get seated. If my veil bothered her or even caused a raised mental eyebrow, it was not obvious.

"You okay, Morg?" Debbie asked as she scanned a menu.

"Yeah. Completely," I said as I scanned mine.

I was as close to insanity as one could legally get. I didn't even know what was on the menu. All I knew was that Tony Slayton was the bartender.

A busboy appeared from the netherworld and slid water in front us. Debbie scanned her menu and said quietly, "Drink the water, Morgahna."

I lifted the veil, picked up the glass and sipped daintily at it while turning my left shoulder and staring at Tony Slayton who was working behind the bar. I slipped the veil back down over my face and stared at him. He was behind a well-stocked bar, few customers in front of him. It *was* only three o'clock in the afternoon and that may well be why there were only four people around it. He was chatting amicably with a woman who sat at the end of the bar, a fashionably correct woman who was thirty-five. She sipped what could have been water or could have been vodka. She had nice teeth.

"That him?" Debbie asked.

"Yes," I said as coolly cold as is humanly possible. "One of them anyway," I said.

"Morg? You stay cool. You be the nice unobtrusive broad I've always known you to be. Don't decide to be the hero right now. That's why Billy's here."

Right on cue, Billy walked in like an old west gunfighter, sat down at the bar and waited patiently while Tony finished smiling and winking at the woman who had his eye. As much as I wanted to know her name, I already knew it. She was Karin Hubbell, a lawyer who worked with both Tony and Evan. Putting my head back into the menu, I whispered to Debbie, "The lady at the end of the bar?"

"Yeah?"

"She's a lawyer who worked with both Evan and Tommy."

"Name?"

"Karin Hubbell."

"What's she do?"

"Criminal law."

"Same as Evan?"

"Evan was branching out into corporate law. He actually set up their firm as an LLP instead of the sole proprietorship that it was. That's why he was made a partner so soon. Tommy basically rewarded his hard work with money."

Debbie raised her glass, I tipped mine to it while she said, "Welcome to America."

"Amen," I said as we both drank that short, silent toast.

My anger grew as I considered the obvious: Karin Hubbell was sharing a friendly moment with one of the people who tried to kill me. Karin knew Evan and now I wondered if Evan knew Tony.

Karin was married to a man named Carl. Yeah, Carl Hubbell. I knew more about the dead New York Giants pitcher than I did about Karin's husband. I knew scant more about Karin than her husband. Evan and I did the dinner thing with them a few times but they never grew into

Chapter Seven

friends or even contacts. We saw each other at office parties and a few times around town, but nothing more than that.

Karin carried a weight problem around and I always felt sorry for her. Me? I'll never be fat, but might get bony one day as I grow older. God, I hope not. I hate that look and even considered a donut habit to ward off the possibility of elbows that resembled kitchen knives and knees that could render a man sterile should he ever bump into one. She did, though, know how to dress. Nothing tight that would highlight her weight, nothing too loose that might whisper the word "tent" in anyone's ears, especially mine. She wore her hair short and I always thought that was her one mistake because it tended to emphasize her heavy chin, a chin that would grow double one day. She has that type of chin that makes me hold my head erect in the hope that mine doesn't look like hers.

The waitress showed up and I ordered a Caesar salad, the donut habit still a few years away. Debbie ordered something with chicken that I paid no attention to because I was watching Karin, Tony and Billy. Karin took a sip of whatever she was drinking, put the glass on the bar and actually wiggled her fingers at Tony and said, "Bye, bye."

"Give me your car keys," I said hastily, hurriedly.

Debbie reached for them, produced them but still asked, "Why?"

"Catch a ride with Billy," I said snatching the keys from the table and standing.

"You dent my car and we'll have a real cat fight, babe," she hissed. She almost used my name but caught herself at the last moment.

"Don't worry. I'll take the shoes off."

Just before I left, Debbie stood, touched my elbow and hugged me with, "I trust you, girlfriend. Just be careful."

"I will. Thanks, Deb." I quickly added, "Phone. Billy has one. If I need to call you, I'll need it."

She fumbled for it, found it and pressed it into my hand.

I slid the filmy black veil over my face and followed Karin out the door and immediately re-learned a lesson about short, very tight skirts and very high heels. Don't walk fast in them or your ass will look like a metronome. I *felt* people, both men and women, looking and staring, the men staring, the women looking. That walk, the one where I followed Karin Hubbell was worse than the one that I'd just made with Debbie because that one was done calmly, slowly and we pretended to view the river from River Street. It needed to be casual and serene because that was the longest single walk I'd done with heels that high and I was nervous in them. Throw in the skirt, the way it moved with me and I felt like a walking porno movie. I stumbled once and that just made men want to *help*. Jesus Christ. A girl stumbles in a tight skirt and men get romantically gallant.

The only break I got was where she parked. Along that stretch of River Street, there is only one public parking lot, the one we were in. She was parked there, too, a gigantic white Escalade. I'll admit to being in a hurry because I needed to know where she was going. I understood the very real possibility that she was merely returning to her office, Evan's old one down on Broughton Street. She was parked near the exit but she was a girl for a moment and checked her makeup before she started the big SUV. That gave me time to pull down my skirt in a vain attempt to hide my pubic hair and get behind the wheel. I fidgeted with the shoes but Karin started up and I had no choice but to do some on-the-road training in how the drive with high heels. Twenty-seven years old and I'd never done that before. Being a girl's girl, Evan drove when I wore heels. When I was single? I didn't wear heels when I drove, not even those two-inchers that I owned.

I was behind her as she left the lot, but dropped back several car lengths as she made a quick left onto Barnard Street and a quick right onto Bay Street. She was in no hurry and neither was I.

She was driving in the same general direction that I would have gone had I been going to see Evan in his office. The huge tourist hotels towered around us as the river glistened off to my right. The entire area was studded with nice restaurants, night clubs and places to party. I knew about the restaurants but not about the clubs. I was a dinner waif, not a party animal. Debbie would do both the restaurants and the clubs. I smirked. *Yeah, and I know the stores.* Then I smiled. *Deb? You know them, too, but you know the ones that sell slightly wicked stuff.* Yeah, stuff like I was wearing.

Chapter Seven

Karin passed all the hotels and kept going west on Bay Street. I fully expected her to make a left on MLK Boulevard and was mildly surprised when she didn't. Had she, I might have stopped following her altogether because my assumption would have been that she was going back to her office, to Evan's office and I didn't think I could stand the grief that place would inflict on me. Instead, she kept driving down Bay Street, kept driving toward the workingman's end of that street. There are some hotels down there, a couple of nice ones right across the street from each other and part of me wanted her to pull into one them only because it would mean a sort of gentleness that I craved.

No, that's not where she went.

There is a huge slum down there, down on Bay Street. Ranks of old apartments that attract the poor, the lazy, the infirm, the shiftless, the crafty, the people who know this is their own personal dead end and all manner of filth.

Bay Street.

She made a left onto Fahm Street and was in the belly of the beast. The apartments on either side of her were deep, dark brown and blacks lived there.

Blacks.

I took a deep breath and wondered what I was going to do, especially here. No, I'm not really afraid of blacks because my basic conservatism says that they're merely disadvantaged and can easily help themselves *if they want to*. I have always assumed they simply don't want to. It has nothing to do with white oppression and the stark fact that whites make the rules they live by. No, I was entirely logical about them and always have been.

But. Where were we and why?

There were apartments all around us, but the lot she parked in bordered an old one. Black kids ran around and tried to look menacing. Okay, I think all blacks look menacing and I don't like their music either. There is nothing like good country music and a fiddle. I found an adjacent lot and parked there. Karin got out of her SUV and walked toward an old apartment building, her purse over her shoulder, a briefcase in her hand. It looked for all the world like business and I grew a bit disheartened.

The Package

From the distance I sat from that place, anyone who came to the door would be beyond my immediate notice. I flipped that gauzy veil down and just watched and continued to wiggle my toes inside those damn shoes. As much as I wanted to slip out of them, I wanted to know where she went even more. The grass around the place needed mowing, the building needed painting and most of the cars in the lot needed work of some type, body work mostly. I felt no kinship with these people. They were poor and I was not. Period. Mostly, though, they were black and angry black at that.

Karin knocked on a flimsy screen door and waited for a few moments before the door opened and I saw a black girl standing in the doorway.

A black girl.

The voice on the phone that night was a black girl.

She used Evan's name.

Karin worked with Evan.

All that meant squat and I knew it.

I expected Karin to enter the apartment but she didn't. She slid her purse down from her shoulder, dropped it at her feet and opened her briefcase with some difficulty. If I had to guess, Karin didn't want to go inside and preferred to conduct her business from the sidewalk. She pulled out an envelope, closed her briefcase, reached down for her purse, shrugged it back over her shoulder and handed it to the girl. They didn't shake hands or linger and chat like old friends. Karin turned around, walked back to her Escalade, got into it and left.

What had I just seen? The human being in me was screaming that it was a payoff of some sort. The newspaper reporter in me demanded more evidence than I had. Therefore, I did the one thing I had to do first.

I unbuckled those goddamn shoes, slipped out of them and audibly sighed my relief.

Priorities.

We all have them.

Chapter Eight

I was not raised to be prejudiced against blacks.

I just am.

Now that I've admitted it, maybe I can deal with it. I hope so because I was edging closer to dealing with blacks and while I have always been logical around them I have always been sheepish around them as well. I don't wish to give the impression that I'm KKK-prejudiced because I am most certainly not. Burning crosses on lawns is truly the work of the devil and I will never become involved in anything like that. The voice, however, on the phone that night was black and here I was sitting in a black neighborhood. It made me wonder what sort of mix Evan had at work. I mean, how many and in what proportion did he deal with blacks? I'm sure he did because if my memory serves me as well as it always did, I can remember black associates in their firm, one of them a paralegal named Deneisha. I met her a few times and she seemed extremely competent and that's all anyone can ever hope to be.

Still, it would be wrong for anyone to assume I am overtly prejudiced, so maybe I should back off on that claim that I'm prejudiced at all. Maybe a better description of my feelings about blacks is that I never had a black friend. I call myself prejudiced because until you can treat everyone the same, then you are guilty of some sort of prejudice. I feel it when I'm alone and a group of black men or boys passes me on the street. Am I safe? How come I don't have those same feelings when a similar group of white people crosses my path? I even have the same feelings of inadequacy and subtle fear when I have to pass a group of black girls. I wonder what they think, what they want, where they're going, wonder how they arrive at decisions. I realize and will readily admit that they probably make decisions the same way everyone does; they do what's in their best interest. Not having a black friend, though, I can't verify any of that. I am a product of my environment even if it is racist.

Where is all this going? Well, as much as I wanted to go talk to that black girl, I was entirely intimidated by the neighborhood. Yeah, and me a reporter. In the years I spent working for the Morning News, I had *many* assignments around town, many in neighborhoods like this one. Working as a reporter, however, is far different than working on your own to find out who's trying to kill you. Reporters get a certain amount of cultural protection. When you're talking to a person who can put your name in the paper and make it known to hundreds of thousands of people, your behavior changes. When those same people think you're trying to accuse them of a crime, it changes yet again.

Oh, but it's entirely worse than that. I've talked about Dave Woods, my colleague at the Morning News. I know he has an ex-wife named Merriam and a nine-year-old son named Nathaniel. I know he lives out in Garden City but don't exactly know where because I've never been there. I know he's a Georgia Bulldogs fan because he has a degree in journalism from that school, the University of Georgia. I know he thinks Michael Vick is the best athlete in the NFL, if not in professional sports. We've shared *many* lunches where we've discussed everything from the tides in the Savannah River to state politics. I've met Merriam twice, both times when she dropped off Nathaniel a bit early. I know he lives out in Garden City because that's the most affordable place he can live given his child support obligations to Nathaniel. I know he wants to get back with Merriam because he still loves her but she wants nothing to do with him but I don't know why. It could be another man, another woman and it could be either way given the state of the country. Okay, okay. That's my Republican bias showing through. I never been to his place out in Garden City not because it's so far from Taylor Street and certainly not because it's a mere apartment. Dave Woods is black. That's why I have never been to his place. I suffer from an exceedingly virulent strain of cultural racism. Blacks are wonderful people to work with, lunch with, dine with on late nights, gossip with but make troubling friends. What do you say to a black man? What do you say when you're in his home with friends of his who are the same color? In public, the races mix and we get along fairly well. In private? I think we still have trouble.

So, I'm a racist and it kept me from going in there alone. She would have black men in there and I was dressed like I wanted to party. Well, maybe not but it felt that way, felt as though as soon as I walked into an apartment where black men may be congregating that I would be *expected* to party. In a nutshell, that's why I merely called Debbie and told her where I was and then asked, "You still there?"

"Yep. Great chicken salad. To die for, Morg."

"Uh, I'd rather not."

That was an example of her bleached-blondness. As soon as she said it and I responded, she sounded contrite and answered, "Sorry, Morgahna. I won't say anything like that again."

"You going back to your place?"

"Yeah. We'll meet you there. You discover anything?"

Yeah, Cowardice. "Karin went out to Bay Street. She gave something, an envelope, to a black girl. Then she just left." I omitted everything about how and why I hadn't gone inside or at least to her door to talk to her.

In the past two years I'd talked to hundreds of people, all under the guise of being a reporter and under the unstated protection of the Morning News. Most of those assignments had been done and conducted alone. Working with Dave was a luxury that I loved because he's a knowledgeable man and I've learned a lot from him. Well, maybe not, obviously.

I've never gone under cover like a cop might, never resorted to a disguise either. I've always approached my job openly and straightforwardly. Yes, I've been to Garden City and once down to Florance Street to an urban center that caters to blacks and Hispanics. I did a piece about a year ago down there and a few people saw it and complemented me on it for a job well done. All I did was go down there, talk to the director, get permission from a young girl down there to tell her story and explain how and why she had a baby at sixteen, so these locales are not new. The circumstances were. If I got out now and walked over there, I'd be *alone*.

My feet were sore, I still had twinges from my ribs, if I coughed hard enough I could feel that tracheotomy that saved my life and my legs were still a bit sore from the broken bones in each thigh. As motivation, it was far more than enough.

I got out of the car, tugged at the skirt, smoothed the material over my stomach and straightened my shoulders. I had the hat in my hand and started to fit it over my head and face again, then thought better of it and tossed it back in the car. *Deal with my flat butt, dammit. I have to deal with it; why not you?*

Yep. Barefoot.

I sat down dejectedly on the driver's seat, grabbed the shoes from the floorboard and slid them back on. You have *no idea* how badly I wanted to wear something else besides those shoes and only submitted to them because my *entire* wardrobe was missing and maybe even gone forever. I was at Debbie's sufferance and my guess was that she was going make her more comfortable clothes somehow unavailable for the next few days. I stood wobbly but was determined and the reason was still horribly simple. Anything those people could do to me would not be as bad as anything Tony Slayton did and he was white.

The afternoon's heat was gathering but I was immune from anything as trivial as nature. There was a basketball court across from the parking lot and adjacent to the building where that girl lived. The kids stopped playing and watched me walk across the lot toward the front door. I could assign any motive to them, anything from they were part of the group that almost beat me to death, to watching me and planning a new assault, this more sexually depraved than the last merely lethal one had been. At least I didn't hear anything from them.

The building got worse the closer I got to it. It needed a painting and a few new windows. The door to *her* apartment was 2B. I knocked on the screen and waited. I could hear a television inside and it switched off after a few seconds. It opened to darkness, the screen and dark interior entirely masking her from my view. She could have been anyone and I would never have known. I discovered that being tied to a tree gave me immunity from a lot of implied violence. Don't get me wrong; I don't want another round with that tree or any just like it. I simply mean that I know what pain feels like, know how close I came to death and it was at the hands of white men, the very last people I would have expected to do something the insidiously cruel.

"My name is Morgahna Hamilton," I said to the darkness. "The woman that was just here is Karin Hubbell. She's a lawyer. I have only

Chapter Eight

one question." Without waiting for an answer, I said, "Does that woman know me and do you?"

There are, unquestionably, any of dozens of answers that could be made to that question. She could lie and do a good job of it or lie and leave me wondering if her answer was the truth. She could lie and do a bad job of it and make the real answer quite obvious. She could say, "What? Your name is what?" She could even deny that Karin Hubbell had just been here. She could do any of a number of things. What she did caught me by surprise.

She closed the door.

I took a step backward, looked up at the second-floor balcony, saw nothing above me, behind me or to either side. *Dammit. Learn something.* My job to me, that one I had so long ago with the newspaper, was simple. There was a story out there and my job was to find it, get it and bring it home. Period. Looking back, I think I was more abrasive than effective, more brash than polished. It is very possible that time and experience would have smoothed out those edges that stuck out like barbs on a wire.

Not today. Someone tried to kill me and I tend to take that sort of stuff personally. I needed to get answers to that last question. Someone called me the night I went to Sugarplum's and if it was her, the girl that came to the door, I needed to know why she called me and why she used Evan's name before she hung up. As an emotional ploy, that was a good way to get me to do something as stupid as I did. I was a grieving widow, a woman whose heart had been shattered by an act of unspeakable horror and then made witness to it when I discovered his body.

So, I opened that screen door and pounded on it, pounded until it opened and it was her again. This time there was a face to go with the voice. She was shorter than me but heavier and wore her hair in blond cornrows that dripped off the back of her head like step ladders. "Do you know me?" I asked angrily before she could start.

And she did. Twisting and turning her head like a pit bull mangling a smaller dog, she snapped, "Get your white face out of my door!"

I leaned into her face and snapped back, "Answer the damn question, you fucking nigger bitch!"

That set her off worse than fireworks on the Fourth of July. Before I could get into my first legitimate fight, a body slid between us, a taller and more muscular one. It was a man and he pushed the woman away as she snapped, screamed and snarled in a drawl so thick I didn't hear much besides "kill that honky bitch" and "damn white woman". The man pushed her out of my view and another man kept her away from me. The one who turned his back to me was, like I said, taller and more muscular, but then I've always been a girl and most men are both taller and more muscular than me. Take Tony. He was both and I regretted letting him get that close to me.

Well, the best defense is a good offense as Dave used to say, so I walked up to him, put my nose to his and said, "Don't fucking start! Just answer the damn question. Do *you* know me? Does she? It's a simple fucking question!"

Real trouble started when he put his right hand on my left shoulder and started to say something to me. Well, I suppose you could call it an extreme case of overcompensation, but as soon as his hand touched me, I stomped the spike on my heel into his instep and he howled painfully but still got his hand around my neck and pushed me out the door. No, I didn't go peacefully, not at all, never again. I slapped at his hand, bit his forearm, screeched, screamed and spit until he got me against the wall outside the door and let me loose. "Jesus, lady!" he said as he rubbed his arm and then his foot against his opposite leg. "Settle down."

He was as black as an oil slick and from my position, just as deadly. All black men, except Dave Woods, are deadly. That's how I always saw them and that's why I have no black friends including Dave. His hair was short and that was all. It wasn't styled in any obvious way, just cut short. His face was smooth and shined like an eight ball. No, I have never played pool. I could still feel his hands against my throat so I took another swing at him and snapped, "Prick!" He caught my hand easily because I punch like a girl, too. Had I been carrying a purse, I would have taken a swing at him with it.

Still holding my hand, he said, "I don't know you and I don't think Daydra does either."

Chapter Eight

"That lawyer?"

His face was as placid as a windless lake, his eyes taking all the energy. They were alive but betrayed nothing. His mouth didn't even move. Finally, he said, "That's personal."

"So is attempted fucking murder, nigger!" I snapped, freeing my hand from his by slapping at it with my other hand.

"You gotta broken nose," he said without so much as a stray emotion.

"No fucking shit! You want the rest of the itinerary?"

"Look, lady. Daydra didn't break your nose although she might want to now. Why don't you knock off the insults and just tell me what you want to know?"

"Let her deny knowing me! Just drag her black ass out here and let me ask her!" My hair was a mess because of the way he pulled me out of that apartment. I pulled some hair from my eyes and stared up at him.

His reaction was muted and understated. He stepped back to the apartment and said, "Go fuck yourself, lady. You've been insulting and rude ever since you showed up at our door. That lawyer? She's a shark but you're a cobra. I've seen both and you can avoid sharks."

He started to close the door, so I said quickly, "Look, I'm sorry. Someone half beat me to death two months ago and I still have some pain. Can I ask her?" The door was closed to within a few inches of closing. If it shut, I was dead and would have to follow Karin. While I had no problem with that, I wondered what was here and why. Maybe nothing, maybe something. It was time to turn down the heat. "Can you believe how scared am I? I'm a white girl in a black neighborhood, mister. All I want to know is if she knows me and has ever called me. Answer that question and I'll leave either way."

Savannah, I know from my days at the newspaper, is one of the most violent city's in the country. Gun ownership here is higher than the national average and the crime rate goes along with it step-by-step, hand-in-hand. The chances that I was standing in the doorway of a home that had guns in it were astronomical. If I pushed too hard, he could just point a gun out the door and blow my head off. So, I repeated it. "I'm sorry. Tell her that. I was raised better than this."

I stared hopefully at that door. As a reporter, I never knew where stories would end, nor really where they would begin. Sometimes my assignment was so generic that I simply thrashed around and then stood back and watched whatever happened. I was never concerned for my safety. I was young, invincible and lived the perfectly chaste lifestyle with my husband who simply adored me. If anyone had asked, I would have told them I didn't need advice, just time. Sooner or later, I was going to have the world in my pocket and my methods would wind up proving themselves.

The door opened a few inches and I saw his glistening black face in the shadows. "Daydra don't want you here, lady."

"Let me apologize to her. I'm sorry, mister. I'm just scared, okay?"

He turned his face away from the door and said something I didn't hear. That woman said something because I heard a female voice say something hot and presumably nasty. Then it opened and she shot out the door at me and put her forehead directly against mine. No, I didn't give an inch and that was for several reasons. Primary among them was fear. I was scared but not so much that I couldn't think. She said hotly and angrily, "I don't know you, I have never called you and unless you leave right now, I'll forget I'm a lady! Happy, bitch?" Her eyes were huge and contained more hate than any I'd seen in a long time, her face straining under the weight of anger.

A baby cried inside and only that made me feel guilty. Maybe it was hers and maybe not. My behavior, however, was deplorable so I accepted her answer, nodded and said, "Okay. I just wanted to know. Sorry I bothered you."

It was getting late in the day, the sun dropping towards the tree-lined horizon. I fluffed and preened at my mussed hair as I walked back toward the car, Debbie's Miata. I've been on and through dead ends before, so this wasn't my first. If anything, dead ends are more normal than not in my work so I wasn't really depressed, just anxious to find another way inside the problem. That's how I saw this, as a problem. It always helped me when I was working because I was good at problem-

Chapter Eight

solving. Sooner or later, I'd pick up a piece of information that would go somewhere. All I needed to do was keep pushing. Okay, maybe not that hard but pushing anyway. It was my style. Sure, I can see that I needed to modify it because it almost got me killed.

I leaned against the door and looked out at the grounds. My parents were from a place like this. No, not an apartment, but a place of low expectations and less original thought. Once, just once in my life, I wanted to write a book about something that would shock the public. It had to be entertaining and original, something that was uniquely my creation and now that I had it, I didn't want to tell anyone about it or let anyone know what had happened to me, to us, to my family. This was as personal as anything could ever be and telling people that I drove my husband to suicide, while maybe a good book, would humiliate me for the rest of my life. So, no. I wasn't going to write about this and wasn't going to tell anyone that didn't need to know.

Debbie keeps sunglasses on the visor above the driver's seat. Since the glare was fairly intense, I slipped them off the visor and onto my deformed face. Still, I sat there and tried to find another way around the problem. Going back to Debbie's place seemed like I was admitting defeat and following Karin Hubbell was not something I wanted to do. That felt too much like a stakeout and I don't have the personality to sit in one place all day waiting for someone to do something. So, what then? I didn't know and my brain wasn't giving me any alternatives. *Back to Debbie's.*

The parking lot empties out onto the street between two separate buildings. As I started the car, I noticed the door to that apartment open and that tall black man exited wearing a dark blue windbreaker. His hands were in his pockets despite the simmering heat and he headed toward the driveway. My senses screamed "gun".

Guns are weapons for people who like fast answers and exceedingly simple ones. In all my years of reporting, I have never seen a gun. Is that incredible? Most of us haven't outside of television and movies. They are prevalent nonetheless and I was convinced I was going to see one in the next few moments. I had choices; it seemed as though I always had some. One choice was to punch the accelerator and hope that his gunfire missed me. Another choice was to drive across the lush green grass to the next lot and escape that way. The last choice was the most foolish one.

It was one the one I took. I drove slowly toward the exit and he angled directly toward me as I hit the small ramp that emptied out to the street. His left hand came out of his pocket and he held it up to signify that he wanted me to stop. Fear is cultural in many respects. I was finding that word all over the place lately, Cultural. To me, culture was red wine and clinking toasts over a soft fire. To me, culture was a quiet museum where you walked hand-in-hand and talked softly. To me, culture was a symphony and an elegant dress. To me, culture was anything but a black man holding his right hand deep in his pocket as he tried to get me to stop. All my senses screamed otherwise, but I stopped and even rolled down my window.

"Can we talk?" he asked, his right hand still in his pocket.

"About?"

"That lawyer?"

"Not Daydra?"

"She don't know nothin'."

"You carrying a gun, mister?"

"Yeah."

"You gonna shoot me?"

"Probably not."

"Probably?"

"You gonna call me a nigger?"

"Probably not."

"Then, can we talk?"

His voice was fluid and flowed easily. I've met men with entirely nasal voices that were as educated as Plato but were agonizing to listen to. His voice took no effort to hear. It was a plus for him. "Yeah," I said. "Where?"

"We can go down Abercorn a way and talk in a coffee shop."

Chapter Eight

"The gun makes me nervous, mister."

"White people make me nervous, lady."

It was an interesting reaction to another cultural lesson. I've already alluded to the fact that black people frighten me on some level. Realizing that the reverse was true wasn't startling news but was a revelation nonetheless. If I ever took the time to think about it, our history is not full of black people lynching whites. It was always the reverse. Always. All those gangs wars? All that means to me is that one group of minorities is thinning the herd of another. Either way, I won. And racial profiling? Babe? They ain't profiling me, they're profiling *him*. So, I smiled and said, "Climb in."

I've invited lots of people to ride with me in my life. I mean, why not? Life was logical and orderly, plus I was a reporter. What better way, what more *logical* way to get someone to talk to you than by offering them a ride to wherever they were going? To my knowledge, and I realize I could be wrong, I'd never given a ride to someone who was carrying a gun like this guy was. He got in, closed the door and kept his right hand in his pocket. I extended mine to him and he paused. *Come on, dude. Take your hand off the gun and shake my hand. I'm a white girl that won't enjoy rape quite as much as Debbie would.* "My name is Morgahna."

"King Arthur's sister," he said with his hand stubbornly in his pocket.

"Come on, dude. Take my hand and give me one less thing to worry about. I'm a girl and I rape all too easily." He was nervous and that gun in his pocket made me nervous. So, I smiled and pointedly did not show any teeth. I tried to look meek, submissive and pliant, three things I have never been. "She seduces her brother and bears his child," I said showing the genesis of my name.

"Only in one version. Either way, she's an interesting person and makes a bad enemy."

"I'm not an enemy, mister. I'm trying to discover who wants me dead. If it's you, then I'm already dead and just postponing the moment."

When he pulled the gun from his pocket, I figured I'd chosen badly at long last and sighed. Then he put it in his lap and extended his hand. "Lady? I ain't gonna shoot you unless you give me a good reason."

"And what sort of reason would that be?" I said sighing deeply at my reprieve.

He extended his hand to me and said as we shook, "Lying and making my life harder than it is."

I'm not one of those people that tries to impress my morals on others despite my Republican leanings. I've never had an abortion, think it's wrong but if I ever got pregnant and didn't want to be, I feel a lot better having a choice on what to do. I've heard the old saw about adoptions, but considering how long it takes to adopt a baby in this country – the show Friends notwithstanding – I'd still feel better about having a choice. I'm a Republican but not for that idiotic reason. All that meant was that I wasn't going to make his life harder than it had to be. The only way that was going to happen was if he hassled me or tried to get me to do something I didn't want to do. "I'm not going to lie, mister. And your name would be easier than 'mister', so what is it?"

"LeRay," he said. "Not Leroy. LeRay. Not Ray. LeRay. Got it?"

I smiled again. "I'm still Morgahna."

He nodded forward and said, "Down to Abercorn."

"We could talk here?"

"You're going to buy me dinner."

"Mister? I'm driving someone else's car, wearing her clothes, using her phone and I'm not carrying a purse. No, I am not buying you dinner."

It was his turn to smile. "Then I'll buy you dinner. Just drive."

We headed back toward downtown and I just drove where he indicated. Stupid idea? You have no idea how stupid it was. I knew nothing more than his name was LeRay and that he carried a gun. Okay, okay. I knew nothing more about Billy Ray but he *did* save my life. This guy could easily take it. He kept giving me directions and I kept driving. I know the city and I knew we were in a bad part of it.

Florance Street.

He pointed to a narrow storefront that was stuck between two entirely generic stores, one an antique shop and the other a bicycle repair

Chapter Eight

shop. Momma's Diner. Hell, it wasn't even a diner, it was nothing more than a small place that just happened to serve food. There were two customers and two people behind the counter, one of them behind a grill where he was flipping burgers. LeRay walked up to the woman, an older black lady with hair that reminded me faintly of Aretha Franklin and kissed her on the cheek. "Hi, mom. Need a couple of burgers."

She got ethnic real fast. "You gonna pay, Mr. Big Shot? Whitey there looks good for a couple of burgers."

"No money, mom. Please? It's important."

Well, the burgers came but were accompanied by a long litany of reasons why LeRay Morrison was a no-good son, a deadbeat, a weed-smoking zombie, a no-good snake-in-the-grass and several other slightly more colorful ethnic epithets. LeRay looked embarrassed but then my guess is that all parents embarrass their kids. His mother continued to fume as the man simply went about the job of making two more burgers.

The place was clean but as I indicated, nearly empty. There were two tables near the front window and a line of four booths against the wall. Crowded, the place could not have fed more than twenty people total. Small doesn't begin to describe the place. Had it not been clean, I might not have consented to eat anything they made.

"What's the Big Shot want to drink?" she shouted from behind the counter.

"Cokes, momma."

"Small ones, like your head," she announced to the neighborhood.

We sat in the booth that was closest to the back of the store and waited for the food. I was hungry but not hungry enough to eat just anything. I'd wait and see what they served. LeRay slid into the seat opposite mine and said, "That lawyer?"

"Yeah?"

"I don't know what she gave Daydra but I think it was money."

"Who is she?"

"My sister. I live with her."

"The other guy?"

"Her boyfriend. She's not married."

"Did she have a claim against someone? Why would a lawyer give her money?"

He looked troubled and my mind immediately remembered that gun. Nervous people and guns make for a bad combination. I wondered, and for the first time, if Evan had been nervous about his plan that night. What sort of circumstance would it take for me even to contemplate something like that much less carry it out? But this guy? I had no idea what was on his mind. The fact that he was an adult and lived with his sister was bad enough. That he carried a gun and knew the legend of King Arthur just made things worse. Why? Well, my gut was screaming that people with options they were unable to perform got desperate enough to do things others might not.

"I don't know," he said to my question. "Daydra isn't too smart, lady. She would get involved with people…"

"…who carry guns?" I finished for him.

He clasped his hands together on the table in front of him and said to himself as though he was thinking aloud, "I need to defuse this somehow." He looked up at the counter where his mother and the man stood talking, his mother's look one of extreme disappointment. He got up, went to the counter and said, "Mom? Do me a favor?"

"*Another* one?" she asked sarcastically.

He slid the gun across the counter and said, "Toss it for me? It makes her nervous and I don't want to do that."

The woman didn't miss a beat. She just palmed it and it disappeared. I watched her and her entire demeanor changed. She'd been loud and abrasive. Now she was quiet and subdued. *Good thinking, lady. Being loud with a gun is not the best way to be.* LeRay came back, sat down and said, "I'm just any other guy now, lady. You don't have to be scared. Okay?"

"Okay," I said quietly, easily.

Chapter Eight

"That lawyer? I never saw her before. I saw another guy. He might have been a lawyer but I can't swear to that. This other guy came by a few times and talked to her like he was afraid that a deep secret might leak out. He referred to a thing he called 'the package' and said it needed to be kept quiet. I saw him several times like I said and he was always nervous."

I needed to know. "Was he black?"

"No. White."

"Was he nervous because you're black and he wasn't?"

It appeared that he was thinking, considering his answer before he gave it. Slowly, he shook his head and said as though considering his answer even as he made it, "No, I don't think so. My guess? He never considered race a thing to fear. He was scared of something else. That lawyer? The woman? It would a take a lot to convince me she wasn't there because of him."

"You said you didn't know if he was a lawyer. So, if not, why do you link one to the other?"

"His words. Lady? I didn't finish college because I didn't have the money but I recognize educated people when I hear them. He was. He used words like 'litigation' and 'case law'. Most people who aren't lawyers wouldn't talk like that. If I had to swear on a bible that he was a lawyer, I couldn't. If you asked me to guess, that's what I'd say."

The older woman came out from behind the counter with two trays, a burger on each one. She put them in front of us and then slapped LeRay's head. "Trust you to find the only white woman in Savannah without money," she said bluntly and then walked away only to return with two small cokes. He looked entirely embarrassed and kept quiet as he rubbed the back of his head.

Me? I took a deep breath and said the only other question I had. "LeRay? Why are you telling me all this stuff?"

Since this started I've felt like a leaf in a wind storm, blown from one tree to another, from one lawn to another. Other than Tony and Doug, I had no idea who did this and why. Since I don't know and never met either one of them before that night, I agreed with Billy Ray that they were employed by someone else. Exactly who was still unknown. Did LeRay open a new path for me? I didn't know. All I knew was his answer scared me.

"Lady? I don't know anyone named Morgahna. Never met one before I met you. I knew about the legend and the story because it's a good one, full of evil, good and everything in between. But that man? He used that name. Yours. Morgahna. He said, 'If Morgahna finds out, she'll shit'. He said that and I remembered the name because of the story of King Arthur's Round Table. Then you show up right after that lawyer does and tell Daydra that your name is Morgahna. Lady? That's way too close for comfort. What is my sister involved in?"

It dawned on me that he was trying to take care of his sister, of Daydra. That was his motive for being here. Love of family. That's why I was here. Love of Evan. Did one have anything to do with the other?

I had an idea, a way to find out.

"Can you take a ride with me?"

"Yes."

He didn't ask where we were going and that made him braver than me. I would have asked and then decided based on the answer. It seemed that love exists in degrees. The evidence suggested that he loved Daydra more than I loved Evan. Was that true? Maybe so and maybe not. Time would tell.

We ate the burgers in total silence. Total silence. Not even his mother raised her voice.

My idea? I thought I knew the identity of the man that used my name and Debbie was the only one who had a picture of him since my home had been stripped right down to the bailing wire. We drove to her place, to Debbie's.

I have learned long lessons, professional ones that always served me well. One lesson that I always heeded was never to write the ending of a story before I had all the information that led to it. That was a good lesson and one I applied liberally throughout my career, one that I was going to have to heed once again as events built up. This was just one event, just one. It didn't matter at all if I was right because it would not

Chapter Eight

answer who was responsible for that attack and why it took place. Yes, I was going to get an answer that fit my own prejudices. That answer, in and of itself, was going to mean little.

It was, however, going to upset me more than the attempt on my life did.

It was going to be more deeply personal than I thought it would.

My first problem when I got to Debbie's place was that she was screaming and Billy Ray was nowhere around.

Screaming.

I'd heard too much screaming and I panicked.

I learned why guns are such a bad investment when I burst into her room because I would have shot first and not bothered with questions.

Lucky me.

Chapter Nine

Time for an admission. LeRay *was* trying to stop me and I shook him off because Debbie is my only friend, my only real friend. I actually stared him down and then threw open her bedroom door and *immediately* slammed it shut. *Oh, fuck. Morgahna? You stupid fool.* The admission? I panicked and ruined a perfectly good orgasm. Then I smiled. *No, you didn't. Not even a freight train could stop her.*

Hers.

I stood with my back to the door and waited for that image to burn away. Yeah, the image. Billy Ray was on his back, she was astride him, his hands were on her breasts, her distended nipples sticking erotically from between his fingers as he clutched them, her entire body about to explode in an example of sexual pleasure I have never allowed myself to feel. She deflated as soon as she saw my face come inside the door and then regrouped enough the scream at Billy, "Now!"

With God as my witness, I have *always* been subdued during sex. That's another thing I cannot blame on my parents. They didn't teach me *anything* about sex, not even that it feels good. Yes it does, but I didn't want the neighbors to hear us doing it, doing *it*. Evan was louder than me. You know? In my entire life – and I'm twenty-seven – I have had three sexual partners and the first two never bothered to call me back after we did it, did *it*.

And.

I have *never* been on top. Ever. Not once because good romantic sex was merely satisfying, not slutty and left you with a serene smile, not with the deep satisfaction of being fucked by someone who knows how to do it. Slutty girls – sorry, Deb – got on top. *Sluttier* girls screamed like that foghorn I talked about that's on the lighthouse at Tybee Island. Scenes like that, like the one I just walked into, have always made me nervous. No, I have *never* seen a porno movie. Just the idea of women screeching like that makes me uncomfortable, like ants are crawling all over me.

It took another ten minutes before Debbie came out of her bedroom red-faced. Billy Ray was calm and hugged her sweetly, *romantically*. It looked altogether too chivalrous to me. She walked up to me, shuffled her feet and said, "Sorry, Morgahna. I just…he just…"

That's when it hit me. *She thinks I'm jealous.* I hugged her and whispered into her ear, "It's okay. I didn't want to do anything anyway. Really. It's okay."

She was wearing a Japanese robe, a kimono or something, and wrapped it tighter around herself. "You sure?"

"Yes, Deb. I am very sure."

She rolled her eyes and said, "Great. He is one *fine* lover."

I think the attraction between Evan and me was entirely understated. He knew how to romance me and that's *exactly* what I wanted. I wanted a sweet man, a tender man, one who touched me gently and liked it when I did the same. If anything, he never lost his romantic touch for me. I lost mine. I can remember countless soft caresses in the bathroom as I applied my face, sweet touches to my cheek and soft kisses to my neck. I can remember countless hugs and soft smiles, hundreds of times when he said my name softly and gently after the lights went out at night. I'd like to humiliate myself farther by saying the number of times we made love could be counted on one or two hands but that wouldn't be true. Truer and much more humiliating would be that in almost every occasion where I allowed him to make love to me, I was thinking of my precious Daytimer and my schedule for the following day. In all our marriage, I can remember *one* toe-curling orgasm and that was on our wedding night. One.

Yes, I envied her. No, not because she got Billy Ray into bed or even that she got him to renounce his one-year ban on *anything.* I envied her because she had that elusive ability, or at least the normal ability to enjoy herself and the man she was with. I couldn't even enjoy Evan after we'd been married for a while. My career was *always* more important and I still saw the problem as one created by me. *Every* time I came back to the issue of interpersonal relationships, I didn't think I had one with my own husband. Did I kill him? I still believe I did and I'd heard nothing to convince me otherwise.

Chapter Nine

I hugged her. "That's great, Deb. Don't worry about me. I still see Evan when I close my eyes and that prevents a lot."

"I'm so sorry, Morgahna. You have no idea how much." Then she eyed LeRay and said, "Who's the gorgeous dude?"

"LeRay Morrison," I said almost dismissively. Then, "Do you still have my wedding picture?"

"Sure. Why?"

"Can I see it?"

"Not until you tell me why."

"That lawyer I followed? Karin Hubbell?"

"Yeah?"

"Well, this guy was in that apartment and from his story, I think Evan might have known his sister. How and why? I don't know. I just need him to identify Evan's picture."

"Hmm," she said. "Leave it to me."

"Deb? What are you planning?" I asked.

"A lineup. Just like in the police station. You show him a wedding picture with you in it with Evan and he might identify him for all the wrong reasons. Give him a variety and force him to identify Evan from a crowd."

"Ooh, that's devious," I said with a smile. "Let's do it."

"You wait in the kitchen and I'll bring the pictures."

Billy Ray stuck with her and I dragged LeRay into the kitchen. Was every man in Georgia named Ray? Sometimes I wonder. I motioned to LeRay and he followed me into Deb's kitchen. The room could use some help; there was a lot of potential in it. Silver and chrome set against a black backdrop gave the room a voice that Debbie didn't hear. Why? The table was *white* and the chairs were *red*. It seemed enough for LeRay, though.

"What's up?" he said.

"Deb's getting the picture. Sit tight."

"You really didn't know what was happening in there?"

I sighed and said, "No."

"So, you look hot but are a bit dense?" he asked evenly.

"I guess so," I said. I decided to use the few moments to my advantage. Sylvia, Billy Ray's sister, said my name had been on the television and in the news after I disappeared. I stared at the man for a few moments and asked, "You never heard my name before? Really, LeRay? You never heard the name Morgahna Hamilton in the past few weeks?"

With his tongue stuck against his teeth, he shook his head and said, "No. Why?"

"It's been on TV. That's why? I'm just a bit surprised."

If he was lying, he was doing a good job of it. If he was lying, then why was he here? If not, then how was that possible? I took a long mental step backwards and examined my life. I was a media junkie and always had been. Not much happened around town or around the country that I missed. Call it a newsperson's preoccupation, but I knew most current news and lot of old stuff, too. When I talked to people on the streets, to people I was interviewing for a story or to people I met randomly, I sensed a lot of ignorance but not ignorant people. There's a difference, I think. You can be ignorant of things I know and still not be ignorant. You may know things I do not. It goes both ways. There are, however, some truly stupid people in our country but I didn't think LeRay Morrison was one of them. If he was telling the truth, then I was fine. If not, then I had to step carefully.

"Morgahna? I don't pay attention to TV and such stuff. They package the news to show what and who we should be scared of and I already know who to fear. White people. Cops, especially."

"There are black cops."

He had no answer for that and we wound up staring at each other as Debbie and Billy Ray sat down, Deb next to me and Billy next to LeRay. Deb held a clutch of pictures in her hand and looked at the black man carefully. To her, he was neither black nor a nigger, just a guy with

Chapter Nine

a dick, a potential lover. She spread the pictures out, holding a few in her hand. "Which one is the guy you saw?"

Evan was not one of the men Debbie showed him. He looked carefully at each picture and then said, "None of them. Is this the best you can do?"

She picked up the group, a spread of six pictures and plopped down six more, Evan in one of them, a picture taken on the pier at Tybee Island, the ocean behind him. It stirred old and very uncomfortable memories because we stayed in a motel on the beach that night and *nothing* happened. I talked on my cell phone until one o'clock in the morning as Evan eventually went to sleep on his side of the bed as the ocean rolled in beyond the closed sliding door that opened to the beach, an annoyance I didn't want, a pleasure that escaped me entirely that night. Debbie had the picture because she took it. She was with a guy she met where she worked and we all took turns taking each other's picture.

LeRay pounced on that picture and said, "Him. That's him. That's the guy that used your name."

To Deb, that was enough. Billy Ray was ready to do my bidding, whatever that was. LeRay merely watched. Me? I was fighting a breakdown over that picture and the possibilities that could never ever be again. I picked up the picture from the table and stared at it. *Why, Evan? Why could I not just give myself to you? Why was my career always so important?* It felt like a disease akin to alcoholism. Despite my best efforts, tears began to roll down my cheeks and I began to want to get drunk again. Deb took the picture from me, waved away the men and said, "Leave us for a bit, okay?"

LeRay had no special attachment to either of us and just nodded and left the room. Billy Ray lingered and asked almost timidly, "You sure, Debbie? Can I help?"

"No, Billy. It's okay. It's girl time. Just let me be with her, okay?"

I have no idea what Billy said, what his face looked like, what words he used or even why. I just saw Evan's face in my mind and the entire process started from scratch.

Each of us, I assume, expresses anger and frustration in their own way. Maybe my fuse was shorter than most, but the attendant anger always blew away quickly. I tended not to hold in anger only because life was so full of *possibilities*. Being angry and frustrated took precious time that I never thought I could afford to give or spend. The problem that I had now was Evan. He had always been there as my emotional backstop. No matter what happened to me professionally, or even personally, he was always there, was always my husband and was always dependable.

I screamed.

All that sadness that I burned through in those first two months was still there and I was still dealing with a major load of guilt that blamed me for his death. The old days, the comfortable days, the days where my biggest problem was the color of a new skirt or a bracelet or a necklace were gone. Evan was solid and always behind me somewhere. It always seemed that all I needed to do was turn to my right and he would be there ready to take my hand and hold it tenderly.

So, I screamed.

"I DON'T WANT THIS! I WANT EVAN! I WANT MY LIFE BACK! I WANT MY HOME BACK!"

Another thing each of has is a comfort zone, a space within which we can operate safely and without fear of failure. In a very real way, Evan was my safety zone. As long as I knew he was there and both providing for me and loving me, I knew I could do anything. My job, for example. I got that job not long after I met him and as my relationship with him grew stronger, my performance with it got better and people like Harley Hood recognized me. In a very real sense, I owed my job to my husband and when he took himself out of my life, he took my job as well. All that insurance he left me? It was possible he knew and recognized all this a long time ago, maybe when we first met and he saw my personal dynamics at work. Maybe he recognized he was my safety blanket and took steps to create a hedge against life. Evan? I love you but I didn't deserve you. You deserved someone like Debbie, someone who knew how to balance fun with the serious prospects of a career.

Debbie doesn't want kids either.

She hugged me, let me cry because I needed to and slowly said, "Morgahna, babe? I'm gonna be here. Cry all you need to. When you're ready to work, just let me know."

Chapter Nine

I felt empty inside and that feeling was so alien to me that it actually scared me. That newspaper I made when I was a kid? That was the outward expression of what I felt inside, the energy that took shape as a newspaper. Later when I discovered blank books that could be used for any purpose, I actually wrote a novel about a girl who becomes CEO of a large company by her sheer inventive skill. It was predictably awful and I have no idea what happened to it. Personally, I hope my mother found it and threw it away. It was that awful. Still, for all those years between then and now, my head was never empty, devoid of plans and machinations. There were times I talked to myself at bedtime, holding silent conversations in my mind with any number of people. Sometimes it was a handsome man, one like Evan. Sometimes it was with an adversary that wanted the same thing I did. I always suffered somehow, always was made to bow before I could rise triumphant. How was I going to deal with *emptiness*? Nothing like this had ever happened to me before and it was worse than alien, it was alien and monstrous. It felt like a debilitating disease, one that ate away at my mind and was slowing leaving me aimless and pointless. Was Evan my motivation? Did I get it from him? If so, then what were all those years prior to my meeting him?

Slowly, very slowly, I regained some composure and felt better. In all those four months since his death, I hadn't felt as good or as wonderfully alive as before that date and time. I felt as though I was losing ground and silently wondered if I would ever regain it.

"Deb? I hate these shoes."

"Suffer bitch. You look good in them."

Some friend.

"My feet will blister."

"No, they won't. You're wearing heels. Deal with it."

She was holding me and that conversation was a complete throwaway. As my tears slowly faded and my head remained steadfastly empty, I said, "The skirt, too? I feel like I'm on display."

"Feels goods, huh?"

"Feels obscene, Deb."

"Deal with it, bitch."

I actually giggled. "Stop calling me that."

"Stop being that way."

"Can we compromise?"

"No. You're wearing tight skirts and heels. Pants and boots tomorrow."

The only boots I have ever worn were as a sop to weather and not to men. There was a time I would have fought her, a time when I did. I hate boots and the girls who wear them. Debbie does. So, no I don't hate the girls who wear them, just the boots.

"Why did this happen, Deb?"

I was getting closer to it again, pushing myself back into my own life. I didn't care about high heels, boots, the girls who wore them, only wanted an answer for this. Why me? Why did *my* husband do this heinous thing and then not even leave me a farewell note, one that might have taken me off the hook?

"We'll find out, girlfriend," she said like a lover.

"Will we? Can we?"

"Tell me about the black guy?"

"He heard my name in his home. I followed Karin there, to where he lived with his sister and her boyfriend," I said to her, my head still resting on her shoulder, her right hand reassuringly on my back.

"We need to talk to them. What does he know?"

"Nothing. That's what he claims. He's here, though, Deb. I need to do something with him."

I have *always* discounted Debbie Jenson. Always. More fluff than stuff? That wasn't me, that was her. An airhead with her own frequency to the ozone. I've known her for twenty years and I have *never* considered her smarter than me. Our grades always verified that mental claim. While she was busy getting felt up behind the football bleachers by boys who didn't even know her name, I was busy studying and holding those mental conversations with myself. As I grew older, I desperately wanted her to leave me alone and she never did. Like the herpes virus, she kept

Chapter Nine

reappearing on an infrequent basis. Each time I saw her, I was convinced she was stupider than the last time I saw her.

She got a boob job some years back.

She was *twenty-five* when she had them lifted and slightly enlarged.

Her next job is an ass lift.

So help me god, an ass lift.

What she did next only proved to me how stupid I was. It was almost never her, but me. I was the one shunning friends and fun. I was the one who avoided the sleepovers because they accomplished nothing. I was the one who called her vacant. I was the one who knocked on her head once and said, "Anyone home?" I was the one who sought out a husband for all the wrong reasons.

She unpeeled me from her shoulder and said to my face, "Morg? You were always better than me. Always. You studied harder, you saw things I didn't and now you're going to do it again. No more crying, no more wishing for things you can't have, no more asking pointless questions. Evan did this thing and we're going to find out why. Tomorrow is Sunday and I don't work again until Tuesday. I can take whatever amount of time off I need and we can work together until we have an answer. Right, Morgahna? No more crying. It accomplishes nothing and pushes an answer that much farther away. Right?"

Her eyes are deep blue and she has the face that once must have launched a thousand ships. Helen. She is Helen of Troy. Those eyes are always disguised with mascara and that night was no different. Her mouth is the perfect size and shape that men like, her face as round and as satisfying as an apple. Could I do it? Could I be all the things she expected from me, she wanted from me? Could I stop thinking about Evan in terms that brought tears and helplessness? The problem as I saw it was that bitch was challenging me. That frigging blond bimbo bitch knew that I would respond in some way other than *emptiness*. I always had. She knew me *that* well, knew me far better than I knew her.

God, I love her. Why have I been so stupid about not just her but all my friends? I took a deep breath, smiled, straightened my shoulders and said, "Bitch."

She smiled and said, "Yep. That's me."

It was going to be hard not to cry, not to think of Evan that way. It was going to be a challenge and I always got up for them and she knew it. "Deb? What if I fail?"

"We won't."

I, we. She was pushing me toward a collaboration with her and as she did, a small piece of me began to change. I could feel it. The stubbornly independent woman who kept track of her progress and her opponents was gaining an ally. You could say that Dave Woods was an ally but you would be wrong. Dave's own path was headed toward Sports and the people who reported them. My path was headed toward politics, the city and the maze of relationships that made it all work. Dave wasn't a collaborator. He was just someone whose path coincided with mine if only briefly. Debbie Jenson was not even a reporter and she was doing something no one else had even accomplished much less tried.

"And I'm not doing anything else with the hick," she said seriously.

I smiled, hugged her and said, "Don't worry. I won't hold you to it."

"I'm serious, Morg baby. We're going to find out why this is happening to you, get you a suitably trashy wardrobe with accessories to match and you're going to hump the ball boy at the Westin Inn out on Hutchinson Island."

"We need to talk to LeRay and not about my shoes."

"Agreed. You keep those shoes on, girl. They'll give you attitude."

I slipped them off and said, "I already have attitude, Deb."

She smiled and said, "Yeah, I know."

Before we left the kitchen, she stopped me and said, "Morgahna? Tell me we can do this together. Don't blow me off."

"And Billy?"

"Strength in numbers."

Chapter Nine

"Plus he's good in bed?"

She closed her eyes and said, "Oh, yeah. Very good in bed."

I prompted her. "But?"

"No more until we're done."

"With anyone?" I prompted further.

"Oh," she said stamping her foot. "Okay. With anyone until we're done."

"Or I do this myself?"

"Okay, okay. I'll be as chaste as a nun."

"Say it, Deb. Tell me you agree."

She looked as though I sent her to bed without dinner. "Okay. I agree. No more messing around until we're done." Then she twisted her face into a sneer and said, "Happy?"

"Yes, I am," I said with a deeply satisfied smile.

The men were talking in Debbie's living room, a room that was as mismatched as her kitchen. Tall windows across the back of the room made it a very light place. Naturally, she covered them with insubstantial drapes that had the constancy of gauze. I saw elegant curtains and a globe in the corner. Her furniture was a collection of similarly mismatched stuff, some of it chrome and some of it made from sturdy oak. The couch was a muted blue and tan arrangement that would have look appropriate in a frat house or a dorm room, not her living room. I stuffed my disapproval away and decided to work, decided to be focused instead of little more than a weeping widow.

Billy Ray was talking to LeRay as we walked in and sat in separate chairs on either end of the couch.

"I was talking to him," Billy Ray said. "I was trying to find out how much he knows about his sister and basically, he doesn't know anything."

"How is that possible, LeRay?" I asked. "You live with her."

To deal with this in a coherent fashion, I was going to have to resort to my newspaper persona. He was a story and inside him were all the details that would make it real, would make that story come to life. If I pushed because Evan's memory was more important than this moment, I would lose it, him and whatever he knew. There was no choice but to treat this as business, as business as normal. Therefore, after I asked that question, I retreated behind an impartial mask and waited. Facts are facts, but people interpret them however they wish. That was something I got from Dave. *See the facts for what they are, Morgahna, not for what you want them to be. If you push your own interpretation onto them, you might be popular but never right. It all depends on you, kid. Do what you will, but I will never allow something to be published under my name unless I know it to be true.* That was best single piece of advice I ever got from anyone. It didn't matter that I heard the same thing in college. Testing those lessons we learn in a formally sterile environment in the real world always causes conflicts. I'd had a few and Dave showed and taught me to be true and not popular. Thank you, Dave. While I was always unpopular, I was not always true.

  LeRay Morrison was intelligent and I believe that was obvious for all of us to see. We live in a country that is slowly bowing to the wizardry of religion. Things and opinions are true only because we say they are, not because we can verify them and test them against our expectations. Truth is subjective or has become that way. I always wanted something more substantial than John 3:16. I wanted independent verification and the ability to test those theories in the real world. Being a newsperson was perfect for me because the real world is the best laboratory you will ever get. It is full of contradictions and unreliable sources. To succeed there is to succeed wildly and greatly. God, I miss my job.

  LeRay, though, didn't act or speak like a yokel from the hills. He was clear and precise and said what he meant and not what he thought. "Daydra does drugs, some coke and pot. That baby is getting no real care. The boyfriend deals, carries a gun a lot and Daydra is mostly fucked up all the time."

  "Who takes care of the baby?" Billy asked.

  "I do," LeRay said.

  "Being here must cause you a few agonizing moments," he replied.

  "More than a few."

Chapter Nine

Billy looked at me and said, "I'd like to propose a course of action. You ready, Morgahna?"

"Yes."

"I want you to stay here tomorrow morning and let me go back to talk to your neighbors. Then we can all go out to Daydra's apartment and talk to them."

"Okay, but why? Why do we have to stay here?"

His face was once more as placid as a western desert. He looked at me directly and my knees felt as though they were turning to jelly. I admonished myself and listened as he said, "The person that did this is still out there, Morgahna, and he tore your house apart piece-by-piece and your neighbors probably saw them do it. If they see you there, see you and recognize you, the word that you are alive will certainly spread and our job will become more difficult because some one of them will talk; one of them will certainly use your name and if those people come back to your house and hear those rumors, then your life is at stake each time you step outside the door. That's why."

I sighed and said, "Okay. We stay here until you return tomorrow morning. Then we go and talk to Daydra and find out what Karin gave her."

That night might have been easier to bear had Debbie owned a better computer. Mine was a good one, one that ran off a cable line and was as fast as I needed it to be. Hers was a dialup and she used it only for email. It was so frustrating that I quit and went back to her bedroom and looked for clothes for the next day. I found her absolutely adamant and totally close-minded. She insisted I was wearing pants and boots and we actually argued about it until she stopped, dabbed tears from her eyes and said, "Oh, Morgahna. Our first fight. This is wonderful."

Boots and pants, huh?

Yep. The next morning, that was my outfit.

The pants were bone-white and the boots were black and tall, the worst combination of both. My butt no longer felt like a 757 but the airport at which it landed. My feet screamed and called me worse names than merely vile ones, but ones that were wholly obscene. Worse? I had no underwear and the only way her bra would fit me was with tissues stuffed in it.

At least the panties were comfortable. Think about it.

I was going to learn what uncomfortable meant all over again.

I was going to learn what people will do to cover their tracks.

And the process started as soon as Billy Ray got back from talking to my neighbors down on Taylor Street and we headed toward Daydra's apartment.

I was stepping knee-deep in the worst excrement I had ever seen because this stuff was aimed at me.

Me.

And I still didn't know why.

What I found there, found in Daydra's apartment, was horrifying.

Totally.

Chapter Ten

We spent the morning, Debbie and I did, discussing how to rebuild my life. I had nothing that identified me, no credit cards, no driver's license, nothing that showed my address, no proof that I owned anything at all and was living wholly at Debbie's sufferance.

"My feet hurt," I whined.

"Not as bad as they did," she returned ignoring my complaint.

"I look like a whore."

"You don't act like one. Yet. Now, focus. Do you trust Tommy?"

I wiggled my toes inside those boots and said, "I feel like a storm trooper."

"You look fabulous. Now, Tommy?"

"Why am I dressed this way?"

Her eyes bulged, her face looked exasperated and her voice followed suit. "Dammit, Morgahna! Your feet hurt, you think your ass is misshapen and your boobs are on display but YOU ARE NOT THINKING ABOUT EVAN! NOW, TOMMY?"

I grinned and she smiled. The damn blond bimbo.

Okay, I'd already talked about him but I suppose I could fill in a few blanks, so I did or at least tried.

Tommy Underwood was thirty-eight years old when Evan died. In the last five years, in the years I knew Tommy, I suppose he was a male equivalent of me. Tommy was always working and blowing off the occasional girlfriend. He was married once, maybe twice. I never discovered an answer to that and never felt as though I needed to know either. He was, though, easily as energetic as me. He worked insane hours and saw dozens and dozens of clients. I know he was a good friend to Evan and that he made Evan a partner more out of gratitude than skill. Evan saved them a ton of money by changing their business model. Look,

I don't know what that means but I've already said that. According to Evan – and I had no reason to distrust him – Tommy's business arrangement was precarious because he could be charged in lawsuits that were aimed at people who merely worked for him. Changing the business model changed all that and gave them security their previous arrangement lacked. There were probably other reasons and contingencies but that seemed to be the heart of why Evan set it up that way.

It did not make Tommy and me better friends, though. I was far too busy chasing my own rainbows to worry about his or, for that matter, Evan's. It was always enough that he had rainbows and pots of gold at the end of them just like I did. In my mind I equated Tommy to Dave. Was that true? Maybe this case, this entire sordid affair, would prove whether or not that was ever true.

"Deb? Billy Ray asked me to name people that I trusted and he wasn't one of them. I named three and you were one of them. The other two are people I worked with. Tommy? He could be anyone and I mean that literally."

"How do you feel about him?"

"Feelings are irrelevant. I could feel as warm as a puppy toward him but that wouldn't mean anything if he's guilty of something."

"Okay," she said. "Sorry."

"Don't be. You're making me think and that's good. That's always good." Then I smiled and added, "You're making my feet hurt, too."

"What about Karin Hubbell?" she said with a blond smile.

"No idea. She's a cipher of the worst sort. I know so little about her that it may well be nothing at all."

"Who could do that to your home and not stir up suspicions among your neighbors?"

That was an excellent question. It was entirely possible that Debbie Jenson's intelligence was simply different than mine. Maybe the correct term is complimentary. She was thinking in terms and places where I wasn't and it was possible that the reverse was true. "Well," I said. "Tommy. I can't think of anyone else. He has power of attorney over

Chapter Ten

my estate and always has. If anyone asked, he could always get legal with them very quickly and very easily. Anyone else? I can't think of anyone and that includes my parents and my brother that could do it as easily as he could."

"Then, Tommy is part of this?"

Oh, Lord. I came so close to agreeing with her but the absence of proof kept me from it. I even fidgeted over the answer. Finally, I said as I shook my head, "No. I can't say that. It might be easier just to confront him in his office and ask him."

To that point, LeRay had done little more than just listen to us. He seemed to agree with the way I was thinking and that just sent suspicious shivers up and down my spine. That seemed altogether too much like ass-kissing, a thing I knew all too much about. As soon as I made that answer about confronting Tommy in his office, he just leaned forward across the table where we were sitting and sipping coffee and said, "I wouldn't do that if it was up to me. I'd call him. I wouldn't even call him from a cell phone but from a payphone somewhere. If his phone shows Caller ID, then he would have a hard time tracing your call to a payphone. I know it's possible, but not bloody likely."

Deb leaned forward and said, "Good point, LeRay. You married?"

"Hey," I said. "Your promise. Remember it?"

Her bottom lip came out and she said, "I was just making plans for the future."

LeRay smiled and it looked good on him. "No. Been involved a few times but never been married."

"Why?" I asked.

He frowned and said with his hands spread wide, "What do I have to offer a girl? I baby sit my sister's baby."

"What skills do you have?" I asked.

"Other than a few minor intellectual ones, I've been a busboy, a waiter, worked in a laundry, delivered newspapers for the Morning News, sold insurance for a while, worked retail and that's a thing I'll never do again thanks to the public and their abuse of me, worked for a few fast food places and a few others I won't admit to, a few that were illegal. Skills? None, ladies. I'm a lazy nigger." Then he smiled at me and said, "Right?"

Debbie leaned forward, let him look right down her blouse, a thing he did not do and said dreamily, "Mmm. House nigger."

I was about to sputter my objections but both of them started laughing all too easily. "You don't mind being called that?" I asked.

"Depends on the job description," he said with a smile at both of us.

Deb smiled, still dreamily, and said, "*Horizontal* house nigger."

He pointed at her and said, "Deal. Fringe benefits?"

"Orgasm."

"Mine?"

"Both of us. Simultaneous."

He smiled and said, "You're making this hard."

"Only if I do it right," she said licking her lips.

I nudged her. "Your promise, girl?" And to him, "Knock it off."

Deb got apologetic. "Sorry."

If LeRay was offended, he didn't show it.

The front door opened and Billy Ray walked in and sat down next to LeRay. "No one remembers anything. It's amazing. A moving truck shows up and the neighbors just assume you've moved away and don't even take into account the stories on TV. It's amazing. They all assumed you moved away after your husband died."

"Then we're going to see Daydra?" I asked.

"Might as well. No one on Taylor Street remembers anything. No one even remembers the name of the moving company that took all your stuff."

"LeRay made a suggestion that I want do when we're done," I said.

Chapter Ten

"And that is?"

"Call Tommy Underwood from a payphone. I want him to tell me he had nothing to do with this."

"Okay," he said nodding his head. "That's a good idea."

It was the same deal as before. I rode with Debbie and the men rode together. My knees still felt weak around Billy Ray and I was having to deal with that as we got on the road. Deb started whistling and it took me a while before I recognized the tune from "Shaft". I frowned at her and then giggled behind my hand. "Jeez, Deb," I said. "Maybe I should just take him to bed and find out if that's a good way to forget."

As she drove away from her condo, she said with as much conviction as I'd ever heard her make, "Well, I got two problems with that, Morg. The first is the obvious. Your head is already befuddled and that would only complicate your problems. The second is a bit simpler. You? Seduce a man?"

"Oh, thanks," I said rolling my eyes.

She was, however, correct. I can't really claim any great seduction of Evan. Okay, I'm attractive. So are a lot of other girls my age. It isn't difficult to be that way when you're young. No, if anything, Evan saw something in me that made me more attractive than I felt, than I ever felt. As time went by and sex became less and less frequent, I saw him sigh more and more. There were times that I tried to dress down. You know, consciously wear stuff that would tend to make his desire go limp. Pardon the allusion. I tried baggy sweatshirts and baggier shorts but I still saw him staring at me *that way*. We never talked about the attraction, what it was and why it worked. It just did and it irritated me endlessly because I can remember having sex when I didn't want to, when I had other things on my mind. Yes, those other things always seemed more important than him and now none of them are.

As the city rolled by, I asked idly, "Is sex really that good for you?"

She turned her face to me if only briefly and said quietly, "Yes."

I envied her because I *always* suppressed my response to sex. Always. The kinkiest thing I ever did? Well, not did, but got involved in?

About a year before his death, Evan came to bed one night and said with all seriousness, "Tonight? I'm going to make you scream."

He didn't. I was able – albeit with a huge effort – to suppress anything louder than a soft moan. The irony? That isn't even remotely kinky. That's just sex and love. Love and sex. After that night, he stopped trying and it was obvious even then. Something drained out of him and I chose not to notice. If I am truly to blame for this – and I still think I am – that was most likely the start of his downward spiral. His best effort as a lover was not as good as my best effort to suppress it. Again, I am sorry, Evan. I can't believe that was me. I can't believe I was ever that cruel. Yes, I know we live in a society that condones a lot of sickness that we call sex. Bondage, domination, that sort of thing. But me? I never wore leather, would never carry a whip, would never restrain anyone for my own gratification, yet I so thoroughly cowed and reduced Evan to what I wanted him to be that my name may as well be Mistress Morgahna.

As the remainder of that year crawled by in all its ignominious glory, Evan seemed to shrink away entirely. About four or five months before he died, he took a two-week vacation and didn't shave for the first week at all. That was such a warning sign that it seems criminal I didn't do anything then, do anything like at least sitting down and talking to him. I didn't and I will always blame my own selfishness for it.

"Morgahna?" she said. "Don't. I can see it written all over your face. It isn't your fault."

It *still* seemed as though it was but I had a new focus now. I wanted to find out who was trying to kill me and if this really was all my fault. So, I needed to give voice to it. "Debbie? You know how I feel."

"Yes, and…"

I dropped my hand onto her arm as she drove and said emphatically, "I need to know why he died and who wanted me dead, Deb. If those two things aren't connected then I'll go to the police and report everything. But, Deb? I was pushing myself in this direction ever since I got that job at the newspaper. I was pushing myself to be an investigative reporter and I don't mean on the cleanliness of downtown restaurants either. I mean investigative reporting into criminal wrongdoing. This is where I was going before all this started. This is where I want to be."

Chapter Ten

That was as bluntly truthful as I could be. As I grew into my teenage years, I started getting into very interesting trouble. I found a vibrator under the mattress on my mother's side of the bed and wrote about it in one of my infrequent Morgahna Daily's. Mom read it and hit the fan. I was sixteen and I was told, "That is *none* of your business and if I find *any* reference to it outside of this house, you are grounded for the rest of your life." Unquote. I never found out how she used it, if she did, what she got out of it or even why it was there. For a while, I suspected it was there simply to tempt me. Well, I don't think so now, but at the time you could not have convinced me.

Those years were my crucible. Those were the years I learned about sex, that it was not necessarily unpleasant but that it was no big deal either. That's what I got out of that vibrator. Men were incapable of sexually satisfying a woman and their purpose was to provide wealth and luxury. It made my high school years easier and made sex unnecessary. It also made me exceedingly unpopular and gave me all the time in the world to think about my life, what I wanted in it and for it, who I needed to share it with and my choice of career fields. When I got hired at the newspaper, my hometown newspaper, it was a validation of my entire life and the plans I made for it.

That Daytimer? The yearly one? Inside the front cover was a statement of my future and where I wanted it to go. "Beat reporter for 18 months. Feature reporter after that. 36 months. General assignment reporter in 60 months. Op-ed after that." How did I do? Well, I was a beat reporter for not quite two years and my last assignment was as a feature reporter. Given that I worked there for five years, I was on schedule. At twenty-seven, I was beating my elders to the best stuff, the best sources and the best slots. In any newspaper being "above the fold" is preferable to being below it. What does that mean? Most newspapers on a newsstand show half the page and is folded exactly in half. Being above the fold means people can see your article, your face, your pictures, everything you did. Being below it means being buried. My stuff was more often above the fold than not. Of course, being a feature reporter meant not getting many front page articles. Senior reporters usually got those. I was on my way though.

I saw the op-ed page as the Promised Land. You got your picture next to your column and with it went a lot of prestige. I wanted to redraw the genre, rewrite the stories that appeared there, wanted to tell the public the truth and stop pandering to the lowest common denominator. To do that, I needed to be an investigative reporter who got free reign to do what was necessary and not what would sell newspapers.

That was the key. Newspapers have existed in this country and on this continent for *hundreds* of years and the temptation to write fluffy stuff has always existed. The one discovery I made that cemented my decision to become a reporter was Jacob Riis and his absolutely pivotal work *"How The Other Half Lives"* that was published in 1890. It covered *all* the bases. It was sensational, spellbinding and true. It documented in words and pictures the abysmally appalling conditions that half the population of late-nineteenth century New York City lived in during those times. I read that book at least ten times during my sophomore year of high school and of all the things I lost when my home was stripped to the walls, that was my most prized possession.

I learned about the famous agnostic, H. L. Mencken. I considered him a genius with words and read his surviving Baltimore Sun columns religiously all through high school and college. Then Ernie Pyle and his common man approach to warfare. I disdain war and that is most likely my initial liking for Billy Ray Simpson. He seemed to have it straight. Warfare isn't about patriotism. It's about making that other poor bastard die for his patriotism. Thanks George Patton for allowing me to paraphrase you. Finally, Ben Bradlee, the man who helped to stop The Vietnam War by publishing The Pentagon Papers. Where is a similar man now? I fear there is none and that an entire generation of Americans is destined to die so that a small cabal, an already wealthy one, can become even wealthier.

Deb never understood any of this, never saw my preoccupation with Truth and Justice. Had she been a bit more flexible in her choice of friends, a bit more liberal with her opinions, we would not know each other today. For the record: Debbie? I am glad you saw yourself as a shoehorn into my life. I don't think I could have gotten this far without you. Now that I'm here, I don't think I will ever forget your contribution to this, whatever may happen.

Chapter Ten

As those apartments loomed ahead of us, I said, "He referred to something called 'The Package', Deb. I can't help but wonder what that means."

"No idea, girl," she said as I pointed toward the parking lot nearest those apartments and not the one I used last night. She parked her car and waited a few moments for Billy Ray to park his pickup.

We stood facing that old building and Billy Ray gave the issue. "Which one?"

I nodded at the building that faced us and said, "That one. Middle apartment. 2B."

"How do you want to handle it?" he asked.

LeRay said, "Well, since she's my sister, I can always make the initial demand. You know? Something like, 'What's the deal, Daydra?' What do you think?"

"Will she talk to us?" I asked.

"Nope," he said. "My guess? She got her money from that lawyer and she's isn't going to say anything."

"She thinks I'm dead," I said. "That's the only thing all this can mean. If I show up, it might rattle her enough. Besides, we can always threaten that her lawyer, Karin, will come back and demand her money back."

Billy rubbed his chin thoughtfully and said, "I like that angle. I'd still like to be first into the room, though. Do you have any objections to that, Morgahna?"

"No. Since my self-defense skills are just above those of the Iraqi Army, you can go in first. In fact, be my guest."

"LeRay?" he asked. "You?"

"My momma has my gun. Like the lady says, be my guest."

"Well," he said squinting up at the sun. "Let's go. Just remember, we're after nothing more than information. Okay? We find out what she knows and we leave. Okay?"

That was still okay by me.

The day was breaking with intense sunlight and high clouds. The humidity was gathering force and before nightfall, anyone caught outside of an air-conditioned room was going to be a sweaty mess. It was not a good day to be caught without an antiperspirant.

I still felt as though I was on display dressed the way I was. I suppose that Debbie was right. My feet hurt too much to think seriously about anything other than why we were here. The grass was wet from an early morning sprinkler, so the boots were a good idea. *Yeah, right. I could be just as safe wearing tennis shoes.* I frowned at Debbie and she just smiled wickedly.

All four of us knew that both Daydra and her boyfriend had access to guns. In fact, LeRay admitted that the one he had belonged to his sister or that at least she was the one who carried it around deep inside her purse. "Morgahna? I feel better that she doesn't have it."

"What will your mom do with it?"

"Throw it away. Take the ammunition out of it and toss in the garbage."

"Good for her."

Billy Ray knocked and said loudly, "I'm from the lawyer's office. Can we talk to you?"

No one answered. The first time I was here, there was a television playing in the background and a baby was crying. The silence was, as they say, deafening. He knocked again and got no answer. "Maybe they aren't home," he said.

"Open it," I said. "See if the door opens."

He twisted the knob just enough to verify that the door was both open and could be. He looked at me and I nodded. "Go on," I said with a voice just above a whisper.

When you're a beat reporter, you get the shit assignments. The city council meetings are the shittiest. Nothing happens in them that isn't supposed to and a lot of otherwise good reporters have failed in that testing ground. Not me. I've already testified to what I did to break that spell. That assignment is the worst one, though. Besides flower shows, there are dog shows, monster truck rallies, elementary school meetings

Chapter Ten

and a host other more basically boring jobs. School boards, PTA meetings, cub scout meetings, budget sessions for any legislative group, bankers, insurance association meetings and such others that defy description. I was in all of those and those others that still defy both description and memory. I can remember meetings and assignments when I wished to be *anywhere* else. This was like that. I wanted to be *anywhere* else but not for the same reason as then.

Billy Ray pushed the door open quickly, not shyly. Later, he would tell me that's how they taught it in Iraq. You go in quickly, don't worry about noise because any you make will tend to surprise them for a moment and mostly you peel off to either side of the door after you enter. People standing in the doorway tend to get shot. All of which meant nothing to me.

To be fair and honest, none of us saw anything when we first entered that apartment. The living room was empty and the television was not on. The room looked lived in which was another and more polite way to call it messy. Part of the mess was the newspaper, The Morning News. Pieces of it were on the couch, other pieces on the floor. The carpet was the color of dirt and it was stained darker in some places by what looked like spills that had never been cleaned.

"Maybe they aren't home," Deb said.

"The door was open," LeRay said. "That's not right. Daydra is paranoid about locking her door."

Okay. Obviously. If there were drugs in the apartment, that would follow. I'd never reported on serious crime because I wasn't that far up the ladder yet. A couple of years maybe.

The kitchen was off to the left and it was empty. Everyone seemed to gravitate to that end of the place so I peeled off to the right and approached the hallway back to the bedrooms and bath. The bathroom was small and offended my upwardly mobile sensibilities. The mere thought of applying makeup in that cramped space seemed impossible. Yes, I had totally forgotten my life before Evan because not only was my bathroom this small but I applied makeup in a room similar to it. The world, it seemed, was zeroing in on my weakest points and memory was the worst.

I stepped across the hallway and obviously entered LeRay's room. It was orderly, neat and a book was in the middle of the bed, a book about the war on terror. At least, that's all I saw, that word. Terror. It's the new buzz word and I have an inside track on it because I work – or worked – at a newspaper. Everything is being related to terror in one way or another. We *want* to be afraid and it's becoming more and more obvious.

But, I learned terror when I opened that last bedroom door.

The room was a mess but not because of what happened in there. No, the room was a mess because of the people who used to live in there. There were clothes everywhere and a crib on the corner. The crib was thankfully empty.

As soon as I saw them, I clamped my hand over my mouth and bolted from the room and ran straight for the toilet where I dumped my breakfast in the bowl in long heaving chunks. Everyone heard me and that caused Billy Ray's protective spirit to kneel next to me after he came back from the bedroom and said softly, "I'm sorry. I should have been in there instead of you. This is my fault."

I spit chunks from my mouth and said, "It just caught me by surprise, Billy. I'm okay."

That was very nearly true.

I've seen bodies before in my line of work. It's inevitable, I suppose. The first one was a kid who was hit by a car while he was riding his bicycle. Since the driver wasn't drinking, the story never made it past the local pages. The kid never had a chance, though. He turned a corner on his bike and the driver never saw him and rolled right over him. The left front wheel snapped his spine and the left rear crushed his skull. The boy was eleven when he died and the driver had a nervous breakdown afterwards. The public crucified the driver and made his life so miserable that he moved to Charleston to live with his brother. That boy's body was a mess and I got a chance to see it for two reasons. The first was proximity. I was there. The second was professional. I was a reporter and that incident qualified as news, so I called a photographer and he took the goriest pictures you ever saw, none of which ever made the paper.

The bodies, and there were two of them in that room, were cut open in such a way that they bled profusely. I got up from my spot in front

Chapter Ten

of the toilet and gently pushed Billy Ray out of the way. "I've seen death, Billy. I have to see them."

"It's not pretty."

"I don't expect it to be."

He grabbed a facecloth from the towel rack and said, "Put this over your nose and mouth."

"Don't treat me like a girl," I said.

When he grabbed another one from the shower stall door and clamped it over his nose, I apologized. "Sorry."

LeRay was coming out of the room when I came out of the bathroom. He looked grim and shaken. He looked directly at me but said nothing at all. Written across his face was the unspoken business that brought us here. *This is your fault. In some way, this happened because of you.* Was that paranoia? Maybe but I don't think so. Did he really think that? Probably. In those words? Maybe not, but ones that conveyed the same message. I stopped him and asked, "LeRay? Do you believe me when I say I'm sorry?"

His eyes were moist and a few tears broke loose and coursed down his cheeks. He swallowed hard and seemed to be measuring his words carefully. All he managed in the end was, "Yes." Then he went out to the living room.

I had to see them. I had to know what was in there and what was done to them. Why? Maybe I was convinced I was seeing a preview of my own death and simply wanted a reference point. Maybe I'm as bloodthirsty as you are, but I went with that cloth over my nose and mouth.

The man was on the floor at the end of the bed and lying in an ocean of blood. Even considering his baggy clothes, it wasn't hard to see two major wounds. The first was the easiest. His throat had been slashed clear to his spinal chord. That eliminated any screaming. The second was around his stomach. If I had to guess, someone had sliced open his stomach and let him bleed to death as he tried to breathe through a windpipe that was no longer there. Agonizing? No doubt.

It was Daydra that bothered me.

Billy Ray hovered nearby, but both Debbie and LeRay were outside somewhere. Daydra was on the bed as though sleeping. Her throat was slashed open just like his was and there was blood from the carotid artery, but she looked serene while he looked as though he had been angrily defensive. That thought made me check his arms and hands. Yes, there were slashing wounds on them. He tried to defend himself. Not so, Daydra. She was merely laying on the bed with her throat slashed clear to her spine just like his. Her hand showed no defensive wounds and her stomach had not been cut open. She died from that single wound to her throat, her eyes half-closed, her face gentle in death. How was that possible?

I stepped back through the death scene and stood in the doorway. What was I looking for? Not a motive, but a method. If I was her and knew someone wanted to kill me, why would I just lay there like that? The bedcovers were slightly mussed where she lay, a pack of cigarettes on the nightstand next to her. Her clothes were like his, baggy and disheveled. The room was otherwise simply messy because of who lived here and not because of what happened in it except for that scene at the end of the bed.

It was almost as though…

And my mind stopped. Was it possible? *She's in bed and someone shows up, a person she knows. She makes love with him and he cuts her throat as they lay on that bed, maybe as he's approaching orgasm. He does it, though. He has with him a knife large enough to do the job but small enough to hide from her until it's too late. Then…*

THAT'S IT!

Her pants had been put back on her *after* he killed her. Her shirt was outside them but the first time I'd seen her it was tucked inside the waistband. She was barefoot and that just figured no matter how you looked at it. *Then he came home and found all this and the first thing the killer did was cut his throat so he couldn't scream. Then he cut open his belly and let him bleed to death.*

I felt euphoric because it seemed to hold water. Despite the carnage and the two poor souls in there, I felt good. I stepped out of the room and Billy Ray followed me all the way to the living room where Debbie was talking with great animation with LeRay.

Chapter Ten

"What's up, Deb?" I thought she was going to get queasy or something but that's not what happened.

She looked at me, gave me her house key and said, "Get out of here. Billy will take you back to my place."

"Why?" I said as I took her key.

She nodded at Billy and said, "Because of what he said. We have no choice here, Morgahna. We have to call 911 and if you're here when the police show up, then your secret is out. You can't be here when they show up. I can truthfully verify I was with LeRay last night while Billy Ray gets you out of here." She looked at Billy and asked, "Is that okay with you?"

"Yeah," he said. "That's good thinking. I would have missed that."

"They'll find forensic traces of me here, Deb."

LeRay said, "Well, sure. You were here yesterday. If it comes up, I can verify that."

And so can those kids on the basketball court. They saw me. It might hold water, just might. "The killer's DNA is in his semen," I said. "That seems pretty stupid."

"It will also clear you," Deb said.

I let the idea roll around inside my head and then nodded. "Yeah. I buy it. Billy? You ready?"

"Yep. We need to make sure no one is watching."

That seemed to be the only drawback. It was possible that neighbors saw four of us approach the house. If they canvassed the neighborhood, that fact might implicate me deeper than I wanted to be implicated. If I stayed, then Debbie was right. My anonymity was over. The person responsible for the attack on me would know I survived it and might try it again. From my own vantage point, I seemed to have no alternative but to leave and hope my presence didn't become known.

I hugged Deb and said, "You be damn careful, Debbie Jenson."

She hooked her arm inside LeRay's and said, "Careful doesn't get you dates on Saturday night."

"It's Sunday, Deb," I corrected her.

She smiled. "We're just getting our stories straight. He was great in bed last night."

He smiled. "Awesome is the word I heard."

"Both of you be careful," I admonished them.

Time was going to make that word mean more than a mere admonition. Time was going to make that word a warning. Be careful. Careful. Be careful what you ask for. Be careful for what you want. Be careful because you might get it.

Several people already had.

If you've been following this, then you know there is one person missing here that none of us thought much about.

None of us.

Why was that?

Chapter Eleven

I wanted to be scared but I wasn't and he noticed. I was thinking, my right hand to my chin, my face pointed just slightly out the window on my side of the truck. I was rethinking what happened in there, in that room. "Billy?" I asked.

"Yeah?"

"The guy that did this seems too smart to have left forensic evidence as clear-cut as semen. Could you make love to me without coming?"

He smiled. "Nope."

"Is it possible for a man to do that?"

"I suppose," he said. "Even if I could, forensically, it would still leave my pubic hair in yours. With enough investigating, you could still discover I was with you."

The damn man saw where I was going with this. There was no way, literally no way, the murderer could have made love to Daydra before he killed her. Then what happened if not that? "You got a quarter?"

"Yeah. You want to call Underwood?"

"Yes."

He squirmed, got his right hand into his pants pocket and produced a handful of change that he held out to me. "Take whatever you need."

I plucked two quarters from the jumble of change and we looked for the first phone booth. Considering the way I was dressed, it was likely someone would remember me so I vowed to dress much more inconspicuously from now on. Sorry, Deb. It was a nice experiment but it's over. Also over was my descent into self-recrimination. Well, at least for the present. I had a focus that was taking me away from that downward arc and I felt the first signs that I was fighting back in the only way I knew how. I was going to work toward an answer even though I knew this experience, this assignment whatever it was, could very easily kill me. "Billy? Go up River Street, okay?"

"Sure, but why?"

"I'm not dressed for anyplace but River Street. I'll go into a bar down there, make the call and then we go back to Debbie's place."

"I'm going with you when we find a place. Sugarplum's is down there."

"I know," I said with a sigh. "Give me an alternative, Billy, and I'll listen."

"No, we're cool," he said. "Just as long as I go inside with you."

We parked in that *same* lot only because I knew a few bars down here from where I could make a call. You can't work in a town built along a river without getting to know a few bars. I imagine that's true almost anywhere there is a newspaper with ambitious people working in it, river or not.

The place was named the Golden Rooster and if you have to ask about the name, then you need to get out more often. I wrapped my right arm around Billy's waist as we entered, just to make certain that no other guys got any ideas that I had no idea how to perform. He slid his around my waist and held me tight. With God as my witness, that felt better than the best sex I'd ever had. Okay, not that it meant a lot given my background, but it felt wonderful anyway.

There was a phone in the hallway across from the bathroom doors which only meant I was going to have to be short, blunt and to the point. Billy stood at the entrance to the hallway ready to signal if someone was coming. With him there, I really didn't worry. Was that wise? Look, he hadn't given me any reason to mistrust him, so I didn't. As he leaned against the wall watching the bar, I dialed Tommy's number and made the last few practice lines in my head before the call connected. I knew his number by heart, both his home and office numbers. Like any other professional, he had several numbers and like any girl's girl, I knew them all. Sure, part of the reason was Evan and the fact that he was Tommy's partner. A smaller part of it was jealousy. Yes, jealousy. I found Evan handsome and feared that his eyes might wander, so I called him

Chapter Eleven

randomly and never found him in a place he shouldn't have been. There were some times when I wasn't sure and on those occasions, I submitted to him sexually only because I was nervous about losing him.

I can dimly remember an occasion about a year ago. I was laying in his arms after another bout with sex. He seemed fine, seemed to like our life. At least that's how I saw it. He hugged me and said something odd. I never thought of it before now, before I stood in that hallway looking like a tramp. "Morgahna, my minx, don't worry any more. Everything is going to be fine." Why would he tell me not to worry anymore? Why would he need to reassure me right after he'd emptied his balls into me? At the time, it seemed like a harmless conversational toss-up and I merely remember smiling and tossing the ball back to him. "Oh, I'm not worried, Evan." He said nothing and just held me. It seemed enough and I let it go. Now? I'd give anything to have that conversation back again.

I pushed Tommy back into my mind and focused on him.

That hallway was dark and dingy. There were two photographs of old motorcycles on the wall opposite those bathroom doors, one on either side of the phone. Country music was playing from a juke box in the bar, something by Waylon Jennings. I recognized his voice. The song ended and Johnny Cash came on singing about that boy named Sue. I dialed Tommy's home number and it rang twice before he answered. Consider that I still had no proof one way or the other that Tommy Underwood was involved in this: I needed proof or at least a direction from him. So, my first words to him after he made his greeting was, "Tommy? I want my home back. You took my home and I want it back."

Then I waited for an answer or at least a response.

My only benchmark for this type of phone call was Debbie. That phone call I made to her shoved her from a sometimes and maybe friend to one that seemed a lot more important than she'd been before I made it. I realize that I needed to tread softly on all the ground I was covering because the stakes were no longer as simple as words on paper. The stakes were my life and I was convinced that the people responsible for this would not miss the next time they tried. If it was Tommy, I needed to listen to his voice and judge his reaction with a great deal of caution.

"Morgahna?" he said as his voice made the requisite upturn at the end. "Is that you?"

"Yes, Tommy. It's me."

"Where are you?" he asked. As he spoke, I listened to his voice just as much as I listened to his words. I found it odd that he didn't ask how I was but where. I rolled back against the wall, put my right boot against the it and looked down at Billy. He was watching the bar and the crowd in it as I tried to determine if my dead husband's partner wanted me dead, too.

"Where?" I asked. "Aren't you the least bit interested in how I am?"

There was the slightest hint of concern as he asked, "Well, yes. How are you? Where have you been? The police think you're dead."

"My home, Tommy? What did you do to my home?"

"You been there?"

"Yes. Tell me. Why? Why did you do that and don't bother denying it. You have the legal right to do that and we both know it. Just tell me why."

He would be in his study, in his library reading source material for cases. He lived for the law like I lived for the printed word. He would already have known the name of the business from where the call was coming. His desk phone is right at hand. It has a Caller ID display on it. Would he show up here? Would he send someone else? His answer tended to reinforce my belief to handle him warily. "Morgahna? You're staying with that ditzy friend of yours, right?"

Debbie. Several long moments passed before I simply hung up the phone and stood there wondering if that was a thinly-veiled threat. I leaned heavily against the wall and started considering a course of action. "Hey, Billy?" I said quietly.

"Yeah," he said falling in next to me.

"There's a tourist shop two doors down. Do me a favor? Go buy me some sunglasses that will do more than merely hide my face."

"We staying here?"

Chapter Eleven

"Yeah. No more than an hour. If Tommy shows up, I want to be here. I want to see if he sends someone else."

"Why?"

"I don't know, Billy. That's just it. I don't know."

"And a purse," he said. "You need a purse." He handed me his cell phone. "A purse for the phone."

I smiled. "Whatever you come up with will be fine."

He draped his arm over my shoulder and said, "You mind? You gotta look like you belong to someone dressed like that."

"And I belong to you?" He smiled and my knees did that thing again.

"For the time being."

His face is gorgeous and as we stood in that hallway it was easy to see how and why Debbie did what she did because I certainly thought about it. His entire soul began to cover me. Everything I ever wanted began to get dwarfed by him and whatever he wanted from me. It would be so easy just to roll my arm around his neck and let him do whatever he would, whatever he wanted. His beard was a three-day one and it made him even more rugged than I thought he could be. Was this the man who cried over his wife and child? Was this the man who wanted a year to mourn and grieve?

God. Oh, God. I turned to face him, my arms going around his neck. That strong face I saw two months ago grew in intensity until all my energy, all my resistance fell away. I was going to kiss him and we both knew it. *Who are you, Billy Ray Simpson? Who am I that you can do this?* With Evan, every kiss was a calculation, a way toward my future, another step up a long ladder. Erotic? No, not at all. I never even learned to moan with the anticipated pleasures he intended to shower on me. Moan? Those were things porn stars and people like Debbie Jenson did, not me.

His arms dropped around my waist and his face covered mine completely as he kissed me. It was the same as before with one small difference. This time, I did not allow myself to get lost inside him. I kept myself apart and separate from him and wondered briefly why I was doing this. Yes, it felt ungodly wonderful but Evan had been gone only four months and he knew that. *Yesterday, it was Debbie. Who will it be tomorrow?* I battled for control and felt myself pulling away from him emotionally even though I lingered long enough to taste his lips and wonder why he was doing this.

Was I being the same cold and calculating bitch I'd been? Was I? With Evan, it was slightly different. Evan accepted me in a way Billy hadn't quite yet. Those soft sighs I heard from Evan were blunt force evidence that he would not, could not most likely, push himself onto me. Evan seemed satisfied with what I gave him and I never thought to ask him if it was enough. Billy seemed to know that I had more to give and had no moral qualms about taking it. *Why, Billy? You spent two months with me out in those woods and you never showed me this side of you.* Granted, I was recovering from hideously serious wounds and his attempts would have been lost in a haze of pain. I do not, however, remember anything quite like this, so when that kiss ended and I began to regain my full senses, I dropped my cheek onto his chest, clutched his shirt in my hand and appeared to be in the same amorous clutches as before. I even moaned. Thank you, Evan. I think.

He hugged me and said, "I'll be right back, Morgahna. Don't worry."

"Oh, God, Billy," I said with my eyes wide open. No, he couldn't see them and that was planned. "You make my knees weak." They weren't. I was wary and I only hoped that he didn't think I was being anything but a *girl,* a girl's girl.

"Let's get you to a table then," he said as he slid his arm around my waist and guided me out to the bar.

We found a table in a corner, a nice dark, anonymous corner where he sat me against the wall where I could see the door to both the bar and the street beyond. I felt like a traitor to him and didn't know quite why. Yes, he saved my life and for that I owed him quite a lot. Would I ever be able to repay that debt? That was doubtful. He kissed the top of my head and smiled down at me. "Be right back. I'll bring a surprise."

I smiled up at him and said, "You've already been the biggest surprise in my life. Where would I be without you?" I tried to smile with

Chapter Eleven

my eyes but that seemed like one of the forbidden arts. I hope I pulled it off okay.

"You don't owe me anything but honesty, Miss Hamilton," he said, his face so warm and tender that I wanted to kiss it more and more.

I almost slipped again, almost slid right into his life without so much as a blink or glance. I sighed and that was genuine. I was probably throwing away the best sex I would have for the rest of my life. Sex and what else? But was I? Throwing it away? Yes, I'm afraid I was. Until I knew what was happening, knew why Tommy Underwood would throw Debbie's name into our conversation that easily, I had to walk softly. So, yes. At least for a while, my feet were going to be on the ground and I was going to watch the scenery carefully.

To illustrate my moods concerning sex, maybe a slightly revealing episode from my honeymoon is in order. If you don't understand it, I can only be grateful because I really find my behavior deplorable. We had a great honeymoon planned and I bought the most revealing bikini I could find, then stopped wearing it shortly after we returned from our honeymoon. We went to the Caribbean, Jamaica, the Caymans, The Virgin Islands, that sort of stuff. I wore that revealing bikini *only* to ensure Evan looked at me and not the other girls on the beaches. That was the time in my life when I could have been the woman he thought he married instead of the barracuda that he did. If I learned anything about myself in the past five years, it was that I was a self-centered bitch and a nonsexual one at that.

So, I watched Billy walk away slowly, rhythmically and watched his graceful power leave the bar and my breath caught. Yes, I had to admit to a powerful attraction, but it was no doubt the same attraction Debbie felt. I had to stay away from him and *it* for no other reason than my peace of mind. If I crawled into bed with him now, all my objectivity would be gone and my concentration, my sheer ability to figure out what had happened to me and us would be seriously jeopardized.

The bar was dark but not as dingy as the hallway leading back to the bathroom. It was full of signs from old advertisements, Texaco gas signs, Mobil, Phillips, Philip Morris, that sort of stuff. The booth seemed more like a tomb than a place to sit and share friendships with the world, was made of dark mahogany and was trimmed with vinyl the color of wet beach sand.

It was much more difficult to hold my focus than ever before. That much I must admit. After my sophomore year in high school, I was *always* able to focus on one subject to the exclusion of everything else. That focus changed from day-to-day, from time-to-time but whatever landed in my sights, I was able to track it down and make it mine while everything else became merely secondary and, thus, unimportant. Included in that category that I dubbed "unimportant" was Evan himself. That was why I was having trouble focusing. I wanted to apologize to him and my fear was becoming that I would never quite be able to get his ghost out of my mind.

The day, at least the bar's day, was getting busier as groups of people, men mostly, entered the bar noisily. A few women came in, none alone. There were some islands of femininity around the bar, but none of them were watching the football games on TV, the Falcons were playing someone, plus others from other stations. I was, however, the only one sitting alone. Naturally, men started eyeing me and smiling from across the bar, at least three that I saw. If I got lucky, maybe they would start fighting among themselves. Okay, I was getting grumpy and I couldn't quite identify the reason. All I knew was that something was wrong somewhere but didn't quite see what it was. I knew that it was related to Billy in some way but that was all.

Maybe I should retreat a bit and regroup. I place great faith in consistency, great faith. Of all the people I have ever known, I place myself at the top of my own scale. I have changed very little from my wedding day. Yes, the exceedingly revealing bikini is gone and so is that one night of good sex. Otherwise, I have remained who I was and my goals have only changed by degree not by subject. I was beginning to wonder about Billy Ray Simpson. Why? Well, I measure people by their words and his were simple. *I want to wait a year. I loved my wife.* Among and around those few declarations was sex with Debbie the first time he met her, three kisses with me, ones that were designed to put me in the same position as Deb and several oddly reassuring statements scattered among those disparate actions. The however here was that he *did* save my life. I was safe around him for that reason alone.

Chapter Eleven

A man in a nice polo shirt approached me from the bar. I sighed inwardly because I really didn't like this sort of stuff. I am not a barfly and hate being seen as one. I was the wife of a successful lawyer and my days in bars were basically non-existent outside of my work for the newspaper. The guy was cute enough but I just wasn't interested on any level. Before he could even say anything, I said, "Just go away and I'll pretend this never happened."

He smiled and didn't take the hint. "Sweetie? We can go across the river and have a decent lunch over at the golf course. I'd be honored."

The Westin. It was a huge hotel with an attached golf course across the Savannah River. I'd eaten there many times and he was right. It was a lot more decent than a bar and the view was incredible. Evan took me there many times and I never got tired of it. I don't play golf; Evan did. I can count the times I had lunch there with other golf widows. I never saw myself as a widow like that because the atmosphere was so absolutely perfect. I was catered to, deferred to and made to feel as though my position in society was a right and not a privilege. Stupid me. I didn't work for those things, Evan did. I merely went along for the ride and enjoyed the fruits of his labor. Still, I couldn't. "I'd prefer not, mister." There was still too much Evan in my soul and he wasn't draining away very quickly.

"Ma'am? My name is Todd. I'd very much like it if you accompanied me."

There was no way he was going to get my name. A small and very suspicious part of me wondered if that was the point. Get my name and verify his own suspicion. Did he recognize me? That was the entire reason for the sunglasses. They would help disguise my face. Personally, I felt that my face was disguised enough. I still maintain that it was positively grotesque. The crowd behind him was beginning to thicken, the noise growing louder. Oddly, I saw Billy in the doorway to the bar just standing there watching us as he held a shopping bag. I glanced away, glanced up at the man in front of me and said almost sadly, "I'd rather not. Sorry."

He reached into his shirt pocket and gave me a business card. Well, I'd been given business cards before, but never as a pickup in a bar. I read the card and it identified him as Todd Gilmartin and his profession that of Counselor At Law. Todd was a lawyer.

"Mr. Gilmartin? I don't think I'm going to need this," and tried to give it back to him.

He smiled and held up his hands. "I never take them back, ma'am. You never know where clients come from."

I smiled and said, "Or from where they come."

He bowed and said, "Duly corrected."

Okay, all I'd managed to do was belie my trampy outfit as belonging to a woman who knew correct English. I frowned to myself as he turned and walked away. I never even noticed where he went, just that Billy slid into the booth opposite me and said, "Nicely done."

"Really?" I said somewhat annoyed. "And if he had been on their side?"

"He looked safe."

"You look safe."

He pushed the bag across the table and ignored my annoyance. "Go ahead. Look in the bag."

Well, there were sunglasses obviously, big black ones that not only went with my basic black-and-white outfit but actually looked good. I put them on and stared at him. He was smiling and looked at ease. I had to admit he looked delicious. I took them off, placed them next to the bag and reached down and plucked a man's idea of a purse from inside. Lord, where do men get their taste in clothes and accessories? My suspicion is from porno films. The purse? Well, the *best* thing about it was that it was black and provided contrast with my clothes. That was about it for the upside, though. I gave him a thin smile and said, "Thanks, Billy. It's the thought that counts."

He looked embarrassed and should have been.

There was a wallet and a makeup case inside the purse and neither of them was anything I would have ever bought. Still, considering everything I owned was simply gone, they were my best possessions. I put Todd's business card inside the wallet and it actually made me sad. I had a lot of contacts, a lot of names in my book. I had a case full of business cards and actually took the time to update them on a semi-annual

Chapter Eleven

basis. If the card was no longer of any use, I tossed it. If I could get an updated one, I asked for it. Todd Gilmartin's lone business card was like a single grain of sand in an enormous surrounding desert.

A bar of candy, bite-sized chocolates rolled out of the purse and he said, "Sweets for the sweet."

"Oh, you romantic devil, you," I said with a small smile.

Did he know of what he was reminding me? Did he? I had no choice but to change the subject. "Order me an iced tea, okay?"

"Coors Lite," he said. "You order an iced tea and people will remember the dynamite-looking lady who drank *tea*."

"Oh, fine, whatever."

He clutched my hand, smiled and said, "Get 'em drunk and take 'em home happy."

"Got no home, dude."

"My place then," he replied.

"I'm going home with Debbie, big guy."

"Beer," he said with a wider smile. "The lady just demanded beer."

He turned and headed toward the bar through a herd of people. My guess was that church was out and the men folk were trying to wash the experience from their minds. Me? I can easily profess to be a convenient Christian. You figure out what that means. I already know and I find religion personal. Period.

As soon as he disappeared into the crowd, I saw a familiar figure enter. It was Karin Hubbell and she was alone. She was dressed for the role of barfly as much as possible. This may seem catty, but I can't believe any sober man would pick her up. No offense, Karin. Being alone put an asterisk above her head. She was in uncharted waters and the only person she could be looking for was me.

I slipped the sunglasses on and followed her as she entered and sat at the end of the bar. No one talked to her other than the bartender who gave her something that was probably not alcoholic. It was on the rocks and looked like ginger ale. After she took a sip, she placed the drink on a small napkin in front of her and began scanning the room. She was looking for me and checking every single woman closely. I could see no way she wouldn't recognize me even with the sunglasses and the different face. Sure, there were other girls and women in the place but none of them were alone and from what I could see, none of them looked even faintly like me.

Billy was taking a long time but the sheer numbers were against him. I watched Karin as she continued to sweep the room. How long had it been since I talked to Tommy? Not even a half hour. Given that Karin lives out near Tybee Island and that's farther than Tommy lives, she had been in the area, maybe at their office downtown when Tommy called her and told her from where I called him. Did her work habits include Sundays? Probably. That's the best answer I could find.

Her eyes finally found me and they stuck. She was wondering if it was me. I turned my head just slightly as though I wasn't looking at her. Oh, I was and I hoped she didn't realize it. She had her cell phone in her hand and was tapping it against her palm as she tried to make a decision about me. Billy came back with two foaming mugs of draft beer and slid one in front of me. "Billy? Grope me right now."

"You but ask and I obey," he said as he slid into the booth, cupped my right breast in his left hand, put his face in mine and kissed me.

As a kiss, it was a complete failure. As a diversion, it was perfect. When it was over, Karin was no longer holding the phone and was instead sipping her ginger ale and scanning the crowd. After a few moments, she got up and headed toward the bathroom. I pushed Billy out of the booth and followed her. He had to know what was happening and had to know I was going to confront someone. He stood and watched me head into the crowd.

It was a hasty decision; I've made my share of decisions like that and this one was no different than any of them. I got pinched at least once as I knifed through the growing crowd. It was neither erotic nor thrilling but irritating as hell and I resented it, but not so much that I would stand and argue.

She entered a stall and was closing the door as I entered. Her thick legs and flattened shoes gave her away. I pushed on the door, she made a

Chapter Eleven

startled noise and pushed herself to the back of the small stall as I stood there. "Why, Karen?" I asked taking off my sunglasses.

There were a few others in the bathroom and they no doubt noticed two women go into the same stall. It was possible I was going to face trouble in the next few moments, also possible no one cared at all.

"Who are you?" she said.

Her cell phone was in her hand and I snatched it from her and she began to scream. I gave her an angry stare and she just fell into silence, nervously afraid of me, a stranger to her. The number was already on the screen. She was going to call Tommy. I handed it back to her and said, "Call the man. Right fucking now."

Slow recognition washed across her face as she stood in that cramped corner between the wall and the toilet. Pointing at me with the phone, she said with quiet euphoria, "Morgahna! You're her!" She could have said anything at that point, could have made any wild claim about me, about where I'd been, about my face and about how it got that way. I make no special claims for intelligence, none. I know that I am but know that my strength is in its application.

For the past two months, I'd been working toward this moment, toward the moment when someone from my previous life looked at me, recognized me and did nothing more than blink. To me, when I look in mirrors, I see a grotesqueness that makes me want to cry every time I look. Maybe that's simply because the belief I put in my own face was simply gone. It's possible a good plastic surgeon could rebuild it to where it was recognizable if not the same as it was. I don't know. Karin Hubbell, however, was the first person from my former life that saw me and this face other than Debbie. Her reaction was what I would think anyone would assume. Plastic surgery. Okay, she seemed to think that the surgery went well. I still think otherwise. Karin? She swallowed hard and never even mentioned my face or how it got that way. Yes, I found that odd.

"Call him," I said evenly.

She licked her lips and seemed to be considering the angles, seemed to be weighing her choices. Slowly and without taking her eyes off me, she hit the dial button and lifted the phone to her ear. It rang and he answered. "She's here," Karin said into it. Then she frowned in some small way and added cryptically, "She's different somehow, disguised in some way."

I reached up, took the phone from her and she shrank back against the wall. She was afraid of me and that was a new piece of the puzzle. Why would she fear me? I very carefully, very deftly, removed the phone from her hand and said, "Tommy? Be in your office tonight at six. Just you. Not her, not anyone but you. Be ready to tell me what you did to my home and why."

He, like her, could have said anything. In every step of this bizarre tale, everyone was always free to say whatever they wished. Karin didn't blanche at my new face. In fact, she was so self-absorbed that she didn't even notice it wasn't my face. I will always remember her staring at my clothes and deciding that, for me anyway, that disguise was perfect. Who would ever think that me, good old Morgahna Hamilton would stoop so low as to look like a whore? Tommy had that same privilege. He could have said anything to my offer to meet him in his office. He asked the one question that made me fear for myself.

"Will you be alone?"

I lied. "Yes."

Billy would there. Billy would be my ace in the hole. If anything happened, he would be there to protect me.

As a plan, it was the best I had.

I handed the phone back to Karin and said, "You took Evan's place, didn't you?"

She just nodded and said nothing. She was scared.

It never occurred to me that Evan had been scared, too. It never occurred to me that people who worshipped sameness as an objective always feared the unknown.

Always.

Evan had fears.

Lots of them.

And I was headed directly toward their heart.

Chapter Twelve

Debbie and LeRay showed up at her house just before five that night. I was nervous as hell but not so nervous that I couldn't find a better outfit for my night. I took the time waiting for her to rummage through her clothes and found several outfits that would suffice for a late Sunday afternoon meeting with a man who might be trying to kill me. I settled on comfortable blacks pants and a gray top.

And comfortable shoes. God, I had no idea how much I missed shoes like that.

Billy watched me as I searched and he kept holding up different pieces, stuff like a push-up bra, spandex shorts, a tiny thing that looked like pants, a similar shirt and all the trashy lingerie in Deb's drawers. I finally pushed him out of the room and he laughed all the way. Maybe it was funny to him, but it wasn't to me.

The conversation got serious when I finished dressing and went out to talk to him. He was watching television and switched it off when I came out of Deb's bedroom. I sat in a chair opposite him, a wet bar to my right, black-topped chrome barstools lined up in front of it. "Billy? I'm going to see Tommy tonight. I'm going in alone because I don't believe he's going to kill me. I believe he's going to be reasonable and tell me what I want to know." Before he could object, I added, "I'm not saying I don't want you there. All I'm saying is that I want to talk to him alone. I've known him for nearly six years and I can't believe that he would wait until now to kill me."

I was trying desperately to inflict logic upon the situation and was determined not to take no for an answer. Billy could very easily slide into his romantic southerner routine but I did not believe he could ever sway my emotions quite like he had over the past few days. Maybe that meant I was gaining strength and coming to accept that Evan was dead and took with him a secret that I was trying to uncover.

Billy, to my slight surprise, did not try to talk me out of it. He looked thoughtful for a moment and then said slowly as he looked directly at Debbie's cream-colored carpeting, "Yeah. I agree." Then he looked up

Chapter Twelve

at me and said, "Reluctantly, you understand. What's the layout of that office, where he will be. Windows? One-story, two? What?"

Their office, Tommy and Evan's, is on the south side of Broughton Street where it makes a dead-end at Martin Luther King, Jr. Boulevard and is directly across the street from a place that sells tires. The area is full of commercial buildings, most of them two-and-three story storefronts. Tommy seemed to be a good organizer and manager of money when he set up his practice years ago. Evan found Tommy before we met; the circumstances of that meeting were never important. The money was. Now, I wonder if my naivety about the subject was wise. Anyway, Tommy's finances were always in order and he was making a lot of money. I know from people that talked to me about Tommy that he started small just over ten years ago. I've already alluded to the fact he's a lot like me, a workaholic at the expense of personal relationships.

Yes, I've avoided the word workaholic. It bestows upon the holder the sense that work is far more important than life. Well, that's what I always thought. Work, career and goals, were always more important than anything else. In the first two months after Evan died – and I *still* cannot bear to use that other more ugly and sinister word that describes what he did – Tommy tried to comfort and settle me. Debbie did, too, but I ignored everyone and insisted that I was going to drink myself to death because I am a coward at heart and didn't own a gun. Debbie was easy to deflect but Tommy has that same monomania I did.

My mother came up from Jacksonville where they live and stayed for two days before her own life beckoned her home again. It was an odd visit anyway and I sensed a strain between us that I still ascribe to Evan and what I drove him to do. Mom seemed troubled by what had happened and never talked about the act at all. She took time with me and just said that my father would come up later, but he never did. Mark, my brother, called from New Orleans and offered his sympathy but I never saw him at all. Of my family, my mother was the only one that came to Savannah.

Evan's parents live in New York City and he was an only child. I saw them at the funeral and their brief visit with me was cold and heartless. His mother cried and could not face me at all. His father held back tears that no doubt erupted later when they went home. Of all of them, the only one I wanted to call was my mother but I never did.

As I planned my visit with Tommy, a term that Evan used frequently came to mind. Game face. I think everyone who has grown up in this country knows that term and to what it applies. If you watch any professional sports on television, you can see it. The best game faces are on baseball players because that sport seems to exist without the adrenalin rush that both football and basketball encourage. Lawyers, though, have it, too. If you see any of the news shows, any at all, you see it all the time on lawyers. The case I will always measure game faces by was the Laci Peterson murder trail. All of the lawyers looked grim and grave whenever they spoke about the case and whatever nonsense the talking heads were spewing that day. Lord, there was a lot, too. Being in the news business, I always wanted a chance to cover a trial like that, one that garnered a lot of national media attention. It would have given me national exposure at the expense of some poor fool who was merely unfortunate enough to be the victim of a homicide.

Evan had a game face. He even taught me how to do it, how to both make and wear one, and quite unwittingly sabotaged his sex life. It came up during an extortion case he was defending. He went on local television and looked as dry as any desert and as barren as I'd ever seen him. I'm not stupid and I know why he was doing that. That visage, that face he was giving the world was the only one he could show without tempting trouble from the court. In my business, game faces are sometimes necessary and mine wasn't as good as his by any stretch you can name.

"Teach me how to do that, Evan," I said one Sunday afternoon.

He was willing, was always willing to talk to me. He always claimed that I was an intelligent person and loved my insights and comments. "First, my little minx, you have to remove all foolishness from your mind because, at least in my case, defending people who face prison terms is serious. I don't know any lawyers who take it as any less than serious."

"Got it," I said as we sat in the kitchen eating a breakfast that Debbie taught me how to make. Spanish omelets.

"No matter what I say, you have to remain focused and serious," he said with a wide smile.

"Got it," I said. "Give me your best shot."

Chapter Twelve

"Before we start, I need to tell you that you have beautiful eyes, Morgahna."

I blushed. Can you imagine? My husband tells me I have beautiful eyes and I blushed. I smiled, looked at my empty plate and said, "Well, thanks, Evan."

He took my hand, held it tenderly and I smiled back at him, Then, he said with a wide smile. "You just sent your client to prison for twenty years, baby."

I snatched my hands away from him and said, "That's was cruel."

"Lawyers don't care how they pierce your shield. You have to see every single interaction as an attempt by them to learn something. Ready?"

"Yeah," I said erasing everything from my mind.

He smiled and said, "I love sucking on your nipples."

I couldn't help it. I started sputtering into laughter and said, "Stop it!"

"Your client just died by lethal injection, minxie."

We faced off again and I readied myself for anything he could say, no matter how suggestive.

"We're in bed and I'm licking the insides of your thighs, kissing and caressing as I go. I kiss your stomach and work my toward your neck…"

…and I broke up again because it was so unlike Evan to talk that way. I was twenty-four then and not ignorant of human sexuality, just in how it applied to me. I covered my face with my hands and shook my head in order to get that disgusting scene out of it. Yeah, disgusting. My husband was telling me bluntly what he wanted to do to me and I thought it was disgusting. The problem was that it was, or could have been anyway, quite enjoyable and pleasuring. It is very possible that I would have loved him doing that to me if only I'd allowed it.

We did, however, face off again and this time I was absolutely stone-faced. He said everything he just had and more. He got positively pornographic and while my stomach turned, my face never did. I asked for a chance at him and never even got a eyebrow to wiggle. Of course, my idea of shock was a lot tamer than his. The most graphic thing I described was a blow job and mine were never very good. Oh, stop. A woman knows. When your husband never even implies to you that he would like you to do something like that, you get the message. Me? Well, I was relieved he didn't want me to do that because that is most disgusting thing I would even consider trying with a man.

But, my game face got a whole lot better and Evan kept trying to break mine. I got very good at the game and learned that he had no blemishes in his either. We could go for hours with neither one of us getting the other to break up or do anything but simply react dispassionately. All this meant was that when I went in to talk to Tommy I was going to be wearing my game face. Unfortunately, in learning how to apply that game face, I learned how to deflect Evan's *urges*. Yeah, sexual ones. I got so good he stopped trying after a while. In fact, over the last few months of his life, we had no sex at all and I'm *twenty-seven*.

Anyway.

The first step in the process of getting into his office was telling Billy of its layout. It was a two-story office and Tommy and Evan's offices were on the second story that was accessed either by a stairway against the wall or a freight elevator in the rear near the kitchen. Karin had an office upstairs, everyone else was downstairs. A conference room, a fairly big one, was downstairs, too. The theory was that clients and prospective ones, would not want to climb the stairs for an initial consultation. Evan talked about a better elevator out front for clients with money but Tommy always balked at the idea as being foolish. "If they're guilty and we can force a not guilty verdict, then they'll climb those stairs happily." That was his outlook on a new elevator.

There was a parking lot in the rear of the building that was big enough to hold all the cars employees could park back there. In truth, that building was the only one on that entire city block. Planter boxes stuck up like guard houses at each corner of the huge lot. Tiny palm trees stuck up like sentries from them. A small loading bay for the delivery of legal forms and such was also at the rear of the building. Aside from Daneisha the paralegal, were three clerical people, all women, all well paid. Daneisha is black, so was one of the clericals. Her name was Lisette

Chapter Twelve

Johnson. The others were Shawna Kingsbury and Bridget Haines. There were any number of legal interns but their number and dates of employment changed so often that it was pointless to keep track of them. Shawna was the nearest to my age and she was thirty-one. The others were all over thirty-five, Lisette was in her fifties. All four of them worked for Tommy when I met Evan and his story was that all four them opened the office with Tommy over ten years ago.

Naturally, the ground floor was the most extensive. A law library existed down there as well as a second but much smaller conference room. There was a large room downstairs where the interns worked and another office for associates like Karin. The fact that her office was on the second floor gave her some prestige the others must have felt. The only room I never saw was the IT office, one that was almost always empty because Tommy had no staff for that. He contracted with a local firm for as-needed support. It seemed to work in that the contracted firm was always available. Computers. Ew. Icky. Girl's girls do *not* do computers.

We agreed, Billy and I did, that the best place for him to lurk was at the back door. That led to a long hallway that had been widened and more extensively decorated as time went by. My first memory of that hallway was a ten-foot wide tube that emptied out into the receptionist area. The lunch room and a storage room were on the other side of that wall and both rooms sacrificed some space to make that corridor a bit more user-friendly. I will always believe that I had something to do with that widening. The first time I saw it, my professional instincts screamed insultingly at me. It seemed a place for lawyers whose aspirations were distinctly minor league. The first time I said that to Evan, he actually froze and repeated, "…whose aspirations are distinctly minor league." He smiled, kissed me despite my objections and said enthusiastically, "I love it!" A few months later work started on widening that corridor. They enlarged the receptionist's - who was Lisette - station and moved it farther toward the front doors and put Shawna's desk near that widened hallway. She became the official greeter of people who came in through those doors. Bridget's desk was between them and she did most of the serious transcription work.

I sketched it all out on paper for Billy and he seemed to understand everything implicitly. With his bottom lip curled up into his mouth, he said, "And at that time of night on a Sunday, no one will be there? Is that right?"

Technically, yes. "Billy? Tommy worked all hours. Most of his after hours work was done at home, but he was never much for schedules. All this means is that I expect him to be there but anyone else is your guess."

He nodded and said, "Okay. Expect others. That's how I'll do it."

When Debbie and LeRay came in, Debbie was smiling and that boded well for both Billy and me. She was thrilled at what happened and how well they pulled off their ruse. For the record, I may be guilty of obstructing justice but my life is far more important than Daydra Morrison and her boyfriend and *that* has nothing to do with their race.

"I should have called," she said a bit apologetically. "If I had, though, they may have become suspicious, so I didn't."

"It's okay, Just tell me none of them suspected anything besides what you told them."

"Nah, they think it's a drug hit. Down there? That's more frequent than not."

I sat down on the couch with LeRay and took his hand in mine. Look, I'm not very good at empathy and sympathy. Even though they are opposite sides of the same coin marked "tragedy", I have little experience with it and said so. "LeRay? I'm not very good at this, but I'm sorry for what happened to your sister. If I knew why this was happening, it would be a lot easier to handle. I am, though, as sorry as I can be."

Debbie sat heavily next to him and she commiserated. "Dude? That was harsh. You really handled it well, though."

He clasped my hand with both of his and stared at me as his face began to change, began to melt toward despair and sadness. As inexperienced as I was, I felt that this was something I needed to do because I *still* felt that everything was happening because of me. Had I been a better wife to my husband, I cannot believe he would have done something like that. Had that not happened, then all of the attendant items of madness would not have happened either. So, I felt it was incumbent upon me to try to assuage his pain as much as I could.

Chapter Twelve

"She was always looking for easy answers," he said sadly as tears rolled down his face.

"That's no reason for this to happen, LeRay," I said. "I have a brother. If something like this happened to him, I would feel the way you do. It wouldn't matter that I disagreed with him about a lot of stuff. He's still my brother and I would grieve him the way you grieve her."

He looked like a retreating army so I said with as much happiness as I could muster, "Come on, big guy. Let's go for a walk. I've got time before business calls. Let's go walk and talk about your sister."

Debbie smiled suggestively at Billy and said, "And I'll entertain Mr. Simpson."

Billy looked nervously at me and said, "Morgahna? Do you think it's wise to go outside like that?"

I dismissed his concern with a wide smile and said, "Billy? Right now LeRay is more important than me. He just lost his sister." I looked at LeRay and said, "You game for a short walk?"

He looked as lost as a little boy who couldn't find his mother. Finally, he just nodded and I hugged both Billy and Deb before warning her, "I've got him at quarter to six, girl. Make sure his pants are on."

"Ooh, a quickie," she said with a smile.

I rolled my eyes and left holding LeRay's hand as we walked.

Deb lives near Bacon Park, lives close to the golf course. As soon as we exited out onto the sidewalk, LeRay said, "It doesn't get any whiter than a golf course, Morgahna. Places like this make me nervous."

Majestic oaks and maple trees dominated the area, Spanish Moss hanging from a lot of them. It was a quiet area and spoke of home again. I held his hand as we walked and could not say why exactly. He seemed to prefer it, though, but nothing happened between us. We were nothing more than friends as I talked quietly to him. "What are you going to do?" I asked him.

He seemed to be thinking about that subject nonstop ever since we left the condo. "Move in with my mom, I guess. She needs someone around."

"Daydra didn't?"

He smiled and said, "Yeah, but that baby needed me more."

The baby. I'd forgotten about the baby. It wasn't there in that apartment when we went in. I stopped in the shade of an old oak and said, "What happened to it, LeRay? Was someone babysitting him? Was it even a boy baby?"

"Yeah, it was a boy," he said distantly. "I worry about him, though. His name was Artemis." LeRay was looking out toward Bacon Park when he turned and looked back at me, his hand still in mine. "Can I ask you a question?"

"Sure."

"Do you feel that blacks get equal justice?"

Without a hint of a smile, I said, "No."

"Because of race?"

"Partly."

"What other factors do you see?"

"Money. OJ is black and smart money always painted him as guilty. Why?"

He very carefully and very slowly withdrew his hand from mine. "Morgahna? Are you still a reporter?"

"I don't know, LeRay. That's the best answer I have. Why?"

"If you are, you could write about this."

"LeRay," I said defensively. "I don't know. This is pretty personal to me."

When I look at him I can see hints of Denzel Washington in his face. The same eyes, the same mouth. Maybe that makes it easier to deal with him because Denzel Washington is a man any white person would allow into their home. He's a genuine movie star and his roles make him palatable to most whites. LeRay Morrison, though, was as black as the people who burned down Watts back in the sixties and Los Angeles after the Rodney King verdict was read. "Morgahna?" he said quietly but with his eyes riveted on mine. "What are the odds that one man, one person

Chapter Twelve

whether black or white, would have two sisters murdered in his lifetime and both within the last eighteen months?"

"You have another sister who was murdered?"

"Yes. Artemis wasn't Daydra's baby. He was LaRuth's son."

"Who was she?"

His right hand formed into a fist. "She was beautiful, not like Daydra. She glowed from the inside and someone beat her to death. I saw the body afterward and it was awful. I almost didn't recognize her but she had a very distinctive tattoo on her left ankle, a heart with a bullet hole in it. The cops said she was beaten to death with a club or a pipe, something like that."

"Oh, my god," I said. "Oh, LeRay," I said. "That's terrible."

His brows wrinkled and he said, "They tied her to a tree and beat her to death."

"They?" I asked only because the method of her death resembled too finely the attack on me.

"The cops said at least two people beat her based on the wounds and the pattern they left. One set of blows came from the right and the other from the left as though one guy hit her and waited for him to finish before the other hit her."

Exactly like what happened to me. I turned my back and walked a short way up the sidewalk and asked as my back was to him, "Do you have her picture?" I was suspicious and that was not something I felt very often. The most suspicious feeling I ever had was the day I caught Evan having lunch with Shawna in the lunchroom at his office. They were laughing and clinking Coke bottles in a toast of something they just said. I got cold immediately and treated Evan like an adulterer for weeks afterward. I felt justified and superior at the same time. Evan broke the spell by getting on his knees in front of me and offering me a free dinner at a restaurant downtown along with a gift coupon for a thousand dollars to spend wherever I wished. He kissed the back of my hand like a supplicant and I grinned. "Forgiven," I said. Yep, I was that shallow. Money and food bought his redemption. For the record, they weren't guilty of anything except friendship.

This, however, made me more suspicious than that did. It had to be Tony and Doug and I wondered why. What could link me with LeRay's sister? I turned around and he was digging in his wallet.

He handed me a picture of her, a picture taken in Market Square in Historic Savannah, one where she posed next to a cart full of flowers. LeRay was right. She was gorgeous and photogenic. "Can I ask where she was found?"

"Out in the woods. Hunters found her. Out near Hinesville."

The pattern was still similar. "LeRay? Do you know what happened to me?"

"Just that they thought you were dead."

"No more than that?"

"No, why?"

I was beginning to assimilate some evidence but had no idea what it meant. I know that Evan knew Daydra and most likely the man she lived with, a man whose name I never found out when I had a chance. Did I need to it? I didn't know so I asked, "What was the name of Daydra's boyfriend?"

"He called himself Bounteous T, but his name was Frank Walker."

I let that name bounce around a bit and then shook my head. "Never heard of him."

He actually smiled. "No one else did either."

Did Evan know LaRuth? "Did my husband ever meet your sister, LaRuth? You've already said he knew Daydra."

"I don't know, Morgahna. That's the best I can do. LaRuth was working on a modeling career and I didn't see her much."

"Did she live here?"

"No. She lived in New York City and came back here infrequently. Even if she did, I might not have been here. I have been here only since last November. Before that? I was in Atlanta."

Chapter Twelve

I began to think out the problem. When I worked for the newspaper, my thoughts were always on paper in the form of scribbles. I had little experience with thinking aloud or even in the abstract. Still I tried. *Evan knew Daydra, most likely as a client. After his death, Karin gives her an envelope of money. Daydra's sister was killed at least a year before the attack on me.* It didn't make sense, that attack. I turned around and said, "LeRay? I need to ask you a very sensitive question. I'll understand if you have trouble answering it or even if you cannot. In that case, I'll back down. I don't want to cause you any more trouble than I need to. Okay?"

He nodded but said nothing.

"Can you estimate the number of times she was hit with that club?"

I will always remember the dry analytical way Sylvia described the wounds she found on my body. "Three to the head, at least two to your chest, another to your stomach from what you said, one to each arm, maybe two but no more than that, at east two to each leg, your thighs, one to your neck that almost killed you and maybe one to each of your arms. At least eleven blows, Morgahna. You should be dead. A second blow to your head would have been fatal."

Thirteen. *They hit me at least thirteen times with a metal pipe.*

LeRay looked severe, his face taut and serious. "I can only tell you what they told me."

"And that was?"

"At least fifty times."

Fifty. *They killed LaRuth Morrison by hitting her with a club at least fifty times and I got hit thirteen times.* "How many times did they hit her head? Do you know?"

"Why?" he asked. "What good will this serve, Morgahna. They said it was racial. They called this a hate crime because they felt she was killed only because she was black."

"How many, LeRay?" I asked pointedly. "How many times did they hit her head?"

"At least a half dozen times," he said sadly, said as his eyes began to tear up.

I took his hands and said, "LeRay? If I tell you something, you have to swear not to tell anyone, not even Deb and Billy."

"Okay," he said. "I promise."

"LeRay? What you described happening to your sister? That's what happened to me two months ago, nine weeks and a few days ago. The difference? I was hit thirteen times but only three times on my head. My face isn't even the same as it was."

"What are you saying, Morgahna?"

With God as my witness, I did not know. Were these two crimes even connected? My objectivity was screaming that I didn't have enough evidence to make a determination one way or the other. My selfish side, the bitch that lived within me, was screaming otherwise. I have grown more self-centered as I have gotten older but this madness was pushing me away from that extreme. Now, quite suddenly, I was being handed a piece of information that might belong exclusive to me and LeRay. "Did you tell the police about LaRuth when you and Deb were there?"

"No."

"They'll begin to pick up the thread after a while," I murmured. What did that mean? They'd want to talk to LeRay again. They would verify his alibi and continue their investigation. And me? What did it mean to me? I was very close to making a decision to toss the investigation to them, to the police. The *only* reason I didn't was Daydra Morrison herself. The police knew her sister had been killed and that knowledge did not prevent her from being killed, too. As part of the media that reports on serial killers - not that I ever had – I knew the game all too well. We almost cherished new victims because it gave us something new to emphasize, a new angle to cause interest in what we provided the public, which basically was more of the same. Sales always went up during stuff like this. I can remember the sniper story and how there were some jealousies that the story was happening in a place like Washington DC, a place where a lot was always happening anyway. There were some people who thought Savannah needed a sniper like that. It was sick thinking, granted, but fairly typical for news people.

Chapter Twelve

I gripped LeRay's hands and said emphatically, "You can't tell anyone about this. The police will probably want to talk to you again and you'll need to. Me? If you tell them about me, you might be killing me."

He asked an insightful question. "How can you trust me?"

I smiled. "Because you said you were in Atlanta when she was killed. The only way you can be involved in this is if you killed both of them and you were with us last night. We're your alibi. You're safe as long as we are."

"You're saying what Billy and Debbie don't know won't hurt them, Morgahna. Is that wise?"

The worst days I can remember were Sundays during football season when Evan, Tommy, Dave and a few others would congregate in front our HD television and watch NFL games. Look, I'm a girl's girl and we don't know about football. We know about frilly, silly things, know about shades of blue, waffles on Sunday morning, calf-length skirts, the way we want our bedrooms to look, hair, makeup, the perfect pair of shoes, not about sweaty men growling at each other over a misshapen ball that doesn't bounce true. I know, however, about huddles and how they try to hide what they want to do from the other team. That makes perfect sense. The perfectly pulled surprise, the perfect play, will always result in a touchdown. It doesn't happen often, but according to Evan, it's a thing of beauty when it does. That's what this felt like. LeRay and me were in a huddle and we were designing the perfect play, one that would result in a touchdown. Yes, I know the implication here was that I was putting both Debbie and Billy on the other side. That's as far as I can take the analogy. I had no way to justify keeping it from them on any other basis except one. This was an exclusive and I knew all too well how that felt. I can count on one hand the number of times I had an exclusive and still have five fingers left over. No, it had never happened to me and here it was happening *to* me instead of *for* me. So, I looked up and said, "I don't know, LeRay. I know that Debbie tends to get scatterbrained and I don't know Billy well at all. You? If I had my way, you wouldn't know either. So, can you keep this to yourself?"

He looked decisively blunt. "You remember when you asked me if I was gonna shoot you?"

"You gonna?"

"No, but you remember?"

"Yeah, why?"

"You remember my answer?"

"You said I was okay as long as I didn't lie and make your life harder than it already was."

"That's right."

"So?"

"You've been truthful with me ever since I met you and I'm the poorest man you will ever meet. That gives you some credibility that most white people I meet don't have. Yeah, I'll keep your secret only because you've treated me fairly well up to now. You give me any reasons to change my mind and I will."

I stuck out my hand and said, "Deal."

He shook and replied with the same thing. "Deal." Then he said, "Can I test you now?"

"Go ahead."

"That friend of yours?"

"Debbie?"

"Yeah. Her. That woman is gonna kill a guy someday and the weapon will be just below her navel."

I laughed. "LeRay? That's no secret. Every man she's ever met can testify to it."

"Amen."

We went back to Debbie's arm-in-arm. I was ready for Tommy, as ready as I'd ever be. He had a game face, too, and he was about to use it. The problem with game faces is that you never quite learn what's hidden behind them. The game usually goes to the one who is best prepared. At least that's what Evan used to say.

Evan. He was a smart man. Very smart. And he learned from Tommy. And I was going to face him with a secret that might very easily kill me.

Chapter Twelve

Only if anyone else learned of it.

Time would tell if that secret could remain that way.

Time.

It was running out, though.

For someone.

Chapter Thirteen

The firm of Underwood and Hamilton, Counselors At Law, was still a going concern. Because the way the legalities of corporate life exist in this country, Evan's name would probably exist for decades to come in the name of that firm. The glass storefront had been bricked over and the front of the building looked altogether like an old brick building down in the Market Square. It was an image that meant nothing to Evan but one that Tommy seemed to cultivate consciously. The name was conspicuous across the brick face that faced the street. Hell, I was *still* proud of Evan. Getting your name on any firm at the age of twenty-nine was an accomplishment worthy of note.

The parking lot was on the grounds of an old warehouse of which nothing at all remained except that huge lot and the planters in its corners. I wouldn't know that, but there aren't too many private parking lots in that part of Savannah. It just figures that Tommy Underwood would have one, though.

I knew he was there because that T-bird was the only other car in the lot besides Deb's Miata. I had no choice but to take it because Tommy, if he saw it, would ask where I got it. If I took the pickup, he would know I had company because I do not drive pickups. I parked it next to the T-bird and looked hopefully at Billy. There was a buzzer at the back of the building and security cameras inside the door. All that meant was he should have been safe in the parking lot, but then I should have been safe at any place along River Street, too. "You okay, Billy?" I asked.

"Yeah," he said. "Worried about you. Are you sure about this, Morgahna? You sure you want to go in there alone?"

"Yes," I said firmly.

"My gun?" he asked again. "You sure you don't want it?"

That was the only bone of contention between us. He wanted me armed and I had no time to learn how to shoot a gun. Oh, I know. You just point and shoot. Well, there were many smaller items of training,

Chapter Thirteen

ones like how not to shoot yourself, that I'd need to learn before I was convinced I knew what I was doing with a gun. My greatest fear with a gun has always been that I would shoot someone inadvertently, or shoot someone who was trying to do anything but hurt me. I can think of many situations where a gun was the last thing any two people needed between them. So, I said once more, "No, Billy. Tommy isn't going to shoot me."

It is very possible that he was more convinced than I was. Me? I kept hearing him ask if I was living with that "ditzy friend of mine". Did he know or was he guessing? With Tommy's game face, it was going to be difficult to know one way or the other. The only card I had that might work was the friendship one. The way I saw games faces, you could lie if it was to your advantage.

The entrance to the rear of the building is through double swinging doors. There is a buzzer next to the door for after hours visitors like me. Despite the urge, I could not turn my head and look behind me to make sure Billy was there where we agreed he would be. An unknown camera could spoil everything so I had no choice but to approach the building as though I really was alone. I pushed the buzzer and Tommy's voice said, "Yes?"

"It's me," I said clearly, plainly.

"Say your name."

"You fat frigging jerk, it's me."

"Hello, Morgahna," he said with that same clear and blunt voice.

The door buzzed and I pushed it open.

Old habits die hard. I punched that buzzer hundreds of times in the past five years because Evan worked late just like I did. A better wife would have cleared his desk of the miscellaneous detritus that clogged her desires and just made certain that she sent her husband home happy. All those times, all those chances and now they were all gone. I had no real reason to be here after I was done talking with Tommy. All those chances, all those too human longings went with him, went with Evan. It was hard not to look at the walls, at the carpeting, at the desks scattered at the foot of the stairs, at the deepest and most tangible thing Evan Hamilton was. It was hard not to feel those emotions that seethed and writhed inside me.

As the door closed and locked behind my back, I leaned against it and gave myself the luxury of one last emotional look around. That shortened and widened hallway was mahogany on both sides that contrasted nicely with the plush beige carpeting and the pictures and paintings that were mounted by color instead of subject, another thing I believe should be credited to me. People will notice the décor and the colors long before they notice the details. Those get added only after the brain has worked out the schematics. Yes, I was here in this place and that gave me the strength to do this. *Tommy? Don't be against me. Be a conduit to information that will help me discover the truth behind Evan's death. Please. Be a friend, a good one.* I closed my eyes and said an infrequent prayer, then pushed myself from the door and headed for the stairs.

The downstairs was dark, only the light at the top of the stairs giving me any light by which to navigate. This, too, was normal. After hour lights could bring unwanted distractions to those people working upstairs. The buzzer was in and of itself, however, not enough, so much so that Evan talked about a camera to the outside parking lot, one that would show who was out there. Unwanted guests made their work harder than it had to be. Tommy, though, just scoffed at the idea of a camera whose only purpose was to chase away winos. So, the status was quo - a buzzer that any of the upstairs people could answer and unlocked from their desk. More than that was never going to happen. You can attribute that to the same mindset that outsourced his IT work. Anything to save a buck. Tommy was one of those people who was always screaming about the bottom line. I knew better, knew from Evan that their business made a lot of money.

I passed Shawna's desk and wondered if I would ever see her again, wondered if she even wanted to see me. She wasn't even a person I considered a friend, just someone I knew professionally. As I passed Bridget's desk, I almost missed it. Had the lights been on, I would have. What did I almost miss? Well, like I've said, Tommy is cheap. Well, maybe I haven't said it like that. Okay, Tommy is a cheap bastard. That's one reason the lights are out. Think about it. He runs a business *and doesn't want people to knock on the doors.* Another manifestation of that aspect of his personality is the computers his people use. The price differential between a six-foot video cable and a nine-foot one cannot be

Chapter Thirteen

much. Those extra three feet, however, can be the difference between having the CPU, the actual computer box, on your desk as against having it on the floor next to it.

Bridget Haines does the transcriptions and the serious client mail that any law office generates. I have no idea how old she is, but my best guess is she's between thirty-five and forty. It doesn't hurt that she's absolutely frigging gorgeous and has Miss America hair that is thick, black and *perfect*. When I'm that age? I want to look like her. She wears it shoulder length like I do, but that's as far as the similarity goes. Next to hers, my hair is limp and windblown.

The thing I saw, though, was her computer. It was on. Not all power lights are green, but hers was. I looked over her desk toward Lisette's and hers was off. I turned, went back to the Shawna's and hers was off. Only Bridget's was on. Okay, it meant nothing at all, just nothing. Well, except that Tommy is that cheap bastard I mentioned a bit ago. Running office equipment uses electricity and that was always forbidden. Plus, a law office that keeps computers running can get into serious trouble if someone walked in and the user in question wasn't running a password-protected screen saver. It could compromise the entire network. That meant one of two things. Either she was here or someone, Tommy most likely, had been using it. If he'd been using it, then why was he still upstairs? And if she was using it, where was she?

There are a lot of hiding places in that office, especially downstairs. Yes, I was getting a bit paranoid. I imagined Bridget hiding in the law library or in the lunch room or from anywhere she could spring out at me. Why she would want to do that is beyond me. That presumes I know something or have something they want and I can't imagine what that would be. As I walked up those stairs, I wondered what I was involved in and what Tommy was going to do.

There are three offices upstairs and I immediately wondered if Karin was here, too. The lights were on in his office but no others. The fading light from outside made everything gray or shades of it. His door was open, a sea of light spreading from his office. He was behind his desk and rose as I entered. No one else was in the room.

I knew I was going to get only one chance to judge him as he looked at my new and entirely repulsive face. He's from Irish stock and that red hair of his tends to make him florid at times. The fact that it doesn't trip him up very often is to his credit. But then? My face shocked him which meant another of two choices. Either he knew my face was different and still reacted to it in faint shock or it caught him by surprise. If I had to guess, I'd say the lawyer in him would never allow him to get caught that flatfooted. All that meant was that he had no idea my face was different, or *this* different.

His first remark, after his face settled back down, was the same as Deb's. "Plastic surgery? You found a good one, Morgahna." His hand extended across the desk and his smile was one he saved for clients, not friends. Yes, I knew the difference. My husband was a lawyer and I preferred to think of him as a good one. That meant I was being seen in the same manner he would see a client. His bullshit detector would be up.

"I didn't have plastic surgery, Tommy," I said as I took his hand and shook it.

As we settled to either side of his desk, he stared at me and it made me distinctly uncomfortable. I was still not comfortable with my face and maybe never would be. Before all this happened to me, I only wanted to be attractive enough for Evan. With him gone and my face looking like the bride of Frankenstein, I might never feel comfortable again. *Yeah, stupid. Billy Ray found you attractive enough to kiss…three times.*

He has that same game face, that same one Evan had. One was as good as the other and I never did get Even to break his. "What happened?" he asked, his voice level, his eyes merely open.

"I was attacked," I said and nothing more.

"By who?" he asked. "The police think you're dead."

I leaned back in the chair and felt the weight of his office on me. He has all of his certificates behind him on the wall. They were intended to give the impression that he was a professional and to impress upon you the entire idea of legality and that he knew the process and you didn't. My own college degree and other items? Were all in my office down behind the house. Where are they now? I have no idea. "Two big guys that like to pick on women," I answered calmly.

He leaned forward and that was an old trick, too. It invades your space and requires a decision from you. Most people engage the person

Chapter Thirteen

who leans forward across the desk in a friendly fashion. They exchange smiles with him and get friendly fast. The alternative is undeclared warfare on an entirely subliminal level. I decided to pretend I was European and merely smiled when he said, "It's good to see you, Jaynie."

"What happened to my home, Tommy? You did all that and don't bother to deny it because you're the only person that could."

That was at the top of my agenda with him. Bill Ray's opinion was that someone was looking for something. If they weren't, then what was the reason for stripping the drywall from their places? He smiled and it was another professional one. "Oh, that's easy, Jaynie. Those two that were living downstairs?"

"Albert and Shannon?"

He paused, pursed his lips and said gravely, "Yes, them."

"What about them?"

He grinned and that was calculated. "Geez, Jaynie. You look good. I know you said you were attacked but whatever happened left you prettier than before."

Interesting. I leaned back and crossed my legs. Men take that as an erotic sign and tend to stare. A lot of women do it for that reason. I can't say I never did but never liked having to do it. It turned me into little more than a target for misdirected male lust. Crossing yours legs also has meaning subliminally. I have no idea where I read it but I read that crossing your legs and/or your arms puts up negative signals. That's exactly what I wanted him to see. I wasn't interested in his phony compliments of my face. Maybe I could learn to live with it some day but that had nothing to do with why I was here. "Albert and Shannon, Tommy?" I reminded him.

His face firmed up and he leaned back in his chair again. "They were dealing drugs, Jaynie."

That may be, but Albert never seemed the type. Shannon either. Okay, in my line of work, you cannot assume anything. That holds true in more places than just mine, but when you put your feelings in print, you better be correct. I tried to be and I still give Dave most of the credit for making that lesson stick. Still, Tommy might be right but I had one big problem with his scenario. Their level, their home hadn't been stripped to the walls, just emptied. It was as though they merely moved. I've dealt with the police before and my guess based on what I have seen in the past is that they would search the primary residence – theirs – before they searched any other. Hell, that seems reasonable anyway. So, I merely nodded. "Then my stuff is in storage somewhere?"

He seemed distracted somewhat. "Oh, yeah, yeah. Storage. Yeah. Out near the airport."

"Have I been declared legally dead?" I asked because I began to sense something else and wondered if I should be worried.

"Oh, no. No, you haven't."

"Why not?" I asked. "If they think I'm dead?"

He folded his hands in front of him, leaned over the desk again but this time asked a question. "Did Evan leave anything for you, Jaynie?"

I have just enough experience, professional experience, to make that question ring a lot of bells. *They were looking for something, Morgahna.* That was Billy's opinion of the condition of my home. What better way to disguise that search than by accusing Albert and Shannon of dealing drugs and hiding them in my home? So, I tossed out a throwaway question. "You mean like a note?"

"Anything," he answered in the same throwaway fashion.

That question hurt and I believe it was intended to. He could have used any preamble available to him, anything like softening the question with a warning but didn't. He used the blunt force trauma method of cross-examination on me. It showed that we weren't friends and maybe never had been. Okay, lawyers will treat everyone the same and I know that. So, it was possible Tommy was using that approach as though he was in court and I had information he wanted. That's why I didn't think we were friends. Had he softened the question in any way at all, I might have changed my attitude toward him. Still, whether or not he did, didn't change my answer. "No, Tommy. I got no note, nothing. He didn't leave anything for me."

Those old self-inflicted wounds began to fester again. I felt tears deep inside, felt them as a growing sadness that might never go away. I

Chapter Thirteen

turned my head, swiveled it around the room and saw bookcases of law books, drawers, files and all the reminders of where I was. He was being a lawyer with me, was putting me on a witness stand and expecting the grieving widow to fall apart and spit out things she didn't want to admit. I saw Evan try a few cases over the years only to get a sense of what he did in the courtroom. He was like this – stone-faced, stern, unyielding and altogether too much like a dog after the last bone. I asked him once, "If I was a witness and knew things I didn't want to admit, what should I do? Is it possible to hide stuff like that in a courtroom?"

I remember his answer as being equivocal. He balanced it because that's how he saw it. "Yeah, minxie. I think is possible. I've seen witnesses that wouldn't even admit their mother was a female, so it is probably possible to keep information to yourself. I think the key is being unflappable. You know what I mean by that?"

"No matter what you ask, no matter how you ask it, keep presenting the same face."

My memory showed a wide smile as he put his chin in his hands and said, "Can I suck on your toes?"

My logical answer was, "I'm wearing shoes, Evan." I could have taken them off and let him do *something* to me. I didn't and will always regret it. Always. Thank you though, Evan. Thank you because you taught me enough to handle Tommy and his grim-faced prosecutor's look. Those dark feelings were still there and I still felt them way down deep. I was able to keep them there, keep them just out of the conscious level of my mind that would cause tears to start. Oh, I felt them in my stomach but I built a dam to protect myself from *him*. "What are you looking for, Tommy?" I asked bluntly and dry-eyed.

"Case notes," he replied curtly, shortly.

"For what case?"

"You wouldn't recognize the name. It was an assault."

Hmm. And I hadn't been assaulted? Okay, I'd told him I had been *attacked* and not *assaulted*. To a lawyer, those were probably two different crimes. I crossed my arms and said, "LaRuth Morrison?"

Touchdown.

There were only two names I could give him. Mine and hers. Since my case had never been reported to the police, the only other chance I had was hers, LaRuth's. I've already testified to the fact that I've never been in a fight. That forest? That doesn't count as a fight because I never got a chance to fight back. I hope to God that I never do either but if I do, I can assume that the first face I hit will look like his or at least react that way. He blanched but it was so quick, so momentary, that I almost missed it. Had I blinked? Yeah, that would have done it. I would have missed it because his reaction was *that* fast. Unless I missed my calling as a reporter and my hopes to be an *investigative* one, his next statement should be a lie.

"No, I don't recognize that name."

Which meant he did.

"It was a chance," I said shrugging.

Of course, the problem became deeper at that point. He knew that I knew a name I should not know. How did that name tie in with LeRay Morrison, Evan, Tommy and the entire mess? I don't know. So far, I had no proof that Evan knew LaRuth at all. Sure, he knew her sister and at least met LeRay because he recognized Evan's picture. If my little glimpse into the past was true, then Tommy was telling me that LaRuth Morrison was a client of Evan's, one that, after their deaths, required a payment of money to her sister. What could cause that?

"Have you heard from any of his old clients?"

"No."

"Will you let me know if one does?"

"Sure."

Another small piece of this puzzle was her name, her very name. To that point, I felt I had a secret, an exclusive one that LeRay was willing to keep. Now, I had at least tentative proof that Tommy knew the name as well. According to LeRay, however, she had been dead for a while, at least eighteen months. I tried to assign her name as the reason Evan grew depressed before he died but could not. I'm not saying she wasn't, but there was no proof at all that she was a client of Evan's. The only thing that tied him to her was that little lie and that lie was in the form of a look

Chapter Thirteen

that faded quickly from Tommy's face. I was basing everything I'd learned on that single brief look I stole from his face. If I was wrong – and I had to admit to the possibility – then everything else was suspect.

"You aren't curious how I came to look this way?" I asked.

"Sure, Jaynie."

"I was tied to a tree and beaten with a metal pipe, Tommy. I was beaten and left for dead."

A lot rested on that statement and since I was the one who got beaten and left for dead, I didn't give a fuck about Tommy Underwood and his clandestine girlfriend. Bridget? You can suck his wang all you want, but in my opinion you won't get anything but a foul taste in your mouth. Was that why she was here? Was it even her? Look, I don't know. I don't know how computers work and will avoid that knowledge for as long I possibly can. Still, I felt that the only reason I was here was for what I knew and I didn't know *anything*. I had some suppositions and that was all. Was I in trouble? It felt like it. From whom? Him and everyone I knew.

"Just like..." and he caught himself before he could fill in the name. It didn't matter. I already knew the name. LaRuth Morrison. Suddenly, I needed a computer, one to use and not one to understand. I don't know how my car starts, just that it does. That will always be enough for me. I knew where to get one, too, knew where to find a computer.

"Yeah," I said. "Just like her." Then I stood and said, "Where is my stuff and when do I get it back?"

"How can I contact you?"

"You don't. I contact you."

"You don't trust me, Jaynie."

"My name is Morgahna. I hate it when you don't call me that."

"I'm sorry," he said and pointedly did not use my name at all.

"I expect my home to be put back to the way it was. I expect everything to be the way it was."

"That will take a few days to arrange."

Which was bullshit. Still, I bowed and said, "Tell Bridget goodbye for me." I stared at him for a bit and his face grew a bit wiser. He knew that I knew far more than I was telling and that little aside was my way of telling him. It was also a gauntlet. I had every reason to hate him but hate is a strong emotion and one that opens you to vulnerabilities you might not have had otherwise. That was another thing Dave told me, taught me. *Morgahna? Be as fair and as even as you can be. You'll piss off the extremes on both ends but you'll always be able to reach them from the middle.* That advice had been committed to memory and to my approach to my job for a long time. I had never been involved in a case, though, where I was the subject. It was always easier to be detached when the subject was flowers or the port authority. When the subject is your own survival, it gets tougher to do, to be that way.

When I got to the door, he stopped me by saying, "This can get serious, Morgahna."

"As serious as being beaten with a metal pipe, Tommy? You ever been beaten that way? You ever woke up to find another face in your mirror? You ever find a scar on your throat that wasn't there before? You ever woke and found breathing difficult? You ever woke to two broken legs? Tommy," I said with my back him. "No offense, but the only thing more serious than those things is death."

"I hope it doesn't come to that, Jaynie."

Jaynie. He was telling me where he stood. As much as I would like to know why that was, I might never find out. He was telling me that we were adversaries and I never figured him that way before. Was I scared? Oh, you bet. I am, after all, a girl's girl and we get scared all too easily. Well, maybe not me as much as any other girl's girl after what happened to me, but I had to be aware that he was a man and most men would be able to handle me all too easily. "Tommy?" I said turning my face back toward his. "I hope you never find out what that feels like. It isn't pleasant."

"Yeah," he said. "I hope. If you hear anything, you let me know."

"You get my stuff, Tommy. And don't worry about where I am because I don't think you have any where that is."

Chapter Thirteen

"Skidaway Road."

"Uh huh," I said. "You keep thinking that."

I had to figure out a way to protect Debbie now. She didn't deserve the sort of trouble this could bring her. Her face is already perfect and hitting it with a metal pipe would ruin perfection.

I left his office and walked carefully down the stairs. Bridget was here somewhere and I expected her to jump out at me but she never did. I paused in the hallway downstairs and listened carefully and heard nothing, not even Tommy upstairs. I exited through the back doors and Billy picked me up easily as we headed for Deb's car. I got at least halfway to her place before he asked, "Jesus. Are you going to tell me?"

"He was fishing," I said.

"For?"

"Information I didn't have. He gave me bullshit, too. He said Albert and Shannon, my renters, were dealing and doing drugs and they weren't. Hell, Billy, even if they were, why wasn't their apartment torn up like mine was?"

"Then, I was right. He was after something that he assumed was hidden in your home."

"It wasn't or we wouldn't be here."

"He thinks you have it."

"And I don't have any idea what he's talking about."

That wasn't exactly true. Whatever it was included the beating death of LaRuth Morrison. That was all I had to go on and I needed to pursue that as much as possible. Deb's computer wasn't going to do it, but I knew one that would. I was done, however, with endangering people I knew and loved, so I just said, "I have to think about this, Billy. You understand?"

"Completely."

We got back to Deb's place and she was eating lasagna. LeRay was conspicuous by his absence so I asked, "What happened to LeRay?"

She shrugged and said, "Took a taxi to his mother's place."

I sat next to her and bumped her shoulder. "S'matter, Deb? Let one get away?"

She pushed the pieces of her meal around on her plate and said, "He was cute."

"Yes, he was. I need a ride somewhere, Deb."

"Where to?"

"Oh, just finish up, girl," I said with a wide smile. "It's no big deal."

She pushed her plate away from her and said, "Well, shoot. Let's just go."

I hugged Billy and said, "I'll see you in a bit, okay?"

"You sure?"

"Very."

We got on the road and I said, "I need to rent a car and you've got the only credit card in the crowd."

She grew absolutely still because I believe she knew what I was saying. I squeezed her hand and shook my head. *Please, Deb. Please don't. It's hard enough.* She swallowed hard and looked at me with a tenderness that I believe only women can share. That tenderness when given to a man turns slightly carnal, just slightly. A man might not do anything with it but knows he can. Women will always hold it to their hearts and treasure it. "No, Morg," she said as I pointed her past the hospital down on Eisenhower. "No, please," she said at a stoplight that had already turned green.

I nodded toward the curb off to the right and said, "Come on, girl. Off the road. You'll kill yourself."

She managed but her hands were shaking and she looked panicked. She banged the curb with her right front tire and the whole car vibrated and shook. It didn't bother her, though. I did. "No, Morgahna," she said as tears began flowing down her face. "I'll never see you again. I thought we were friends."

Chapter Thirteen

I leaned over and began wiping her tears away. "Deb? Tommy threatened you and I can't allow that. He knows or suspects we're together and as long as we are, you're in danger. Deb? I will never forget you and if everything works out okay, we're going to be better friends. This time? I'll listen to you. I'll even let you buy me some trashy clothes and shoes. Okay? But please don't think I'm never going to see you again because you've helped me more than anyone except Billy and I can't tell him for the same reason."

"No..." she cried and reached out to me, reached out and cried on my shoulder.

I held her as her entire body shook with the suddenness of it. I said softly into her ear, "Deb? I don't know what's happening but I can't let it hurt you. You're perfect and I need to make sure you stay that way."

"Morgahna..."

"Deb? I can't. Please understand. Please," I begged her. "If anything happens to you, I'll go nuts. You're my best friend and friends watch out for each other. I have to do this because it might hurt you if I don't."

"Who..."

I shook my head. "Don't ask, baby."

Her entire face fell apart and she cried until she was hoarse. We went to a rental place where I rented an Explorer on her card. Okay, maybe I was guilty of fraud again and maybe she was complicit in it, but she was safe.

After she cried and I held her one last time, she drove back to her apartment and I parked under a huge oak tree and cried until I, too, was hoarse.

Then I made a phone call with her phone. She's a girl's girl, too. Well, maybe better than me. She has three cell phones.

As time would tell, I had made one horrible decision and as I sat there trying to reassemble myself, I had no idea which one it was. As time would tell, one of them was horrible, as horrible as the one I made the night I went to Sugarplum's.

But that phone call?

Well, the person I called answered.

Oh, yes.

The stakes were getting a bit too rich for me, though. The problem was that I had no idea how rich they were or what that even meant. Had I known? I might have gone back to Tommy's and thrown myself on his mercy.

Not that it would have helped.

Not that.

Chapter Fourteen

I was on my way to Garden City when I called Dave Woods. He would have a good internet connection and would let me use it. While I didn't know where he lived, I knew his cell phone number because of that girl business I've alluded to many times. It was after nine o'clock Sunday night when I dialed his number. When it connected, I heard the TV in the background, either ESPN or their Sunday night game. Either way, he was being true to himself. Atta boy, Dave. "Hey," I said into the phone. "How about lunch?"

I heard the clatter of something hitting a hard floor and then, "Oh, my fucking god! Oh, my fucking god! Oh, my fucking god! It's you! You're alive! Where are you! Jesus Christ in Heaven, HOW are you alive?"

"Dave? Are you sitting down?"

After I slight pause that probably put him on the edge of his chair, he said, "Uh huh."

"Where do you live?"

"Here," he said stupidly.

"Dave?"

"Uh huh?"

"Your address?"

"Oh. dwoods@charter..."

"Dave," I said smiling broadly. "Where do you live? The address?"

"Oh, my god. Oh, my god," he kept saying. "You're alive. Oh, my god."

"Dave? Settle down or you'll start hyperventilating."

Well, it went like that. I finally got the address from him and it was predictably near the airport, Kessler Road. I got really stupid directions and had to stop and pin him down a bit more than I had. I finally

Chapter Fourteen

got him calm enough to give directions that could be understood as English by an American. When I got there and parked in the lot, he was pacing up and down in front of one of the buildings. When I parked and got out of the car, I can only assume the darkness masked my face because he jumped straight up and ran toward me. Another assumption was that he'd stop when he didn't recognize me. Well, I got nothing there because he hit me full speed, lifted me off the ground and held me in the biggest bear hug this side of Tybee Island.

"You recognize me, Dave?" I said quite breathlessly.

"Nope," he said.

"What if…"

"You aren't," he said and didn't let me down, but kept holding me fiercely. "Oh, sweet Jesus. Oh, Good Lord. I thought you dead. Everyone did."

"Well, unless you let me down, you might re-break my ribs."

That did it. He dropped me and stepped back staring. "What?"

I offered my elbow to him and said, "C'mon, dude. Let's go inside and I can bring you up-to-date."

Dave is a big guy. If I didn't say that before, let me make up for that oversight right now. He might be taller than me, but that about ends it. He's weighs in easily at two-fifty and that's not because he works out unless you call pizza a good workout. "You look like shit, Morgahna," he said.

Finally, someone who saw the real me. "That's what I've been saying, Dave. Finally, a man with some smarts."

"Tell Merriam," he said. "Now what happened?" he said as he took my arm and began to act like a prom date.

It felt absolutely delicious to be with him, to be with someone that I could work with and not worry about being a girl around. As near as I could tell, Dave had a bad case of Merriam Woods. "Dave? You aren't gonna try to sleep me are you?"

"Well, of course I am. It's part of the contract."

"Contract?"

"Didn't you read it?"

"Nah, I think I missed that one."

"Well, let me translate it for you."

"Okay, please."

"Men fuck women and they enjoy it."

"Really?"

He smiled. "Yeah. I mean, there's a test and everything."

I plopped cheek against his shoulder and said, "God, it's good see you, Dave."

"Who hit you with an ugly stick, Morgahna?" We were right outside his apartment door and he took my face in his hand, pinched my cheeks together under the light by the door – I wouldn't dignify it by calling it a porch light – and stared at me. "Good god, but what the hell happened to you?" Then he shoved my arm and said, "And where have you been?"

"Got time for a story while we work?"

Dave has the best "serious" look of anyone I know, Harley included. If God has a face, it probably looks a bit like Dave Woods. As we stood beneath that miserable light, I got it full blast. His eyes look positively Old Testament with a bit of Charlton Heston thrown in as he came down from Sinai. "Morgahna? You could pull my nuts off one at a time and I wouldn't care. That's how I glad I am to see you."

"Well, your nuts are safe with me," I said with a smile.

He put his hand to my cheek and said, "Do that again."

"Do what?" I said from newly-pinched cheeks.

"Smile."

"You gonna let my face go so I can?"

He did and so did I.

Chapter Fourteen

"Jesus," he said staring hard. "That's awful. Now, what happened?" He opened the door and I went inside to the most meager looking home I ever saw. The floor was black-and-white tile and there wasn't a rug anywhere. The kitchen was as barren as any I'd ever seen. The only decorations in the entire place were sports photos with one huge poster of Michael Vick over a futon that served as a couch. He sat me on it and said, "Beer?"

"Wine."

"Beer?"

I looked up and said, "Wine."

He looked down and said, "Beer?"

"Gee, Dave. You gotta beer?"

"Why, yes. I think I do."

There wasn't even a coffee table. An end table, one only, that was home to every Sports Illustrated printed in the last decade was on it. At least there wasn't any porn. He went to the smallest refrigerator I'd ever seen and pulled two Coors Lite's from it. He opened them and handed me one that I immediately was sorry I'd asked for. "Jesus, Doug. That's awful. You drink this stuff?"

"Recycle it, too." He sat next to me and the entire structure moaned under his weight. "Now. What happened to your once-beautiful face."

You know? This felt so much better than all those others telling me how good I looked. I smiled at him and said, "I could always count on you, Dave."

"Knock the chit-chat. What happened to my gorgeous buddy?"

Lord, I felt almost euphoric. I was hideous and here was a guy agreeing with me. I actually nuzzled his arm and said, "I got attacked, Dave. Over two months ago." I recounted the entire story through the meeting with Tommy Underwood. He listened and did something none of the others did. As I talked, he ran the backs of his fingers over my shattered cheekbones, across my broken nose and around my eyes. Finally, he held my chin in his hand and commanded me to continue telling the story as he looked at me closely. He saw the scar on my throat and fingered it tenderly.

He murmured, "That could have killed you." He looked at me and put his index finger over my mouth and said, "Shh."

I stopped cold because I had no idea what he was going to do. He reached for me and hugged me again, this time with something else involved. I was never frightened around Dave, never. To be honest, I still wasn't because we'd done so much together in the past two or three years that I'd long ago dropped whatever nascent racial mistrust I had for him. "Morgahna? You realize I love you."

"Um…"

And he pushed me across the futon to the end of it. "Jesus, not that way!"

"You had me worried, Dave," I said.

He stood and looked down at me. "You are one tough broad, Morgahna."

"I had help, Dave. I'm hoping I still get some."

"What do you need?"

"Your computer."

"Okay."

It sat in a corner near the front door, an explosion of books and papers around it, most of it on TV trays. The wall behind the small hutch was covered with more sports pictures - Braves, Falcons but no Hawks. I stood and he stopped me and said, "Gotta take you in the bathroom first."

"Why?"

"Need to show you something."

"Okay."

The bathroom was like Daydra's, small and ordinary. I loved my bathroom on Taylor Street because it was custom-made for me, to my specifications. The last time I saw it, it was entirely empty, even the designer tub was missing. He stood me in front of the mirror above the sink and said, "Look at that face."

Chapter Fourteen

"It's ugly."

"Baby?" he said putting his hands on my shoulders as he stood behind me. "You were never ugly and you still aren't. All those people you know? They're all right. You're a very handsome woman, Morgahna Hamilton. Whatever happens to you, I hope you don't let this interfere with your life. You were a major league screwball before all this happened, babe. I never met anyone as materialistic or as cunning as you. Now? You sound different as well as look different. Your voice sounds more humane, more willing to think of others. Is that true? Or am I just another nigger with an attitude?"

He has huge hands and a gorgeous face. I looked at his reflection in the mirror and said, "What was all that crap about me being ugly?"

"This is your chance, Morgahna. Your big chance. You always cultivated your image carefully. You always pictured things in your mind before you did them. Now? You have a rare chance to start over, to give your life some meaning it never had. Evan probably left you with enough money to put your face back the way it was and you've got enough talent to talk Harley into doing whatever you want him to do. You can go on with your life the way it was or you can use this opportunity to do something for us, do something for people who have been victimized just like you were. Morgahna? I won't stop considering you a friend if you revert to the way you were, but a small piece of respect will be gone if you do. Do you understand any of this?"

Oh, yes, sir, I did. "Dave?" I said into the mirror. "I'm a woman. That's first."

"That's irrelevant," he said. "I can introduce you to any number of women who aren't like you were."

"My appearance..."

"...is totally irrelevant."

I felt my face just like he did, put my hands and fingers against it just like he did and it still felt as though it belonged to someone else. Maybe those nine weeks out in the woods meant more than I thought, meant more than mere physical rehabilitation. I can remember countless sessions with Billy Ray's mirror as I stared at myself and tried to find me in the reflection. During all those nine weeks, I never managed to see me in there one single time. My face had been stolen, my life with it and now I was being told all that pain was giving me a chance actually to be another person, not just look at her face on a daily basis. Could I do it? Heck, did I even agree with his outline? Did I?

Well, yes, I did. Weaving all through the last two months before Tony and Doug tied me to that tree were every kind and sort of recrimination a human being could feel. I know I've leaned on the sexual things I withheld from Evan, withheld either consciously or not, but there were others as well. For example, I chose his clothes for him, chose them on the basis of how I wanted *others* to see him. No, I didn't want children because Evan was my child. Silly, huh? We would go shopping for clothes and I'd choose his shoes, socks, accessories and every single thing about what he wore publicly. I chose restaurants based on who ate there, chose them after doing research on the types of clientele and who ate where and when. I told him when he needed a haircut, sometimes chiding him for not shaving twice a day when I knew he had important clients coming to his office. You know? He never complained either. He never chided me on being anything but able to make his own decisions and never made my machinations seem anything but loving.

And then he put a gun in his mouth.

So, all during those nine weeks when I failed to see my face in that mirror, I realized that what Dave Woods was going to tell me one day was correct. I had a chance, that rare chance he mentioned, to judge the life I'd led and inflicted upon the man I presumed to love. The judgment I declared on myself was guilty as self-charged. That was the heart of my conviction that I killed my husband. I gave him far too little happiness and far too much structure. You know? I can't remember sitting in his lap one single time and that included the time before we were married. I can't remember being silly with him, being a girl with him, going to movies that weren't somehow appropriate to my career and, hence, my life. We never went for Sunday afternoon drives in the country, never had a picnic, never laughed spontaneously. Mostly, and I find this the most heinous of all, never allowed him to show affection to me and for me. That included sexual affection as well.

Debbie once told me that the best single time in her life was with a man who simply made love to her and lay there with her, even after they

Chapter Fourteen

finished. She said with a faraway look in her eyes, "He seemed to know how important it was to me that he remained *with me* as long as possible. I felt him leave me slowly, felt it in my heart as well as my genitals, Morgahna. It was the best thing that ever happened to me." At the time, I took it as mere sex and dismissed it as totally unnecessary. Now? I see that moment as reaching for another person and coming as close as is humanly possible. She described how they snuggled and watched sunrise through her window. He went to Iraq and never came back.

You would think that someone who worked for a newspaper would see the connectedness in people, the way we are all together in some way. No, I always saw life as the ultimate Darwinian struggle to reach the top of the food chain. Kill or be killed. Survive or die. But change? How many of us are given that chance in a fashion that is quite as stark as the one given to me. Religious? No, although there are those among us who would ascribe supernatural powers to what happened to me. I cannot believe a truly just God would sacrifice Evan for me. If anything, it is I that should have been sacrificed. No, I believe it is life and the way it rolls around us and sweeps us along in its path. My life *always* intersected with Evan's and always was fated to do something I never saw coming. All of us are fated that way. Despite living in a country that tries to limit the merest exposure to risk, it is all around us and we must be ready for it, be ready in the way we face life and the decisions we make regarding it. I am afraid I took not only Evan for granted but life, too. I am afraid that life holds all the cards and *always* assumed I could cheat my through it if only I planned deeply enough, hard enough and maintained a rigid outlook at the world. Yes, I was quite rigid in a way that defines that term.

You remember the incident I described in my pantry, the one where Evan came inside, grabbed my right breast and kissed me? You remember that one? You remember that I slapped him? Well, I did and I am sorry for it, but even sorrier because when it happened, for the briefest possible second, for a moment in time I will never get back, it was *wonderful*. Then I reverted to form and pushed all that pure pleasure aside and slapped the man I loved. There was a time when I would have said I loved him more than life itself but life itself has shown me how much more there is to love.

"Dave?" I said into that mirror. "Let me finish."

"Okay," he said but did not remove his hands from my shoulders. It was a reaffirmation of our friendship that he did not.

"I'm learning to live with this, Dave. Yes, I have, or had anyway, enough money to put it all put back the way it was. Hell, I don't know if that's even possible. I haven't made a decision, though. I want to get to the bottom of this before I make a determination. I understand, though, everything you're saying. It's hard, Dave," I said as all those old pains reminded me. "It's hard to change but I'm trying."

"Personally, I don't care what you look like. You believe that?"

"Yes."

"You could be ugly, you could be beautiful and I'll still love you like a sister. Now, where do we start?"

I turned and hugged him, turned and just buried my face, whether ugly or not, in his chest. He put his arms around me and I said, "Dave? I've never called you a friend before, but I'd like to think you are."

"You were a pushy white woman before. Now? I'd like to be your friend."

"Why did you put up with me?"

"For same reason you put up with me. Our professional lives depended on how well we could work together. That, fortunately, was never a problem. You would work with the devil himself if it meant getting Harley's notice."

I giggled and said, "Lord, that was true."

"You never laughed like that before."

"I was never grateful enough to bother."

"Well, bud? Let's go to work."

I held him, kept my arms around him. "Give me a second, jerkwad." He stood still and we just hugged one another. Then, I smiled against his chest and said, "This would be a bad time for Merriam to show up, huh?"

"No, baby. I'd see Merriam at the bottom of an alligator-filled well. She's all I think about when I'm alone."

Chapter Fourteen

"Maybe, one day."

"I don't think so, Morgahna."

"What happened between you and her?"

He fidgeted, shifted from one foot to the other and said quietly, "This."

"Me?" I said a bit quizzically.

"No, not you. Another girl."

"How did you feel about her?"

"Piece of ass."

"Pig," I said behind a giggle.

He sighed and said, "She was, baby. But Merriam? She's always been special and now that I'm here in this place? I'm in purgatory, baby. This is worse than hell because it's nothing, just nothing at all."

"She won't talk to you?"

"Calls me a snake. Calls me worse and I deserve it, too. That girl was nothing to me. She showed up in a short skirt and low-cut blouse, called me 'her Tarzan' and I fell for it. It wasn't even that great."

"Can I talk to her?"

"Won't matter," he said gravely. He sighed again and it felt final somehow, felt as though he was giving up the fight. "Morgahna? Can I complement you in a way?"

Smiling to his face, I said, "I'd rather you didn't. My new face might not be able to handle a blush."

"Well, I have to anyway," he said to me. He's a bit taller than me, but I already said most men are. A few women, too. As he held me, his massive hands on my waist, he said, "If anyone could survive anything that savage, it would be you. Still, I have to wonder how you did."

He knew about Billy Ray and already knew about Debbie. The point is that I've had help and now I was getting his. Prior to this happening to me, I don't think any of them would have gone to these lengths to provide it. I was always the calculating one in the crowd, the one who spied the clothes others wore, the cars they drove, the way their hair was cut, the language they used, the words they spoke and how well they spoke them, the people they were with and every other inanity you can name. "Dave? I saw two bodies out there near the port. These people are playing for keeps. It might get dangerous."

He stroked my cheek and said, "This is pretty serious, baby. The person that did this to you deserves justice."

"It isn't always as simple as that. Saying they deserve justice and giving it to them are two different things."

"Are your panties wet?"

"What?" I asked as my face twisted into a question mark.

"Well, you keep hanging onto me and I keep trying to get you to work and the only thing I can imagine that would account for that is wet panties. Are they?"

I grinned and smacked his arm. "That was mean."

"Does that mean 'no'?"

"It does," I said pushing him out of the bathroom.

"Thank god," he said. "I was afraid I was going to have to make love to a white woman."

"Not today, sorry."

Dave gave me his chair in front of the computer and grabbed a thin and rickety one from the kitchen which immediately made me switch with him. "Fat bastard," I said as we settled into our new chairs. "White woman," he chided me with his own smile.

I told him the story of LaRuth Morrison and how she was killed. I didn't know which police agency handled the investigation or even if the story itself ran in the Savannah paper. As much as I wanted to call LeRay and pump him for additional details, I didn't and the only reason was Caller ID. It's so pervasive that any number can be traced. Sure, you can block your number but his mother owned a business and any calls he made from her home or business would have her company name on it, so I passed on that detail.

Chapter Fourteen

The Morning News has a better archive section than a lot newspapers do. They put every story from every day for the last six years online and that meant the story should be there if they ran it. The only details I knew were her name and that she had been killed near Hinesville, out near Fort Stewart. If the story ran in that newspaper, the Hinesville daily, and not the Morning News, we might be at a dead end. The Hinesville daily does not post archives online like the Morning News does. We would never find out who reported the story without driving out there and asking someone from the newspaper directly.

The search function on the website wasn't all inclusive and made finding a match headline-intensive. Also, the only stories that get posted are ones written by the staff of the Morning News. National, even regional, stories written by stringers and freelancers never get posted. You would have to get a hardcopy of that days paper to read a story done by one of them. All which meant we had trouble finding anything with her name in it.

The beer got cold and ignored as we worked. It got to be twelve-thirty in the morning when I finally stretched and yawned. I'd noticed a decline in my stamina ever since the beating. I can remember times when I could do this sort of work until sunrise. Hmm. Times change and so did I.

"Can I crash here?"

"Wouldn't have it any other way. I'll pull out the futon and sleep there."

"Nah, I'll..."

"No, Morgahna. As a matter of fact, you will not sleep on the futon. I will. You will sleep in a real bed with real covers and sheets and if you argue, I can cause you great pain." He tried to look serious but as I smiled at him, he finally broke up and pushed me. "Damn, white woman."

We'd been working for three hours and checked every murder story, every local story for all of the last two years. We even went back three years just in case LeRay was wrong on his dates and times. My suspicion was starting to build in a particular direction and I didn't like where it was pointed. A crime like the one LeRay described was a classic hate crime if you looked at it that way. It was very possible that the story was reported to the newspaper but possible the editors killed it for no other reason that that. Hate crimes that involved blacks and whites are all too easily suppressed. I'd like to assign southern motives to it, but I fear it's national.

Before we shut down for the night, I decided to check the obituaries that were listed as a separate forum. I started looking in January two and a half years ago. The deaths are listed alphabetically by last name. I was weary as I started looking and got all the way to March of that year before Dave said, "She was a model? She might have modeled under a different name. We need to go back and check each name again."

I sighed and he heard it.

"You okay?"

"Yeah. I'm fine."

"You gonna make me hurt you?"

I grinned and said, "Yeah, big guy. Hurt me."

He pushed me again and said, "Just go back to January."

Well, there was nothing even remotely suggestive of a stage name on that list. My fear was that since obituaries are purchased by the family or by someone else and not automatically included, was that the family didn't pay for an obituary for a family member that lived in New York City. I went slower through the list checking every name and even looking at a few in detail before going on to the next one. The site listed all the names first in sequence and then linked that name to the actual obit. It made the search a lot easier to perform, something I probably would not have done had it been organized in any other way. Dave pointed out a few names and none of them were LaRuth Morrison.

I was getting bleary-eyed as we crossed into November, a bit less than two years ago. Twenty-two months to be exact. On the alphabetical list was the name L. P. Morrison. The link went to a LaRuth Patricia Morrison and the information contained in it was sketchy at best. Other than the name of the funeral home that handled the service, its time, and the date of her funeral, there was nothing else at all. It gave me a clue, however, and made wonder why I hadn't thought of it before. Well, sue me. I've been sick.

Chapter Fourteen

Her mother. I knew her mother and even knew where she worked. Dave saw my smile and asked, "Okay, what?"

"Tell me I'm ugly."

"No."

"Tell me."

"No."

"Dave? So help me, I'll scream rape and a white girl in a black man's apartment will not go well for you."

"Okay, okay. I give."

"So, say it."

"I already did."

"No, you didn't."

"Mentally. I said it mentally."

"Dave..."

"MORGAHNA HAMILTON! WHAT DID YOU FIND!"

"Her mother," I smiled, my hands behind my head.

"That's not in there."

"Did I forget to tell you about LeRay Morrison?"

"Yeah, you did. Who is he? Husband?"

"Brother."

"And?"

"His mother owns a burger shop down on Florance."

While it sounded like a triumph, it didn't feel that way. I was making a lot of decisions and missing a few things as I did. I can't really blame Dave for not noticing the holes in my story because the parts I told him were harrowing enough. Recounting the story of being tied to a tree and being beaten with a metal club - by two of them in fact because Tony Slaton didn't work alone - was bad enough. It still gives me chills when I think of it and even as it fades into deep time, I can still feel that pipe as it bounced off my head and the sizzling sound it left in my ears. It's possible that it has affected my memory, or at least my judgment, because I can't remember being that sloppy in my work. I was always more meticulous than that, than how I had been that night.

The problem, I was going to find, was that I was making decisions and the work I was doing based on those decision was affecting other people. Maybe I should have stopped as soon as I even entertained the notion that I was being sloppy. Maybe. I can remember making lists and making check boxes next to each item I investigated. I can remember a far more meticulous person than I was being. True, I was still recovering from a major trauma – several of them, in fact – and even realized I was doing sloppier work than I'd done just five months ago, but the fact is I didn't do anything to check my progress or recheck my work. I knew LaRuth Morrison died on November 2, just under two years ago. That seemed enough.

I'd like to believe that Dave might have noticed and maybe he did. That's likely because we worked together so many times in the past. He knew my habits and knew them better than anyone except maybe Evan. Dave didn't stop me, challenge me or even ask me any questions about my methodology, though. As much as I'd like to blame him, I can't. He was like the rest of them; he was worried about me and was simply glad I was okay. Me? I didn't know what to do because my emotional anchor – namely Evan – was gone and working without either him or the home we shared was harrowing.

Can you believe that? I mean, can you? That home we shared down there on Taylor Street was his as much as it was mine. He was proud of it, too. Even if I manage to put that house back together, I wondered if I will ever really feel as comfortable with it as I once did. I wonder if I will ever be the dynamic person that could do twenty-four hour days. I fear not. I fear I am a totally different person than I used to be and will always wonder in some small way which person was better. The one I was, the one that was going to do these things that were just around the corner or the one that buried her husband because she was too materialistic and self-centered.

Time had already run out on one and a judgment day was coming for the other.

Chapter Fourteen

I knew about one and knew how she got that way. The other? Well, she was still a mystery and I was still learning about her. In and of itself, that is never a bad thing, learning about oneself. However, no man is an island. John Donne? I owe you for that, for teaching me that. It is still debatable if I am more effective than I used to be. Tradeoffs. The world, life itself, is tradeoffs and we never quite get an answer if any particular one was worth the agonies that went into the choice that made it.

Suffice it is to say that I didn't sleep well that night.

At all.

Chapter Fifteen

Dave gave me a huge Hawks t-shirt that I used as a nightgown. He said they played like girls anyway, so why not. In my entire adult life and for several years before those, I cannot remember wearing the same clothes two days in a row and that included underwear. In the last four months that had happened more times than in all my juvenile years combined. The stupid part was that my underwear belonged to Debbie. Every single stitch of clothing I'd worn since I came out of those woods belonged to her. Yeah, I had some stuff in Billy's pickup but I couldn't afford to go back and tell him I needed them.

As I lay awake in Dave's bed, the small practicalities of life began to intrude. Dave was living here because he didn't have a lot of money to spend on people like me who just dropped in at the last minute. He had a picture of Merriam on his nightstand next to the phone, an old white one from the last century. *It would be so easy, Morgahna. You can do it. Just call her.* Who? My mother.

Her name was Evelyn and no one ever called her Eve. She intimidated me so much that I actually took a shower first. Actually, I would have done almost anything rather than admit I needed anything from her. No, I don't hate my mother, so don't think that. It was more that I've always been self-sufficient. Always. Even as a young girl, I was proud of the fact that I could take care of myself. I didn't believe in ghosts only because I had no time for them. I believe my mother was proud of me, too. Having an older brother who was far more normal than me made her more amenable to having a daughter whose first priority was learning how the spell the word "unabashed" and then testing it by using it in at least a half dozen sentences.

I sat there on Doug's bed cross-legged with his old phone in my hand, fear making its presence known as a rumbling in my stomach. Being the girl's girl that I was, I knew *her* phone number, too. She was my mother. I had no choice but to know it. Being my mother, though, I wondered what her reaction to my death had been. If this entire case had

Chapter Fifteen

been the other way around, I do not believe I would have grieved her death endlessly like I grieved for Evan. Why? Well, that was easy – she's older than me and she's *supposed* to die before I do. Now? Well, things had changed a bit. How? Well, those nine weeks had changed my perspective more than I assumed was possible before this stuff happened. I was finding solace in people who had no reason to harm me, people like my mother and father, my brother, Debbie, Billy and Dave. Yeah, the people I should have given more attention to before all this happened. My fear was that she would not cheer my survival, but take the news with some small irritation.

The apartment was quiet; Dave was still sleeping. Otherwise, he would be in the room with me. For some reason, I couldn't dial her number easily. Yes, part of it was that strain of self-sufficiency that I carried with me like a cross. A much larger part was rejection - hers. I never turned to her for help, not even as a child and now I needed it more than ever and was scared she would remember all those unspoken and totally unused options that I never used. *Call her, Morgahna. She's your mother.* I put the receiver to my ear and found the effort hard and put the receiver back on the phone. My palms were sweating and I realized another part of the problem was the danger I posed to her. I was entirely unwilling to risk Debbie's life – even Billy Ray's – yet was ready to risk hers only because she could give help in the form of money.

That thought – endangering my parents – caused me anxiety on a scale that left me helpless and more alone than I'd ever been. When Evan did that? I didn't feel alone so much as *deserted*. He left me and that caused so many of my first problems that had Tony and Doug not taken me out into the woods and beaten me far more than half to death, I might have succeeded in my own death wish.

But should I? Should I go and see them? I was with Dave because I was so worried about Debbie. Was this any better than that? If I did this, if I went there, I realized I was going to have to be aware of being followed. If anyone did, then I was going call her, call my Mother, and cancel my visit. It was the best I could do because I needed to see her as much as I needed a loan.

My second attempt was no better. In retaliation for my own mood, I almost called Debbie. I rationalized it as that I could jeopardize a friend easier than I could jeopardize my mother. *You don't need anything from either of them.* That was my answer, at least my temporary answer. I even began to believe I could do this without Dave. For what it's worth, that was the one thing that convinced me at least to try one more time. To talk to Harley, I was going to need Dave because his presence would make getting access to him that much easier.

Third time is the charm, lady. I picked up the receiver and tried to clear my mind of all the guilt I'd built up around that phone call and just dialed it without thinking. Nothing remained in my head as it rang. Then, magically, there she was. She said with a brightly happy and professional voiced, "Larsen Builders, Evelyn Parker." Her voice held magic, was the only force that could dig into me so deep that would get that reaction.

I started crying. "Mom?"

I saw nothing, heard nothing, sensed nothing, just sat there crying as I waited for her reaction. Her voice broke a bit, then shock set in and she cried out, "Morgahna?"

"Yes," was all I managed as tears rolled down my face and I became far more helpless than I'd ever been around her. Maybe those metal pipes had beaten all the nonsense out me. Maybe they had beaten some sense into me. Either way, I can't remember ever crying like that to her, not to her. There were endless times in my youth where she got *parental* with me and I cried a few times. All kids do. All those tears, though, were from having my wishes broken, my goals curtailed and they exhibited themselves as tears of frustration and a bit of adolescent anger. I never went to her room in tears of pain, sorrow or teenage heartbreak. I can only remember being focused and she was only one of two people who could put my future on hold. The other was my father.

My mother, I realized with a shock as I listened to her voice remained broken but controlled, was a lot like me. Maybe that makes me a bit like her. "Morgahna? Will you be at this number for a while yet?"

"Yes," I said as my hands shook as though they had been exposed to a hurricane force wind.

"This name on the Caller ID box? That's your newspaper friend? Woods? Don? Dennis? Dave?"

"Dave, yes. I'll be here."

Chapter Fifteen

"Morgahna Jayne Hamilton? I will call you right back. Do you hear me?"

"Yes, ma'am."

She hung up and left me sitting there on that bed wondering why she had done that. The number I called was her cell phone and not her work phone. That meant she could be anywhere, anywhere at all. As much as I tried to think of reasons, I could not think at all.

When the phone rang, I picked it quickly and said, "Hello?" My voice was nervous and frightened. Why? Lord, I don't know. Maybe I was turning to her for shelter. Maybe I wanted nothing more than to be taken care of and she was the only one left who could do it.

It was her and she began crying, began shedding tears as she said, "Please, dear. Please talk to me. Please. Don't let this be a delusion."

"Mom? I'm okay but I need help. Can you?"

"What's wrong, Morgahna? Tell me," she said as she began to panic. "Is that man…"

"No, mom. Dave is great. He let me stay here last night. Someone tried to kill me, mom, and I don't know why. I can get to Jacksonville, mom. Can I come home and talk to you?"

"Yes, yes," she said. Then she broke down entirely after she said, "Oh, they said they presumed you were dead, Morgahna. They said you were dead."

It was a sobering moment for me. I had almost entirely ignored my parents ever since I married Evan, ignored them so much that calling my behavior neglectful would be warranted. Why was I that way? The only thing that makes sense now is selfishness and the entire feeling that my life belonged to me and me alone. Events were beginning to paint my life as being connected to everyone I ever met. Combine that with my mother's tears and it was a sobering moment that allowed one emotion to bubble to the surface ahead of all the others. "I love you, mom," I blubbered.

"Oh, little girl, I love you so much. This is like Christmas."

"I can be there late tonight, maybe five or six. I have to go talk to my boss first." I could hear traffic outside. She was calling from her car. "Are you safe to drive, Mom?"

She started crying again and said, "No. I called you back so that I could talk in my car. Morgahna? I came out to my car. I thought you were dead. I've been calling the police everyday for the past month. Morgahna? Are you really coming home tonight? You never came home before."

"Yes, Mom," I said nervously. "I need to see you, to be with you."

"I'll be there, darling. I'll call your father, too."

"Mom?" I said. "I got beaten pretty bad and my face took a lot of it. I don't look the same anymore."

"Morgahna? I don't care what you look like. The fact that you're alive at all is a miracle."

Yeah, I felt that way, too. It was a miracle and I was living in it.

Before I could say anything, she asked, "Have you see a doctor? Do you need one?"

I had no idea if I needed a doctor. I had vague fears of bone chips floating around my face and causing trouble one day in the future. I had fears of my ribs puncturing my lungs, fears that my concussion was far more serious than I imagined. In a way, I felt like a time bomb. Billy Ray might have kept me alive but a doctor and good CAT and MRI scans could be crucial to my survival even if this story went my way. "Mom? I don't know. Maybe I should see one, but later. Okay?"

"Are you sure? I can call my doctor? I can arrange everything."

"Mom? Thank you so very much for your worry, but I need to do these things first. Okay?"

"Well," she said and let her voice drop off into uncertainty. "Okay, but the offer is still open. I can call him and arrange an appointment."

"Maybe later, okay? Mom? I'll be there as soon as I can."

"Oh, god. My baby came back. My baby came back."

Chapter Fifteen

"Mom? I need one last favor and this one might be the biggest one of all."

"Just ask."

"Don't tell anyone but Dad. Please? Not even the police. Please? I don't know what is happening and any attention that gets drawn to me could cause trouble for people around me. Please, Mom? Don't tell anyone? I'm still missing, okay?"

It was hard for her. It was obvious that she wanted to trumpet the news, wanted to dance on her desk and cry the happiest tears in creation. What I was asking was hard and I knew it. I was counting on her deep professional sense to do this, though. It is possible I learned my sense of discipline from her. My father had a quixotic sense of reality but one seemed to balance the other. For what it's worth? I have no idea what my father is doing now. A carpenter by trade, he could have gone to medical school for all I knew.

"Then, it's still dangerous for you," she said, her voice seeming to rise to the occasion.

"Yes, mom. There are some funny things going on and I don't know what they are. I don't have any idea why someone would want to kill me. My biggest fear is that if this becomes public, then they will go underground and no one will ever know who did this. Then, one day he'll pop up and do it again and this time he maybe succeed."

"I can call your brother."

"I have help, Mom. All I need is time to figure this out. If I think I need to go to the police, I will but I need that decision to be mine and no one else's. You understand? Please tell me you do."

"Can we talk tonight?"

"Yes, mom. All night if necessary."

Mom has a pretty smile on an otherwise ordinary face. Given my basic nature, I can't say I gave her a lot to smile about. Oh, all those academic accolades were nice, but we were never really friends. I had no friends of note, not even Debbie. Like I said, she was my friend but I did not return the favor as much as I should have. My greatest remaining goal now is that I will be a better friend and daughter to them, to her.

"Oh, this a miracle," she said happily.

I smiled into the phone. "Mom? You need to tone it down a bit. You go back inside with that smile on your face and people are going to ask questions."

"Then, I need to do this with you. I need to be silly with you. Morgahna? I don't care that we were never closer. I care, I love you, and nothing else matters. I am so, so, so happy that nothing else matters."

"I'll see you tonight, Mom," I said happily. "I love you."

"Morgahna? You always made me proud. I don't think I ever said that to you but I never worried about you either. You always had a sense of yourself, a sense that most others don't have. You have always made me so very proud and when Evan died, I could see that a piece of you died with him. I pray you will be okay. I will pray that from now on, now that God has given you back to me. God bless you, Morgahna."

That conversation was pushing me toward humanity. As odd as that sounds, it sounded even odder to me. I never thought much of others, just in what they could do for me. That's as bluntly arrogant as I can possibly be. Yes, I had airs and I freely admit that now. All those pretentious dinners both at home and in any restaurant you can name around town, meant nothing more than I was advancing my career at someone else's expense. I tried to put it in terms of a win-win situation but I really don't believe in those scenarios anymore. We love them, though. We believe with the devoutness of the converted that in any contest there is a winner and a loser. We believe that. We do not toast the loser of the Super Bowl in any way except that they played a good game. They still lost. However, in business, we use that phrase – win-win – a lot. We use it because we want desperately to believe that the ass-whipping we just received was a good thing in *some* small way. As this applied to me, I saw all those win-win situations that I discussed with so many dinner companions brought both equal terms and equal justice to both sides. Had that been true in *any* way, I would not have been tied to a tree at all, much less left to die.

For what's it worth, I do not believe we have equal justice in this country. In my line of work, that is almost impossible not to see it. The justice we have in this country is like everything we have. The more money you have, the more justice you get. It is no secret to anyone I know

Chapter Fifteen

that our prisons are full of poor people. In some way, we feel they deserve what they got. In the overwhelming majority of those cases, we don't even know what happened to them to put them in jail. All this meant to me was a sense of my future and where it was going.

I got up and wandered out into the living room and found Dave up and already dressed. I hugged him, patted his butt and said, "Morning, big guy."

"You were talking to your mom. I heard and decided to butt out."

"I gotta go see her later," I said as I opened his refrigerator and looked for *something*.

"We'll both go."

"It's not necessary, Dave."

"I know. I'm going anyway. You were the one that involved me. Now? You're stuck with me."

Pushing around all the beer and packaged ham, I said, "You have anything even remotely resembling orange juice?"

"No, sorry."

"Any kind of juice that isn't fermented?"

"I could go buy some while you're in the shower?"

I grabbed his hand and said, "Deal. Bring bread, too. I love toast in the morning."

"Where we going today?"

"To see Harley."

"Oh," he said. "I see you're still a basic masochist."

I pushed him toward the door. "Out. And you better have shampoo in that shower."

"Ain't that poor," he said breaking in to a huge grin.

I hated taking a shower and then being faced with the prospects of wearing the same clothes. Okay, Billy bought me some stuff, I had access to Debbie's wardrobe and I walked away from both of them. All that meant was I was going to have to deal with it for a while. I couldn't even lean on my mother for a clothes and a place to sleep because she was too far from Savannah to make it work anyway.

Paranoia is not something that I ever lived with. There has never been a time in my life when I felt someone was out to get me. Well, not until nine, almost ten, weeks ago. I had adversaries only because my outlook on life required them. You can't get to the top without stepping on a few toes as you climb that ladder. Even so, I never lived in paranoid fear of what they would do to me if they ever tried to get even. Standing in that shower, however, and knowing that Dave wasn't there caused me to have a paranoid attack that left me unable to do much more than weakly wash my hair and listen to everything outside the rushing noise of the shower. It was my worst night since Billy's house out in the woods. Just turning off the water in the shower was stressful. The water dripped from the nozzle with the slow insistence of the tides out in the river. Nothing happened, or at least I heard nothing.

The sliding door on the shower made a quiet rumble as I slid it aside. Was someone out there? Jesus, I actually stood on that small rug he had outside the shower stall door and did nothing for several long minutes but drip. Then I smelled toast and breathed *so* much easier.

My only remaining problem were my clothes. I was wearing the same stuff and that still offended my sense of femininity. Blacks pants, gray top and nice shoes. As bad as that was, the underwear was the same, too. All I could do was put a good face on it and brush out my hair because Dave didn't own a comb. When I walked out of the bathroom, he was sitting at that ridiculously small kitchen table. He jumped up and indicated a plateful of buttered toast that fronted three different types of jams and jellies, all new. Then he pushed a glass of orange juice to me and said, "It's from a carton, not concentrate. I hope that's okay."

I sat and smiled. "It's perfect, Dave. Thank you."

He sank back down and smiled. "You had me worried. I expected the old Morgahna."

"I should smack you for that," I said as I sipped at the OJ.

"I kinda wish you would. This is like waiting for the other shoe to drop."

Chapter Fifteen

It saddened me a bit, that expectation even though it was made in jest. I doubled my fists and held them out over the table and said, "I woke from unconsciousness four days after the attack, Dave. Even after four days, you could still see the marks around my wrists from where they bound me with wire. That tends to change a person, Dave. If it doesn't, it should."

"I don't mean to make fun of you, Morgahna."

It was okay, much more than okay. That little remark was deserving. I smiled and said, "Don't worry, Dave. I think from now on if I yell, it will be because someone deserves it."

"We really seeing Harley?"

"Yeah," I said. "I've been thinking about this. If I try to see him and he won't, then I'll probably call the police."

He poured himself a glass and asked, "Why? I mean after everything you said, why?"

"Because I'll probably move, that's why. If they want to follow me around the country, they can."

"You'd move and leave me without a partner?" he said putting his glass down firmly and then staring at me just as firmly. "I figured we were Woodward and Bernstein, doofus."

"Hamilton and Woods?" I joked.

"Woods and Hamilton. I'm older and have more experience."

"I'm a woman and, thus, superior."

To my surprise, he yielded, lowered his head and said, "Okay."

It troubled me, that reaction did. He's a big man and entirely able to make his wishes both known and real with most anyone he meets. He dropped his hands into his lap as though they were live hand grenades and hung his head. "Hey," I said. "This is me, your buddy. What the hell is this?"

"Merriam says I act superior and that's one of the reasons she doesn't want me in her life. She says I need to be more understanding."

I slid the grape jelly over to me and couldn't open it. I slid it back into place and began eating the toast without the jelly I loved most. Dave saw me slide the jar back into line and gently grabbed and began to remove the top. "What the fuck are you doing?" I snapped angrily.

"Opening the jar."

"Did I fucking ask you to open it?"

"Um…"

"Answer me, Goddammit."

"Um…"

"David Leon Woods, you answer me right now," I said biting into the unjellied toast and winching at its blandness.

He watched me eat that toast as I winced and grimaced as I did. Then I took another bite and actually acted as though it was too much to bear but was enduring it anyway.

"Okay," he said. "What the hell is this?"

"Did I ask for your fucking opinion?" I snapped. "Big fucking black nigger and doesn't even understand basic fucking English." I snapped off another piece of bland toast and winced as I ate it.

"Hmm," he said. He reached out, twisted the lid off the jelly and held it out for me. "Okay. I get it."

I smiled as sweetly as I could because Dave Woods is not a nigger, not to me anyway. "Why, thank you, Mr. Woods."

"What does this have to do with Merriam?"

I took a knife, dipped it into the jar and spread some jelly on a piece of toast and it was heavenly. "You should do this with her, Dave."

"What? Jelly toast?"

"No, just do something that you can and she can't."

"What the hell does that mean?"

I gestured at him with the knife. "You know how different my life would be if Evan just did something *one time* that he wanted to do and I didn't? Now, mind me, I'm not talking criminal assault here. I'm just

Chapter Fifteen

saying, women don't screw themselves. In all the years I've known you, you have never stood up to her one single time. She wants you out of the house? You leave. She wants you to live in a dump that makes her look superior and you allow it. She defies the court order by dropping off Nate at your job and you allow it. Merriam is bitch," I said licking the knife.

"Hey..."

With the knife empty of any stray jelly, I gestured at him again. "Not exactly a cocksucking bitch, but a bitch nonetheless. You could put your foot down on small things like child care and your home. Act like you have a girlfriend, a nice white one whose initials are MJH and loves to decorate apartments. Make this place look more livable. Put Michael Vick in a less conspicuous place and hang a set of cheap landscapes behind the television. Let her think you've gone on with you life."

Then I bit into the toast and smiled.

"I love her," he said.

I shrugged and chewed.

"She'd call a cop."

"Why? She doesn't like landscapes?"

"I don't have the money for landscapes."

"Pass up beer once a week."

"I don't know what would look good."

I smiled and took another bite.

"You? You'd help me?"

"Yes, massa," I said.

"Hey..."

"You remember when you took my face in your hands and stared at it?"

"Yeah?"

"You ever touch her that way?"

"That wasn't romantic."

"Exactly."

He looked past me at the rest of the apartment, at the walls, the cheapness of it, the way it just screamed failure. He sighed and said, "There's this little store down the road? A convenience store? They sell cheap prints for like ninety-nine cents a piece. I could buy some of them and hang them."

"Group them by subjects. Landscapes, portraits, still life, that sort of stuff. Think like a girl, too. Put your own touch on it, too. Find pictures that appeal to you and buy them." After a heartbeat, I added, "A rug wouldn't hurt either. And stash the magazines."

"Act like a girl," he said grumpily.

"No, a human being that isn't sitting home waiting for his ex-wife to magically appear. Dave? You're a handsome man and there are other people in the world. Don't be foolish like yours truly. Be a real person and meet people. One of them might surprise you by agreeing to discuss your etchings."

"My etchings?" he said with a smile.

"Exactly. Any excuse to be alone with a man that interests her."

"And if her name just happens to be Merriam?"

"So much the better."

"Woods and Hamilton," he said looking over my shoulder.

"Let's go talk to Harley," I said as I licked my fingers.

With a distant look on his face as he saw his apartment as somehow different, he said absently, "I'd rather talk to a live chainsaw."

"Yeah, but you have a job."

"Maybe I should ask him for decorator advice."

I stood and said, "You do that. I'm sure he'll give you good advice."

He grinned. "You have this way of being obscene without ever once using foul language."

Chapter Fifteen

Obscene? I was about to beg my ex-boss for my job back, the only job I ever had, the only job I ever wanted. If he turned me away, I had no choice but to go to the police with what I had. I'd tell Debbie I was leaving town and I didn't even have a destination for a second career. Yeah, I was scared and I believe I had plenty of reasons to be that way. I was a girl playing in a man's arena and I vaguely knew it.

We left in my rented Explorer only because Dave was thinking about decorating.

Wow. There's a bet I would have lost.

Chapter Sixteen

Harley Hood is the Government and Business Editor for the Morning News. I have no idea how old he is, just that he scares the piss out of me and was the only one who could do that prior to not quite ten weeks ago. I can't say for certain because I don't and never have thought that way about myself, but I believe I scared people I worked with, too. That's a hard thing to admit because intimidating people was never my goal. My career was my goal, not sending co-workers into shivers of fear. It is possible, at least in retrospect, that Harley managed that way, not by fear but by goals. He had his and assumed you had yours. Still, he is a fearsome person. Well, at one time he was. After you've been tied to a tree and used as target practice, your fear of a lot of things drains away or is beaten out of you. In my case, it was beaten out of me.

Dave was scared of his ex-wife and that left little room for others to intimidate him. We talked on the way there and he was quietly reassuring or tried to be. I smiled and said, "Dave? Don't worry. I'll be good." Yeah, he was scared of me, too. He was scared of what I'd say, how I would act and what the consequences would be for him.

"I'm not worried," he said. "I worry about Nate and Merriam. You? You have this deep seventh sense about what to do."

The newspaper facilities are out on Chatham Parkway just south of the I-16. Built across the street from an industrial park, it is an imposing set of buildings but I still prefer the old building down on Bay Street. They're turning it into a hotel or something, It's a pity that a landmark building like that is being cut up piecemeal.

Anyway, the production building is off to the left and that's where the money comes from. I have no earthly idea what they do down there with all that equipment but I know that newspapers live on their advertising income and that building over there is where all that advertising you pull out of your morning paper gets put together. Harley makes all new employees go down there and watch them work in the morning – and I mean like one o'clock in the morning, too – as a condition

Chapter Sixteen

of hire. I did it one night almost six years ago now and didn't understand any of it. This big machine takes all those lovely ads and sticks them brutally into a newspaper before sending them to get stamped, clamped, bundled, handled and thrown into the back of trucks. No one read them and no one looked like they wanted to either. It saddened me and I knew exactly why. That type of work deadens your curiosity and puts upon you a burden that you never quite shrug off. I have avoided that building ever since. Now? I wonder if I was as wrong about them as I was about everything else.

Dave was more worried about my new face than I was. He actually whispered to me as we entered, "You want me to introduce you to people?"

I smiled and said, "Nah. Let's see how many recognize me."

"You look good, babe."

"Wow, that's one vote."

Despite my flippant attitude, I was curious if any of these people would recognize me. I so casually castigated the production people for not having any of that quality when I first met them those many years ago. Now, those same qualities were being tested on people that I gave higher marks than them. As we walked past desks, cubicles and the general office crowd of people, many recognized Dave and said hello to him. A few stared at me as I passed but no one talked to me at all. You know? Not that many ever did. I mean as a friend, not as a colleague. It is likely that I made no friends here and that saddens me as I think about it.

Harley knew Dave was coming but there was no mention of a friend. That was planned. That much was fear. I was scared that if he knew I was coming, he wouldn't see me and I wanted to see him more than anything. I know I've said that I was prepared to beg for my job but that ardor was waning fast. I felt I had leverage on Harley in the form of a story, my story.

Every secretary to every executive anywhere in the world is overworked to a point of exhaustion and Harley's was no exception. Her name is Sue Cole and she's easily as old as Harley and her age is just as indeterminate. While I've computed Harley's to be in his early fifties, Sue could be thirty-five or seventy. I don't even know if she's married because there are no feminine touches on her desk at all. No childish pictures from either children or grandchildren, no pictures of gap-tooth kids, no flourishes that mark her space as belonging to anything or anyone other than an organized secretary who is ready to handle any emergency. She was there when I got hired and I have always felt that she would be there when the newspaper moved to its next facility fifty years hence.

She wears her blond hair swept away from her face and there is just a hint of wrinkles around her eyes, a slight variation in texture that calling wrinkles is probably misleading. If you ask her, like I did once, if she's had plastic surgery, you would get the same answer I did. "And this information applies to your job how?" Classic Sue Cole. She's a beanpole and always has been unless that, too, is a matter of surgical precision. There will be a day in my future when pounds will be the enemy and I will fight them relentlessly and most likely lose. Sue will never have that problem. She has the ice cream luxury. Oh, you know. She can eat a quart of ice cream everyday for a year and never gain weight.

Dave walked into the office and nodded at her. "We're here to see Harley."

Harley's office was a glass cage. That's how I always saw it. Windows are most of his wall space. When Dave walked up to Sue, I was looking in the window and Harley was looking right back at me. He never winked, budged or made any effort to show that he recognized me but he did. I don't even know how Sue reacted or what she said to Dave. All I knew was that Dave approached the door with the reverence of an acolyte, opened it and we were in his presence.

Harley wears old-fashioned red suspenders and a bow tie. In the years I have known him, he has gained at least fifteen pounds and he was already fighting a weight problem. Well, he wasn't fighting it. He had already surrendered to it. His hair was black at one time but that was long before I met him. Most of it is gone and what remains is flecked with gray. His chin is strong and his neck is thick and meaty. He leaned back as we sat in front of him and said to Dave without so much as a preamble, "Dave." Then he looked at me and said, "Morgahna."

Underestimating Harley Hood is never in your best interest. I'd like to say it was time for a game face but I didn't think so. Newspapers

Chapter Sixteen

and the act of reading them are supposed to elicit a reaction. Passionless reporters are never remembered unless your name is Bob Woodward. Sorry, Bob, but you don't show your passion quite the way I'd like you to and that has always bothered me.

"Mr. Hood?" Dave said. "You seem to recognize Morgahna."

"I would recognize you if I was blind, lady," he said to me bluntly as he leaned back in his chair and put his hands behind his head.

"Want me to drop the pretenses, Harley?" I asked.

"Yep."

"I want my job back."

"Denied. What else you got?"

I crossed my legs and smiled. "A story."

"For which you will be paid like any other stringer if we publish it."

"I could go to the Trib, Harley."

The Savannah Tribune is a weekly newspaper that is owned by blacks and caters to their interests. They make a bit of money but are so minor league compared to the Morning News that it wasn't much of a threat and he knew it. "Go ahead," he said bluntly, blithely.

"The story involves blacks and a bit of racial homicide."

"Never heard that term before. Racial homicide."

"Hate crimes, Harley. Similar to one this newspaper passed on when it happened two years ago."

"You accusing me of a cover-up of some kind?"

"Arrogance, Harley. Blind arrogance. I walk into your office with someone else's face and you aren't even curious about how that happened."

He leaned forward, punched a button on his phone and said, "Sue?"

"Yes, sir."

"How much did you pay for your new face?"

"Five thousand dollars, sir."

"Thank you very much, Sue."

"You're welcome, sir."

I smiled. "Mine was free."

"Interesting conversation, Morgahna. Interesting but it isn't going anywhere."

"You could throw me out."

He hadn't and that was the whole idea. Like a vulture waiting to pick the bones of a carcass, he had all day when he needed it and no time at all when something wasn't going his way. The mere fact that he had made himself so damned comfy was a sign I had something he wanted. The only thing that editors want is copy, good copy. They don't care about personalities and how clever they are. They want all that white newsprint turned into copy, turned into stories that can win them Pulitzer Prizes. Harley never won that award and never stopped to think about it either. The consummate newspaperman, he was always angling for people who knew how to write and knew how to do it daily.

"Maybe I should," he said not moving.

"Did you kill a story about a woman named LaRuth Morrison?"

"Nope."

"Do you know who she is?"

"Nope."

"Then how do you know you didn't kill it."

He leaned forward. "Twenty-one questions, Morgahna? I don't have time for games."

"She was beaten to death with an iron pipe on November second not quite two years ago. Her brother saw her after the crime was committed and he said the only reason he knew it was there was a tattoo on her ankle. Almost ten weeks ago, I was taken out into the woods near Fort Stewart and almost beaten to death in the same manner. That's why I don't have to pay for a surgeon unless I want to put myself back the way

Chapter Sixteen

I used to look. Harley? If someone came to you with a story about a black woman being tied to a tree and beaten to death, what would you do?"

"Report it."

"Why didn't anyone report this, Harley?"

"Circumstances. We can't be everywhere."

I had him and I knew it. He knew it, too. Technically, all I had was his interest and not my job. He had a heinous crime on his hands and nothing in print. Harley Hood knew every story published by every reporter who worked for him or ever had. "She was hit at least fifty times with a metal pipe. Harley? Her obituary ran in this paper soon afterward. Her family paid for it. It's on your frigging website. How is that possible? The victim of a homicide that monstrous and all you have is her obituary and nothing about the crime or who committed it?"

"You're suggesting the willful withholding of news."

Ignoring him, I said, "Then yesterday morning her sister was found dead in her apartment with her boyfriend at the foot of her bed. Two homicides in one family?"

His face was still as immovable as a rock. "Practically the Kennedy's."

"Without all the power thrown in."

"How does this relate to you?"

"Evan was her lawyer."

"Her? Who?"

"The sister. Daydra is her name. Was her name."

"Put it together for me, Morgahna."

"No."

"You can't have your job back."

"I'll give it to the Tribune, Harley. They'll love a story that the mainstream media won't print and I'll be a competitor."

"They do flower shows, Morgahna."

I smiled again. "Just like I used to do, huh?"

"You aren't giving me anything."

"When I came back to town a few days ago, I went home, went to my place down on Taylor Street. Everything I own was taken out and nothing was left except the timbers. Even the wallboards and drywall were removed. Evan's partner has already admitted that it was done because he ordered it."

"They were looking for something."

Billy Ray said that as soon as he saw the place. "I had tenants downstairs living on the first level. I was told that they dealt drugs and that's why the interior of my home had been stripped. When I pointed out that the downstairs hadn't been stripped like the upstairs, I got nothing back. Those two people were not dealing drugs. They were students at SCAD." That was local slang for the Savannah College of Art and Design. SCAD for short.

"Students do drugs."

"Maybe so," I replied evenly. "I do not, however, believe they had anything to do with my home. Without further investigation, without going to SCAD and asking them where those two people are now living, I believe they merely moved from that place after my disappearance was called a homicide."

He stood and held his hands behind his back. The pose reminded me of Churchill. He was looking out at the department, at the cubicles beyond his window. He wiggled his fingers behind his back and the effect was one of deep restless thought. Without turning around, he said, "You still haven't said how this relates to you."

"I don't know."

"Conjecture?"

"Is another word for guess and that's bad policy."

"Smart-assed broad," he murmured.

"Take out the ass and you have a quite descriptive picture of me."

Chapter Sixteen

"Smart broad," he murmured. Then, still without looking at me or Dave, he said, "Wait here."

He left the office and just disappeared.

Dave had remained quiet the entire time and that was not by design. Dave might fear Harley Hood but he is a good reporter and he's been on a lot of assignments where information was the result of a barter or a negotiation a lot like this one had been. He recognized what I was doing and even recognized that Harley was a willing and witting partner to it. As soon as Harley left the room, he said, "What do you think?"

"I think it takes an awful big dog to weigh a ton."

Which only meant I was thinking and he knew it.

If Harley left the room, that meant he was going somewhere to talk with someone privately. An underling would have been ordered to his office and the discussion would be held here. Since Harley went elsewhere, that implied that he went *upstairs*. There are only three people in the news division that have a higher rank than he does. The executive editor is the person that makes the decision regarding the news division. The managing editor makes it work and the senior editor does all the planning for the daily news that gets printed. The senior editor is Nick Pruitt and he is Harley's direct superior. The managing editor is Francesca Wolf and hates to be called Fran. The executive editor is Joseph Blanchard and does not mind being called Joe *if* you know him. I have never called him anything but Mr. Blanchard.

If Harley was looking for advice, he would go to *his* superior and that was Pruitt. Nick had the power to do hiring, but then so did Harley. That meant something else was brewing and my best guess was that gelding reporter they hired in my place. That poor slob would get those interminable flower shows and city council meetings. To be absolutely precise about it, those two jobs are handled by two different people. Government and Business reporters handle city hall and Community News reporters handle flower shows. In the pecking order, both jobs go to bottom-feeders. I worked for a woman named Ana Monroe. She is the community news editor and I transferred from her department very early on when there was an opening. I discovered after my transfer was approved that such transfers are against company policy. You have to complete your probationary period before you can transfer. What struck me when it happened was I had to sign a legal agreement that basically extended my probationary period another ninety days into the future. I asked Evan if it was legal and he smiled and said, "Only if you accept it. All law is that way. Everything is legal until someone contests it."

All this means is that Harley Hood, that old bastard, liked me and figuratively climbed the stairs to take my battle to his superiors. That was my take on his absence from his own office and his command to, "Wait here."

"Do portraits of football players count?" Dave asked talking about his décor out loud but thinking about what had just happened.

"No," I answered the same way.

"Why?"

"Because they speak to you and not her. It's her you're trying to impress, not yourself."

"So, in order to get into her pants I have to think like a girl?"

"Forget it, then. If all you want is sex, you'll never get her back. Use your hand and stare at Michael Vick's picture."

"Who do you stare at?"

"Michael Vick."

"What the hell is going on, Morgahna?"

"I'm getting my job back."

"Really? That's cool."

"I don't want my job back."

"What? I thought that's why we were here?"

"Change of plans, big guy. Woods and Hamilton? That's what I want."

"They would have to promote both of us."

"Yep. Exactly."

"You gonna get me fired?"

"Probably. One day, anyway."

Chapter Sixteen

"Just don't be the other woman in my second divorce."

"I won't even be the woman in your second divorce."

"How do you spell 'premarital'?"

"Dave? You were always fun."

His smile was a small and almost invisible. "Have that engraved on my tombstone."

"Wow. You're getting a tombstone. I figured you for the marker type."

"Are you nervous?"

"I'm about to puke in Harley's garbage can," I said.

"You don't look like it."

"Neither do you."

"Well, the can is on your side. The fat man flying over you shoulder would be me."

"Noted. Never come between Dave and a garbage can."

"Can we talk about sex now?"

"No."

"Why?"

"Because I have no outlet."

He smiled. "I think I've been insulted."

"Let me be straight then. No."

"Can you talk about sex?"

"Yes."

"Will you?"

"No."

"Does this conversation count?"

"No."

"Why?"

"There has been no mention of either bodily fluids or body parts."

"So…"

And I stared at him hard. "David Woods. Stop it." Then I started giggling. "Oh, Dave," I said. "If this falls through? We still have to be friends because I miss your sense of humor."

He turned and looked over his shoulder at the door. "At least I have one."

"So, we're friends, right?"

Looking back, he said, "I don't know. Can we talk about sex now?"

"You need lessons?"

"Yeah, you going to give them?"

"Not to you."

We were both looking over our shoulders when we saw Harley coming back to his office in the company of Nick Pruitt. Neither was saying anything. I noticed many people glance up at them and then at us, at Dave and me. *Okay. What happens now?* I already had an answer for that.

They entered the office and neither of them sat down. Harley stood behind his desk, Nick beside him. It was Nick that spoke first. "You're lobbying for your old job back."

"I don't want my old job. I have a good story, I'm trained and I want to pursue it."

"You don't need to work for us to pursue it."

"The Tribune?"

"Is not a threat and don't try to use it as one."

"Why are you here, Nick?"

"To offer you your old job back."

"Harley doesn't need to consult with you to make that determination."

Chapter Sixteen

"He did."

"Harley is a good boss. There's another item on the table and you're hiding it."

"Your old job. Take it or leave it."

I stood and extended my hand to him. "Thank you for your time, Mr. Pruitt. I promised my mother I'd be in Jacksonville by five. I must leave."

He did not take my hand and said, "Harley asked you to form a conjecture about what happened to you and you refused. If I make it a condition of your employment with us, will you tell me?"

"No."

"Why?"

"Because that's crass yellow journalism and I won't do that. I'll write the story as a book and sell it to a publisher."

"You wouldn't be the first reporter to do something like that, to publish something entirely yellow."

"Granted, Mr. Pruitt. The difference between a good reporter and a bad one, however, is a good reporter will do his best to report the truth and will push herself to ensure anything that appears above the fold on the front page is more that just sensational."

I'd just told him what I expected from this and he knew it. The story was front-page above the headline. Nick has hair the color of used motor oil but at least it's styled. Maybe he works out, jogs. You know the type. Growing old and fighting it all the way. Me, in other words.

I sat back down and stared up at him. There was something else here and everyone in the room knew it. I looked up at Dave, patted his chair and said, "Have a seat, Dave."

He sat and looked at Pruitt. So did I.

Harley looked at Pruitt but Pruitt was looking at me as he sat down in Harley's chair and folded his hands on the desktop. "Mrs. Hamilton? This is all I can do for you. I can offer you your previous position with the company. The job comes with a new probationary period and you must report to Mr. Hood weekly and show him your notes."

"No. Sorry."

I didn't budge and neither did he.

"That's not negotiable."

"My husband was a lawyer and he taught me that everything is negotiable."

"This isn't."

"How about this? Dave is my partner on this and every other assignment we get. That means he gets a promotion and so do I. No probationary period because that's an admission on your part that you're going to fire me for some trumped up reason when this is over."

"That's ridiculous."

"Which part?"

"All of it. Mr. Woods has a position with the company which he will keep and continue to fill."

You never realize who your friends are until circumstances call for one of them to step up. Since, in my own opinion, I had no friends, I expected nothing. Dave took that moment to speak for the first time. "No, Mr. Pruitt. The Savannah Morning News is much more than a company. It's a responsibility we have with the public. If Mrs. Hamilton chooses to leave here unemployed, I will accompany her in that same state."

"You, Dave," Pruitt said. "You'd quit over her?"

"Yes, sir."

"You may have to. I'm not hiring her to be your partner."

I put my hand on his and said, "Don't, Dave. Nate needs you."

"Morgahna?" he said as he stared directly at Nick. "Mr. Pruitt is a busy man and has a human resources department that does these things. The only reason he's here is because this is personal to him in some way." Then he looked at Harley and said, "And to him, too. I have never been anything but a loyal company boy, never did anything to ruffle the bedcovers and now we have two editors in here trying to find a way to

Chapter Sixteen

hire you back on their terms. Why is that? Morgahna? I'd take a pay cut to work with you. I'd even listen to your stupid theories on interior design. And your speech about truth? They could start being truthful right now and just tell us what this is about."

That was strange. He enunciated my position exactly and furthermore, I knew it. To my knowledge, that had never happened before mainly because I wasn't interested in anyone's opinion but my own. It was possible Dave had been on my side all along but I rather doubted it. I can't say my demeanor was any different than it had ever been but my goals were. I don't think I ever ranted and raved about how I wanted things to be, just pushed forward with all my might and did things my way to the exclusion of everything and everyone else. While Dave's position was a bit startling, Harley's was positively baffling when he said, "Hire her, Nick. She'll do a good job."

Pruitt chewed on his lip and looked at me with the eyes of a man who was measuring things carefully. His eyes looked judgmental and full of hidden secrets. While that might sound melodramatic, it fairly summed up everything nicely. Of course, I didn't know it and in the end agreed to his terms when he said, "No promotion for either of you but you work on this together until this is over."

"Probation?"

"None."

"For either of us?"

"Neither of you."

"Twenty percent raise?"

"Four."

"Twelve."

"Eight."

"Done," I said.

Then we shook hands and I felt better about my life. Of course, I'd felt the same way about my life before Evan did that to himself. No, I still couldn't stand to say that word, that evil-sounding word that hints at so much weight upon frail human shoulders. It begged for help, begged

The Package

people to look closer than they do and no one did, not even his wife. I was getting closer to the reasons and there were more than just one of them. At the time, my empathy, sympathy and ability to see others and help them was drowned out by the glare of satisfaction. I'd gotten my way almost completely. Woods and Hamilton would have to wait, but we would be working together again, at least one last time.

I was going to learn what that meant.

One last time.

They used to say that, or a version of it, before the firing squad did its final job on you. Any last words? A cigarette? Anything but life? They used to say things like that. Now? There are no last words anymore.

None at all and I know words.

None that I knew could describe this, could describe what was coming.

And for someone, time itself was running out and that time would be on my shoulders almost exclusively.

Almost exclusively.

Almost.

Chapter Seventeen

We were as giddy as little kids on Christmas morning when we left the building. I was still carrying that awful purse Billy bought me but it was literally the only game in town so I had no choice. I slipped my new identification card into my wallet next to Todd Gilmartin's business card. I was back. Jeez, we even did a high-five in the parking lot and did a thing with our hands that was either Male Dirty or an expression of love. I didn't know and Dave never said only because we were both so damned happy.

"An eight percent raise," he said, his black face shining like an eight ball under harsh light.

Jeez, it was sweet. "I woulda held out for ten, but I had to use the bathroom," I said happily.

"I hate to rain on your parade but we need to go see LaRuth's mother. You said you knew where she worked."

That's why I liked Dave. He kept my focus straight and my goals on track. So, even though I felt pretty good, he was right. Depending on LaRuth and LeRay's mother, I might be late to my Mom's house but I had to do this. When I explained everything to him, he thought about it and came up with that item and called it, "Important, Morgahna. She might be able to tell us what the police are thinking about all this. If Daydra is her mother, then we have to talk to her."

Following an evidentiary trail is not something I should be neglecting and with Dave's gentle prodding, I wasn't going to either. "Right. Let's go talk to her."

"Morgahna? We're employees now. We need to take better notes than we have been. You agree?"

"Yeah. You play secretary to my high-charging bitchy female executive."

"Do I have to sit in your lap, too?"

"That will be the day."

Chapter Seventeen

We pulled away from the parking lot and Dave said, "Are you really okay?"

"I feel okay. Why?"

"You're really different. If I didn't hear your voice coming from that face, I'd be suspicious."

He'd been saying that and stuff like it ever since last night and I believe I knew why. He was used to the old me, the one that seldom joked and never smelled the flowers. I was worse than taciturn. I was positively barren of any touches of random humanity. If you got a compliment from me, it came from the cynical part of my brain and not from the heart where such things should originate. "Dave? How's this then? I'm going back to your place, then to see LaRuth's mother. You need your laptop because this is officially an assignment now."

"That's the pain-in-ass I remember," he said smiling at me.

We talked about the story all the way to his place and didn't make a real dent in it anywhere. He turned it on as we drove and started making notes. As he entered data both factual and theoretical, it gave me time to think. LeRay took me to his mother's place to talk. He could have taken me anywhere but he took me there. I was beginning to suspect he wanted me to meet her, wanted her to get just a little larger than life so that she would stand out from the crowd.

"You smile more than I remember," he said suddenly.

"Yeah," I said quietly. "My life seemed pretty shallow, Dave. Calculating, I mean. Ever since I came back from that cabin out near Fort Stewart, I've been thinking about why this happened and I still think it's my fault."

"That could cloud your judgment."

I nodded, bit my lip and said, "Yeah. I know. Dave? You may have to slap me to keep me in line." Then I smiled and added, "Metaphorically speaking, of course."

"You mean I can't actually slap you?"

Still smiling, I said, "I'd much rather you didn't."

The Package

The neighborhood down where LaRuth's mother ran that burger stand is almost entirely black. I felt nervously conspicuous even with Dave being there. I parked along the curb in front of the building and fully expected to see LeRay inside working at some menial chore. He wasn't there and I worried about him. His mother was there with that same black cook and they were talking as he flipped a few burgers. I wondered why she didn't serve barbecue since it *was* the south and this *was* Savannah.

There were a few people eating burgers and sucking on shakes and such, their numbers no better than the last time I was here. With Dave trailing behind me, his laptop hanging from its case in his right hand, I approached the counter, held out my ID from the newspaper and introduced myself to her. "Ma'am? My name is Morgahna Hamilton and I'd like to talk to you. I work for The Morning News. Do you have a moment?"

I've approached a lot people, *a lot* people, with that line in the last few years. I've gotten responses that ranged from sudden joy to outright hostility when I identify myself. When she neither smiled nor sneered, I wondered about LeRay. The way my brain processed that scene was in his favor because it seemed she wanted to yell at me and tell me to get lost but didn't. LeRay could be the only reason that happened. I don't presume to understand the black ethic or whatever it is because my own ethic, my own life, was always so much more important than anyone else's. Her face seemed to firm up, seemed ready to snarl given the first reason when she said, "I got a bit of time. Sure. Go ahead and talk."

"Your daughter was murdered yesterday morning," I said and then watched her face. She seemed sad and that was understood. There was more, though. If I had to guess, I'd say it was expected. "The police have talked to you?"

"Yeah."

"And you're still here?"

"A person has to work."

"Did you mourn LaRuth like this?"

She came so close to losing her temper with me, so close but didn't. Again, I think that was LeRay's doing. For some reason, he paved the way for me. Otherwise, I do not believe she would have talked to me

Chapter Seventeen

at all. Instead of anger, she broke down and started to cry. Turning away from me, she walked toward the back of the restaurant and stood just inside a door that led to the back of the building, her face in her hands, her entire body quaking as she cried. I looked at the cook, then nodded toward her and asked, "Can I?" He nodded but said nothing. Dave was still behind me and that always gave me a sense of security even though I have no idea how he would respond to a fight.

I've seen that singular black reaction to such things; I've seen the screaming and shaking, heard the wails and saw the tears. Maybe she did that once, maybe she didn't. She looked as though she wanted to scream and do all those things, however. What she did, what she managed, was subdued and quieter than I expected. Look, I'm not trying to be racist. I'm just trying to be straightforward. I've seen those funerals and watched those scenes as though they were middle eastern ones instead of funerals being held in twenty-first century America.

"Ma'am? Two daughters? Both murder victims? What happened to LaRuth? Can you talk about it?"

She was standing next to a cart full of hamburger buns and other bread. I kept expecting that flashpoint, that pain that turns into anger because I'd felt it and turned it inward on myself as others tried merely to talk to me and help me. I treated them horribly and might have succeeded in killing myself had Tony and Doug not tried. Had I been here in this position, in this place five months ago, I would have reacted much differently to her. I would have pushed her and not cared that my questions and the way I asked them were causing old wounds to fester. Now, I merely added, "Ma'am? I sympathize because what happened to LaRuth happened to me. The only difference is that I did not die."

Dave reached into his back pocket and withdrew his wallet. Flipping through old pictures, he found the one he wanted and showed it to her. "Ma'am? This is what Morgahna used to look like. Imagine how bad you would feel if you woke one day and the face you saw in the mirror wasn't the one you remembered. That's what happened to her and I can only assume that these two crimes are connected somehow. Please, tell us what you know."

Circumstances and life push us in directions we never anticipated. I am proof of that. I tried with every waking moment to push my life in the direction I wanted it to go. Then all those things that happen just off stage, just out of our sight, began to drag me in their wake and I am still struggling to pull myself out of it. Should I assume that blacks have a much different view of life? Would that be fair? Look, I don't know. Do they live expecting things to happen to them? Possibly. Such things never occurred to me before and I was born in Savannah, a southerner by birth. What I knew, what I felt I knew anyway, was partially just that. As a white woman living in a place where enslaving human beings was once legal, I was never sensitive to their feelings, their emotions or more importantly, their expectations. What do black mothers tell their children? Beware of white people? Are their nightmares full of whites and that color instead of the colors of white nightmares?

We are told that money will set us free. We aren't told that in those terms but we expect money to cure everything else. We expect money to raise us above the level of the personal. With enough money, we hire people to keep us separated from life and from its harsher realities. This woman whose name I did not know, was awash in those realities and perhaps drowning in them.

She's a big woman, hefty but not fat. Had Dave not been there, maybe things would have been different but I don't think so. She looked briefly at Dave then looked at me with bloodshot eyes and said, "She was so beautiful."

"LaRuth?" I queried.

"Yes," she said mournfully.

"What happened to her baby?" I asked because I knew and remembered him from the first time I'd been there. I asked for no other reason than politeness. A small part of me expected her to reassure me that she had the boy.

Across the hallway was an office, a small one. With the eyes of a person who was lost in the desert, she entered it, looked at the wall behind the desk and just cried and shook. I put my hand on her shoulder and had absolutely no expectations for her reaction. She could have done anything from outright violence at me for having touched her to passive acceptance. What she did surprised me. She turned and cried on me, on my shoulder, on *my* shoulder. Has that ever happened to you? Has anyone ever cried on your shoulder? It bestows upon you a responsibility that

Chapter Seventeen

changes you just slightly. That is, if you listen. With all my heart, all my soul, I wanted to push her away from me and just ask all those far too personal questions. I did not do that, though. I put my arms around her shoulders slowly and almost fearfully. She was old enough to be my mother and I can't imagine doing this for her or having to do it either.

"Artemis is gone," she cried with an accent so thick I almost didn't understand her. "He's gone and so is his momma and his auntie and now my boy is missing."

"LeRay is missing?"

She stood on wobbly legs, wiped tears from her eyes and said, "Yes. I gave him my car and he's been gone with it since last night."

I guided her behind the desk only because the only chair in the room was behind it. She fell into it and sagged. I can't describe it any better than that. She just sagged as though gravity had finally won.

"He hasn't called you?"

She shook her head slowly, her eyes riveted on me as tears rolled down her face. I imagined my own mother feeling this way, looking like this when she thought I was dead. I was seeing *her* performance, seeing *her* tears and it much better prepared me for when I saw her later that day.

I moved to her side and knelt next to her. "I don't even know your name, ma'am. Mine is Morgahna."

"Alease," she said. "Alease Morrison," she repeated with dead eyes. "They was twins," she said. "You know that? Not identical but fraternal. Still, they always acted like they were identical. I'd dress them different and they'd show up dressed the same. They loved each other more and more everyday and when she died, he took it hard."

"Can you tell me what happened? Can you tell me what the police said to you?"

I dimly heard Dave tapping on the keyboard of his laptop. He was doing his job and I didn't have to worry about him. That much was still there between us. I can't say I never took him for granted but I suppose I did. The big difference between then and now was knowledge and a bit of compassion. I needed to be more verbal with him, needed to tell him that I appreciated his work. I always did but always knew that someday we'd part company for entirely professional reasons and I'd never think of him again. Now? Even if life pushed us apart, I wanted to remain friends, contacts, wanted to be able to have lunch with him and just talk. Okay, a part of me was lonely for companionship but that's not his fault. He didn't force me to be the way I was. If his life got pushed into Merriam's orbit again and he had no time for me, I could live with that. I wouldn't like it, but I would live with it.

Alease looked full of old pain and memories that grated against her life. Tears coursed down her dark cheeks as she said, "She met someone. She was so happy and so alive."

"She met a man?"

She smiled. "Yes. I didn't see her for a long time because she was in New York City and working there, working on her career. I knew she was pregnant and worried that it would interfere with things. I can remember her words. 'Oh, momma. I'm going to have my baby and take care proper care of it. It's a baby, not a curse.' Just like that. She never told me who the father was and I worried about that. A baby needs a father. That's how I feel even though my kids don't have one. Lamar died years ago, an overdose. That man, whoever he was, was worse than Lamar. He just left."

Almost as though a voice whispered in my ear, it became obvious. "She came to Savannah to show you her baby."

It was too much, those old memories. She put her face in her hands and cried again. When she was okay enough to talk, she said, "LeRay wouldn't let me see her body. He said it was too awful. He wanted me to remember her the way she was and not the way she died."

That news stopped me and I looked up at Dave. No, it wasn't as though the story suddenly wrote itself, just that the issue, whatever it was, resided here in Savannah and not somewhere else. "Alease?" I asked gently. "Did she come here to Savannah often? Did she get pregnant here?"

"That's what I thought, that she got pregnant here and then went back to New York City."

Chapter Seventeen

Then LaRuth came here not just to show the baby to her mother, but to the father as well. Is that what killed her? "Did she ever mention the father?"

She shook her head slowly and said sadly, "No."

There was a connection here somewhere, something that connected LaRuth Morrison to me. Whatever it was, I couldn't see it and by the look on Dave's face, neither did he. "What did the police tell you?"

She sneered and said, "The po-lice. They're always talking about evidence and proof. All they said that made any sense was nothing at all. They ain't even looking for her killer. You want my opinion, white lady? One of you did this. If a brother killed her, then they would be all over this. A black man kills a black woman and everyone knows about it. A black man kills a white woman and it's the same. A white man kills a black girl and no one knows. You want justice? You go find yourself a white man."

It was as cynical as I expected but maybe even true. I had absolutely no experience with investigations into homicide, none at all. I'd been a reporter, though, for long enough to withhold judgment until I had some sort of proof. If this was my introduction, my stepping stone to a job that made more sense than city council meetings did, then I had to step carefully.

Was there anything else I could ask? Any more questions that might lead somewhere? I took the time to consider everything carefully and came up with, "Did she see any old friends while in town? Do you think she talked with anyone while she was here?"

She began to apologize. "I'm sorry for what I said. I had no call to talk like that. I just lost my second daughter and the police called it a drug hit." Her face fell into her lap and she said, "It might even be that way. I don't know."

"Daydra used drugs?"

"Like they was aspirins. Lord knows LeRay tried to talk to her about them but she never listened. She was willful and paid the price for her pride." She smiled but it was full of ironic pain. "You met her. LeRay said as much. Would you want to be her friend?"

All I could say was, "I don't know. I didn't know her very well. Maybe she had sides to her personality that were okay."

It was possible, I saw, that her death was drug-related. That would eliminate any evidence that could be left on the body. If the killer did not sleep with her but instead gave her drugs that killed her, then he could very easily be invisible. The man at the scene, Frank Walker, probably had a record. While I didn't know for certain, it was a fair assumption to make. I am, however, a product of my culture. I knew of forensic science and that a crime like the one that killed him would leave trace evidence. What types, I did not know but considering the timing of their deaths, the killer knew we were coming and had to eliminate them as quickly as possible. Maybe he made mistakes; maybe he made assumptions that weren't warranted. He wouldn't be the first murderer to underestimate the power of science to find killers. Television is full stories of their prowess and dedication. All I know is that if anyone of them are as dedicated as I am, then the killer has no chance. Of course, the offside of that is me. I may not survive to talk about it. I may be his next victim.

"That boy is all I got left," she said with dead eyes. "I don't even know what he's doing or where he is, lady."

"LeRay seems smart, Alease. He seems to have common sense. That might be enough."

"LaRuth had sense, too. You want my opinion of what happened and why?"

"Yes, I would."

"I think the only reason she came back here was to talk to Artemis' father. She was struggling to live and having that baby must have been hard. I think she came back here to talk about child support. It's possible she talked to the father and that's what killed her."

"You have any proof of that? Anything like diaries, records, maybe phone records. Anything?"

She shook her head sadly and said, "No."

"Would she have spoken to Daydra about this?"

She shrugged. "Don't know. Maybe. My opinion is no. They weren't close like her and LeRay was. Still, maybe."

Chapter Seventeen

"So, it's possible the police found something in her apartment that might link them?"

"Maybe. Don't bet on it. If Daydra had anything on her sister, she would have told LeRay and I don't think that boy knows much about what happened to either of them."

It didn't feel like I was getting anything from her. Time would tell, though, That was usually how things worked. If you turned over enough rocks, you eventually uncovered something that went somewhere. To this point in my career, those rocks were never very big nor did they cover much. Still, I savored every single story, every single assignment and did so much homework that it still astounds me. I can remember listening to Evan snore as I worked on my laptop chasing down *anything*. When I was first hired? I actually spent two hours researching a particular type of rose for a flower show I covered at the fair grounds. Another time, I had to write a short biography of a man who was going to be highlighted on our community pages. He was quite a hero in both Vietnam and Korea and I wanted to know as much about him as possible before I visited him. No, work was never a problem nor was focus. I could always do both to exclusion of everything else. My condition, my physical condition, deems a note, though.

Dave has already commented on that condition but I never had to worry about it before. Now? Sure, I didn't sleep well or very long last night, but that had happened so many times in my life that I entirely discounted weariness. This, though, was different. I *felt* weary and couldn't shake the feeling of it by the simplest tasks available to me, namely just by moving around. All of which meant I could very easily make a mistake and never get to the bottom of whatever was trying to kill me. That was still the one thing pushing at me with the greatest force. Self-preservation usually is.

I looked up at Dave and said, "You got any business cards?"

"Yeah."

"Give her one."

His laptop sat on top of file cabinet just inside the door. He finished another note on it and then fished for his wallet again. Once he had it, he took a card from an inside pocket and handed it to Alease.

She took it and reads his name. "Dave Woods. I read your stuff."

He smiled and said, "I promise to try better, ma'am."

"You write real good, Mr. Woods."

"Thank you."

"Call him if you hear anything or can think of anything, okay?" I said as she fingered the card.

"I will."

As we stood to leave, she looked at me and said, "This is about you, too."

"I know. "

"He'll tie you to that tree again and next time won't leave you alive. Girl? You're too pretty for that to happen to you. Leave town before whatever happened to my girls, happens to you."

In all this time, for all these months, I have never lost nor taken off my wedding ring. Why? Well, most likely – and because I have no other explanation - I have not grieved enough nor allowed myself to declare Evan finally among the dead. Should I take her advice and simply slip away somewhere, it would be an admission I was not prepared to make. I fingered the ring on my finger and wondered if I would ever be able to take her advice. I wondered if I would ever be able to remove it either. As I fingered it, just rolled it around and around on my finger, I said quietly to her, "I have to stay and figure out what happened. Why me? Why did this happen to me? Part of this is my husband. I don't know why but it would be an admission that I never loved him and I did. I need to know what happened to us and if that means risking myself to find those answers, then that's what I'll do."

"My heart will never be the same, girl. It will bleed for the rest of my life. I buried two daughters and now my son is missing, too. The devil don't care and he won't rest until his trouble is done."

"The devil might not care, ma'am, but I do. I cannot run away and pretend my husband just got tired one day and decided to play with a gun. I have to find out why all this happened. I truly apologize if anything I

Chapter Seventeen

ever did hurt your girls. Call it a lesson I learned too late, but I will never be that person again."

"I'll pray for you."

She wasn't the first person ever to say that to me. She probably won't be the last especially if that killer finds me because then I'll pray for myself. Still, I do not believe in divine intervention, not in stuff this trivial. God would most likely just as soon have my soul as not. I believe He put us here to do our best and whatever we do comes down on us and not Him. Her sentiment seemed heartfelt, though, so I knelt next to her and hugged her. "Alease? When I find out what all this is about, I'll come back and tell you. I'll make sure you understand at least as well as I do."

We left into the warm Savannah afternoon and I felt even more weary than I had. A large part of that was simple empathy with Alease Morrison. She's lost two daughters and doesn't know why. Now, her son is missing and she's more alone than ever. I'd like to say that we shared a common bond but she has lost far more than me.

We usually review our notes after we interview someone for a story. Often we see different things and we need to reconcile them. If Dave gave in to me because I was the story, then it added *another* level of complexity we didn't need. "What did you think?" I asked hesitantly.

"She told us everything she knew."

"Did I ask everything?"

"Of course not."

"What did I miss?"

"You won't know until it's both too late and too obvious."

I considered his answer and nodded without replying. Then, "Should we go back inside and ask more questions?"

"No. She would see it as intrusive and we wouldn't learn anything."

"Should we ask about friends of hers, of Daydra's? We could snoop into her life and maybe discover she had enemies that had nothing to do with me," I asked pointedly.

"You're saying Daydra's death was a coincidence. Is it? Was it?"

That was an excellent question and not one either of us had ever asked the other. In my own work, that done without him, I'd seen a few coincidences. They did happen and I saw a few even though no one ever counted on them. Was it wise to count Daydra's death among them? "I need your opinion here, Dave. Do you want to start asking around about him and her?"

He tapped his fingers on the laptop console and he looked preoccupied. "It's either your mother or Walker."

"Yeah."

"You willing to pass on your mother to do this if we decide it's necessary?"

No, I wasn't. I needed to see her and needed her badly. Maybe she needed me, too. I put my hands on the steering wheel and said, "You want to talk to Walker's family."

"Yeah. I think it needs to be done."

"Okay," I said feeling so utterly vulnerable that I felt naked. I stared through the windshield, my hands wrapped tightly around the steering wheel. I couldn't look at him and didn't really understand why. The longer I stared, the more the reason began to coalesce into something recognizable. He was betraying me because he *knew*. He knew I needed to see her and was willing to push me into something I really didn't want to do. I closed my eyes and tried to see a way past the problem and just couldn't. Those woods, that meeting with Tommy, Nick Pruitt's strange introduction into the story, all those things mashed together into one huge and horribly repulsive picture and I couldn't do it. I couldn't agree to it and it had nothing to do with my urge to do things my way. I wasn't even being a girl's girl. I was being a very vulnerable human being that needed the security of someone I trusted completely and implicitly and he knew it.

He got out of the Explorer, walked around to my side as I slowly began to melt, opened the door and said, "Out. I'm driving."

"Dave," I said looking out and up at him. "I can't."

"I know. That's why I'm driving."

Chapter Seventeen

"What?" I said as tears slid down my face.

"Morgahna? I want to talk to Frank Walker more than I want my wife back. You know that? Does he know anything? We won't know until we poke around. But you? You're pushing yourself, you're probably in more pain than I will ever know and this isn't much to give. Let me drive. You just tell me where she lives and how to get there."

"You're pretending I'm Merriam?" I said trying to put some light back into the day.

"Yeah," he said smiling. "She's a bitch and so are you. You seem to handle it okay. Maybe she will, too."

I wiped the last few stray tears away and said, "Don't count on it."

"I won't," he said.

Maybe we were both learning.

That would help because things were getting closer to flashpoint.

Much closer.

Chapter Eighteen

"Dave? I've never asked her for anything. I got a scholarship for college. I never needed anything from her." Yeah, I was babbling because that was highest order of nonsense that ever escaped my mouth.

Dave just smiled as we pulled into their driveway.

I don't know what sort of relationship men have with their mothers. Maybe that's something I need to talk to Mark about. Maybe they don't need mothers, just fathers. Maybe I've been delusional all my life, too. I know that I've had no relationship with my mother at all and I mean that literally. I never call her, never invite her for lunch or dinner, never share stories on the phone with her, never go shopping with her. As bad as all that sounds, I haven't spoken to my father in over a year and it isn't because we share a common antipathy. I just don't see him and never think about him.

Naturally, Mom was out the door before I was even out of the car and had me in her arms crying and wailing as I stood likewise in hers. As I cried, I said, "Mom? I love you."

"Oh, baby, baby, baby," she cried. "I thought you were dead. Oh, my good god. I thought you were dead."

I was easily as emotional as I was at Evan's funeral. I know I haven't talked about it, but maybe I should. To say I was in shock would be an understatement. It took seeing his body to make me believe he was really dead. I mean when they put him in a casket and readied him for burial. It was a closed casket only because the back of his head was missing from the gunshot. As ugly as that sounds, I demanded to see his body and I was entirely sorry I did. I believe he planned his exit for long enough to know *exactly* how to do it without leaving himself both alive and a vegetable. He angled the gun just right and simply obliterated everything that enables a human being to live, exist and think. The exit wound was predictably huge and I fainted when I saw it and him. That was the price I paid for my insistent arrogance. I still see it, still see the

Chapter Eighteen

wound that blasted him out of my life. Am I sorry? I have no words for how sorry I am for ranting and demanding "the widow's rights". That's exactly how I phrased it. I had rights and I wanted to exercise them. Sometimes we get exactly what we asked for and I did. I got to see him, got to see how fragile we are, how thin the line of human life really is and how easily it is erased. If any good came from that horrible night, the only thing I can see is that it pushed me closer to my mother. Otherwise, it is probable that I would see her so seldom as to make every meeting awkward.

My father's name is Phillip, Phil Parker. He was there when we walked into the living room. He slipped from Mom's arms and I hugged him. He hugged back and that was all I knew. That simple act of hugging him happened so infrequently in my life that I had no way to judge his response. Actually, I didn't care. He hugged back and that was enough. "I love you, Daddy," I sniffled.

"I love you very much, Morgahna," he said calmly.

That's how I heard it and I have to admit it bothered me a little. He thought I was dead and yet he remained calm about my sudden revival. I clamped my eyes shut and decided to take what he gave me and left it at that.

Mom was delirious though. Practically jumping up and down, she grabbed me again and hugged me. "Welcome home, baby," she said. "You need a good dinner."

"I need pizza, mom."

"Okay," she said in an untypical surrender.

We spent the next hour eating pepperoni pizza and winding down. I told them as little as possible for no other reason than to protect them. Dave was his affable self and he talked to dad about men stuff. I don't even know what that means. What is "men stuff"? Well, whatever it is, they talked and held each other's interest right up until Mom looked at Dad and said, "Okay, Phil. She's all yours."

We'd been talking about Mark when suddenly she just smiled widely and said that. What did it mean? Well, I was about to find out.

The Package

"Can you come out to the garage with me, Morgahna?" he asked gently.

"Sure," I said. "What's up?"

"Just stuff I need to say, that's all."

I got up, hugged Mom again and wondered what was going on, especially after Dad said to Dave, "Just us, okay?"

"Sure," he said. "I'll be in here with your wife."

"That would be fine."

Mom and Dad are essentially the same height and he is why Mom doesn't wear higher heels than she does. He's stocky but will probably never be fat only because he has been so active all of his life. He loves fishing and has even hunted a few times in Louisiana with Mark. He taught Mark all about guns and never got around to me for the simple reason that I was never interested in guns and hunting. I wouldn't even go target practice shooting when we were kids.

We walked through the kitchen, through Mom's world and out the back door toward Dad's. I always thought he had every tool known to mankind in his workshop. We grew up in Savannah and our home was as small as my dreams were big. They moved to Jacksonville after I started college only so Dad could have a larger workshop.

The garage is detached from the house and was originally a two-car setup. They expanded it out behind the house and that room became his workshop. Easily as large as the original garage, Dad seems to have found his niche and it isn't construction. He makes furniture, stuff made to order and was working on a table and chairs for someone. It's gorgeous but I have no idea what is involved in the creation of furniture. I'm sure he uses a hammer but that's about my only guess. "Please, sit," he said indicating a chair at a table in the corner. I could see clients sitting here looking at plans and drawings. Every tool he owned seemed to be on display somewhere. Mostly, though, what I saw was order. The entire shop was clean and I remember him always keeping it that way.

I sat at the table, the entire shop spreading out to my left. He sat opposite me. Behind him was a desk, cabinets above it and a terminal in

Chapter Eighteen

the corner of the desktop. Dad probably knew more about computers than I did and I'm not sorry for that admission.

"Coffee?" he asked.

"No, Dad. I'm fine."

Anything I ever needed to know about life came from my mother. Dad paid more attention to Mark than to me but the opposite was also true. I got a mother and Mark got a father. What was he up to? Why were we here and not back in the house? And why did Mom put it that way? She's all yours?

He clasped his hands in front of him and said, "Do you remember when your Aunt Laura died?"

"Yeah," I said. "Why?"

My Aunt Laura died when I sixteen. Dad's sister, she was a district manager for an insurance company in Savannah. She contracted lung cancer and died from it ten years ago, almost eleven. I thought the point of bringing her up now was her age. She was forty-three when she died. I remember that distinctly because I computed her age off the funeral announcement. The way I saw this going, he was going to give me a speech about dying young, about Evan dying young like his sister did. I appreciated the thought but didn't think I needed it.

That's not what happened.

"She left an estate large enough to finance this workshop and all the tools in it. She made it possible for me to do something I've wanted to do and I am very grateful to her and I will never speak ill of her."

"I liked her, Dad. She was cool."

Married and divorced twice by forty, she had no kids and her estate went to my father. True, anything Dad gets is half Mom's but it doesn't have to be legal for that to be true anyway. That mere fact of that workshop was a testimony to Mom's diplomatic skills. Allowing Dad to build that workshop with money left to him by his sister was both gracious and genius.

"She had a lawyer that handled her estate and he did a good job."

Dad has a face like a football helmet, namely devoid of anything of interest. A long narrow nose, thin lips – thank you God for giving me Mom's beautiful mouth – dark hair that's almost black but not quite, powerful shoulders and strong hands.

"Well, that seemed reasonable. Given your workshop, I'd say he did a good job."

He sighed and said, "He works for a firm in Savannah. Seigler, Barrows and Thomas. Those three are the partners and Harold Thomas is the youngest of them and he's fifty-three."

I knew of them but only by name. "Okay?" I said shrugging my shoulders. "Aunt Laura had good lawyers."

He nodded but kept his face on the table in front of me.

"Harold and me have known each other for almost forty years. When Laura needed to make some decisions because her condition was not going to improve, I took her to him and everything went well. I'd much rather have my sister than the tools she bought me, but that's life. I don't like it but I accept it."

"That seems reasonable."

His face came up and it held a power I seldom saw. "Your name came up between us."

"Mine?"

"To be precise, Evan's."

My skin started to tingle and that feeling spread to my face. "Um, why?" I asked quietly, softly as though I was walking through a minefield.

"Morgahna?" he asked. "Are you strong enough to talk about this? I will be entirely understanding if you cannot. I have no desire to upset you. I know what has happened to you only because your mother told me the story. If all that is true, then there are parts you never divulged and I fully understand why that would be. You're trying to protect us and I thank you for that. Are you strong enough to talk about this?"

I have been given secrets before. Sure, low-level ones but a secret still feels that way. If you make enough friends in those interminable

Chapter Eighteen

council meetings, you get fed stuff on a fairly regular basis. The key, I believe, is conduct. If someone gives you a piece of information that no one else has and that person knows you can easily print it the next day, then you have a chance to mine further into that mother lode only if you resist the newsman's temptation to print whatever he is given. I have speaking relationships with three council members only for that reason. Each of them needed a friend in the media and I was always smart enough to realize that. Still, the temptation to print those minor secrets was extraordinary. That first secret was special and this felt like that.

"What, dad? What's up?"

He didn't smile and didn't reach out for me. He remained steadfastly calm and said, "Just tell me. Can you talk about Evan or should I wait for another time?"

That feeling crossed my face again and settled in my stomach. I stared at him for the first time in my entire life, stared because he was sealing himself off from me and demanding an answer that was mine and not one influenced by him. I wanted to say no and just runaway. It would be so much easier than telling him I was strong enough to do this, to talk about my husband. A part of me was already gone. What was left was stark naked fear that left me speechless for a few moments. If he had eyes, he already knew the answer. The fact that he hadn't folded his hand and surrendered to me was a multi-fold answer. On the one hand, he knew I was still grieving but on the other he needed to talk to me. There were so many other variations of those same positions that they began to fill me with dread. I fumbled. "I don't know, Dad. Why?"

"Do you remember Richard Blessfield?"

I smiled. "Oh, god, yes."

"Your first boyfriend. Your mother and I did not like him and forbade you from seeing him. You saw him anyway and then dropped him a few weeks later. Why was that so easy while this causes you angst that I haven't seen since you were a little girl?"

"I'm older. I was a kid then, Dad."

"You're an adult and you can only hide behind pain and femininity for so long. If you cannot talk about him, then say so."

"Will you lose respect for me?"

"Absolutely."

That wasn't just blunt but cruel as well. "I can't mourn? Is that so wrong?" My voice was raised a little, piqued a little.

"All I asked was if you are able to discuss Evan. You can mourn his death endlessly if you must."

"This seems cruel, Dad. Why are you doing this?"

"Why can't you just give me an answer?"

"Isn't this an answer?"

"This isn't worthy of you, Morgahna. You have more balls than the entire family put together. You do what you want and don't give a holy fuck about anyone but yourself. You were always that way and now I see a girl where a woman used to sit. Morgahna Hamilton? I have had nothing but respect for you ever since you got married. Hell, even before that. You could grow a dick a foot long and it wouldn't surprise me at all. Nothing is above you but sky."

"I'm as human as you, Dad," I said hotly.

"You're as human as you wish to appear, Morgahna. Can you talk about your dead husband or is this simply a way to get out of a situation that will profit you nothing at all?"

That entire conversation taught me a lot about him. Mom swooned around him and always had. They would be arguing about something Mom wanted and Dad would say something in her ear and her face would turn red and she would yield whatever point she was arguing about. Most of the time, he gave it to her anyway and I never understood it. This, though, was something I understood and understood all too well.

This was about power.

What was about to descend on me was an avalanche that swept away my mother in the years before they married. My father respected me because I had a sense of it, of power and how to use it. The things he wanted to talk about were going to require an effort to withstand and that's what I saw. He was trying to prepare me for something I might not want to hear. In effect, he was saying that he would yield to me, too, if I

Chapter Eighteen

found the needed strength missing. With God as my witness, I wasn't going to be beaten by a *man* even if he was my father.

"Very good, Dad. What do you have?"

"Answer the damn question."

"Yes. I am strong enough to talk about my husband."

"You're going to assume this about you. It isn't. Don't make that stupid mistake."

I smiled at him and said, "Daddy? Everything is about me. You taught me that every time you made Mom blush."

He leaned back in his chair and said, "Interesting."

"Why? Why this, Dad? Why now?"

"Evan was a thief," he said bluntly and to my face without so much as a preamble.

That tingling feeling crossed my face again and I had to remain silent to combat it. When I was sure I could contain my outrage, I said, "Explain that."

I will always remember that conversation and that particular point in it as the time my father pulled his punch. With Mom? Probably never. I learned there are winners and losers, but also leaders and led. Mom *loved* being led but only by him because he would never hurt her. No, I'm not referring to kinky sexual games where pain is momentary and the thrill is short-lived. I'm talking about following someone for love, for dedication, for hope, for strength, for companionship, for the insatiable desires that return again and again, for dignity, for self-respect, for love and commitment and for the knowledge that this man, this human being is so deeply embedded in her soul that seeing one without the other is nothing more than a cruel joke. With me? He taught me compassion and forgiveness, two things that would turn the entire story sideways.

He stood and moved back to his desk, opened the bottom right drawer and opened a file folder within it. He took a file, an envelope actually, then turned and put it on the table in front of him. "Morgahna? You look me in the eyes and tell me you're strong enough to do this."

"Evan made love to me once and despite everything I felt, the hotness, the heat, the intense longing to explode, I merely lay there and smiled benignly. Why? I wanted a new car and he said we couldn't afford it."

"What color was it?"

"Black. That was my Z3."

He tapped his fingers on the envelope as though considering my words. That occasion happened *exactly* that way. I wanted that car and he wanted to deflect my attention from it. At the time, it did not seem to be a measure of my power over him. It seemed nothing more than a sexual tantrum, a way to turn the tables on a man both bigger and bulkier than me, a way to win and get that car.

"This isn't a car. This is truth. This isn't something you can bend to your will. This simply is and must be accepted that way."

"You're saying Evan came here to see you."

"Yes."

"When?" I asked out of curiosity and nothing more.

"About three months before he died. He made certain I was the only one here when we talked."

"What was the subject?"

"This envelope," he answered tapping it with his fingers.

"And he convinced you he was a thief?"

"No. I already suspected."

"How and why?" I asked because this was getting disturbing.

Maybe I should stop and regroup. God knows I needed something, some sort of a break.

I was completely on pins and needles when we came to see my mother. That much I have already related. I expected my mother to give me enough money to survive for a few days in a motel somewhere. That's what all this was about. Yes, I could have stayed with Debbie and that is something she will hold over my head for years to come if I survive this. Oh, not seriously. She'll hand me a lunch check and say something

Chapter Eighteen

flippant like, "Here. This will help repay for your disrespect." I'll pay it, too. I'll be a better friend and we'll talk about things I never found time for before.

This, though, was frightening despite how my father approached the subject. Maybe he saw me that way, saw me as a nascent bitch who simply needed unwrapping. Maybe he saw me as wanting power and decided to show me how it's wielded. Maybe he loves me and this was its manifestation. Maybe when I reached out for his hand and he took it, he saw the girl was still there and needed some parental affection. Thank you, Dad, for noticing it.

"Are you sure, baby? We can do this some other time."

"Dad? You know what's happening. You also suspect that if you don't do this, then I might not know everything I need to know."

"I don't have all the answers."

"You have enough of them to get me started."

"I might also have enough to crash your mind. Evan had problems of which you know nothing. The one thing I remember him saying and remember it word-for-word was, 'Please tell her this wasn't her fault'. If I had known what that meant, I would have stopped it. Do you believe that? If you do not, then I fear this is all pointless."

I smiled. "This would be a bad time to tell your first lie, Dad."

"It would," he replied without a smile.

"What did he tell you and is that different from what is in the envelope?"

"Both are essentially the same. One is a reflection of the other. Morgahna? I do not think he told me everything. I suspect that what he told me and what you might already know will give you direction. Before I continue, I need you to tell me why there have been no police here, no one trying to solve this?"

"That would be easy, Dad. It would chase away whoever is doing this and I would have to face it all over again."

"You want to survive this?"

To that point, I was merely trying to survive. His question made me think. If I survived this, then I had a life without an anchor. I always saw my life in terms of portrait photography. I saw myself on the arm of a successful man who doted on me and never looked away when I smiled at him. I did not see all those idle moments when he was alone and wondering about his life, his wife and how they did not sometimes fit together very well. I saw nice clothes and just enough cleavage to arouse interest without passion. I saw a man who would take only what I gave and never seek anything else from anyone. I saw a man that did not exist and never would.

Surviving this meant taking a different picture and committing it to memory the same way I'd committed to that one, that entirely false one. It meant thinking about the people in the photograph and how they saw the camera. It meant changing my image, the one I saw of myself when I closed my eyes. Could I even have a successful relationship now? Was a man even an option anymore? Would my life simply be the same one that took Evan?

I leaned back in the chair and asked, "When did you realize you had Mom under your thumb?"

"The question is preposterous and you know it. Why would you believe I even want her under my thumb?"

"She is, Dad."

"Not because I put her there and you know it."

"How does it work? Do you beat her?"

"I have never touched her in anger and I never will."

I smiled again. "You avoided that one, pop. Now it's your turn to answer the question. Do you?"

"No."

"You aren't angry."

"I merely satisfying your carnal curiosity. I don't own a whip either."

"Yet you manage her very well."

Chapter Eighteen

"We manage together, something you and Evan did not do well."

That brought a frown. "Touché."

"I have no desire to hurt you, Morgahna. I love you and I will do whatever is in my power to help you."

"Does she scream?"

"It is enough that I know you do not."

Lord, I was avoiding it and I think he knew it. I looked down at the table and said, "What was her name?"

"Janine Pruitt."

Slow tears welled up from inside and began their long slow course down my face. *Janine. A simple name. What did she give him?* That was such a stupid question that it caused even more tears. *Sex. Maybe love. Maybe I'll never know.* I looked up at him, at my father and he actually said it. "I'm sorry, baby. I didn't know until he told me."

"Anything else, *Dad*?" I said sarcastically.

Yeah, I thought that was it. I thought this was why he brought me out here to his domain, to tell me about my husband's affair. I thought he was going to tell me that was the underlying cause of his death, of his death wish. To avoid me, to avoid the confrontation with me, he killed himself.

He got tender for a moment, got emotionally sympathetic and said kindly, "Morgahna? If it was that simple, I don't think any of this would have happened. A divorce is a lot easier than this. Baby? Please. You've been so strong. Don't fail or fall apart now, not now. Okay, it's hard, it's painful and it hurts. It happens to the best of us, to the worst of us."

"To *you*, Dad?"

"Patty and Wally."

God, that stopped me. *Both* of them had affairs? I turned my head because obviously he and they handled it and *that* so much better than Evan and I had. I pushed the table angrily and stalked toward the door. I wanted out, wanted an end to this and *would not* accept anything less than what I so dearly wanted.

That, however, was Evan and that is the *only* reason I stopped just before the door. "Quick, Dad. Why? Why did he fuck someone else?"

"For the easiest reason. Because you wouldn't."

"Did he love her?"

"No."

"How do you know?"

"He told me and I believed him."

"Do you love Mom?"

"Deeply and completely."

I laid my head against the door jamb and wiped tears from my eyes. When I turned, he was standing behind the table, his fingertips on that envelope. "What else did he say, Dad?" I asked sadly, numbly.

"That he would try to work out everything but he feared he would not be able."

"Maybe it's time for me to see that envelope."

"Maybe it is."

Before I took it from him, I had to ask one last question. "Why didn't you hug me stronger back when I first got here?"

"Fear."

"Of?"

"You. You have a powerful personality. I have tried to nurture it, to shape it in a way that is beneficial instead of bitchy and I have no idea if I have succeeded."

"You? This is the longest conversation we have ever had."

He smiled. "Your mother was my proxy."

"If I hug you now, will you hug back stronger?"

"Let's find out."

Chapter Eighteen

He did. He is much stronger than he appears, a thing to which my mother can attest. As we hugged I heard faint tears coming from him and I asked quietly near his ear, "Why, Dad? Why cry now?"

"Anticipation, daughter. What happens now will be more painful than what has preceded it. I will do everything to help you. I will move heaven and earth to bring you through this and finally give me grandchildren."

I giggled. "Is that what all this is about? Grandchildren?"

"Mark's are pretty lame."

We broke and I asked, "Why was Evan a thief?" That was as blunt as I could be. My eyes were dry and my tone was serious. I wasn't done with Evan yet and I needed his memory to be clear.

"He stole six years of your life."

"Dad? We stole from each other then. I wasn't the perfect wife."

"Aunt Laura's lawyer?" he asked slowly, reminding me.

"Harold Thomas. Right?"

"Yes, that's right," he said as he sat back down. I did the same opposite him and waited. "He told me that he made partner at the age of forty-eight and did a lot of work before that time to earn it. He was entirely skeptical of Evan making partner by twenty-seven. The *only* reason he saw me was our friendship. Otherwise, he would not have stooped to something as menial as estate planning."

"What are you saying, Dad?"

"That something fishy happened between Evan and that partner of his. Underwood?"

"Yeah. That's him."

"Hank's opinion was that Underwood had no choice but to make Evan a partner. Why? Neither of us ever figured it out. I figure the answer is in here," he said tapping the envelope again. With his hand still resting on the brown paper, he slid it across to me. "I do not know what is in it. I believe he is telling only part of the story. Why? I do not know."

I picked it up and it was heavier than I thought it might be. A lump in the bottom betrayed something but I didn't have any idea what it might be. I looked at him and asked, "Why you, Dad? Why did he trust you with this and not me?"

He sighed and looked at the envelope and not me. "Baby? I've thought that ever since he gave it to me and then asked me not to say anything, not even to ask why. He just made that little speech, shook my hand and left. Why did he give it to me and not you? The only answer I have is that he hoped he could do something about what was happening, make it work out somehow. Obviously, that didn't happen." Then he looked at me sadly and said, "And I'm real sorry, Morgahna. I wish it was different."

Rather than retreat into tears, I ripped open the envelope and said, "Well, let's find out what's inside."

An audio tape slid out as I pulled out a folder, a legal-sized file folder that was several pages thick. Interestingly enough, the top pages were a long note to me from him.

I couldn't help it.

I cried.

I think you would have, too.

Chapter Eighteen

From the File Of Janine Pruitt

My Dearest Morgahna,

Should this ever fall into your hands, then it is safe to say I have succumbed to cowardice. I have much to lose and on that list, you are at the top and always have been. I see you sitting, working, thinking and I am totally enthralled by you. You do not second-guess yourself, do not imagine the worst that can happen simply because you do not think that way. You decided long before I met you that the world belongs to you and you will fashion it into a shape that is pleasing to your eye. I love you and will miss you with the certainty of sunrise. My purest Morgahna, the simple act of writing this is an admission of weakness that I cannot withstand. To be brave, to stand against the tide would mean to lose you and that is the root of my spinelessness. I cannot live only to lose you and I cannot live because you would find me reprehensible.

Janine is only part of the reason. No, I did not love her and found being with her only reminded me of what I was losing by the merest of physical acts. It was unsatisfying and made me ashamed to admit to a weakness that base and so far beneath myself. Please, do not berate yourself, do not wish for things to be different because Janine had little to do with you.

You will most likely ask your father why I talked to him and not to you. I cannot speak for him, but my reason is simple. I was terrified to face you with her between us, terrified to lose you because of what I have done.

This unpleasant tale starts with Tommy. You will probably learn to hate him. I already do. He is a competent lawyer but it is his reputation that sweeps up people who want him to plead their case. I cannot expect you to understand this because your own career always took center stage in your life. In that way, our marriage and our life together was perfect. Our careers seldom crossed only because you were so busy pursuing yours. My own career was fine until that rape case.

Janine was raped down on River Street below Factors Walk. The weather was nasty, rain and wind sweeping the street of most onlookers.

Despite our best efforts, no witnesses were ever found to corroborate her story. It descended to the level of DNA and a finger pointed at her accuser. He was a student, a law student from Florida who wanted to see the St. Patrick's Day parade as it wound down River Street. He rented a room in an inn on the street and that is where the trouble started. I will not mention his name because I was never convinced he was guilty of anything but intercourse with a willing partner. In that way, he was much like me with the same girl.

It was not difficult to prove intercourse because we got a sample of his DNA through a subterfuge that was wholly successful. Janine was, indeed, guilty of intercourse with that unnamed man but Tommy explained his case succinctly. "Janine? All we have are two people, neither with any of the identifying marks of a rape."

She was livid and said she was going to report our conduct to the bar and have us removed from practicing law in Georgia. Had we allowed nothing but that, these events would not have happened. I was entirely willing at that point and I encouraged her to report us and allow the system to plod onward as the investigation proceeded. At that point, we were not guilty of anything but practicing good law.

Tommy, however, had issues with such things. From his point-of-view, I can understand them. From anyone else's, his concerns were feeble and short-sighted. He was my friend, however, and I began to feel his panic at what her allegations could do to our firm.

Our firm.

I was a partner and only recently so.

Before I continue, I need to be clear on one point. I am guilty of several crimes, not the least of which is murder. No, I did not kill anyone. I simply know who did and who the victims were. My crime is not the worst, but being culpable in my mind is clearly as bad. I know of many crimes and I said nothing to anyone about them. That means, I cannot tell you out of fear you will sit on your knowledge and makes yourself as guilty and as culpable as I am and always will be.

That is why I will do what I will do. That is why I cannot tell you what I know. You will need to discover these things on your own or take this note and the accompanying file to the police and let them handle the

Chapter Eighteen

investigation. My fear is that should you give this story to the police, that you will be under the gun and I mean that quite literally.

Those things said, I humbly apologize for what I will do. It will leave you alone and I believe you always loved me. Believe this then: I have always loved you and that love will follow me to the next world.

My partnership, though.

The circumstances of that paint me as somewhat less than honest. My fate was sealed during a case involving the rape and murder of a woman named LaRuth Morrison. She was another rape case, another one that was quite real and left the woman pregnant. Her rapist was frantic when she disappeared, evidently returning to New York City where she mended, had the baby and returned to her modeling career. That career was the only reason she did not report the incident to the police. She was serious about it and wanted to be successful at it. A few months after the baby was born, she returned to Savannah and attempted to blackmail her rapist into paying child support. Personally, I think that was the most foolish thing I have ever heard. The mere idea of expecting a rapist to pay child support is outlandish.

She disappeared while she was visiting and her body was found by hunters in the woods out by Fort Stewart. She had been beaten to a point where the only identifying marks left were some tattoos. One on her ankle was the one her brother finally used to identify her. Her killer went unidentified until he admitted it in our office, the downstairs conference room.

I am, however, getting ahead of the story.

During this time, we hired a private investigator to do little but foot work for us on Janine's case. We needed witnesses located and interviewed and we had one on retainer. I talked to him about Janine and that conversation was no more than an idle one. Maybe he thought I was asking for something else, a way out of my problem. Morgahna? I did not know he was going to do these things. That man killed Janine because, in his words, "She was going to blackmail you with your wife." That was probably not true. Janine was a hateful person but did not hate me. She simply wanted nothing to do with me. Our office was, however, in a conflict of interest vis-à-vis Janine Pruitt. I had a personal relationship with a client and that alone was grounds to disqualify us either from defending her and litigating against her. We should have handed off her case to another firm, but that would have sealed my legal career and I could face that. I am and was a coward.

What happened next sealed my fate and left you a widow.

They, the private investigator and Tommy, brought her to the office and interviewed her on tape. It got ugly and I walked into a murder scene. The investigator snapped her neck as he raped her yet again. Tommy took turns. No, I did not but I conspired in the removal of her body from our office. Bridget Haines helped clean the mess and I remained silent. You may remember my two-week vacation where I did little but vegetate. That case was on my mind but my job was so important to me that I could not see it end that way. I had no contacts the way Tommy did and still has, so I felt incapable of building a successful practice, or one quite as successful as the one he built.

It was during this time I approached him about changing the business model from sole proprietor to an LLP. Personally, I cannot believe he failed to do this years ago. An LLP would limit his liability and almost certainly exempt him from personal disaster. In any case, any judgment against the investigator would not fall on Tommy because the investigator is merely an employee of the company and not a member of the LLP. I hope you see this the way it was intended. It was intended to protect Tommy from that investigator but when Tommy became a part of it, the purpose went out the window.

Naturally, we had a meeting and it was one called by me.

I taped a mini-recorder under the table where I sat and allowed the conversation to proceed as it would. None of us mentioned Janine and none of us really wanted to either. The investigator was gruff, short-tempered and vulgar. I will always wonder how and why Tommy knew him and allowed him to investigate cases for him. I knew the capacity of that tape and wanted something on it that might help you one day. My own life was over because that scene in that very room ended whatever chance I had at being a lawyer and practicing law.

So, I baited him.

Chapter Eighteen

It took less than fifteen minutes for him to admit to his role in killing Janine Pruitt and even in the death of LaRuth Morrison. That admission shocked me. His opinion of her was vile. "She was a nigger."

Morgahna? I, like you, grew up here. Are we complacent racists? I never thought so. I viewed myself as a balanced man, as an individual who judged fairly and on the evidence as my profession decrees. I never saw myself as a man who could be swayed by racial motives. I saw myself as being above that sort of medieval nonsense. You worked with Dave Woods and he's black. Did you ever see him as a nigger? I would suspect not. Neither of us would stand accused of being racists. We saw money. We would be accused of being capitalists or at least of following that creed.

I am, I suspect, proof that money finds the lowest common denominator.

Morgahna? I love you and I always will.

While I have admitted to the omission of facts that are designed to shield you from legal problems later on, I have already admitted more than I should have. My life is spinning out of control and I already sense it. That investigator has friends that he has already warned me about.

"She'll wind up in the woods, Hamilton."

That thought sickens and horrifies me; it makes me physically ill and I believe Tommy sees it. Shawna snuck me a note that contained but one word. "Beware". I find myself watching my back, watching the shadows and worrying about you. It is inevitable that you will hear these things one day. That is why I have written it down and made you a party at least to this much.

Stay away from Sugarplums.

Stay away from River Street.

Stay away from investigators named Simpson.

Billy Ray Simpson.

He has a sister with a package for you.

Simpson is a psychopath with a license.

He used to be a cop.

A Savannah police officer.

Talk to Mike Hardy. I believe you know him.

Mention my name but not the tape. That is the golden fleece. That is manna from heaven and should be hidden carefully because both Tommy and Billy will kill to get it back. Tommy knows of it.

Stupid me. I told him of it in a fit of anger.

I cannot stand this much longer. I watch you sleep and see your face. I see you and sometimes my hand hovers just above your face and I cannot stand to withhold my touch. I hug you more than I used to, hug and expect nothing but silent condemnation. You are my angel, my savior, but nothing can save me now.

I must sleep.

Forever.

With you on my mind for eternity.

Eternity seeing your face.

Your beautiful face in my mind forever.

I can live with that.

Chapter Nineteen

Voices from the grave are harrowing and tormenting. As I read that letter and heard his golden voice in my head, tears made me retreat several times. I loved hearing him talk; his voice was cultured, mellow and gentle. If I ever needed a lawyer, he was the type I would want. I always thought that and now I wonder if I always will.

My father pulled his chair around to my side of the table as I read. When I needed to retreat because what I was hearing was so unlike the man I remembered, he was there to hold me and I let him. The first part of the letter was the hardest. He was telling me things my mind did not want to accept and that had always driven me frantic. Whenever I was confronted with something that made no sense, that was out of my control or simply displeased me in some minor way, I worked until my calluses bled to make those things into something I could stomach. This was beyond me and would forever be that way, so I cried out of mixture of frustration and loss.

It took at least half an hour to get through that first page. I cried for many reasons and Evan wasn't in all of them. I cried for myself because despite his words, he was validating why men fool around. *If they got it at home, they wouldn't be on the streets looking for it.* Or anywhere else either.

Dad was as strong as I needed to be and I didn't even care if he lost respect for me. I didn't feel like being strong and that was because of a woman named Janine, a woman who gave my husband things I did not. That was difficult to read and not hear from his mouth. His voice in my head not enough so I retreated many time as I read. Dad just held me every time it got too much. Slowly, though, I began to gain the strength to do this, to be strong enough to be the person he remembered.

The story about Janine Pruitt was so full of holes that I stopped reading and tried to picture an attack like that in Tommy's office and couldn't. What time of day was it? If it was during working hours, then there would have been other employees there. After hours? Would Janine go there after hours? Would she go there even though she'd had relations with Evan? It didn't compute.

Chapter Nineteen

Dad was reading over my shoulder and he said as though he was reading my mind, "No, it doesn't."

"How could that happen, Dad? How could they assault someone in their own office to a point of death? I don't see it and that bothers me more than anything that I've read."

"Maybe he explains it later on. Keep reading, baby."

That seemed like a good idea until I read that name.

Billy Ray Simpson.

My brain froze and I don't think anything registered until my thoughts turned to...

...Debbie.

Despite my weariness, I jumped straight up and screamed, "NO!" In my panic, I forgot that Dad had a phone on his desk. I was running back to the house where my purse, that stupid one that Billy Ray bought for me, was on the dining room table where we had been sitting, talking and eating pizza.

Dad caught me and said, "What is it, Morgahna?"

"HE HAS DEBBIE!"

"Who?" he asked because he simply did not know.

"SIMPSON! I left her with him last night!"

The late afternoon sun was behind me, shadows lanced through the doorway like angry knives as I watched him come to terms with the news. He didn't know the name, had never heard it. All he knew was my reaction to it as I read it, as he read it over my shoulder.

"Where are you going?" he asked in an attempt both to slow me down and to get me to think a bit more clearly.

"A phone! I need to call her!"

"The desk. Use that one."

I rushed across the room, past the tools, past the table and saw none of them. I saw her, my belated friend. I dialed her number and it rang twice before someone answered it. "Debbie!" I shouted into the receiver.

"Hi, darlin'," Billy Ray said sweetly. "How you doin'? You have a nice visit with your momma?"

"Where's Debbie!" I screamed.

"Oh, she's around. Don't worry about her. Do you have it, Morgahna? Did he give to your mother?"

I sank into Dad's desk chair and said, "I need to hear her. I need to know she's okay."

"I can make her scream," he said as kindly as a face full of acid.

"I NEED TO TALK TO HER!"

"Well, it's against my principles but I suppose it would settle your mind a bit."

I heard a rustling of the phone and then her terrified voice. "Morgahna? He has this knife…"

…and then a muffled scream.

He came back on and said, "I love hurtin' her. She squeals so nicely. Don't you think? Girls have so many parts you can hurt. Just choose one. It don't even matter which one. Just reach out and touch someone." There was another muffled scream. "See what I mean?"

"You bastard," I said with as much venom in my voice as I could manage among the terror.

"I get that a lot," he said with a happy voice. "Goes with the territory, I guess."

"Why? Why did you do all that for me?"

"The tape, stupid. As long it survived, I was in trouble."

"So is Tommy Underwood."

"Yeah, but who cares?"

"Not me," I said, my voice still full of hate.

"See what I mean, baby? No one likes lawyers."

Chapter Nineteen

"If you hurt her…"

She squealed again.

"You mean, like that?"

I've never known anger like that. It made everything dimmer including my mind. I've already mentioned that I feel weaker than I did before that attack in the woods. Combine this with that and I was practically newborn. I turned and looked at my father. He was watching me and saying nothing. I licked my lips and tried to see myself through his eyes based on what he said to me earlier. *You could grow a dick ten inches long and it wouldn't surprise me.* Expectations like that weigh on a person especially when that person is a girl. *It's time to be a woman.* "You killed Daydra Morrison," I said. "Why and how?"

"Gimme a sec," he said.

My heart froze as I heard Debbie's moan turn into a quietly muffled and entirely blood-curdling scream. "God, I love doing that," he said. "Makes my dick hard."

With the phone still in my hand, I put my elbows on the table and took a long mental step backwards. *You can't help like this. You have to find out where she is and then go there. It's just that simple. He's hurting her to keep you from thinking clearly.* Even knowing his motives, it didn't help much. Debbie's screams hurt almost as much as though he was hurting me. "Why, Billy? All those speeches about Iraq? About being a medic? About your wife and child? Why? And why kill Daydra? She was as stupid as a post and didn't need to die."

"Yer right there, girlie. She truly was stupid as a post. Greedy post, but still stupid. I mean, would you let a man into your bed with a syringe full of death? That heroin killed her quicker than a bullet." He snickered. "Well, not that quick, but it sure was fun watching her die."

"Walker?"

"Just happened to walk in. A walker. Get it?" His voice broke up into cackles.

He has this knife…

Yeah, it fit. He was threatening Debbie with a knife and that was a sure way to terrify a girl whose entire life was her face and the business it brought her. Look, I'm not that stupid. Hairdressers don't make *that* much money, not enough to afford that wardrobe. She was practically prostituting herself for her profession and I think I always knew it and that was the basis of my distance from her. I disapproved of the way she lived and loved.

It was then that I finally admitted it.

At least she didn't drive someone to suicide.

"Why did Karen Hubbell give Daydra money and why?"

"Oh, shoot," he said. "Here we're busy tormenting this bottle blonde and you want to talk about niggers. You turning liberal on me, Morgahna? You? A white-bread southern Republican? You? I expected better from you."

"Just tell me, Billy."

"Oh, why not. Gimme a second."

I closed my eyes tighter as I listened to that muffled scream gain in intensity. *He has her gagged somehow. Otherwise, the neighbors would hear.* It *still* didn't help, that effort to put objectivity between Debbie and me. It *still* hurt almost as much. I bit my lip and fought back tears. The only thing that helped was seeing him dead and that was an emotion he was fostering consciously.

"Ah, that was fun. Did you know she has quite perfect skin? Her cheekbones are perfect, too. It would be a pity to smash them."

"Daydra?" I said even though my voice betrayed a warble.

"Ah, the nigger. Well, if you must keep asking, then I guess I'll have to tell you. I killed her sister and had her nigger baby. Well, the baby came first. That baby? He's in the swamp now, sleeping with the 'gators. Gave him to Tony and he did the deed. Good man, him. Anyways, that nigger was taking Tommy's hush-money and I couldn't trust her to stay quiet. You got money somewhere because your damn husband was such a pussy and money is money. You might have offered her more than Tommy was giving her. Can you imagine? A nigger bitch blackmailing a white man and expecting to get away with it? In *Georgia*?"

Chapter Nineteen

"Billy? I almost slept with you."

"Jeez Louise, girl. That was the whole fuckin' point. You got a powerful lot of willpower goin' for you. Girls get all squishy and emotional and they're so easy to control. Just tell them whatever they wanna hear and they do, they hear it. You? You heard a widower with a dead baby. Gets 'em every time. I still figure if we'd had more time, you'd be around my little finger."

"That's never going to happen, Billy."

"No, I don't suppose I'll ever find out how tight you really are. Might have to force my way in, if you get my meanin'."

"That won't happen, Billy. You're going to have to take my word for that."

"Well, time will tell. I kinda like my odds, though. You got dark blonde pussy hair, huh?"

"You'll never know, Billy."

"Well, until then, girlfriend. I'll call you."

"Where? When?"

He sneered. "Well, jeez Louise, girl. If ya have to ask, then yer dumber than I thought. Tomorrow, noon. Me and yer friend will be havin' a party."

And he hung up.

I have never hated anyone in my life. I didn't even hate the high school physics kids who figured out how to color my hair green by spraying a chemical on it. Don't ask, because I don't know. I didn't hate them, but I was angry at them. It took three weeks and some gentle prodding from an über-geek named Kenny before I knew how to turn their skin color the same shade of green. Mom laughed her butt off even *after* one of their mothers' called the house and screamed at her and threatened legal action. No, I've never hated anyone in my entire life until now.

Billy Ray Simpson? I have no means to kill you, not even a gun. Somehow, though, I will manage it. I slowly place the phone in the cradle and sat there trying hard to find an answer to this. Dad sat next to me and said, "That sounded extreme, girl."

"Real," I said numbly.

"Can't talk about it?"

"It won't help, Dad. He has my friend and I need to get her away from him."

"Look at me," he said.

When I didn't but just stared at the hutch on his desk, he reached out, took my chin his hand and forced me to look at him. "Morgahna? I'm way past trying to change your mind about things, because you won't. You tell me, though. Can you do this?"

I gave him a small smile and said, "Nope. No chance. If I don't find help, he'll kill my best friend. If I call a cop? Debbie will dead before the choppers are airborne. Dad? I have to do this. Do you understand?"

"Not at all. This is why we pay the police."

"This guy was a cop, Dad. He knows the game and how it's played."

"Come with me," he said.

We went back to the house where I found mom in stitches, laughing so hard she couldn't breathe. Dave saw me, my face and patted my Mom's hand and said something soothing to her. She relaxed, smiled and saw where his gaze went. He got up and followed me. I was simply following my father. Soon, all four of us were in their bedroom, in their closet. Dad reached up onto a shelf, took down a box that looked heavy, or at least one that held something weighted. I didn't even have to ask what it was. He opened it and showed me a gun, a pistol. That's all I know. "No, Dad."

"Morgahna? From what I saw, from what I've heard, you have no chance without a weapon."

"I'll find another way. Dad? If you give it to me and I take it, I'll leave it behind. I won't use a gun, especially one that's registered to you."

"It isn't registered. No one will trace back to me."

"I'd know, Dad. No."

"What are you going to do?"

Chapter Nineteen

"Talk to Dave. We'll think of something."

That's when Dave surprised me. "I'll take it," he said.

I looked up at him and regarded him as though I'd never seen him before. Maybe I hadn't. Maybe we didn't know each other and this was the first sign of that. "Dave? I won't allow you to jeopardize my father."

"I won't allow anyone to kill you either, Morgahna. If you won't talk to the police, then we need another answer."

"They trace stuff like this, Dave. They'll loose forensic people on this and they'll know exactly where it came from and who used it."

"But you'll be alive," Dave said, his face dark and unyielding. "I'll take the gun if your father wants to give it to me."

Dad wanted to give it to me and I was furious not just with him but Dave, too. I turned to leave the closet, a big walk-in one that held mostly my mother's clothes, and into a roadblock named Evelyn. "Take it, Morgahna. Take it or I will go with you and do it myself."

"No, Mom," I said. "I don't know anything about guns and both of us know it. I could shoot myself." Then I looked back at Dave who towered above me and said, "Or him."

"Give it to me," she demanded of my father.

He did.

"You ever hear that line Bill Cosby used in a routine once? 'I brought you into this world and I can take you out?' That one?"

"You're not going to shoot me, Mom."

"Phil? Take the man out to the dining room. He's absolutely delightful," she said to me with the deadest eyes I've ever seen.

"Let's go, Dave," he said clapping him on the shoulder.

Dave turned to leave yet stopped and looked down at me. "Morgahna? You were always a fool. Now, I have witnesses."

Mom said to Dad, "Phil, please close the door. I don't want the neighbors to hear."

He closed the door and it was just us in that closet. Ranks of clothes were all around us. Sunday suits, things she wore for business, swim suits – no bikini's – shoes of so many types that I wondered if she'd worn them all. Okay, okay, I had nearly as many and I wore every single pair I owned. I have no doubt she did, too.

She backed me up to a wall at the end of the closet and said directly to my face, hers not more a few inches from mine. "I found a good man and I gave myself to him, Morgahna. I am not, however, helpless. He made certain of that and I will not allow some stupid redneck to kill you when I can it do myself."

"Then, kill me, Mom. Don't bluff. Either kill me or get out of my way."

I did not grow up scared of them, of either of them. For the record, I do not bluff easily. You can't be me that way. A lot of people have tried and not many have ever succeeded. Of course, the stakes were never life and death before either. So, when my mother tried to bluff me, I paused, thought about it and disregarded her threat as worse than silly. She wasn't going to kill me and we both knew it.

She started undressing.

"What are you doing?" I asked even though I felt I knew.

"Going with you. I'll shoot the bastard myself."

"Mom, you are most definitely not going with us."

She smiled and looked entirely ironic. "You going to shoot me?"

"Mom…"

"Just let me get dressed, sweetie."

It boggled my mind, her attitude. She took off her jacket, hung it on a hanger, unbuttoned her blouse and did likewise while I just stared incomprehensively. Nothing in my life prepared me for anything quite like this. I mean, we were *girls* together. We used to laugh at the same jokes and even did that hideous, "Here taste this," junk with the other as we ate. When we went shopping, our taste in clothes was eerily similar. Sure, we had those infamous mother-daughter spats like all of them do, but mostly, she fed my desire to be better than anyone else with a long

Chapter Nineteen

tirade of advice. "Never show your hand too early. Never give away the store to the first shopper. Strength over weakness always wins. Blonde are more popular, brunettes get more dates. Big bosoms are wonderful but your back will complain. A good bra can topple an empire. Knowledge is wonderful but money can afford answers."

"Mom? You are not going with me."

"Oh, dear," she said brightly. "You're never going to give me grandchildren, so I might as well."

"Mark has two daughters!"

"And both of them think décolletage is what the French have with burgers."

She slipped out of her skirt, then her shoes and began donning dark clothing. If I didn't know better, I'd say she was serious. She slipped into black pants and a maroon sweater. "What do you think dear? Appropriate for a night of mischief?"

I rolled my eyes and left the closet.

I walked right into Dave; Mom asked him, "What do you think, dear?"

"Lovely, ma'am."

"I'm going to accompany you kids."

"No, mother," I said. "You're not."

She hooked Dave's arm and said, "Exactly where are we going? I'm packing heat. Is that the correct term?"

He looked at me and said, "Morg? Tell me this isn't happening."

Dad actually kissed her forehead. "Babe? You keep dry."

"Dad!" I said incredulously. "You can't be serious. I am not taking my mother!"

"She's a lot like you, Morgahna. Once she sets her sights on something, it's tough to change her mind."

I stalked toward the door and she followed. Heck, Dad followed, too. Dave was getting nervous and I was getting mad. I turned to her and was ready for a fight. I was *not* going to get my mother killed. Period. That didn't even need a qualifier. Period. I put my finger in her face and screamed, "You are not going with me!"

"The only way I'll stay here is if one of you has a gun! I will not send you off to get killed just because you like quiche!"

"WHAT! WHAT DOES THAT MEAN!"

"I THOUGHT I LOST YOU ONCE AND THAT WAS ONE TIME TOO MANY! I WILL NOT SPEND THE REST OF MY NIGHT WONDERING WHAT HAPPENED TO MY BABY!"

Dave stepped between us and said to me, "That's it? She wants you to take a gun and unless you do, she's coming with us?"

"Dave..."

He turned around, faced my mother and said, "Give me the damn gun."

She looked up at him and said, "Watch your language young man. My daughter is a lady."

But she gave it to him.

And he took it.

Then he turned around, looked down at me and said, "There better be a good story here, Hamilton."

I grumbled and stalked the door. Behind me, I heard, "Thank you very much, Mr. Woods. I was terribly nervous."

"You hid it well, ma'am."

"Thank you again. You take care of my daughter, okay?"

They *hugged*. With God as my witness, I wondered what they did in that dining room while my Dad was busy outfoxing me. To top it off, she actually kissed him on the cheek like he was old friend who was simply going home. "I will, ma'am. Don't worry about her."

"Oh, mother's do."

My mother *never* worried about me because *she didn't have to.* I threw open the door and almost walked off without asking her the one

Chapter Nineteen

question I'd gone there in the first place to ask. It felt worse than bamboo shoots under my fingernails to turn around and ask her. I could find no other justification for being here unless I did, so I asked, "Mom? I came here to borrow some money. Can I have a few hundred dollars?"

"I'll give you my ATM card. Just a second," she said turning back toward the dining room where she left her purse on the table.

Dad stood in front of me and looked as grave and as concerned as I'd ever seen him. He knew things Mom didn't and I felt fairly certain he wasn't going to tell her either. Without having to ask, I knew he was the strong one here. He would tell Mom just enough to satisfy her curiosity and answer any doubts she had. He nodded imperceptibly at me and I knew exactly what that meant. He was telling me he had faith in me, was telling me I had enough fortitude to do this.

You know? He hadn't even asked me how I felt physically. Maybe it was one of those imperceptible "man things". Maybe that's the way he was when he was with Mark. Maybe that's all how men are – totally impervious to pain or at least not enslaved by it. I can't dignify that one way or the other because I just don't know. I know that illness seldom slowed me down, know that having two broken ribs was ungodly painful but that I survived them. Did those things count as "manly"? *You could grow a dick ten inches long and it wouldn't surprise me.* That phrase kept bouncing around my head like a ping-pong ball. My father was always a man of few words – around me. I can remember him having endless conversations with Mark and having them over the most inane things. Monster trucks, tires and wheels, torque, "balls", zero-to-sixty, hooters, heels, shorts, first-and-ten, TOUCHDOWN!, girly-man and so many references to Arnold Schwarzenegger that it simply boggles my mind.

My father, I saw in a display of logic so perverse that it disturbed me, saw me as a better man than my own brother. How and why that perception came to me I cannot say because I don't know. Maybe it was the way he looked at me, the way his gaze seemed to firm up and instill within him a confidence I never saw before. Maybe it was just everything that happened out in his workshop, the words he used, the tone of his voice, everything. If I had to guess, my father was easily as worried as my mother but he knew as well as I did that no one could do this but me. Our police are fine in almost every case of which I can think except as bodyguards. They will find your murderer with quiet precision, investigate the facts of your death but are helpless to keep you alive. The police clean our streets of the detritus of our society, of the trash that accumulates. My father agreed with me on one point. Don't become trash. Don't become something that gets flushed down the drain.

Mom came out with her ATM card and said, "The password is 'PHIL1204'. Can you remember that?"

"Dad's name and birth date? Yeah, I think so, Mom. Thank you."

She put her hands on either side of my face and said, "I want it back. I want you to give it back to me. Do understand me, Morgahna Jayne?"

"Yeah," I said with a smile and a hug.

I went to dad and hugged him, too. It was strong and meaningful. "I'll see you later, Dad?"

"Yes. Call first."

"Sure."

Dave drove to the first McDonalds only because I requested it. As soon as we got into the Explorer, I opened my purse, the one Billy gave me and dropped the wallet into my lap. He knew I'd been in Jacksonville talking to my parents and that was far more than a lucky guess. He *knew*. Maybe I've seen too many movies, but I thought I knew why he knew where I'd gone. Dave watched wordlessly as I searched every compartment in that wallet and found nothing. I dropped it on the floorboard and started on the purse. It didn't take long. A GPS tracking device fell out of an inner pocket and I said some things that would have been standard language down on the docks in Savannah.

"GPS?" Dave asked.

"Most likely. With a good setup, he even knows the address where I went."

"We," he corrected.

"Okay, mother," I said with a small smile.

"Where are we going and don't say to bed either."

Chapter Nineteen

It was after nine o'clock in the evening. "Gimme a sec," I said and got out of the car and dropped the device into the bed of a pickup with Alabama plates. With luck, that truck was headed anywhere but back to Savannah. I got back in and said, "I'm driving."

"No, you're not."

"Yes, I am. This is a story and you're taking notes."

He grimaced and said, "Busted."

We switched sides and as we got back onto I-95, he asked, "Where are we going?"

"To see a cop named Hardy."

"Who is he?"

"He's old, irascible, mean as a junkyard dog and might be the only cop in the southeast who both knows me and might even give me some information."

"Ah, a contact."

"Yep. The oldest trick in the book."

"Where did you meet him?"

I smiled. "Sleeping in a meeting of the city council."

"Must be a lot of that."

"Well, he stood out. He was snoring."

We both laughed. Mine was cut short by the memory of Debbie's screams. Even though I felt faintly tired, I knew I had no choice but to do this. I only hoped my instincts on Mike Hardy were correct.

That flashpoint was drawing very near.

Very near.

Chapter Twenty

It was ten-thirty by the time we got back to Savannah. I'd been looking for Mike ever since I dropped that GPS tracking device into the bed of that truck. Finding a particular cop is not easy even if you're a reporter for the daily newspaper. I finally found him in a coffee shop on Whitaker near Bay Street. When he saw us walk in, he recognized Dave but obviously had a hard time with me. He followed me as I walked, his gaze hard and penetrating. I slid in opposite him and said without even a hello, "Tell me about Billy Ray Simpson."

"Christ, Hamilton. You're supposed to be dead," he said as he searched my face closely. I suppose I was going to have to get to get used to people doing that.

"I had a religious experience."

"Not with you, Woods," he said looking at Dave.

Mike Hardy is an Internal Affairs cop. Is he any good? I have no idea. He could be the most corrupt cop in Savannah and I wouldn't know. The only recommendation I had that gave him any credence at all was Evan's reference to him in that note. He could have dropped any name at all, any and I would have given it the same respect I would have given to Jesus. Also, being a vice cop and Billy Ray being a *former* cop seemed a match made in a shit pile. Where you find *former* cops, you also find IAD cops. It might mean Mike and Billy Ray were on opposite sides, but also might mean they were old friends that still drank beer from the same bottle.

Dave looked entirely nonplussed. "Nope. Wouldn't work. I need a black woman. White ones break too easily."

"Simpson?" I said gently nudging the conversation back to Billy Ray.

Mike Hardy has a thick face. I suppose that's a politeness for fat. Do they have fitness drills on the police force? If so, how does Mike Hardy pass them? Was I looking for reasons to paint him as dirty?

He took a bite of his sugar donut and then said after he wiped his mouth with a thin napkin, "The mere fact you can ask that question means you're in over your head, Hamilton. And what happened to your face? You get hit with an ugly stick?"

The shop was busy. It faced City Hall and that only guaranteed traffic. It could serve sewage and the cops would still come here for their daily ration. I'd eaten many sloppy meals here and if my life resumed its former course, I imagined many more. "I have a rather interesting plastic surgeon," I said. "He uses a metal pipe."

If Hardy was going to bite, that was it. You would swear that all the background noise dissipated as soon as I asked it. He was holding that flimsy napkin in his hand and crumpled it slowly. "Hamilton? You say one more word and I'm going to arrest you for obstruction of justice."

"Ah," I said. "A crooked cop. That's how you stay fat and a cop at the same time."

His eyes never flinched. "My brother-in-law is on the fitness board," he said as nothing more than a time waster. "You tell me right now how you know that name," he said as his face began to look like the Lincoln Memorial.

I smiled. "He saved my life."

It was the ultimate *non-sequitor* as far he was concerned. He looked at me, then at Dave. "That man is worse than a rabid dog. Hamilton?" he said as his gaze settled on me. "How do you know him?"

My smile got wider. "I told you, Mike. He saved my life." I reached over the table, picked up his cup and said just before I sipped from it, "His sister, Sylvia, helped." I grimaced. "Je-sus, Hardy. How much sugar is in this?"

"It keeps me going," he said absently.

"Why is Simpson a former cop and not a present one?"

"Metal pipe? I figure you already know the answer to that one."

"I told you. He saved my life. He didn't use a metal pipe on me. Two other guys did."

"You've heard about LaRuth Morrison then."

Chapter Twenty

"A model who had interesting surgery."

He reached across the table, took the coffee cup back and sipped at it and watched as Dave took notes. "I haven't said anything that is on the record, Woods."

"We live in a society that keeps re-writing history, Mr. Hardy. Who knows? This might soon become public record."

"Is that a threat?"

"It's a fact, sir," he said, his words indicating subservience while his tone suggested a slight menace that I'd never heard before.

"Officer Hardy?" I said. "I've had an interesting few days. The last few months of my life have been even more interesting than those last few days. Do me a favor and tell me why Simpson isn't in jail or at least under investigation."

He looked at Dave and said, "Off the record."

"Does that mean I can't take notes?"

"It does."

I looked up at Dave and said, "Humor him, Dave."

Dave slid his pen into a shirt pocket and folded his hands on the table. "Officer Hardy?" he said bluntly. "Nothing is going to happen to her. Am I clear? She isn't going to get killed and she isn't going to jail because she defended herself either. Am I correct?"

"No."

I found that exchange interesting and as Dave started to object, I put my hand on top of his and said, "Really? Self-defense no longer works?"

"This seems more like personal vengeance."

"What have I said, Officer Hardy, that leads you to that opinion?"

The sounds from the café began to filter back around us. The sounds of silverware on plates and saucers, idle bits of conversation and the distinct smells emanating from the grill began to surround us. A flotilla of young people, probably students from SCAD, rolled through the door in a huff of laugher and energy. I sighed. I wondered if I would ever feel that way again and wondered if that feeling of dreariness was physical or mental.

"You're asking for information in an ongoing investigation, Mrs. Hamilton."

I leaned back in the booth and said, "You don't know where he is, do you?"

"Do you?"

"Probably."

"Probably?"

"Yep."

"I can force you to talk to me."

"Legal pressure? Is that it?"

"Of course. I would never touch you otherwise."

"Ah," I said. "The power of the press."

"So, where is he?"

"Can we exchange information? Mine for yours?"

"No. Where is he?"

I drummed my fingers on the table and said to his coffee cup, "I'd have to see a map in order to tell you."

"Is he on the military reservation?"

"Fort Stewart?" I asked.

"Yes."

"Nearby. I'd have to see a good map in order to tell you. I spent nine weeks there and that is the only place I know." Before he could say anything, I said, "Tony Slayton and a man I know as Doug." Then I watched his face *closely.*

I've been watching politicians for years in those council meetings. Had I done *anything* but take them seriously, I don't think I would have had a clue as to what he was thinking. I had, however, taken those meetings seriously. I saw outright lies during them saw them for what

Chapter Twenty

they were and watched how they said them. Help the poor? *All* politicians vow to help the poor. Many of them consider themselves in that rank and, thus, help themselves. How did Hardy fare on the Hamilton Monitor? Well, he said, "I don't know them." He said it, however, with the face of a man who vowed to help the poor and couldn't keep from laughing.

"Sugarplums?"

"Nice restaurant. Shitty bar."

"They have interesting questions on their employment exams."

He looked at his watch and said, "Hamilton? You were always a pain in the ass, but I'm glad you're alive. I need to cut to the chase here. Why aren't you dead and how do you know Simpson?"

"Officer Hardy? My guess is we could make each other's life much easier if we just cooperated. That maniac has a friend of mine and I know *exactly* what he's going to do to her if he gets the chance. Mike? Please. Please, tell me that you've got Billy Ray Simpson under surveillance and that you have enough evidence to bring him to trial. Please tell me that."

"Blunt?" he asked.

"Yes, Mike. Please, be blunt."

"No one has ever accused him of anything. Witnesses refuse to talk, men with wives refuse to deal with us. We've put so many bugs around Savannah we'll probably start fumigating soon. Hamilton? We don't have anything on him. Until you sat down with that face and mentioned his name? No one in the Savannah Police Department even suspected he might be involved in your case."

"And now?"

He pushed aside the small plate that held nothing but donut crumbs and covered his coffee cup as a waitress came around and offered him more. She asked us if we wanted anything and neither of us did. Only when she turned and walked away did Hardy's face change. Something in his look made me wonder how Evan knew him. He might have seen him as a father figure, as a contact, as anything at all. The mere fact that he knew him at all, however, pointed right at Billy Ray Simpson. That seemed obvious. In what context did they see each other? I might never know because my dealings with Mike Hardy showed a tight-lipped cop, one that could still be anything from a crook to a saint, a dedicated cop to one so long on the take that he no longer even had a sense of justice, just greed. He leaned forward and said with a low, deep voice, "Exactly what do you want, Mrs. Hamilton?"

I leaned forward until we were no more than a couple feet apart and said, "I have evidence I believe is exculpatory and will put Billy Ray Simpson behind bars for a long time. It's in the form of an audio tape whose veracity can be attested to by a woman named Bridget Haines. I have case notes from a case my husband was asked to help defend and those notes will go a long way to proving the guilt of several people, not the least of whom is Thomas Underwood, my late husband's partner."

That envelope hadn't left my hands ever since my father gave it to me. It rested in my lap and I'm certain, if Mike Hardy is any kind of cop, that he knew about it, too. That guess became reality when he swallowed hard and glanced down between Dave and me. He suspected it was sitting in the space between us. Even though it wasn't, he *knew* and that marked him as observant even if those powers escaped him during city council meetings.

"What will it take short of a court order to get those items from you?"

"Help."

"We can get a SWAT team put together…"

"…within the next hour," I said interrupting him. "That friend? He'll kill her and he'll do it soon. He expects me to try something tonight and I am going to oblige him either with your help or without it. Mike? Help me."

"You can identify Slayton?"

"Both Slayton and Doug. I'll never forget either of them."

"From a lineup?"

"From a casket, too."

"Gotta piss," he said.

Chapter Twenty

When he got up and headed toward the bathroom, I said, "Follow him, Dave. Don't do anything but watch."

He nodded and slipped out.

That left me to think about the only piece of this puzzle that made no sense. The voice that called me on the phone all those weeks ago? That one I identified as black? Well, I can attest that it wasn't Daydra. That poor unfortunate's voice was like a sledgehammer. The voice that called me was timid and uncertain, but also identifiably black. Who was she? I ran every name through my head I could think of and nothing and no one appeared. I even considered people I knew and met before Evan took himself away from me. Still, nothing happened. There were no cosmic flashes of insight.

It was also the first time I'd been alone since I read that awful note from Evan. I picked up the envelope from my lap and stared at it wistfully. He said he loved me and could think about me forever, that he could live with that. The problem was I didn't think I could. Life, I saw in the far abstract, was going to keep pushing him away from me. It was inevitable even though I didn't like it and wondered if I would ever fully agree.

I reached into the envelope and pulled out that letter again. It was impossible, entirely impossible, to read it because it felt like torture. I tried and got no farther than the opening paragraph where he referred to himself as a coward or at least succumbing to cowardice. Tears rolled around my eyes before slipping down my face. It was vivid proof that I wasn't done with him yet and had no outlet for him. I took a deep ragged breath and put the letter back into the envelope and turned my face toward the dark street outside the window. I know I've said Savannah feels like home but in truth, I wondered if it would ever fit quite the same way. To me, Savannah was magical, or had been anyway. It was a place of beauty and endless possibilities. All those possibilities revolved around Evan and the genteel life we had planned for ourselves. That life was now able to be inspected under the harsh light of reality and it came up short. Gentility was a state of mind, not an act of being. I was going through the paces of gentility without ever once feeling the part. To me, gentility was supremacy and endless battles for dominance and not a gentler way of being. Yeah, kinder and gentler, the old conservative mantra. It was neither as kind nor as gentle as I would like to believe it once was.

That tape was still heavy in the bottom of the envelope. I was smart enough to know that the contents of that tape was the reason, *the reason,* Evan did what he did to himself. It implicated him in a heinous crime and that was not something he could live with or inflict it on me. Could I have divorced him? Lord, I don't know. Even knowing what happened one and two years ago, it is difficult to consider a living Evan Hamilton and me not being married to him. Could I? Probably not. I would have screamed, threw the Southern Belle of all tantrums, would have demanded an answer to the question, "How could you do this to *me*?" Sensitive, right? Without even considering alternatives, that is how I would have seen his crime. It was committed against me and neither poor Janine Pruitt nor LaRuth Morrison.

With God as my witness, I wanted to burn that letter and throw that tape into the Savannah River.

Mike and Dave came back from the bathroom, Dave sliding in next to me and Mike sitting across from us. Mike folded his massive hands on the table and looked prepared to give a speech. He looked at the table directly in front of me, then quickly looked up into my eyes. "Hamilton? I am neither in the shape nor have the disposition to run around in the woods with you all night. I cannot do this."

I sighed and said, "Okay. Dave? Let's go." When he didn't move, I looked up at him and said, "What is this?"

"An English lesson, girlfriend."

"What?"

He smiled. "What did he say?"

"That he can't help me…us."

Mike dropped a highway map of the Savannah area on the table and said, "A buck fifty which you owe me, Hamilton. Show me where this place is and I'll get someone to go with you, a cop who can play both bodyguard and legal advisor."

"Who?"

He took his own deep breath and seemed to become tentative. Maybe the word I was looking was legal. He's IAD and therefore on the legal side of law enforcement. He held that breath as he said, "Don't

Chapter Twenty

know. I'm walking a thin line here, Hamilton. On the one hand, you're a live hand grenade. On the other, I should report this fully and allow the department to deal with it. I have to find a middle path through this mess and my fear is that your reputation will prove all too real."

"Meaning?"

"You'll screw me."

My instincts were urging me to jump and jump hard. Those same instincts urged me ten weeks ago to call Sugarplum's and that foray into the hard science of reality did not go well. I forced myself to lean back and smile like an ingénue. "Oh, come on, Mike. I'm not that bad."

"Do you remember how we met?"

I blushed. "Yeah."

"I feel asleep in that council meeting and you woke me with a two-fingers-in-the-mouth shrill-as-midnight whistle. Hamilton? I know better than to get a promise out of you because you'll still do whatever is in your best interest despite whatever promise you give me."

"Officer Hardy?" Dave said. "That might have been fair once upon a time, but not now. She's proven to be a bit different."

"All I have to go on is her past, Mr. Woods."

The inside of my head was filled with the worst sort of franticness. Like fingers were clawing on the inside of my skull, I wanted to start pushing against him, wanted to start telling him whatever he wanted to hear if only he'd give me whatever I wanted. I dropped my hands into my lap and with an effort of will, kept silent as the two men talked about me as though I was a salt shaker.

"Being tied to a tree and beaten half to death has changed her, Officer Hardy. I would think it was obvious."

"It can be an act for both of our benefit."

"I think not. You haven't read that file."

"Will I get that chance?"

It was my turn and I knew it. "Officer Hardy? I need to play that tape first. If it holds what I've been told, then I need to make a copy of it."

"We can go to my house, play and copy it," Hardy said.

"Agreed," I said. "Let's go."

"You follow me," he said. "First, show me on the map."

He unfolded the map, had to move the sugar bowl, cups, saucers, plates and napkins before he had enough room to unfold it completely. I was looking at an area map and not a city street map. It showed all the major highways and even the legal boundaries for Fort Stewart. It took no more than a few moments before I recognized the general area where Billy Ray Simpson was torturing my best friend. It made me both cautious and zealous at the same time. "Promise me, Hardy. Before I show you, you promise me that you won't turn this into a SWAT show. My best friend is out there and she's being tortured even as we speak. Promise me that this guy you'll give me will be nothing more than a competent cop and not an IAD drone."

"My promise wouldn't mean anything, Hamilton."

"Your best effort is all I want, Mike. If someone above your head betrays you, then I can't blame you for that. Just tell me you won't lie."

"I won't."

"Broken promises tend to find their way into print, Mike."

"Stop using my name. We aren't friends."

I idly licked my lips as I stared at him. He's old cop, one who has spent his best years in their employ. He's too old to change his spots and all his training is too engrained. The best I could do was elicit that promise from him. Did his word mean anything? I was going to find out and Debbie's life might depend on how he honored his promises. "Promise me then, Officer Hardy. Tell me that your word is golden."

"I already have."

"Say the words."

Chapter Twenty

"I promise that all my efforts will be exactly as I say they'll be. Is that good enough?"

"Yes," I said and turned my attention to the map. I pointed to Highway 196 just after it splits from the 25 and said, "It's in here. The military reservation is behind and parallel to the road, offset several miles beyond it. His cabin is in here. It's remote and as I remember, there is a pitiful track that leads back there, not a true road at all. His sister used a Range Rover to get in there and he had a pickup. If you drive back there? You'll need one or the other because that land was terrible. Tree stumps, swamp lamp and all manner of wild game is back there. The best I can do is indicate an area. I'd have to see it up close to know exactly where it is."

He looked at the map and said, "That's way out of my jurisdiction, Hamilton."

"You throwing in the towel?"

"No, that just makes the officer off-duty is all."

"Will he actually be off-duty?"

"Yep."

Well, as near as I can tell, no cop is ever off-duty. Maybe they are legally off-duty but not professionally. How do you turn that off, that insistent nagging to correct illegal behavior? I had an inkling of what it felt like because even on my days off, I wasn't off-duty. I was always writing and scanning the headlines for possibilities. In the end, I nodded, watched as he folded up the map and we left.

Hardy lives on the eastern fringes of the Historical section of Savannah near the intersection of Victory Drive and 36th Street. The Bonaventure Cemetery is down 36th Street and I imagine Hardy gets his share of funeral processions past his home because he lives on the route to it.

His home was empty and barren of any female touches. I began to wonder where all those nice feminine homes were or if our society is that bifurcated? The head of a deer adorned the wall above the front door and a gun cabinet was against the wall behind the dining room table. Since it was close to midnight and no other lights came on in the house, I had to assume he lived here alone. As much as I wanted to stop and gossip, his words were clear; we weren't friends.

He flipped on the lights in the back of the house and we walked back to a study or library. One or the other. An old stereo system was in a shelf next to a television, an old tape deck predominating it. He turned and said, "The tape?"

My concentration was broken by a knock at the door.

"Give me a second," he said and went to answer it. There was no one it could be but our babysitter, the off-duty cop.

"Do you trust him, Dave?" I asked quietly.

"Yes."

"Why?"

"We have no choice. Me and you aren't going out there alone. Not with a guy like Simpson running around."

"Did he make that call to this guy when he went to the bathroom?"

"Yeah. We discussed it first. Morgahna? We have to trust him. Legally? He's holding all the cards."

That was true.

Hardy walked in with a man who ordinarily would make any woman stop and look. He was tall, handsome to a point of distraction and his smile should have been able to highlight my day. Hardy nodded toward me and said, "John? This is Morgahna Hamilton." Then he turned toward Dave and said, "And this is Dave Woods. They work for the Morning News so anything you say can be printed and used against you."

His grip was as firm as one you would expect to get from a police officer. "John Newell," he said with an all-American smile. He was not wearing a wedding ring, damn the luck.

"Morgahna," I said. "Enemies tend to refer to me as 'That bitch'."

Dave took his hand and said, "Dave. She's right. I've done that a few times."

All of us laughed but John's gaze remained on me. "I was told you were the one that was going to make the decision here."

Chapter Twenty

"What decision, Officer Newell?"

"First, my name is John because I'm off-duty. Second, the decision on whether I go with you."

"If you do, in what capacity will you go? Even an off-duty cop is never off-duty."

John Newell was as handsome as I remember Evan being. Was Mike Hardy doing this on purpose? He was tall, short-brown hair, a hard stomach and powerful legs. If he started talking about legal statutes, I'd cry.

"I'm a bodyguard, Mrs. Hamilton. I've been told this outing will be a rescue operation. If we determine the young lady is being held against her will, we bring her back safely."

"And if we meet resistance?"

"Legal force may be used."

"Define legal force."

"If we determine the young lady is being held against her will and that her life is in danger, we may use whatever force is necessary to free her."

"Legally?"

"I'm not a lawyer, ma'am."

"Are you armed?"

"Yes."

"Have you ever been out there? Near the reservation?"

"Many times."

"How do you know Hardy?"

"He's my uncle."

I looked away annoyed and said to Hardy, "Copy the damn tape. Then we listen to it."

I gave the tape to him and he found an old used cassette and used it to make a copy. The copying process was quick but entirely harrowing.

He could be erasing the tape and setting me up for a kill, a most legal one. Worse, if he was erasing it, I'd never find out what was on it that Evan ran from, would never be able to determine if grief was warranted or not.

The tape snapped to a quick stop and Hardy said, "Ready, Hamilton?"

"Yeah. I'm ready."

He rewound the tape and punched the Play button.

It hissed, popped and began.

I heard Tommy's voice first.

Before it was over, I'd be crying like a baby.

Chapter Twenty

From Evan Hamilton's Audio Tape

The tape began to hiss and snarl as though it was a live being. The four people stood as though enamored of something quixotic and as lethal as a bullet. The speakers, nice ones from Harman Kardon, continued to hiss as the audio began.

"We're here, Billy," Tommy's voice spoke like a traffic cop, "to plan an exit strategy. We need for things to settle down and we need for you to become much less active than you've been."

As Morgahna stood listening, Billy Ray Simpson's voice seemed full of an old anger, old anger that was pointed at the world. "Less active?" he said with a voice full of disdain and misplaced hate. "You want out of this? Then stop talking about it like it was a real thing."

As Evan spoke, her voice caught and she tried hard not to cry. Still, slow tears rolled down her face as she heard his wonderful voice again. "Simpson? Why kill Janine? I can understand how you feel about blacks, but Janine? Her father is my wife's boss. They'll put it all together and we'll be worth less than dirt at low tide."

"She was a bitch, Hamilton. Worse? You know it firsthand. She did everything but blackmail you and she was planning on doing just that. You want your wife to know? That sweet little piranha you're married to? Think what she'll do if she ever finds out? Your nuts will be swimming with the fishes. They way I hear it? They already are. Hence Janine."

Tommy tried to calm the waters but Evan seemed to smile as though his words could not harm him. In a fashion, nothing could anymore. "Mr. Simpson? Your future business with us, your retainer in fact, will be determined by how well we feel you can carry out future assignments. Janine Pruitt's basic disposition has nothing to do with whether or not she's anathema to me or Mr. Underwood. She could be Lizzie Borden for all I care. Our requirements in the future will be simple. Do you job and nothing more. Having relations of any kind, no matter whether they are black or white, will no longer be allowed."

"So, you can fuck 'em, but I can't? That's it?"

"Mr. Simpson? I wouldn't call what happened to Janine Pruitt as 'fucking'. That was first degree homicide. LaRuth Morrison, too."

"Morrison was a nigger, Hamilton. That don't count for anything to me. Getting her taken care of was fun, about as much fun as a person can have. Do me a favor. Get me another one."

"She was a client and a witness to a crime."

"The mere fact you fucked her screwed up your case good, Hamilton." His voice seemed to change, maybe just changed direction. "And you, too, Underwood. Your dick was so far inside her it may well have come out her mouth."

The audio, or at least the voices paused and fell away for a moment. The faint sound of writing could be heard, maybe a transcript of the meeting, but all four of them doubted that. The content, the purpose of that meeting entirely warranted against anyone taking notes. Had Simpson known about the tape recorder under the table, all four of them had no doubt the man was capable of making the meeting both short and to his own liking.

Evan spoke and said, "Yes, I agree. Tommy was involved and so was I. It matters little whether her involvement with me was voluntary or not. I am as guilty as Tommy in that regard." He paused and the faint sound of finger drumming on the table could be heard. Morgahna remembered that drumming he did, remembered he did it when he was thinking. The harder he thought, the harder the drumming became. The drumming, as she listened with tears rolling down her face, was gaining in intensity as he spoke.

Simpson sounded angry, still angry and dismissive of him and them. "You want me to admit I killed them and then promise not to do it again. Okay. I promise not to do it again. Just don't get clients with pussies like theirs. Them was too sweet to ignore."

"It's supposed to be business, Mr. Simpson. You're supposed to be an investigator and not someone dabbling among the frozen fruit. Please, no more of this. What sort of business will you have if we go out of business ourselves?"

"Fuck," he said haughtily. "Don't matter to me whether you lose your license or go under. The world is still full of sweet young things. Hamilton? One day, me and your wife are gonna tangle in bed. Count on it. That is one piece of sweetness I'll enjoy when it happens."

Chapter Twenty

"Are you threatening my wife?"

"Nah, don't worry, Hamilton. Just havin' some fun."

"Well, don't, Simpson. If I even think you're planning anything against her, I'll go straight to the police."

Underwood spoke up then. *"Now, now, guys. Settle down a bit. Everything's fine, cool and no one knows but us. Let's leave it that way."*

"What about that other cunt. Haines?"

"Ms. Haines is fine," Underwood said. *"Leave her out of this."*

"Wrinkled anyway. Who would want her ass?"

Evan's voice returned and it sounded calm and refined. *"Mr. Simpson? We simply need no repeat of what happened. Can you promise us that?"*

A loud hollow sound happened so suddenly that it took all four of them several long and confused moments before Morgahna at last mumbled, *"He put his feet on the table, the smug bastard."*

Simpson's arrogant voice spoke up again. *"The way I see it, you two are up against a wall. Okay, I killed both of them. Who are you going to tell? In fact, you'll be hearing from me before long. That nigger? She cried like a swamp rat. I would have killed her myself but Tony wanted some black ass and I figured, 'Why not?' Pruitt? She just got away from us. I didn't want to break her neck 'cause I like 'em flopping around the way that nigger did. I love it when they fight back. Pruitt just up and died. Never fucked dead pussy before. It didn't seem that different than live pussy. You two? I figure you'll do whatever I say, jump however high I want you to jump. In fact, you make certain that the good Miss Haines knocks on my door real soon or I'll be havin' a chat with some friends of mine named Tony and Doug."*

"No," Evan said. *"Miss Haines will not knock on your door. You will leave her alone and you will act according to your mission as spelled out by the State of Georgia. That doesn't include murder, rape or kidnapping. You will be an investigator and nothing else."*

"Really?" he said, that arrogance still alive in his voice. "And what are you going to do, Hamilton? What are you going to do if I choose to go to Tony and Doug?"

"Whatever is necessary to stop you. I will not allow you to harm anyone else ever again."

"You threatening me, Hamilton?"

"Absolutely, Simpson. What I did was bad enough. What you did was criminal. You ever do anything like that again and we'll see each other in Hell."

The sound of something scraping dominated the audio. Most likely, Morgahna thought, it was the sound of Simpson removing his feet from the table. "You listen here, Hamilton. You fuck with me and you're wife will know real pain. You, too, Underwood."

"You going to do to her the same thing you did to those two women?"

"Sweet little Morgahna will squeal like a pig, Hamilton. You know how many ways there are to torture cunts? I love hearing them scream. It makes me all excited and such. Screaming women. Imagine the power you have over them. You're stronger, healthier, better and nothing they can do can beat you. The ultimate aphrodisiac, power over women. Your wife ain't no different. She'll squeal, too."

His voice grew louder and more distinct as Evan leaned forward and said, "With God as my witness, I will stop you."

"A lawyer? That will be the day."

"A lawyer will stop you," he said. "Count on that."

"Not you," he said hatefully.

"Me," then he added almost cryptically. "And your sister."

There were no more words spoken. The tape continued but the sound of the door closing was an indication Simpson had left.

The tape ran for several more minutes before it clicked off.

Morgahna fainted.

Chapter Twenty-One

Have you ever forgotten to breathe? Well, I think that's a symptom of hyperventilation. The longer that tape ran and the longer I had to listen to Evan's voice, the worse it got until I just fainted dead away. I loved listening to his voice, loved its mellow quality as though he was in charge and nothing could phase him. In the end, or at least the last thing I have any evidence of, was his last promise to protect me. That put me out because it showed a concern I always took for granted. Husbands are *supposed* to love their wives. That was proof, however, of exactly how much he did and was willing to give for it. A cynic might charge him of insincerity. *He knew Simpson was a maniac and killed himself rather than face him.* I can understand. Still, we choose our wishes and my wish was to remember his last act as the ultimately romantic one.

As I regained some of my consciousness, I began to realize my head was in Dave's lap and I was looking up at him, my body laid out on that couch.

"Hey, gorgeous," he said, "Just breathe deep and normally."

"I'm sorry…"

"Don't be. I should have foreseen something like this. I was thinking like a reporter, though."

I took a deep breath and began to feel better. Both Hardy and Newell were standing and watching as Dave comforted me. I rubbed my face with my hands and sighed deeply. Embarrassed, I said, "Sorry. I didn't mean to act foolish."

Dave being there was a comfort but a small one. It wasn't him that acted like a fool. It was me. I slid from his lap and felt faintly dizzy. Maybe it was the concussion and maybe it was just me being a girl. I was never ashamed or embarrassed to be a girl before. It won me many battles, some because men won't fight with a girl. This, however, was a case where that was not true. Billy Ray Simpson was going to fight with me and was going to kill me unless I had some sort of plan that didn't include fainting.

Chapter Twenty-One

With my head down, Dave put his hand on my back. "You okay?"

"Yeah, It just hit me hard. That's all. I wasn't expecting his voice."

"I understand. Take your time."

I looked up and felt faintly dizzy still. "Dave? We don't have time. At noon tomorrow, he's going to kill Debbie and make me listen to it."

"Debbie is the young lady?" John asked.

"Yeah," I said. "Perfect. She's perfect."

"I'll have to meet her to make that determination, ma'am."

"Well, let's get started," I said with as much determination as I could muster.

Dave stood but looked at Mike. "Was that tape of any legal use?"

"I'm not a lawyer, Mr. Woods."

"You're a cop, Officer Hardy. Your opinion counts."

All three of us watched him as he turned toward the front of the house and just stood as though thinking. Slowly, he said, "There was a name on that tape, someone named Bridget Haines. Evidentially, she's a material witness to whatever happened in that room. You provide her, make her talk and provide expert testimony and, yes, that tape might very easily be the thing that will turn this case. Morgahna? Ms. Hamilton? I will need that original if this is going to happen. They will insist on a chain of evidence and I will need to know exactly where it's been since you received it. You understand all that?"

"You're asking me to give the tape to you."

"Yes," he said with his back turned.

Trust was never something I gave easily. Jesus, not even to my own husband. I held it to myself as though it was a vestal virgin, a thing sacrosanct unto me. Now, a man I knew in a vaguely professional way wanted me to put the lives of myself and Debbie Jenson into his hands. It felt like sandpaper was rubbing against my soul. I did not want to do this but if I went out there and killed Billy Ray Simpson, I could easily be charged with murder. On the other hand, if Mike Hardy was crooked in any way then I was dead and so was Debbie.

"Trust him, ma'am," the young cop said.

I didn't feel as though I had much choice. Debbie's life was slipping away from me the longer I dallied and acted like a girl. She may already have been dead. I just didn't know. "Okay, give me the copy," I said and felt as though I was sealing my fate.

He walked back to the den or at least the back of the house and came back with the copy. I didn't even know if there was anything on it and didn't feel as though I had the time to spend to check it. It was worse than being naked in public because even after you are, you're still alive and I had no idea of I was going to see another dawn.

I dropped the tape into my purse and fought off the biggest attack of panic I can ever remember. That attack in the woods? I didn't have time to think about it and that made it less stressful than this was. That attack? It just happened without any warning or preliminaries. This? Well, this had been building for most of the last three days.

The road back to where Billy Ray's cabin was located took maybe forty-five minutes to reach. I drove for several reasons, not the least of which was that the act of driving took my mind off Mike Hardy and what he was doing with that tape. His nephew, John, sat in the back seat and asked several questions that he called "tactical notes". Actually, I couldn't fault him for asking. He was taking me on faith as much as I was taking Mike Hardy. Yeah, the fact that Mike Hardy's nephew was in the back seat and I didn't fully trust his uncle was on my mind like nothing else quite was. I was nervously worried and Dave knew it but was as helpless as I was to do anything about the situation.

I drove slowly along the shoulder of Route 196 looking for that opening into the woods. When I left here several days ago, I wasn't really paying attention because I still had so much ahead of me. To say that I wasn't interested in where I'd been, but more interested in where I was going would be very close to the truth. It was, therefore, very possible that I wouldn't recognize the place even if I saw it, so I drove slowly along the shoulder just watching the tree line pass endlessly.

Chapter Twenty-One

There are many businesses along that road and that can mean people who work there are at least familiar with the surrounding area. The fact that I spent nine weeks out there and never saw anyone but Sylvia and Silas could only mean the place wasn't near any commercial businesses or homes. Every time we got in an area that was completely devoid of any businesses, I slowed down and watched the area closely. I knew Hinesville was ahead and also knew that we hadn't really been close to it. We were much closer to Fort Stewart, at least to the land around it, than we were to anything else. Considering that the fort is almost deserted of military personnel because of the war in Iraq, Simpson couldn't have picked a better place to hide.

As I crept along at no more than five miles per hour, I finally saw a place in the trees that looked familiar and stopped. I put the Explorer into park and got out. Standing near the front of the heavily idling vehicle, I scanned and said weakly, "I think this is it."

Dave and John were both out of their seats and watching the trees but saw nothing. Dave finally said, "If this is the wrong place and we waste a lot of time out here, it may not go well for Debbie."

Didn't I know it.

Heavy trucks blew passed occasionally with rugged gusts of wind. Lord, it could have been the Seventh Cavalry and I wouldn't have noticed. That much, that part of my brain really hadn't changed all that much. I was still able to concentrate albeit not as hard nor as long as before the attack. Given that I was already a bit weary before all this started that night, I was even more tired now than before. It didn't matter though. I was committed to this because every time I closed my eyes, I heard her screams and they sounded altogether too bloodcurdling for my taste.

"Yeah, I know, Dave," I said a bit wearily. I looked to the west and said, "Hinesville is off in that direction." Then I looked back toward the east and said, "And Savannah is back that way." Nodding directly toward the trees, I said, "And Fort Stewart is a few miles straight ahead. Nine weeks and no one found us except her sister."

"Who is she?"

"An army doctor. The way I see it? Billy Ray knew enough medicine only because he listened to her, his sister and she's a doctor.

Maybe cops know some stuff because of their unique circumstances, but he knew some specific stuff and I think it was because of her, Doctor Sylvia Morris."

"Do you suspect her of anything?" Newell asked.

I shrugged and said, "I didn't even suspect him until yesterday."

"Well?" Dave asked. "Are we going?"

I nodded slowly and finally said, "Yeah. I think so."

"Flashlights?" Newell asked.

It was so dark that if we didn't take something like them with us, we'd get lost anyway. The woods were thick, dark and full of animals that were foraging. I couldn't speak for them, but I didn't want to be anyone's meal. "Yeah."

"They may signal our approach," Dave said.

"You got a better idea?" I asked.

"No," he said a bit abashed.

Newell said, "We keep the lights pointed straight down. In the dark, they'll be difficult to pick up that way, at least more difficult than if we pointed them dead ahead of us."

"That makes sense to me," I said.

We had two lights between us and I decided to let the men play boy scouts and walked between them. Before we started, though, I hugged Dave tight and hard and said, "You can always go home, Dave. You don't need to be out here."

"Up yours, Hamilton. You were always trying to scoop me."

"Thanks, Dave," I said as I held that hug.

"S'okay, kid."

"Kid?"

"I'm older than you."

Hugging John was awkward but I forced myself to do it. He may have been trying to kill me, or at least conspiring to it, but I had no proof

Chapter Twenty-One

of that. All I had was his willingness to do this and be here with us, so I hugged him and said, "You just make sure Debbie is okay."

"I'll make sure all of us are okay."

"Her first. She didn't ask for this to happen to her."

"Neither did you, ma'am."

"Just make sure she's okay."

"Let's go," He said finally.

We got back into the Explorer and I drove it off the road and toward the trees where I parked it maybe fifty feet from a faint track that went into them. I left here in the daylight and things always look different then no matter how hard you look. I was fairly convinced I was in the wrong place but I could find and saw nothing else even remotely familiar as we drove out from Savannah. If this wasn't it, Debbie was dead and I killed her. The way I saw it, I was already guilty of killing Evan and now I was guilty of killing my best friend, my only friend. Sorry, Dave. Our friendship isn't that old and we don't share all the memories that Debbie and I do.

We debated walking along that faint track that was little more than a memory of a real road. In the end, Newell was right. "If we walk along the road, Simpson will be able to see us much easier than if we stay in the woods."

That made sense to Dave and me but then anything would. I had *no* experience at this sort of thing and had no choice but to trust the man. If Dave knew anything, he kept silent.

I know I've already mentioned my issues with trust, but as we stepped into those woods, they began to eat away at me even harder. My basic personality was screaming at me to turn and run because Newell and his uncle were on *his* side. All those trees around us reminded me of that terrible night out in the woods when all this started. I actually rubbed my wrists because I still felt that wire around them and imagined myself tied to every single tree as big burly men kept hitting me until my face was nothing but raw meat and no longer recognizable as a faintly attractive human female. Yeah, I was a mess.

THE PACKAGE

Our progress was slow and I didn't even think to wear a watch or ask anyone what time it was. We were on a deadline was all I knew. If this wasn't done before noon, I may well be dead. That's how I felt.

Dave was off to my right, Newell to the left and he was paralleling those faint tires tracks that would never pass as a road anywhere. The light beams pointed straight down as we walked and that just made our progress difficult. As I remember, the trip away from that house out here was a long one. Still, memory is a bad barometer because everyone's is different. If I had to guess, however, I'd say that house was a couple of miles from the road anyway.

We moved through land that was becoming more swampy and more damp. It was September and that only meant the summer heat had dried up a lot of the swamp. In another couple of months when the rains returned, the swamp would get thicker and wetter. Maybe I should have been thankful for small favors but my girl's girl brain was still screaming, "ICKY!" I wanted nothing more than to change course, go back to the Explorer and find a bed somewhere. Again, Debbie was the only reason I did not. She was depending on me and she was the only one I would trust my future underwear selection to. Yep, I was saving her life, or at least attempting to, for the simple reason that she knew which bra to buy for any given situation. Well, what are best friends for if not to help you with your non-existent sex life?

Trees stumps began to poke up through the muck and my female brain, or the girl's girl version of it, had no idea they represented old fires that burned through years ago. The forest thinned for a while and I could see dim outlines of taller trees beyond the burn area. I looked over at Newell and he was concentrating on the road next to him. To lose sight of it would spell doom not just for Debbie but for us, too.

"How far have we come, do you think?" I asked as quietly as possible.

"Half mile, maybe."

"My guess is that we're at least another mile from that house."

"Gotcha," he said.

I turned to Dave and said, "Did you hear that?"

Chapter Twenty-One

"Yeah. At least a mile."

We were all on the same track, all three of us.

The moon was nearly new which only added to the basic gloominess of the woods. I looked at Dave and asked quietly, "You got the time?"

"Nearly two in the morning."

Ten hours to Rama.

Yeah, it's a reference to an old movie about the assassination of Ghandi. It felt that way, though. It felt I was on a deadline and that should it come, would mean the death of a person who was important to me. *Debbie? I'm doing the best I can. Please don't be dead. Please, don't give up hope.*

I know I've referred to her as my best friend but the blunt reality is that I had no idea how she or anyone would react to something like this. Would she fight back? Would she submit and pray for mercy? Would she be like me and act as though the situation was so preposterous that it couldn't possibly be true? I just didn't know. The objective side of my brain was telling me – and truthfully, I think – that no one could guess or judge something like that. Maybe if you had prior experience with emergencies, maybe you could predict your reaction. I didn't think Debbie had any experiences quite like this, though. Who did?

As we got farther from the road, the terrain kept getting wetter until we were walking in ankle-deep water that was probably filthy. If I stopped to think what might be swimming in it, I might not have continued. Hell, if it was daylight and I could actually see the terrain, I might not have been able to continue. I kept telling myself, "It's just water, a swimming pool maybe." Yeah, I knew better but it kept me going, that little fantasy I was enacting in my head.

Newell said, "Stop."

Dave and I did and my heart began racing and I felt the first twinges of panic. Why had we stopped?

"Just listen," he said finally. "Let me know if you hear anything."

"Do you?" I asked a bit louder than I wished I had.

"No. Now quiet. Just listen."

In retrospect, I suppose it was a good idea just to listen to our surroundings. As I stood there, however, I had one emotion and one only. I was scared, not quite to the point of terror, but still scared. Maybe it was simple apprehension. I don't know because this endeavor was entirely too new for me. Maybe all soldiers feel this way before a battle. Again, I don't know and there was no one there to salve my fear and help me along. In the dark, I guess we were all alone with our fears and apprehensions. I looked at Dave and he looked busy somehow. Okay, that meant he was actively listening and that was always something I knew how to do. *Just start, stupid. You can listen to anything and anyone to the exclusion of everything else. Just listen and hear whatever is there.* True, in the past, that listening was to spoken words and to speaking faces. This was a new type of listening and I didn't know what I was hearing.

Sounds both faint and loud began to creep around me and invade my girl's girl sanity. I realized I was hearing animals of all sorts but I was never a nature lover. To me, a visit to Fort Pulaski at the mouth of the Savannah River was a trip into the wilds. It was an old Civil War-era fort and I had to go out there once for a speech some asshole politician was making there. Even then I found it entirely ironic that a speech about national defense should be given on the site of a spectacular defeat. That fort was a Confederate one and was pounded into submission by rifled Yankee artillery. If you know what rifled artillery is, then maybe you can compare that to the artillery the Confederates had, stuff that was smooth-bore. I don't even know that stuff and I know a spinning projectile will travel farther and straighter than one shot from a smooth-bore rifle. That shot will tumble and go off course easier than one from the other type. It didn't take the Yankees long to take that fort. A bit less than a year after the start of the war, the fort fell and cut off Savannah as a port to the Confederacy.

And I'm a *girl*.

This, though, was spooky, eerie and unnerving. Owls hooted, animals growled in the night and I imagined all manner of swimming things eating my ankles. Dave put his left hand on my shoulder and asked quietly, "You okay?"

"This is creepy."

Chapter Twenty-One

"Do you shave your pubic hair?"

"What?" I snapped much louder than I should have.

He clamped his hand over my mouth and said, "Think of that now, Morgahna, instead of this place. Okay?"

Well, damn. I bit his finger and said, "It's bushier than your friggin' head."

Newell laughed but it was subdued. "Shall we continue?"

"Yeah," I said grumbling.

Still, as I walked, my irritation at Dave erased most of my fear and I knew it. In all the time I've known him, he never got that personal, not once, and those stupid questions he asked in Harley's office didn't count because we were both nervous. We hadn't gone ten yards and I hugged his arm as we walked through the muck. "Thanks, Dave."

"Bushier than my head? Girl? You *need* to shave it."

We'd gone farther than a mile from the road and if my calculations were correct, we had at least that much farther to go before we reached Billy's house. I noticed the farther we went, the slower Newell progressed. Maybe that was wise. I had no choice but to defer to him. I had a hard time deferring to Dave and here I was deferring to a total stranger only because a casual contact that I knew to be a cop told me this guy was both a cop and his nephew. A better and more complete road to a disaster I couldn't think up myself. With God as my witness, I wanted to tackle him and just start demanding answers from him. Yeah, a bit late, that thought was.

I began to have private fantasies about Newell and Dave tying me to a tree and doing whatever they wanted to me. I mean, what could I do if they wanted to do those things to me? Scream? Jesus, we were at least a mile from the road, probably farther than that, and if I screamed, the surrounding trees would muffle it and I'd die out here. Lord God, I wanted to cry so bad that it took a gargantuan effort to hold it in. The girl's girl within me was practically hyperventilating like she did back in Hardy's home.

Still, we kept on.

The night got louder the farther we got from the road. That much, I noticed. Crickets and smaller animals got louder although I never saw anything. I didn't feel those invisible animals eating my ankles either. Had we been able to talk, I would have screamed, pulled my hair and run off toward the road and *any* sign of civilization. Girl's girls *demand* civilization, civilized conduct and this was neither civilization nor civilized. It was taking all my fading willpower to keep going into the deeper darkness of the forest.

Despite that previous visit to this place, I have never been raped. That was becoming my fear, of being raped *and then* killed. Every racial stereotype I'd ever heard was shouting in my ear and I *expected* Dave to grab me and put me against a tree where he would take sloppy seconds to John. Alone? I have never felt that alone before and I have felt that a lot in the past two months. Every stupid decision I'd ever made from refusing to go shooting with my dad and brother to my decision to let Dave carry the gun was kicking me in the groin over and over. I was getting weak with fright and didn't know where we were. I couldn't see the track that I presumed was still off to our left and kept expecting John to scream, "Now, Dave!" That he didn't just kept postponing what I saw as the inevitable. I was a girl in the forest with men who could do anything to me that they wished. What could I do? I could scream and make their ultimate goal harder to get but what if they were like Billy and relished a struggle with a girl? Should I just submit to them and let them do whatever they wanted? In the end, all I could do was keep up with them and keep moving through that ankle-deep muck.

Newell signaled another stop and my senses screamed, "This is it! Prepare yourself, Hamilton!"

All he did was listen and watch the forest. Nothing happened and I breathed a sigh of relief and felt in my soul that all I'd been given was a temporary reprieve. Newell switched off his light and waved his arm at Dave who quickly turned off his. I was terrified and not of Simpson, but of them. I never liked sex all that much and was sliding headfirst into a terror of being raped.

I probably made a noise, a soft cry probably because Dave turned to me asked, "You okay?"

Chapter Twenty-One

Oh, God. I would have screamed but I was far too terrified to do anything but cry and whimper.

"Newell?" he said quietly. "I need a second."

"Please…" I managed to moan expecting his hands to rip apart my sweater and grab my breasts.

No, he hugged me and felt my terror. "Hey, it's okay. You need to stop?" he asked gently.

"I'm so scared," I cried.

"Don't be," he said.

"You're going to rape me, huh?"

He actually laughed softly, "Yeah, my ultimate goal. To get you in the forest with a man I don't know and have sex with you. Morgahna? Did it ever dawn on you that I could have done that back in my apartment in a neighborhood crawling with other blacks? Jeez, girl. Give me a break."

I buried my face in his thick sweater and muffled my cries against him.

"We can stop for a bit."

"Okay," I said as my breath came in fits and starts.

He just held me close as the night slowly faded away. He whispered to me, "You're being brave, girlfriend. This will make a great story. You'll see."

"You aren't going to tie me to a tree?"

He hugged me tighter and said, "No. Just tell me when you're ready. We can afford to wait for a while." It was possible that he could both sense and feel my fear. As we stood together, our ankles covered in slime, he asked, "You remember our first assignment together?"

I smiled into his chest. "Yeah. Fort Stewart to report on the troop assignments to Iraq."

"You thought the guards were cute."

"Did not."

"You got a bird colonel to break discipline and that's when I decided you were more than a cute butt."

"My butt has never been cute."

"Girlfriend? You have no idea, women don't seem to realize it."

After a few beats of his heart, I asked, "Really? I have a cute butt?"

"Merriam was always jealous of you."

"I should talk to her."

"Maybe you should."

"We have to survive this first, huh?"

"That would help."

I sighed and said quietly, "I'm sorry, Dave. I'm sorry for being weak and expecting you be someone you're not."

"Hey, I'm scared, too."

Newell's face hovered over Dave's shoulder. "Just for the record? This is no picnic for me either. You guys ready?"

"Dave? If anything happens to me…"

"Nothing will," he said interrupting me. "Let's go."

That short talk helped but we were still deep in the woods and I still had no idea where we were. I was taking an awful lot on faith and that was an entirely new idea for me. I had so little experience with putting my fate in the hands of others that I could do little but walk between them and hope at least one of them knew what he was doing.

We hadn't gone ten yards when Newell stopped and went into a crouch, one that both Dave and me followed. I slid a bit closer to Dave but didn't look at him. Instead, I concentrated on hearing whatever there was around us. When I did look, it was at Newell. Obviously, he heard something and was trying to locate the source. In the dark, all I saw was an outline and little else. His arm was parallel to the ground in a classic rendition of, "Shh!"

Chapter Twenty-One

A flash of light, a room light I thought, flared for no more than a moment and all three of us crouched a bit lower. Newell crept near to me, to us, and asked lowly, "Did you see it?"

"Yes," both of us said.

He pointed off to the right and said, "That way. We need to circle around behind them."

Dave waited for Newell to lead and put me between them, his hands going to my waist and forcing me to follow Newell. The brush and trees were as thick as I remembered and we had to go slow because of it. Trees towered overhead and all around us as we moved slowly and silently through the woods. Animals and owls sounded like foghorns as we moved through the trees. I was no longer scared or terrified, just wary about my chances of surviving something I couldn't even begin to guess at or fathom how deep the hatreds lie.

Our movements were slow and deliberate because we felt we were close and that was reason enough to make every movement a careful one. I kept watching my left where that brief glimpse of light came from and saw nothing more. My mind was telling me I'd seen a cigarette being lit but I knew Billy Ray didn't smoke. Well, for nine weeks he hadn't. Would he start now? If not, then he had help and I always figured that he would and even knew who it would be. Tony Slayton and that man I knew only as Doug were here somewhere. The mere thought of their coldness and the way they treated me so impersonally made me shiver as we stepped over fallen trees and old logs. The muck was no longer ankle deep but had changed to solid ground. That was what I remembered around that cabin. I suppose that made sense. You never build a cabin in the swamp but on the shoreline that bordered it. It made our progress easier but we still went slow and deliberately as we kept moving off to the right and then way around the back of the building that none of us even saw.

Newell moved a bit farther ahead of me but I still saw him clearly. He was angling slowly to his left when I saw a dim flash in the night and the sickening sound of a metal bar meeting the back of a head. Newell went down immediately and I felt an arm go around my waist and Dave carried me off into the deepest forest as shouts behind us betrayed both Tony and Doug following us.

Suddenly, he stopped, wrapped his hand tightly around my mouth and said absolutely nothing.

Then, I heard an old voice.

Billy's.

"Welcome back, Morgahna. Too bad you'll never leave alive. Debbie was fun, tight and fun. I hope she's sleeping."

Dave's hand dug into my mouth and he turned me against his chest but remained silent as we crouch under a huge tree. As scared as I was, I was about to know fear beyond any I have ever known. That fear was for my friend, Debbie, and what he'd done with her. Well, with and to her. I was about to step ankle-deep into a human being's worst fear.

You figure it out.

Chapter Twenty-Two

Dave had his right hand clamped around my mouth and I could feel that gun in his left hand. Since his own survival depended on my ability to remain quiet, he kept his hand over my mouth. Look, I can't blame him. I already had piss in my underwear because I was absolutely beyond terror and all the way to paralysis.

Voices filled the night.

"Morgahna? You ever been butt-fucked?"

No. I couldn't imagine Evan doing it to me and could *not* imagine anyone else even asking.

"Debbie admitted to it," he said. "She was under some duress, so maybe her answer doesn't count. I mean, I was butt-fucking her when I asked, so maybe she counted that as prior experience. I shoulda asked."

Then Tony.

"You figured it out yet? I wasn't supposed to kill you like I did that nigger."

Then Doug.

"Her head just kinda got all squishy. I guess you hit something that hard and that often and it gets that way. You be sure to let me know."

They were close and Tony was closest based on his voice. Billy was off to our right and farthest from the house. Doug was off to our left and closer to the building. They were spread out about ten feet apart with us just to Tony's right.

"I don't know, but I think Debbie's fake boobs exploded. We'll probably never know," Billy said as his voice grew closer and more threatening.

Dave's hand dug deeper into my mouth as those voices got even closer. My knees collapsed and Dave had to hold both me and that gun at the same time.

Chapter Twenty-Two

"You know?" Billy said. "You can fuck a woman so many times it isn't fun anymore. I learned that from LaRuth. I wouldn't exactly call that a gang-bang because there was just the three of us and it was spread out over three days. But I musta fucked her a dozen times in those three days and got so tired of it that I had no choice but to kill her."

"Speak for yourself, Billy," Tony said. "That was sweet pussy."

"Start out real tight and got kinda loose after a while," Doug said.

Tony couldn't have been more than fifteen or twenty feet from where I was, from where I cowered behind that tree. Tears of absolute stark terror rolled down my face and over Dave's hand. I pissed again and felt the dampness between my thighs as it rolled toward my knees and slowly got absorbed by my pants. Jesus, if they got much closer, they'd be able to smell it.

Everything got quiet and the voices got still and all I heard was Dave's heavy breathing and the woods around us. I felt Dave turn his head try to look behind us. From over his hand, I tried seeing things in the dark and saw nothing at all, nothing but the dark woods and the noises in the night.

Then a sudden voice said gruffly in our ears, "Drop the gun, nigger."

Don't, Dave. Please, Dave. Don't. Please fight. It will be worse for me than you. Please, Dave, fight. Please.

He dropped it.

It was Tony and he was meaner than I remember. Look, I don't remember much of that ersatz interview in his office before Doug drugged me with something that simply smelled musty and sweet. Doug came up behind him and dragged us from the tree where we were cowering. Well, I can't speak for Dave but I was cowering. Doug pushed us into a clearing and Billy came out of nowhere and hit him with the same sort of pipe or metal club that Tony and Doug used on me. It took two to his head and Dave didn't move anymore. Me? Doug held that club in his hands, pointed it at my face and said, "You want another dance?"

I was terrified and didn't answer. My silence bought my a shot to my stomach. The worst part of it was seeing the blow coming and not being able to do anything about it. I crouched a bit and the impact knocked me to the ground. Billy Ray put his foot to my neck and said, "Where is it, bitch?"

"A guy named Hardy has it," I said, my voice practically begging.

He stepped down on my neck and my hands gripped his calf almost involuntarily. I couldn't breathe and my terror began to build to levels where I would say anything if only he would stop. "You better have it, bitch. You better have it close by." The copy was in the Explorer back where I'd parked it near Highway 196. The entire envelope was there, the entire file. He leaned on my neck and my throat just cut off entirely. "Now. Where the fuck is that tape?"

Doug's foot came to rest on my groin and he stepped gently all around it. Then he kicked me right there as hard as he could and I saw stars. I've heard stories about men and how much that hurts. I'll never know because I'm not a man. I can attest that it hurt enough to take away my breath, though. As I writhed on the ground, my hands between my thighs, Billy let up on my throat and I started wheezing badly, just gasping for breath as I tried to fend off the pain or at least make it go away.

"Now. Again. Where is the tape?"

I would have agreed to almost anything at that point. My fear was that Dave was dead and the way Newell got hit, his fate was probably the same. I was alone and my fate was clear as soon as I told him what he wanted to know. His foot was still on my neck and not even my worst moans, writhes and wiggles had done anything to remove it. He reached around to the small of his back and produced the biggest gun I'd ever seen. Okay, it just looked that way. It was, however, pointed right at my face.

"You'll cover up just nicely out in that swamp." He cocked it and re-pointed it at my face. "Now. Where?"

"Back in the Explorer," I said. "It's parked by the road near that track." Yeah, I felt like a coward and would no longer accuse anyone of being one, not after that. My groin still hurt and his foot was still on my neck.

"Tony?" he said as he stared at me. "Take the pickup back to the road. Break the windows if you have to, but bring back that tape."

Chapter Twenty-Two

"You got it," he said.

He removed his foot from my neck and said, "Doug? Bring her to the house."

"Gladly."

Doug reached down and picked me up easily, then twisted both arms behind me and forced me to walk back to the house with my arms pointed backward at the sky. It was painful and I stumbled many times. No matter how awkward I felt, he kept his grip on my arms and those falls just made my shoulders scream that much more painfully. I screamed once and he kicked me in the stomach with his knee; I fell gagging to the ground, my arms still twisted painfully behind me.

"Scream again, bitch," he said, "Please." Then he slapped me again and again.

A long stream of drool that was mixed with blood escaped from my mouth and dripped to the dirt. The house loomed above me as my face was pressed toward the dirt. I wanted to beg but was terrified even to speak. He grabbed my sweater just behind my neck and pulled me into the house where he threw me through the front door. I came to a stop in front of that old couch where Billy kicked me in the ribs as I rolled onto my back again gasping for breath. His foot went back to my neck as he told to Doug, "Drag the nigger back here. Then check that other one. If either of them are conscious, just fucking off 'em. Otherwise, bring 'em back here. Debbie might just get lonely."

"You got it," Doug said and he left.

"Morgahna? You and me never partied like me and Debbie did. That's gonna change as soon as I have everything and all the loose ends are taken care of."

My literate mind was screaming, "Poor grammar!" My emotional side was winning, though. "Why, Billy? Why tell me all those lies? Why kill those girls?"

He smiled and it was nothing like I remembered from ten weeks ago. Gone was that man who cried about his dead wife and baby. The trouble was that I knew who that referred to now and knew what my own future was. I would end my days looking like mashed potatoes.

"Girls is pussy," he said. "Girls is pussy and the world is full of it. You take what you want and pass along the rest. Girl? You got a fine pussy because during those four days you were unconscious? I checked it out and it looked inviting as all hell. It took a lot of willpower to withstand it. That night I crawled in bed with you? That was the key. I knew I had to cry and let you see me as a girl and not as a man. That's what women want. They want men who cry and wail and carry on and act like weaklings. You bought it hook, line and sinker."

"You killed her baby, too? You killed LaRuth's baby?"

"Fucking nigger kid. Wasn't worth the effort either. He just sank like a rock and the 'gators ate him."

I was looking up at a triple murderer. LaRuth Morrison, her baby – Artemis - and Janine Pruitt. He was going to add me to his list. It was possible that John Newell and Dave Woods were already dead.

"Take your pants off, lady," he said as he pressed his boot against my neck.

That was not something I could do easily. It was a graphic reminder of what he was going to do to me before he killed me. When I hesitated, he stood on my neck until I could neither breathe nor move my head at all. My windpipe closed entirely and I began to panic as my lungs slowly emptied of air, slowly but assuredly emptied of my ability to live and do anything to protect myself.

He repeated it. "Take your pants off."

With clumsy obedience, I began to struggle to get them off. Yes, I was willing to be raped if only he would let me breathe. The worst part was the button. I fumbled, closed my eyes and kept trying to get it undone. Finally, it popped open and I slid down the zipper and squirmed and wiggled until I realized I had to take off my shoes first. Then I got out of them and rolled my legs up toward my head.

"The panties, too."

Those were easier.

Finally, when I was naked from the waist down, he relented and I gasped in deep gulps of air and actually felt I was getting the better of the

Chapter Twenty-Two

deal. When my lungs were full and getting more of it that way, I put my hands over my genitals and he pressed down again.

"Don't do that. I want to see it."

I dropped my hands to my sides and was entirely willing to let him look if only he would not choke me again.

Doug came in dragging a lifeless Dave Woods by his ankles. He dropped him near the door and Billy asked, "He alive?"

The man smiled and said, "He's breathing. I wouldn't call what we got planned a life, though."

They laughed together and Doug said, "Gotta go check that other one."

The boot came down again and he asked, "Who is he?"

I squeaked, "John. His name is John."

It came harder and I almost could not breathe at all. "Who the fuck is he?"

"A friend of a friend," I said weakly as my hands pressed against his leg as he stood on my neck and made even speaking difficult.

"Who the fuck he is, Morgahna? Why is he here?"

I was frantic, my arms flailing about then gripping his leg that would not move from my neck. The way I was squirming and flailing, I felt worse than a bug on a pin. "The nephew of a guy I know," I wheezed as my hands kept trying to dislodge his foot from my neck.

Everyone I suppose gets sloppy. Everyone. I'd like to say I'm a sloppy drunk but the evidence points to me being a belligerent one. I was sloppy with my inter-personal relationships, the primary one being with my husband. Billy was sloppily arrogant. Maybe I would have been that way, too. You know, standing there with my foot resting tight against the neck of girl's girl. Maybe I would have smiled a bit nastily the way he did because he *knew* he was going to get what he wanted. When you force a girl to take her pants off, the rest is easy. So, Billy got arrogant and failed to ask the one question that would have killed me then and there. The stupid part of it was I didn't even see it, didn't even realize that I'd withheld a crucial bit of information from him. The way Billy looked at it, John Newell was simply a horny friend, one who liked my butt and the re-shaping of my face. What did I withhold? That John was a cop, was a cop whose uncle was also a cop. Given that my background was politics and business, it was easy to ascribe John's clean-cut appearance to a stock brokerage or some foolishness as that. All it did was buy me a short reprieve.

He stared at me and licked his lips as he did. It was an entirely silent message for his plans for me. Scared? Lord, I couldn't even think. You know? I was actually glad to get out of those piss-stained pants and underwear. That's how far into psychosis I'd gone. I kept panting a mantra over and over again in my mind. *Please don't rape me. Please don't rape me. Please, pretty please. Please don't.* Yeah, the school of wishful thinking. Maybe that works in civilized society but not in one where the animals rule. In that kingdom, raw power wins every time.

Doug came in an dumped John on the floor where the drop stirred him. He began to become conscious and Doug pulled out his gun. "Pop him?"

"Nah. Club him. That might do the job anyway. I want to drop all three of them at the same time."

"We waiting for Tony?"

"Yeah. When I know I have everything, then we share the cunt and pop the other two."

Doug smiled. "You know what?"

"Tell me."

"The stud here wasn't carrying a gun."

"Maybe he dropped it in the swamp."

"Maybe so. Stupid bastard thought it would be easy."

Doug knelt next to me and stuck his index finger up inside me as far as it would go. "Tight."

"Not used much from what I hear," Billy said.

It hurt because I was so scared and he was so careless. Well, maybe not careless exactly. He simply had no reason to be gentle because

Chapter Twenty-Two

he didn't care if I got anything out of it. When I grimaced, he stuck two fingers inside me and didn't care how much it hurt. "I think she likes it, Billy."

"Don't matter none," he said dismissively. "Just leave her until I'm ready."

Doug stood and said, "You were easy. I'll never know why you showed up there that night because we'd been discussing how to get you there. Tony figured he'd have to follow you and pretend to pick you up or something. That always seemed pretty lame because no one ever described you as easy. The thing that has us baffled is the phone call you said you got."

It seemed like an opening and I decided to wiggle through it. You know, anything to wiggle off that pin. "I did!" I said as I slowly strangled. "I got a phone call from a girl!"

"Who?"

"I don't know. That's why I went there. She called me and used Evan's name! She knew him and I wanted to know why!"

His boot heel was starting to hurt besides simply cutting off my air. The space between the heel and sole was digging painfully against that old tracheotomy. I wondered if Billy actually did it or if Sylvia did and he just took the credit. I grimaced and squirmed, my butt naked against that old wooden floor. I was going to die with splinters in it.

Anger spread across his face in a great wave as he removed his boot heel and dragged me to my feet and threw me against the wall near the kitchen table where I'd had so many breakfasts' with him. I was convinced I was going to be killed and I started begging. Tears and terror filled me in equal portions as he clamped his left hand around my neck and looked as evil as anyone I'd seen. "Please, Billy," I cried. "Please, don't kill me. Please."

When and how he dropped his pants I'll never know but when he entered me and it hurt, I knew what rape felt like. He just banged me against the wall over and over and over, my head bouncing painfully off the wall as he did, his hand still wrapped tightly around my neck. At some point he just came and I never knew. I was terrified and simply stood there with my legs splayed and my hands spread wide against the wall with fear. He head-butted me three times, just hammered me with his forehead until I became woozy and began to slide down the wall. He kicked me in the face with his knee and pain exploded across it as I began to lose consciousness.

Someone said faintly, "She's all yours Doug."

I have dim memories of being thrown on the table and raped again but with little memory of anything except more pain. Doug was harsher and said things that are still painful to hear even in my mind.

Somewhere I heard a scream and I don't think it was me. Maybe so, but I don't think so. I will always remember hearing Debbie's scream in my mind. That's who I thought it was. I was hearing her screams, those screams I heard over the telephone, was hearing them in my mind. My heart went out to *her* and not to myself and that was the first time I can honestly say that I'd thought of someone else first.

I heard another voice, another man. It could only be Tony and he raped me, was the third guy that did. Then Billy came back, lifted me off the table, turned me over and took me anally. My face hit that sugar bowl and shattered. I tasted equal parts of sugar and blood as he kept at it, kept grunting as he just hammered me over and over. When he finished, he picked me up and threw me over the table where I landed under it and on the other side. I was weak, in pain and had totally given up. It was the most humiliating and painful thing that had ever happened to me and I waited for him to kill me. For what it's worth, I actually wanted him to do it because it was so thoroughly humiliating. He grabbed the table and heaved it out the way, actually threw it across the kitchen where it bounced off the refrigerator in pieces.

He was getting angrier and I think it was only because I was a girl, a female. They were talking, probably inspecting the evidence they had gleaned from the Explorer. There was no way Billy could miss the reality of that tape, that it wasn't an original but a copy. Mike Hardy used an old used cassette that showed the name of a band, one I'd never heard of before. The original, the one Even recorded, was professionally labeled and clearly marked as evidence. I heard a voice say, "Shit. Now we gotta find the original one."

"She'll know," Tony said.

Chapter Twenty-Two

Without bothering to answer, Billy picked me up and backhanded me with his fist. Blood splattered from my mouth and when he backhanded me, it splattered again. My lip swelled and he kept hitting me. "Where is it, you rotten whore."

I was so terrified that I actually said, "Mike has it."

Things began to get confused. Noises from the room began to filter through to me. One of the men began to regain consciousness. Billy turned away from me when he heard the noise behind him. Where Tony and Doug went was beyond my scope. They could have gone to the Moon and I would never have known. My left eye was puffed and partially closed. My concentration was shot and I knew only pain and the possibility of a quick death.

Then I heard what my brain interpreted as a gunshot that was quickly followed by another one. I saw Tony slump toward the floor and Doug follow him. Billy grabbed me quickly and hugged me to his chest in a protective embrace and dived out the kitchen window back-first, his face down to protect himself from flying glass.

Hollywood has it all wrong. Those windows that simply disintegrate when you fly through them? Well, in films, that glass has the consistency of beach sand and no one gets hurt by it. I know Billy had cuts all over him and I had a big one running across my right shoulder from which blood spurted down my back. I heard another shot and Billy grabbed me and headed toward the woods using me as a shield from *someone*.

I was groggy and had no idea where I was but my mind, the one that always saw every situation to her own benefit saw a chance and I wasn't going to lose it. Despite my condition, the pains and crimes committed against me, I screamed and bit into his hand with all my remaining strength. He screamed dropped me and I fell to the ground and landed on my hands and knees. Another shot sounded and someone – Billy, I thought – grunted painfully but I knew nothing of the others and their attempts to settle old scores. I knew only that something basic had changed and I launched myself up at him and actually got my teeth into his neck and bit down so hard that a piece of flesh tore away, one that I spit out as I screeched and fought back.

He punched me but its impact was far less severe than before. I didn't care why, just kept pushing myself because my mind seemed to grasp that this was my last chance at life. He fell backwards and I landed on top of him. Even though he seemed weaker than before, he was still stronger than me and easily threw me off of him where I landed against a tree.

When he stood over me, he had that metal club in his hand and I will never know where it came from or how he came to wield it like he did. I remember him standing over me, that club in his hands ready to strike down like God. Something splashed in the middle of his chest and he stopped as though frozen. Blood began to spurt from a wound that had obliterated his breast bone. He slumped to his knees and looked at me before he died. "You will never find her. She might as well be dead." Those words frightened me as nothing else quite had. Debbie was my friend and I promised myself I would find her, free her and take her home. His last words before he crumpled dead at my feet were harrowing and full of the darkest evils human beings can relate to another. "I buried her alive."

And he was dead, taking his secret with him.

For a few moments, for a few agonizing and sinking moments, I was beyond words. It seemed incomprehensible that his words meant what my heart heard. He buried her alive? Despite my seeming lack of an imagination, I saw that scene in vivid detail. I saw her laying in a coffin six feet underground and heard every heartrending scream and shrill cry she could manage before her air simply ran out and left her to die by asphyxiation. As a way to die, it was easily the most fearful one of all. *Oh, my God. Oh, my sweet God. Buried alive.*

I didn't even care who fired that shot, the one that saved my life. I was beyond words and beyond caring. Everything I'd ever grown up with, every horror movie I ever saw, every midnight hour, every corner around which I could not see lumped into one undying horror that would consume me long before I died. I would lay awake in bed at night and see her as her mind slowly dissolved in an abyss of blackness and uncontrollable horror.

Someone knelt next to me and it was LeRay Morrison. "I heard," he said sadly, sympathetically. "Oh, god."

Chapter Twenty-Two

There was no need for more. I knew exactly how he felt and knew exactly the stakes he felt. His choices in that split second were far beyond slim and none. He could kill Billy and Debbie simultaneously or leave Billy to survive only to kill me himself. Either way, Debbie was dead yet would live the remaining few hours left to her in absolute raving terror.

Tears rolled from my eyes as I fell against him.

I looked up towards the window through which we had crashed and saw John Newell standing in its frame, blood running from a terrible wound in his temple. LeRay said quietly, "I have to get you dressed, Morgahna."

"Dave?" I asked weakly.

"Groggy. They'll both need doctors." Then he caught himself and said, "So will you."

"I'd rather be dead."

"Let's go help Dave," he said.

He helped me to my feet and I looked down at Billy who lay dead at them. I wanted to kick him but knew with a deep sadness that it would make no difference. I managed to spit a wad of bloody spittle on him and that did not begin to erase the horror from my mind.

"Come on," LeRay said gently. "Dave needs us and you need to need to dress and cover yourself. Please, Morgahna. Help me here. I don't think I did all I could have done."

The living should have meant more than Debbie did but somehow didn't.

Dave was sitting on the floor, his head in his hands, blood clotting around two huge wounds in his head. I knelt next to him still naked from the waist down and cried on him as we held each other. LeRay produced my underwear and smelly pants and handed them to me. Dave just moaned painfully as John knelt next to us. It was a moment dry and devoid of anything hopeful.

With a final push, I asked LeRay, "Where did you come from?"

"I've been following you ever since you left my mom's place. I knew you'd figure out what this was and would try to take care of it. Morgahna? You have to believe I'm sorry."

John said painfully, "There's a truck load of police on the way. I've been carrying a GPS transponder and they've been tracking us. The code was to come in unless they heard from me by sunrise."

It was a faint hope. "Maybe they'll find her."

"Yeah," he said. "The first people should be here in about an hour."

It was still pitch black outside beyond the immediate house. The darkest hour before the dawn. LeRay said, "They couldn't have buried her very deep because this is swamp land and any deep hole will quickly fill with water.

Oh, great. She could drown in a box.

LeRay saw what he'd said and began to apologize even for that. "Oh, Jesus, Morgahna. I'm sorry."

I must have put my clothes on because I found myself standing in the dim light beyond the back door just looking out at the swamp beyond the trees. She was out there and I was never going to find her. As bad as I felt, I felt nothing. Contradiction? No, that was the truth. I was numb and finally stumbled back to the house, LeRay escorting me because I was in so much pain. Blood was running down my arm from that cut across my shoulder and all I wanted to do was cry because I already missed my friend.

I sank on the couch next to where Dave was hold his head and trying to remain conscious. John sat heavily next to me as LeRay hovered nearby helplessly. John hugged me and I felt nothing because those woods were enormous and Debbie could be anywhere in them.

"I love you, Debbie," I said to the air miserably.

They say there are angels, but I think I stopped believing in them. Life in those first few minutes was no longer any fun and I seriously thought about fighting LeRay for the gun.

But.

Chapter Twenty-Two

Angels.

They say there are angels.

I believe now.

Oh, God. Do I believe.

Chapter Twenty-Three

My angel appeared in the doorway crying hard, his nose running with snot and his eyes flooded with tears. He was carrying a shovel and walked into the house with his hand extended toward mine. I reached up and instinctively took his hand in mine as he said, "I know where he put her, Miss Morgahna."

It was Silas, the kid whose first words to me were profane and suggestive.

All my pains evaporated and I jumped straight up and followed him out the door as LeRay followed with a flashlight. I think John hobbled along with Dave but I was so mesmerized by Silas that I just followed like a believer. Yes, he might have been taking me to my doom but I'd already died at least twice in that house and one more wasn't going to hurt much.

We walked out into the darkness and followed the swamp line until the woods were as dark as hell itself with only that flashlight enabling us to see anything at all. We walked up a slight hill and he pushed the shovel into the ground and started digging. "She's here."

LeRay gently took the shovel from his trembling hands and started digging in earnest. I squatted next to a fallen tree and watched as Silas became the boy he'd always been. I am not a mother and can't pretend to have those feelings in stock somewhere, but it seemed to me that Silas was a boy who was trying to be a man and his only model was a psychopath. The boy cried hard as he watched LeRay dig like a madman in that soft earth. I held the light in my shaking hand until John took it from me and held it in his own unsteady hands.

As LeRay dug with the ferocity of a man possessed by the images he knew to be below him, I watched John and Dave and they seemed to be as mesmerized as I was. Dave seemed to be in worse shape than John but he knew the score here and was prepared to help in whatever way he could.

Chapter Twenty-Three

Dirt flew from that shovel as LeRay kept digging. John kept the light focused even though his hands shook. My shoulder was screaming, my lips felt like balloons, my nose was leaking blood, my vagina was sore and my bottom was probably bleeding. Still, I'd let Billy Ray do it all over again if only Debbie was alive.

Silas stood crying as LeRay dug. I stood and went to where he watched that dirt flying from an ever-enlarging hole. He looked up at me and seemed to know I was hurting and why. One day, he will be a handsome man and I have to wonder what this episode has done to him. Will he see women like Billy Ray did? His face was streaked with old tears and his eyes looked haunted by things he'd seen. "Ma'am?" he said pitifully. "I'm awful sorry. I never wanted anyone to get hurt."

"You saw what they did?"

"Yes, ma'am," he cried even harder as those images began to eat away at him.

"You understand that your uncle was a bad man?"

"Yes, ma'am."

I nodded toward LeRay, then John and Dave. "These are men. If you need a role model, choose one of them. Don't memorialize your uncle because he isn't worth your tears."

"Ma'am?" he cried. "Are you okay?"

"I let you know when LeRay is finished digging."

"Who is it?"

"My best friend."

That seemed to strike a chord with him. He grew more sober and watched as LeRay dug. The hole was maybe six feet around and was nearly three feet deep. He kept digging and not showing any weariness. He knew the score and was willing to do all in his power to uncover that sunken tomb.

I put my hand on Silas' shoulder and said, "I can't blame you."

"What if she's dead?" he said looking up at me. "I watched them bury her and didn't do nothing, lady. I watched them do that."

There were so many things I needed to ask and couldn't. He knew things, probably knew what had been done to her. He probably saw her screaming and fending off madness as they used her and then just buried her like old news.

I heard a dull thunk and jumped straight up. LeRay beat the shovel on a hard wooden casket and began digging around its perimeter as he saw that he'd come down midway along its length. I'd heard no answering sounds, no knocks, screams or tapping and my stomach sank like a rock in a deep pond. John crawled down into the hole and began digging with his hands. Dave slumped down, just slid into the hole and John had to help him out. I saw the effort and appreciated it.

They had no way to know which end was the top, which end was where her head was located, so they dug all along its length until the entire coffin was freed from dirt and then LeRay dug the tip of the shovel under the lid and began prying. Nothing happened as I watched, nothing for several long and frustrating minutes. The lid seemed tight and I kept listening for sounds and heard none. *Please, Debbie. Be alive. Be alive and well. Survive this.*

I heard the sound of nails being pulled loose. He was pulling frantically on that lid with his hands until the whole thing tore loose and there she was. She lay still, her head leaning to her left, her eyes closed and we all thought she was dead. I started crying until LeRay said, "She's breathing! John, help me."

John's face was covered with dirt and blood as he helped LeRay lift her from that coffin. They laid her on the ground and John began CPR but that seemed pointless because I could see her breathing. I stepped around him and said, "Let me."

She looked awful. Both eyes had been blackened and her left one would probably not open. Her lips were bruised and puffed; she was entirely naked. Her body was bruised from her shoulders to her thighs and there were assorted cuts and bruises to her entire body, none bleeding any longer, all of them clotted and dirty. I knelt next to her, got her head in my lap and brushed her soft blonde hair from her face.

They say it's always darkest before the dawn and it was darker than I care to remember around the hole. I vaguely heard all those animals out there in the forest but I screened them out as I looked down at her.

Chapter Twenty-Three

She was the only thing I saw or heard because she needed a friend – me. I would stay there, stay with her head in my lap for the rest of the day, the week, would stay there forever if that's what it took. I lost a husband to this madness and I was not going to lose my best friend, my only friend.

She looked so small, looked too insignificant for anyone to do this to her or want to. We are all that way. We are all insignificant and alone. What did she do to deserve this except know me? Tears began to fill my eyes as I looked down at her. Why would he do this? Why would any man do these things?

"Oh, Debbie," I said as though we were getting ready for a date. "I saw this cute little white dress that would look gorgeous on you. And these sandals? Oh, you could dance all night in them. I went into a store and got a sample of some perfume and I can't wait for you to wear it so the men will think you're special. When we get home? We're going to eat an entire quart of chocolate chip ice cream and eat a bagful of Hershey Nuggets. Just you and me. We're going to watch television and laugh because it's so stupid. Girlfriend…"

…and her right eye fluttered open and she saw me.

I wiped away tears from my eyes because she recognized me. "Mor-gah-na?" she said weakly.

"Yes, baby," I said. "It's me.

"I…don't…feel…good."

I looked up at John and said, "Tell me something, Newell. When will they be here?"

"Soon."

"There's a phone back in the house. Call someone. I don't care who."

He limped off toward the house and I looked down at her. Her gaze, from little I could learn of it, seemed to disappear. It seemed she was reliving the nightmare and saw the darkness instead of the dawn. "Girlfriend? I'll be with you until you're okay."

"Billy…" she said as panic began to take control of her.

"He's dead, doll. They're all dead."

I looked at Dave and he was slumped on the ground, probably unconscious. I looked up at Silas and said, "Get me something to cover her with. A blanket, a sheet, anything,"

"Yes, ma'am," he said and raced back toward the house.

I stroked her cheek and said, "It's over, baby. Don't worry about anything.

They say you should shouldn't lie to friends and that was a big one. Removing Billy Ray Simpson was only half the problem. There was no doubt John saw it and maybe even Dave did. Tommy Underwood was still a problem and I had one chance to do something about him, just one. If the police weighed me down with endless questions about what happened, Tommy was going to slip away, maybe off that hook forever. I had one chance to stop him and I didn't know who else knew it. Maybe Dave, but probably not John.

Her breasts were bruised and probably sore. I can only imagine what those three maniacs did to her and them. As sore as I was, they'd had her far longer than they'd had me. I could see her being in the hospital for a while. I could see them insisting I follow her but I had no time for that.

"Is…it…really…you, Mor-gah-na?"

I smiled at her. "Yes, baby. It's me."

"You…look…bad."

I laughed and wiped away tears. "Oh, thanks. Just what every single woman wants to hear." She faded again and I added quickly, "We have to do something with your hair. I can't imagine going down Broughton Avenue looking like that. Maybe a new cut?"

"Morg…" and she began to cry and I picked her up and held her to my bosom and let her. She cried hard and her entire body shook with staggering emotions, shook with a power I would hopefully never know.

"It's okay, baby," I said as I rocked her gently. "It's okay.

She wrapped her arms around me in an embrace of both fear and reassurance. I held her tightly and kept talking to her happily and brightly until I heard a helicopter above us and then saw a spotlight stabbing at the

Chapter Twenty-Three

ground. They could only be looking for us and I waved an arm at them as Silas came running with a blanket, one from the bed I'd slept in. I began covering her with it as she kept crying. A loudspeaker said from the hovering craft, "A TEAM IS EN ROUTE."

I lifted my hand into the air, my thumb up in a classic sign that I understood the message.

John came limping back and knelt next to us. "They're about five minutes away."

"I need to leave, John. As quickly as possible. As soon as I know Debbie is okay, I need to leave."

"That won't happen."

"You fucking make it happen, Newell. This is Morgahna Hamilton talking and I can make you look like a dogcatcher in tomorrow's paper. You fucking make it happen. There is still one person out there who is responsible for this and I need to do this myself."

"The police can do this, Morgahna."

"This guy will slip away and we'll have to do this again someday."

It caused him to slide into thought and he said, "Let me talk to my uncle."

"Make it happen, John."

The wash from the circling helicopter made the trees wave and bend as we huddled under its protective embrace. Flashlight beams lanced through the night from off to my left. A team of three people emerged, their guns ready but not drawn. John yelled, "HERE! WE NEED MEDICAL ASSISTANCE!"

"On the way," a police officer said, a sheriff.

I looked down at Debbie. "The good guys are here, baby. I'm going to settle this first, though. I'll see you before the day is over. Don't worry about me. LeRay is here, John and Dave are here. The police are here. You'll be okay."

Dave struggled to his knees and said harshly, "You need a doctor, Morgahna. You were raped."

"You need one worse than I do, Dave."

"Morgahna," he said. "I'm going…"

"No, Dave. You're going to the hospital."

A familiar voice came through the trees. I looked up and saw Mike Hardy emerge from them, a flashlight in his hand. He looked at John and grimaced. Then he looked at Debbie and me and his face froze for a moment. He knelt next to us and said, "A doctor…"

"…Won't help me," I said. "You and me are a taking a trip, Hardy. You, me and no one else."

"Why?"

"There is one last person that we need to bag and if your types do it, he'll disappear, maybe to the Caribbean and we won't see him until he kills one of us, Debbie or me. Probably me. I'm the one with evidence against him."

"Lady? You look like hell. You probably feel worse."

"Okay, Granted. I've been raped, I don't want to be pregnant, not by them but I've got time to do that, to take care of it. There is one person who can help and we're going there, just you and me. Me because I know the person and you because you can make it legal."

The scene began to flood with people, cops mostly.

Dawn was breaking hard and fast and I knew if this was going to happen, I didn't have long. An ambulance appeared, its lights turning the whole scene slightly surrealistic. Hardy was huddled with a plain clothes type and the two men made no obvious references to me or anyone else, just talked with their hands stuffed deep inside windbreakers that clearly identified them as police officers. Hardy's was labeled "SPD" and other one "LIBERTY CO SHERIFF". The sheriff was holding the envelope in one hand and the tape in the other. Hardy, to my knowledge, still had the original.

I knew where the buck stopped and only hoped Hardy could sway his opinion. They finally looked at me. Debbie was rolled onto her side

Chapter Twenty-Three

and was clutching at me as though she was drowning. A pair of EMTs approached us with a gurney and I said, "The cavalry is here, girl. You're in good hands."

"Morgahna?" she cried. "I'm scared I'm not going to see you again."

"No chance, Deb. You're stuck with me."

"I'm scared."

"Don't be. They will take good care of you or else."

"Promise?"

I smiled at her. "Oh, yeah. No one is going to hurt you ever again."

"You?" she asked looking up at me.

"How about this for a promise. You can rent my downstairs apartment for half of what those kids paid. Then we can sneak upstairs to my bedroom whenever we want and be girls."

She smiled. "Live with you?"

"Yeah."

"I'm a…"

I smiled put my index finger over her lips and said, "My best friend. You're my best friend. I don't care about anything else, Deb."

"I was…"

"…Always doing your best, girlfriend. I'll see you at the hospital. Don't worry about me. Worry about those pounds you're going to gain eating all that ice cream and cookies."

"Chocolate chip?"

"Anything you want."

"Russell Crowe?"

I smiled. "Well, almost anything."

The EMTs took her from me and began to get her vitals signs first. I kissed her forehead, squeezed her hand and said, "I love you, Debbie."

One of the EMTs said, "You need help, too."

"And I'll get it eventually," I said and walked toward where Hardy was still talking to that sheriff. I was sore and wanted to cry and be a girl, a girl's girl. Considering what I needed to do, I didn't have time to be one. My shoulder was getting sore and I felt bruised from my waist down. I touched my face and it hurt. My lip felt twice its normal size. These were things I was willing to sacrifice for Debbie.

"Hardy? Can we leave?"

Mike looked at the sheriff and said, "Well, Ronnie?"

"She's a material witness, Hardy."

"She'll be available. She'll also be with me."

"She needs a doctor."

"She'll get one."

He seemed to shrink a bit and said, "Christ, Hardy. Get her out of here. Just don't forget you owe me one."

"Thanks, Ronnie."

As we walked toward the house, he said, "You look like hell."

"I feel like hell, Hardy."

"You gonna faint or anything?"

"Not until we're done and not even then."

"John has a concussion and Dave has a fracture. They're both bad. You sure we're doing the right thing?"

"Absolutely, Hardy."

We stepped up onto the porch and the place was crawling with official Georgia. All three bodies were covered with sheets and the weapon, that one LeRay dropped outside, had been recovered. If anyone tried to turn him into a criminal, I'd get Harley to smear the entire sheriff department.

He stopped me on the steps and said, "Well, convince me. Where are we going and why? Who are we going to talk to and what are we going to say to him?"

Chapter Twenty-Three

I needed to sit down and sank to the steps in front of the house. He sat next to me and said, "This stinks, Hamilton."

"Doesn't matter, Hardy. I'm doing this. Even if I have to do it alone."

He touched my lip. "Tell me that doesn't hurt."

"You want the full itinerary? I have places that hurt that aren't visible. You want me to tell you where they are?"

"You were always this way, Hamilton."

"The only reason I'm this way now is my friend over there. She was buried in that coffin and I can't imagine what her night is going to be like tonight and tomorrow and for the rest of her life. Nightmares? It would scare me silly being in that box and waiting for my air to give out. And being confined like that and being underground in a box that small? I'm this way because of her and I need to stop the man who could have stopped this a long time ago."

"Your husband's partner."

"Yes."

"So, convince me."

Silas hovered on the fringes, a forgotten boy. I smiled at him and patted the space next to me. He hurried over, sat down and I put my arm around his shoulder. "This kid is a witness, saved my life, saved Debbie's and should be a hero. Hardy? You make sure something good happens for him."

"Okay," he said. "Now tell me where we're going."

I started my story and told him everything I knew and suspected. He listened and nodded at the appropriate times and as I talked, his face grew more serious than it had been.

In all my life, I never figured on the unexpected. My life was planned, perfect and I was prepared for it only because I made myself that way. I remember my high school graduation vividly. I went to the auditorium where it was going to be held and paced off how many steps I had to take to the podium to get my diploma. I remembered my college days and the dorm I lived in, the girls who shared it with me and almost never invited me to go anywhere with them. That was always okay because I had other things to do that were always more important than the tediousness of their lives. I can't say they were wrong and I was right, just that I should have taken some time with them and tried sharing with them more than I did. I spent four years in college and don't even know the name of one person I went to school with, just the names of professors who helped me along the way. While it isn't wrong to know teachers and get their help, it's wrong not to know classmates and share experiences with them.

I was, I think, the quintessential American. I wanted a nice, safe life and wanted guarantees that no one can give. I can remember my first flat tire when I was eighteen and driving home from a trip to the library. I was livid and it ruined my entire *week.* Yeah, a flat tire. Rather than learn how to change one or call AAA and let them worry about it – which they did, by the way – I allowed it to scramble my entire life for a week. It was as though that flat tire targeted me for misery. That's how I took it. *How could you do that to me? I am so careful. I don't drive over nails.*

The most extreme thing I can remember was Evan's sexual state. He got horny at all the wrong times and just made things difficult for me. I'd be sitting up in bed and he'd be smiling at me and I'd get annoyed only because he loved me and wanted to express it that way. I don't remember hugging him very often either. No, I tried to plan everything and unexpected surprises were not welcome. I had more than one argument with Evan over such trivial stuff that am I now embarrassed and not a bit humiliated. What was different? Well, I can't expect things to turn out the way I want them to anymore. Except this. This was my last foray into the world of certitude. This was not for me, though. This was for Debbie. She needed my help and I knew I could give it, so as I explained the next few hours to Mike Hardy, he began to see that we could do it.

Finally, he nodded. "Let's go."

I hugged Silas and said, "Stay with John and Dave. They'll go to the hospital. Don't go home."

"Okay," he said.

"Silas? Do you trust me?"

Chapter Twenty-Three

"I think."

He was a child and I knew I was going to have to learn about him because my guts were telling me things were going to be different even though I could not see quite how. I was going to know him and be with him more often from now on and didn't have any expectations at all. It was perhaps the first time in my life I could say that and be entirely truthful.

We left in Hardy's unmarked police car and drove back toward Savannah. The hinge on my entire morning was going to be an address that I'd used only once in my entire life. Evan and I had to go there once to pick up someone for a Christmas party. That was two years ago. If that person no longer lived there, I was going to have to resort to a computer search and that meant going to the office and asking one of the IT people to help me. In that respect, I was still a girl's girl. I could see that changing.

If my prey, my object, still lived there, I'd know from the car in the driveway. I knew that car, the one I was looking for and could only cross my fingers and pray. Hardy talked to me and kept asking if I was okay. I finally grumped and said, "I was raped four times, Hardy. I'm surprised I can even walk."

He stopped asking.

I know I looked awful and that was part of the plan. My current appearance would make a better impact on people I wished to challenge than if I'd taken the time to clean up. That glass cut across my shoulder was starting to pound with every heartbeat. Okay, I can buy an infection but it wasn't going to stop me. I remember a sprained ankle once and complained that I couldn't wear two-inch heels anymore. I'd settle for that type of pain now rather than the various ones that kept competing for prominence.

I directed Hardy to the address and he just drove. He'd covered all the legal angles and what needed to happen to make this work that way. I nodded and closed my eyes because I was in more pain than I thought. Still, I was used to pushing myself and this was so minor that I could go all day if I had to.

The house was exactly where I remembered it being and we parked behind a nice Lexus. Getting out of the car was painful but I did and even shook off a proffered arm extended by Hardy. When I realized that my rebuff looked a bit hard, I smiled and said, "Sorry. I'm not used to accepting help."

He nodded and we went to the front door. I knocked and waited for someone to answer. I knew at least five people lived in that house and knew that it was unlikely or at least improbable for the person I was looking for to answer it. That person did not. A kid, a boy of maybe twelve or so did and his face turned white as Alpine snow when he saw me and mine. I told him who I was looking for and the boy turned and went to look for them, the door hanging open. It was a nice home, one that I remember as a kid. There were no aspirations and no pretenses here, just a comfortable home amid more of them just like it.

When the person I was here to see approached the door, things got interesting. I expected a strong reaction and I got one. Hands went to a face and it grew even whiter than Alpine snow, just blanked entirely.

"Can I come in?"

"Morgahna?"

"Yes."

"Oh, Lord."

"This is Officer Mike Hardy of The Savannah Police Department. We'd like to talk to you."

"I…"

"We have an offer for you, one that you should hear before you say anything more. Okay?"

"Okay."

We stepped inside and Mike closed the door behind us. My legs wobbled because standing was difficult. I wanted to fold up like an old tent and couldn't. I needed to be straight and tall, wanted to do this from strength and not weakness. Still, Hardy sensed my difficulty and said, "A chair for the lady would be a welcome thing."

Chapter Twenty-Three

A hand waved and a chair was produced that I sat in despite my best wishes. I was tired, nearly broken and had to force myself along the path I saw just like it was the old days where Evan was home in bed waiting for me, needing me and seldom getting me. As a reproach, I can now see needing a man at some future time and not being able to attract one. I shook off that last-ditch bout with pessimism and decided to be as strong as I willed myself to be.

I started to lay out what I wanted and the condition of my lips kept stopping me as I tried to speak. Hardy put his hand on my shoulder and said, "Allow me."

"No," I said with a small smile up at him. "I need to do this."

I took a deep breath and laid it all out as all five of them crowded together and listened to my story. The one that was the object listened to me closely and fearfully. They needed to be scared because it was intensely legal now. There were too many witnesses to what Tommy Underwood allowed to happen and the person who I talked to needed to know what might happen in any case.

When I finished, I got a reply.

"Okay."

I looked up at Mike and said, "From your point of view?"

"I will recommend what we discussed."

"Are you ready?" I asked.

"Yes."

And what I presumed to be the act last was about to begin.

But then, I have always been presumptuous.

That needs to change.

Needs to.

It makes me smaller somehow and entirely deserving of what happened to me.

Therefore, it needs to change.

I have no choice.

I'm too young to die.

Debbie faces a long life and I will not leave her alone.

Not now.

Not ever.

Then I made one phone call and that was to a lawyer I'd met a few days ago, Todd Gilmartin. I introduced myself, told him what how he could help me and where he could meet us. He agreed.

Everything was set.

Chapter Twenty-Four

Tommy Underwood's back door was open for business but he would not be checking for visitors because most of his staff was already at work. I was going to see Shawna Kingsbury first and while that was not by design, it was propitious for me. Shawna heard the back door open and would be wearing her professional smile when she saw us. When I turned that corner and she saw me, saw a woman who wore darkening bruises and dried blood still clinging to her face like old camouflage, she blanched like everyone else had. "We need to see Tommy, Shawna. I know he's up there because his car is in the lot."

There were four of us including Gilmartin. She nodded and did not buzz Tommy's office

We headed up the stairs and I grew stronger with each step. His office is the first one on the left and he was there if only because the light was on in it. By agreement, the fourth person remained in the hallway and make certain Karin Hubbell stayed out until and if we needed her.

Mike was on my right and Todd was to my left when I went into his office. He looked up and probably did not recognize either of them. I stood and despite my weariness, did not sit in one of the chairs that fronted his desk. He did a double take because I have found it impossible to look at me the way I was, the cuts and bruises, the dirt and my general appearance without *noticing*. Without waiting for a response, I said simply and blunted, "I found it, Tommy. Evan gave it to my father."

I had all the power and motivation I needed to do this because, in my mind anyway, this was the end of it. As long as I held that fiction in my head, I could go all day and had many, many times. My shoulder was insisting I pay attention to it, but I ignored it and the attending pain that radiated out from it. I was more interested in Tommy and his reaction than to that nagging pain.

Tommy, I realized, was a handsome man and I should have noticed it long ago. The sad fact is that I didn't even notice my own husband was handsome until he'd been dead for four months. When he held my arms at my side all those months ago when I was hung-over and

Chapter Twenty-Four

looking forward to another bout of oblivion? I believe it was his way of trying to seduce me. What easier way than to touch and hold a grieving widow? He misjudged me and I never noticed the attempt at seduction, the hope that I would blurt out something he would recognize as important. It painted him as even more despicable than he'd been in my mind already.

A seduction with two other men present in the room, one of whom I met when he tried to pick me up in a bar, ended any attempt he might have wanted to try to pry from me any information that would loose him from my hook. That's exactly the way I saw myself. I was angling for him and he knew it because he knew the contents of that envelope and what was recorded on that tape. He is, however, a lawyer.

"Morgahna? Are you okay? You look terrible."

As an attempt to push me back in the girl's girl corner, it was feeble at best. "On that tape you are heard admitting to the death of Janine Pruitt."

One of the first things I remember Evan telling me back when he thought I might be even faintly interested in his work was an old, old saying. *Know your enemies, Morgahna.* Well, I wasn't interested in his career; I was only interested in my own and never learned that lesson as well as I might have. Yes, it was inevitable that Evan would talk about his partner and also inevitable that we met socially because I was big on social events. So, I knew a bit about him and among those pieces of flotsam was the primary fact of his professional life. He was a lawyer and had argued many cases in front of juries. That meant he had the ability to be impersonal and detached. As he settled back in his chair, that's how he became almost immediately.

"Are you accusing me of something, Morgahna?"

"Yes. I am accusing you of murder."

"Interesting. Whose?"

"Janine Pruitt."

"You must be referring to that meeting."

"Yes."

"The one attended by Evan and Billy Ray, that meeting?"

"Yes."

"Evan, who reported it, is dead and Billy Ray? Who knows. Do you? Morgahna? You have no case. It boils down to he-said, she-said."

It didn't seem to matter that he didn't know Billy was dead.

"What's your version of that meeting?"

"Janine showed up for our meeting and we had it. The events are protected under client privilege."

"She was alive when she left that meeting?"

"Of course. She was nursing."

She was nursing. That bit of information had appeared nowhere else. Was it even true? "She had a baby with her?"

"Of course. She even had a towel over her shoulder because she was nursing during the meeting. She had a baby."

That tape betrayed no mention of a baby. Tommy was trying to use emotional blackmail against a woman who never wanted children. I smiled. "You killed a woman who brought a baby to your office?"

If that was true, if it was true they killed Janine and she had a baby with her when they did, then it begs the obvious question. What happened to the baby? The only infant mentioned during the entire story was LaRuth's and by common agreement, that baby wound up in the swamp. A baby would mean a relationship with someone approximately two years ago, a time when LaRuth Morrison was pregnant with Billy Ray's baby. I know that Billy Ray did not meet LaRuth until Tommy and Evan hired him to follow Janine. I already knew that they had asked Billy Ray to follow-up on a rape case when he was already guilty of raping and killing LaRuth Morrison. It was akin to asking a fox to guard the henhouse.

The difference between them were obvious or should have been. Billy Ray had no love lost for blacks. It was easy for him to be totally dismissive of LaRuth and her baby. Killing either of them probably did not count as murder in his mind. I'll never know, but I'll never care either. He was a triple murderer and held more hatred in his heart than anyone I

Chapter Twenty-Four

ever knew before. But kill a white baby? Was that beyond his capacity? I can't say. If he did not, then what happened to it? Who has it?

The one person who knew the answer to that question was outside and I hadn't even asked that question. Actually, it didn't really matter to me. Getting Tommy, nabbing him for that crime was paramount to me because my own motive was Evan.

"You could have stopped that crime or at least called the police and reported what happened, Tommy. Had you, Evan would still be alive."

"Why, Morgahna? My version is that she was alive when she left that meeting. You need to chase Bill Ray Simpson, a man who was already guilty of rape and murder." Then he looked at Mike and said, "Might I ask your name?"

"Officer Mike Hardy of the Savannah Police Department."

"And yours, sir?" he asked of Todd.

"Todd Gilmartin. I represent Ms. Hamilton."

"A lawyer?"

"Yes, sir."

He smiled at me. "You don't trust me."

"No, Tommy. I don't."

"Well," he said smiling. "In the absence of any corroborating evidence, I'd say you have to excuse me. I have people that need to work."

I held up my hand and said, "I just want to make certain that I had your version of the events of that night straight. You claim that you had that meeting with Janine Pruitt and that she left this building alive that night."

"Yes, I do. Anything else is subject to prosecution. I will not allow myself to be slandered."

"Mr. Gilmartin?" I said.

"Yes, Ms. Hamilton?"

"Would corroborating testimony to the facts of that tape show cause to arrest Mr. Underwood?"

"That would be for the police to determine, but in my opinion, a crime and a witness would warrant an arrest."

"Mr. Hardy?"

"I agree. Ms. Pruitt is presumably dead. A witness to that crime would be sufficient grounds to place Mr. Underwood under arrest."

It was now or never.

If my witness was no longer in the corridor, my allegations would hold as much water as a badminton net. I opened the door and that person was still there. "Now?" I said into the hallway.

The person that entered the room was identified on that tape as being present the night Janine Pruitt died. She was taking notes on a transcription machine and I have no doubt those notes no longer exist. Actually, I know they don't because *she* told me.

Bridget Haines.

She was in the building the night I went to talk to Tommy, the night Billy Ray waited outside for me. Billy Ray would have concocted some sort of story anyway for that night had I not offered to talk to Tommy alone. They needed that tape and if I had walked into a room with them together, Billy Ray might have killed me even inadvertently. Maybe he knew himself that well.

But why was she there when I walked in?

Well, those five people that were at her home when I went there to talk to her? One of them was her husband, Porter. The other three were children ranging in ages from eight to fourteen. Bridget is thirty-eight. She has a family and the price of her cooperation was my silence about her being there that night. Tommy might bring it up and try to destroy her credibility, a thing to which I alluded when I talked to her earlier that morning. "Bridget? He might tell stories and try to ruin your credibility."

That was the key to her being here. "Morgahna? Do you miss your husband?"

"Yes. Dearly."

Chapter Twenty-Four

"All these things have happened to you," she said thoughtfully. "Would they have destroyed your marriage?"

"Maybe."

"But he would be alive to argue with, correct?"

"Yes."

"Was he reasonable?"

"Very."

"You would have been hurt, right?"

The question itself hurt. "Yes, Bridget. I would have been hurt and I might have turned into a real bitch, but he would still be alive and maybe we could have salvaged something for ourselves."

When I am thirty-eight and staring at forty like a pending death sentence, I might do what she did. I might give myself to the first man who complemented my sagging bust line. Porter Haines does not know about the various meetings, both clandestine and otherwise, Bridget had with Tommy. She was aware even before she stepped into that office that Tommy would try to ruin her credibility in a court room. She knew she was at least as culpable as Evan himself felt because she was the one who cleaned the room after Janine was killed.

"It was a mess, Morgahna. She hit the back of her head on the table and it bled profusely all over the place. My reward was my job. If I didn't help, I felt as though I might be next. Billy Ray threatened me and I got scared."

Todd interviewed her very briefly and Bridget proved to be adept at being succinct. His questions were to-the-point and her answers were just as good. His opinion was that she was credible and I proceeded on that point alone. A baby being part of the mess never came up. It really didn't matter. The fate of that child could proceed through legal channels at its own pace.

The basis, however, of Bridget Haines doing this, of her appearance in that room was what happened to me. My husband committed suicide rather than face a life that would assuredly have been different. I can understand and feel fear of the unknown, can understand the basic conservative ethic because I have always identified with it so strongly, but what happened to me spurred her to do this and live to have those arguments with her husband. She cried briefly when she admitted what she had done and where she had done them. It was still me that was pushing her though. Despite the dire circumstances and the dim future she saw, she was alive and wanted to fight for her marriage and her man.

Tommy's reaction was subdued because he's a lawyer and trained to be dispassionate. My own city council chambers training was a good place to learn about people and their agendas. Everyone has one. When Tommy saw her, saw Bridget, his own agenda popped out as slight bulges around his eyes. No, it and they did not last long but I saw them. Politicians and lawyers make good bedfellows. One is as good as another, or as bad maybe.

"Bridget? What's your opinion of the night Tommy, Billy and Janine met in the conference room downstairs?"

As she answered the question, I watched Tommy's face. He was watching me when I asked, but immediately switched to her when she started to answer. Maybe Bridget was uncertain when she started an affair with him, uncertain of her power to woo a man, to win his heart, to be attractive anymore. Maybe she was all those things, but I know you get to a point where none of that matters as much as self-respect and the dignity you can manage for yourself. Sex is sex and nothing more. It makes you feel good for a few short moments but those moments dissipate all too quickly. When you live in a society that shields sexuality and holds that it is a private affair, then the things that matter most become how you walk in that society, become how you see yourself or even if you can. Evan lost the ability to see himself under the glare of that societal spotlight. Bridget examined herself and maybe would have succumbed just like Evan had except that he *had* succumbed and she knew it. It made her think and made her see that even a life led badly is better than a life not led at all.

Her attitudes that morning made me think of my own conduct like nothing else quite had. She was being brave and was willing to make whatever changes her life was going to require. She was not willing to be led by her genitals quite the way Billy Ray and Tommy were. She decided

Chapter Twenty-Four

to take herself in a conscious direction rather than allow herself to slip away under a cloud of hormones and empty desires.

"Janine was a nasty little bitch," she said bluntly. "She tried to smear a boy, tried to accuse him of rape only to force her father to see her sympathetically. He seemed to have plans for her and that episode with that college boy tarnished his plans and made them unable to happen. I don't know what that means, but she was nasty and vehement because the evidence of her allegation did not support itself."

Tommy just stared and said nothing.

"Billy Ray got angry when he confronted her with the truth. She spit at him and called him a 'hillbilly'. Tempers flared and she actually ripped open her blouse and exposed herself to them." She sighed, closed her eyes and said, "I have been trained to take notes like that. Just record whatever happens. You cannot transcribe a meeting if you get emotionally connected to it. I always removed myself and became a rather disconnected piece of furniture."

Then she looked at me as I was staring at Tommy. "Yes, there was a baby in the room that night. Hers. That's why Evan walked in when he did."

"He saw what happened?"

"Yes," she said rather weakly. "He saw."

"He saw both Tommy and Billy Ray rape and kill her. Right?"

"Yes, he did."

"He did not take part?"

"No."

"Mr. Gilmartin? Is this credible?"

"Yes. It will, however, be challenged."

"Bridget? You understand that?" I said to her while continuing to stare at Tommy.

"Yes."

"Mr. Hardy? Is this grounds to arrest him?"

Mike said, "Finish the story, Ms. Haines."

Bridget sighed and said, "Billy took it personally, the name calling. They were on opposite sides of the table and he actually leaped over it at her. Tommy didn't do anything to stop it and when Billy ripped her pants off, actually took part. Evan didn't do anything, didn't engage with them but didn't stop them either. I will always believe that he saw the practice going under instead of a life being taken. When Janine was dead, her neck broken, Tommy ordered me to clean up the mess and Billy actually said, 'Or else'. I got scared and for my life, not my job. Morgahna? When you came to the office that night? I had been with Tommy sexually that night and I am willing to admit to that in a courtroom. I was there because he told me to be there. I was under his thumb as long as that death remained quiet. Billy Ray disposed of her body and no one discovered what he did with it."

"The swamp," I said.

"Most likely," she answered quietly.

Mike said, "A forensic examination of that room will uncover any traces of blood down there."

"Was the death accidental?" Todd asked.

Bridget paused and said, "Probably. I don't think Billy Ray meant to kill her. I think the violent impact on the side of that heavy table down there killed her. She looked as though she had a broken neck and I can believe it happened that way. All Billy wanted was to control her, to intimidate her and killed her in the process. It intimidated me and kept me under Tommy's thumb ever since it happened."

"And Karin Hubbell?" I asked.

"Under the same thumb."

"How?"

"She isn't a partner and probably won't be, wouldn't have been. She really had no choice but to do stuff Tommy wanted her to do."

"My home?"

"Is being restored. Your belongings were in storage over in Garden City near the airport. The storage was paid by the firm."

Chapter Twenty-Four

"My car?"

"Is there. A black BMW Z3."

Mike said, "That will be easy to confirm."

Todd said, "I concur."

"Well?" I asked Mike.

Tommy frowned at Bridget and said, "That's nothing more than your opinion."

"Tommy?" she said with the rest of her life hanging precariously over her head, "My opinion is going to send you to jail. My opinion is going to ruin my life. My opinion might have ruined Evan's but I kept it to myself and now he's dead. I have a widow next to me that will live with that omission for the rest of her life, will wonder if I might have saved her marriage and helped repair a damaged life. I'm done with secrets, even ones that might keep my own marriage alive. Tommy? Your conduct was criminal and I will testify to that in any courtroom you care to name. Can I be tried as a co-conspirator? I really don't care. I've had nightmares about that night because I see her head splattered, her blood all over that table and her dead eyes. Mostly, I see her dead eyes and they will always haunt me."

"You have no motive to search my office," he challenged Mike.

"I have a record of a meeting where you admitted Janine had been present. Since that meeting, no one has seen her and this location is the last identifiable one where she was seen. Mr. Underwood? I have a lot of motives here."

Todd said, "Technically, Mr. Underwood. All Mr. Hardy needs is evidence of a crime and a reasonable set of circumstances to make an arrest. Motives are things that prosecutors will argue over and assign."

"You don't have a body," Tommy challenged Mike.

"We have reasonable evidence, Mr. Underwood."

"How much time has elapsed since that meeting?" Todd asked.

"Almost a year," Bridget said.

Mike stepped in front of me and began reading Tommy his rights. Mike Hardy was a cop, a most diligent one. Then he cuffed Tommy and placed a call to the police station who sent over a car to have him booked.

It was over.

I was safe.

I slumped into a chair and began to cry.

No, they were tears of happiness.

Even though I thought it was over, I had other problems.

Problems? Well, maybe *issues* is a better term for them.

I had issues.

Chapter Twenty-Five

I spent the next three days in the hospital right next to Debbie. While her immediate injuries were far worse than mine, my prior injuries had never been examined and that's what they started doing as soon as they did the first MRI. The bones of my face had fused nicely, I was told, but any attempt to make me look the same way I once did now fell under the umbrella of plastic surgery. They said it was up to me and I decided since my life was so different that I would start that new life with a new face and I passed on any surgery, plastic or otherwise.

The wearying effects of that concussion, I was told, would fade over time as long as I didn't have the urge to start playing football. Whatever memory problems I had would fade, too.

My broken ribs healed nicely. My worst remaining injury was that slash across my shoulder. It required nineteen stitches that required another decision about plastic surgery. I passed only to give myself a reasonable reason why men would not want me.

Debbie was a chatterbox.

John and Dave healed but John likes football and the prohibition about contact sports caused his reply to be, "Well, it didn't hurt Troy Aikman." Dave high-fived him and they seemed like new friends.

A lot of people came to see me and that was the most reassuring thing that happened during those three days. Dad was proud and Mom was just glad I was alive to be with her.

Oddly, the one person that did not come to see me was Nick Pruitt, Janine's father. Even Harley came to see me and joked, "You owe me a story, Hamilton."

"Which I will write," I answered in the same tone.

My brother brought his family and we had a good visit.

In all, everything was set for my last two visitors. LeRay Morrison showed up with Silas Morris as I was putting my shoes on to go home. They were still working on my home, still hammering up wallboard and

Chapter Twenty-Five

drywall. Debbie, who was already dressed, was planning on me staying with her until the lease expired or my home became habitable. For what it's worth, I was looking forward to being with her, to talking with her, to being able to go on with my life. Besides, hospital food is shitty at best.

LeRay was working for his mother and was expanding their menu to include several barbecue dishes. I was looking forward to going there to eat.

While it was good to see LeRay, it was Silas that brought the message.

"Miss Hamilton?"

"Yes, Silas?"

"Um, my mom wants to see you."

"Sure. I liked her."

LeRay looked a bit worried and I asked a bit fearfully, "What is it, LeRay?"

"Silas has been living with me."

I looked at LeRay and almost asked *him*. Then, I asked Silas, "Why? What's wrong at home?"

"Kanita."

"Who?"

"She lives with my mom. Mom heard what happened to Uncle Billy on the TV and she's real upset. Kanita's been living in her bedroom ever since mom heard."

"Is that why you're living with LeRay?"

"Missus Hamilton? She's been AWOL."

"From the army?"

"Yeah."

"Where does she live?"

"Hinesville."

"You know the address?"

He gave me an address on Madison Street in Hinesville and I looked at LeRay. He seemed to understand what I needed and just nodded.

"Deb?" I said.

"Yeah?"

"Can you take Silas with you to your place?"

"Sure," she said but had that nervous look on her face.

I hugged her. "She's a doctor, girlfriend. I'm alive because of her. She won't hurt me."

"Morgahna? I think I'm going to need you tonight."

"I'll be there."

"I ain't going to bed until you're home."

"Silas is a good kid. He'll take care of you."

We hugged and it was one of the best ones I ever got. Neither of us cried, sobbed or showed any pain despite the fact both of us knew better. "Love, ya, girl," I said.

"Me, too," she said with a smile that was as perfect as she was.

I checked out and LeRay drove me to Hinesville, a small town directly adjacent to Fort Stewart. A map of the area showed Madison being directly behinds the military's property. Michael Vick could throw a perfect spiral from Sylvia's backyard into the fort.

Her home was small and I wondered why she picked that neighborhood when she was a doctor. It was two o'clock in the afternoon when I parked in her driveway next to that Range Rover I recognized from Billy's house. It took a good five minutes for someone to answer the door and when someone did, it was a black girl. She looked frightened. That's the only word that registered when I saw her. I looked up at the facing on the house and said, "I'm sorry. Does Doctor Sylvia Morris live here?"

"Uh huh," she squeaked.

"Is she home?"

Chapter Twenty-Five

"Who are you?"

"Morgahna Hamilton. I met her…"

"Oh, Lord," she said quickly. "You're her," she said and became immediately confused. She turned and looked toward the back of the house and said, "She's back there, lady."

"Can I talk to her?"

"I don't know," she said.

The longer she talked, the more I realized it was her. "Did you call me a couple of months ago, lady?"

She got confused, emotional and upset and just started crying. She threw open the door and said anxiously, "You gotta do something!" Then she ran off toward what could only be a bedroom toward the left end of the house.

There was a time when I lived the perfect life. I was self-centered and totally so. I really didn't care whatever you thought of yourself as long as I was okay. I mean that literally, too. Murder, mayhem, common theft, abortion, adultery, any human weakness was okay because I was focused and none that stuff happened to me. Being self-centered left me alone to live comfortably and not worry about you.

The last few days pushed me so far from that life and that way of being that it scarcely seems like that was me. What once seemed like a perfect opportunity for career advancement now seems worse than anathema. Maybe I'll get used to that stranger I see in the mirror, but I hope not. She is a constant reminder that life is short and precious. She is a tool for me to use, one that will pry open old wounds and see what caused them. That person in the mirror is fresh, clean and is giving me a chance to live a very connected life, one that never seemed very important before now. That person looked out the kitchen window and saw a woman sitting alone in her backyard. She smiled at her and thought what anyone would think. *Ah, Sylvia. I really need to thank you.* Yeah, that's all I saw. I didn't see the pain, didn't see the reminders of my reflection, didn't see what was there until I opened the back door and went to where she sat.

She had a gun in her lap and when she looked up me, said calmly, "Go away."

I don't know guns and I hope I never do. They prove fearsome weapons and sometimes provide easy answers. I looked back at LeRay who stood in the doorway and by his expression, saw the gun. "LeRay? Go check that girl and find out if she's okay. Don't give her any more to panic about, okay?"

"You got it," he said. Then he stopped and asked almost timidly, "Are you okay?"

"Yes. Sylvia and me are going to talk a bit, be girls, Okay?"

He looked at me and then at her and said slowly with a firm nod, "Okay. I'll go talk to the girl."

The chair Sylvia was sitting in was one pulled from a patio set that rested on a empty cement slab. Maybe she once had ideas about doing more out here. Maybe. The location, though, didn't matter. She did. I took another chair from the set and sat it not more than six feet to her right and oriented it in the same direction.

"Morgahna?" she said. "If you try to stop me, I'll shoot you, too. Just stay out of it."

"Okay," I said. "You care if I talk until then?"

"Be my guest."

"Who's the girl?"

"Kanita."

"Where did she come from and why did she call me and start this?"

"Don't blame her, Morgahna. This is your fault as much as it is mine. In fact, you should shoot yourself, too."

It was warm and a few mosquitoes darted about.

"Well, sue me, but I'll pass. I've been close to death several times recently and I think someone wants me to live."

"Or keeps trying to kill you and you keep getting in the way of his plans."

I actually smiled. "Free will, I guess. Never counted you as one of those religious types."

Chapter Twenty-Five

She snorted. "Go away. If you're going to be cute, you're wasting your time."

I crossed my legs at the knee and said, "There was a time I couldn't do this. You helped put me back together and I never thanked you for it. Well, thank you, Sylvia. This whole ordeal has taught me things no one and nothing else could have. Without your help, I wouldn't be here to thank you."

She snorted and looked away, just looked toward the base beyond the trees. "Did you know he was an all-state running back twelve years ago? Did you know he was at the top of his class in the police academy? Did you know he could speak five languages fluently?"

I looked up, shielded my eyes from the sun and said, "Billy? There's a cocksucker that deserved to die."

"He was my brother, dammit."

"Evan was my husband, dammit," I replied calmly.

I realized that she was pretty in a very unaffected way, the type of woman that makeup would destroy, would limit and prove no answer at all. Her black hair sparkled under the warm sun. "People will blame me, Morgahna."

"Fuck," I snorted. "I already do."

Tears rolled down her cheeks. "See? If you cannot forgive me, then who can?"

"I blame myself for Evan's death, too."

"You should."

I grinned. "Well, perfect minds." Then, shielding my eyes again, I added, "Well, with one exception. I'm not going to kill myself."

She looked at me for the first time and asked, "I'm curious. Why not?"

"Tomorrow."

"That's exactly why I'm going to do this. I don't want anything to do with tomorrow and the future."

"Doctor, huh?" I said still squinting.

"Go away. That won't work."

"Don't expect it to, Sylvia. Just confirming things for your obituary."

"All you need to remember is that I failed at everything I ever did."

I smiled. "Kinda like me, huh?"

She shook her head and said, "You're going to have to explain that one, Hamilton."

I pointed across the yard and through the fence. "What's that big thing over there?"

"Water tower."

"Ah."

We didn't speak for several moments. Finally, I said, "You probably seen a whole bunch of dead people, huh? I mean, a doctor and all? Iraq? A crazy war? I'll bet they really mangle 'em, huh?"

"Nice try. After I'm dead, I won't care what my body looks like."

"Didn't think so. I was just saying."

"So, what happened?" I asked.

"What do you mean?"

"Well, just that. I know what happened to your cocksucking brother. He tried to kill everyone in Georgia that didn't agree with him. I mean, you. You're a doctor, knowledgeable and serving your country. I would think the service you provide whether for your country or your people would be enough. Me? Well, I can sympathize. Being a reporter is a noble profession and I wrote some good shit, Sylvia. I mean, really good shit. That's all it was, though. Shit. I was looking toward a promotion, was looking and angling how to get past my boss, Harley Hood. I figured he was an old fucker and would die soon and if my stories and credentials were in order that I'd be promoted. I didn't give a fuck about Harley. I actually took him to lunch a few times and encouraged him to eat steak sandwiches. Still, I was a reporter and that's a respected profession. I know where I screwed up. Where did you?"

Chapter Twenty-Five

She was wearing an old army t-shirt and dark blue shorts with running shoes. You would have sworn she was returning from a jog around the neighborhood instead of planning her last exit. She looked at me and did not smile. "You're a pain in ass. I should have let you die."

"Why didn't you?" I asked even though I felt I knew.

"It doesn't matter. Go away."

"No really, Sylvia. I don't believe you conspired with him to kill Evan, LaRuth, Artemis, Janine and those stupid friends of his. So, why didn't you let me die?"

That gun was too comfortable in her hand as she held it tightly in her lap. I had no intention of wrestling it away from her either. I wanted nothing more than friendship from her. I wanted nothing more than to share lunch gossip with her. She picked up the gun and pointed it at me.

"I was raped four times three nights ago, Sylvia. Pointing a gun at me won't scare me. Either shoot yourself or put it down. All I'm doing is talking and pointing a gun at someone is pretty damned rude."

She jammed it under her chin and for a moment I thought she was going to do it. "GET OUT, MORGAHNA!" she screamed. "I COULD HAVE STOPPED THIS AND DIDN'T! THAT'S WHAT THEY'LL SAY! MY LIFE IS OVER!"

I turned my head, closed my eyes and prayed silently. "Selfish bitch," I said loud enough so she could hear me.

"GET OUT!"

I paused, looked at the yard and said quietly, "Evan was a bastard. That's what I learned from this. He cheated on me and kept it to himself. You know what, Sylvia?" I said sadly. "You know what I learned while I was in the hospital those three days?"

"What?" she said despite her anger and pain.

"They were going to fire me and replace me with Janine Pruitt. Nick Pruitt's daughter was going to be my replacement. Yeah. I was a good reporter, too. And these were things Evan knew. You know?" I said idly, almost passively. "I think Evan knew and didn't know how to tell me. I think he wanted to let me know but was scared of me. I was stronger than him and that's what killed me. Me. I've been trying to blame myself all along for his death and in the end, it really was. I was just stronger than him and his sin was so great in his own eyes that he couldn't face me with it." Tears rolled down my face with easy grace. "I was stronger than him and now that I miss him, that strength is nothing more than an illusion. Sylvia? You do whatever you want, but I'll miss you."

I got up and said with my back to her, "Women were made for days like this, Miss Morris. A gentle breeze, trees for shade and lemonade. Days like this were made for you and me, made so we could share and laugh and cry without the reminder of the world looking over our shoulders. Sylvia? I have friends now, but you can never have too many of them. I'll always wonder what you would have said to Debbie, my friend. You know? She's going to have nightmares for years because of that box she was buried in. You didn't do that to her and I'd didn't pull the trigger that killed Evan. Am I responsible? Yes, but my penance is life and remembering what I did to another's. My penance will be memory and sandy brown hair that I can never twine in my fingers ever again. My penance will be you, too. We could have been friends, all of us. LeRay, Dave, even John Newell. I can't speak for them, but I'll miss you. Professionally? Yeah, maybe it would have been hard but doctors are a dime a dozen, right? I can relate, though. I gotta quit a job I wanted all my life and now find the price way too high."

I walked back toward the house and expected a gunshot. With God as my witness, I did. Instead, I got a question. "Why quit?"

"Because I did a good job, Sylvia. I was a good reporter and it wasn't enough."

"What are you going to do?"

"No idea."

"You called me Miss Morris, Why?"

"Distance. I need to forget you now and I find it might be hard."

"I thought he was telling the truth, Morgahna."

"Shoot yourself, Sylvia," I said. "I really don't care. I can learn medicine on the internet."

"Is that how you treat a friend?"

Chapter Twenty-Five

I turned and got angry for the first time. "Friends don't fucking shoot themselves, Morris! Friends tell all the reasons over ice cream and cake! Friends cry and scream and use profanity! FRIENDS DON'T FUCKING SHOOT THEMSELVES!"

She stood and held the gun at her side. "Fucking? That's profane."

"YOU AREN'T MY FUCKING FRIEND EITHER! YOU'RE PROVING THAT!"

"Can I tell you about him?"

"Why?"

"BECAUSE IT HURTS, MORGAHNA! HE HAD ME BELEIVING HIM!" she said as tears erupted from both of us. She took a step toward me and held out both hands, one that held a gun and one that didn't. "He told me that he wanted to help you because it would help him to forget! He told me that LaRuth was his wife and called him 'William'. He said he couldn't stand the memory and cried! I WAS IN IRAQ AND I BELIEVED HIM! I WAS THERE FOR EIGHTEEN MONTHS AND HE SENT ME HER PICTURE! HE SAID, 'THIS IS MY WIFE'. THEN HE SAID SHE DIED IN CHILDBIRTH AND I BELIEVED HIM!" She put her hands to her face and cried as she held that gun against her face.

I took a step toward her and said, "Is your pain so much worse than mine? Tell me, dammit! Tell me why this is worse for you! Tell me why I must face this and you just leave like he did!"

"Maybe I'm not strong! Maybe I'm like Evan!"

"And maybe you're a goddamn coward!"

As words began to lose their effect, as they began to fade, she said something I did not expect. "How will you respond to Alexis?"

I looked at her and everything about my life finally changed. Everything that had been pushing at me for almost five months came full circle. I suppose to that point all those changes I attributed to myself were mental ones. When she mentioned that name and saw I didn't recognize it, she stopped whatever course she'd been on and saw that I needed her and that need was palpable. She put the gun on the table and said, "Follow me."

No, I couldn't. "Lose the gun, Sylvia. I don't know what that means, but I'm not leaving you here with a loaded gun."

"Would you really let me scream if we were friends?"

"Of course."

"I could call you names?"

"I would expect it." We stared at each other, two fractured women who each knew more pain than fragile humans should be able to withstand. Me? I had the death of my husband. Her? The knowledge of what she permitted. Between us? Only friendship could heal us. Everyone involved in the story had been hurt and dented in some way. All of us were in pain. It was possible that what she knew was the one ingredient that would enable all of us to move on and away from the horrors of the last several years. Those years had moved relentlessly toward a climax that left all of us weak, spent and empty. Me? I can't say I was the worst of us because I never held a gun to my head and threatened myself with it. I was simply one of them and the one almost directly in the middle of that vortex. I was the one being pushed from all sides. Sylvia saw herself as above it, Debbie apart from it, LeRay trying to navigate through it and Dave merely as a spectator that got caught up in it. All of us have been transformed by it, though. All of us have been changed in some fundamental way.

And I was about to be shown the price of my arrogance.

She took the gun apart so fast that if my life depended on putting it back together, I'd be dead. Actually, I didn't care about the gun, just that it was no longer a threat. "Is that okay?" She asked with a smile.

"Yes."

She put her hands on my shoulders and said, "Morgahna? How strong are you really? Can you change that thoroughly?"

I actually smiled because I had no idea what she was talking about. "I don't have much choice, Sylvia."

"Yes, you do. You stopped me but that is only half the puzzle. Do you want to see the rest?"

I tried to laugh and it sounded nervous. "I don't know. Do I?"

Chapter Twenty-Five

"Yes or no, Morgahna. You give yourself high marks for being strong. How strong are you?"

It was put up or shut up. Those were the stakes and I couldn't back down, not after everything I'd said, done and all the pain I'd endured. I could not claim to be that quantitatively different person and not answer her challenge. I licked my lips nervously and said, "Well, I survived your brother."

She looked sad for a second and then said, "Yeah, you did. Are you ready for what Evan left you?"

"He left me something?"

"I believe he called it 'the package'. Do you want it or do you want me to keep it?"

I smiled. "And if you kill yourself? I get it anyway?"

"Bitch," she said simply.

"Okay, okay. Let's see this package."

We walked back into the house and angled back toward the bedroom. Sylvia nodded toward a room on the left, knocked briefly and said, "Kanita? You okay?"

"Yes," she said, her voice sounding happy.

LeRay was sitting in a rocking chair and holding the last thing Evan Hamilton would ever give his wife. I looked at him, looked at that baby and somehow knew everything I needed to know. "Alexis?" I asked the black girl.

"Uh huh. Alexis Jayne Hamilton."

"Can I hold her?" I asked.

LeRay got up and changed places with me. "Kanita called you because she felt guilty about the baby."

The baby. *There was a baby in that meeting. Janine was nursing. Billy Ray couldn't kill a white baby. He took her and gave the baby to his sister.* Alexis was maybe fourteen months old if my math was correct. *She has his eyes.* "How…" I said with some confusion.

"You already know Evan and Janine had an affair," Sylvia said.

"And the baby is theirs?"

"Yes," she said. "Kanita has been living here helping me raise her ever since that night. I was told that the baby was his, Billy's. That's why I helped him. To me, it was justice. It seemed that way. Life took one child and gave him one in its place. It wasn't until after Evan's death that I learned the truth."

She was sucking on a bottle, feeding. "I can't just take her. What's her status? I mean, legally? Who has custody of her?"

"If you do this legally, you have to give her to the state and adopt her. You're not her mother but could have been her stepmother very easily. Morgahna? Do the right thing here. Give her to the state and then adopt her. You might get temporary custody until it becomes permanent."

I had no illusions about my life if I did this. *Little girl? Who better to tell you about your father? You'll grow up hearing the most vile things and I might be the only one that can make your life anything but gloomy and dark. I might be the only person who can tell you about your father and why he was a great man.* She smiled around that nipple and I wondered if I was up to it, up to the task of raising a baby. Would the state even grant me that custody at all? I looked up at Sylvia and said, "I don't know anything about babies. I never wanted to be a mother. They have to know that."

Sylvia sat on the bed and looked at me. "Morgahna? I can make a nice speech here and get you all pumped up. In the end, though, it's up to you. She is Evan's daughter and you were his wife. What better person to raise her than you?"

"What if I make a mistake?"

"Everyone does. The whole damn story has been full of people making mistakes. Babies, I think, might be a way of correcting them."

Was that it? Was I being given that rare chance to correct the mistakes I'd been telling myself I'd made and had been making all along? Was that it? I smiled at Alexis and she gurgled around the nipple and kept drinking. "I'm not her mother," I said not to her but to them.

"A mother is the person who loves, adores and nags at them," Sylvia said.

Chapter Twenty-Five

"Are you okay, Sylvia?"

"I'm going to need friends, Morgahna."

I smiled. "I'm going to need help."

Kanita smiled and said, "Wow. And me needing a place to live."

Can a baby have four mothers? Sylvia, Kanita, Debbie and me? Is that possible. Maybe. "Can you keep her for a few days, Sylvia? Debbie's going to need me."

"Yeah."

I looked at Kanita. "I don't know you."

"I heard that speech about friends. Did it only apply to white people?"

"Of course not," I said smiling. "I have Dave and LeRay."

"Uh huh," she said. "Men."

But we all smiled. "We're going to have great lunches," I said.

I looked down at Alexis and said, "AJ. Alexis Jayne. My first daughter is named after a stock car driver." She smiled and that made everything worthwhile. Five months ago my life was hurtling straight as an arrow and I was missing all the details that were in the peripheries. I think, at least in retrospect, that everything happened for this moment, the one where I held AJ and burped her. All the sadness, all the pains, all the misdirected hatred all conspired to make me realize that AJ needed more than an upbringing; she needed a family that needed her and wanted her as badly as they wanted life itself. I can't say I didn't give AJ much thought because I did. She deserves as much as I always gave myself. AJ Hamilton is my atonement. I will be her mother, her friend and her confidant. I will love her, cherish her and help her be the person I never was. I will encourage her to have both friends and goals. I will teach her that both are necessary and both are attainable. I will teach her that values aren't things bandied about by moralists and politicians; I will teach her that values are what we see and come to respect about each other.

I will teach her that Mommy Debbie likes pink.

I hugged her to my chest and cried a few tears of happiness. No, I will never be quite as healthy as I once was, but that is such a small price to pay to the life that has been given to me, the life I have been asked to help shape and guide.

AJ? You have the best family in the world.

The best.

Chapter Twenty-Six

I can't say that everyone lived happily ever after but I can say that we lived ever after. That first night? Debbie woke at one in the morning when the night is the darkest and all the nightmares and threats that humans create for themselves are hidden in the corners where the night is the darkest and most threatening. She woke screaming, her hands clawing at a wooden lid that was just above her face, woke screaming into my arms. I held her as she cried and never allowed her to believe that it was an imposition.

She loved AJ.

Those fears and nightmares gradually faded and our friendship gained a solid foothold on Taylor Street. Yes, she lives downstairs now and is happier than ever. Kanita lives with me and I will not allow her to call herself a nanny. She is Mommy Kanita.

I see Sylvia rarely because her job makes her life hectic. We do have lunch and she has settled into the role of Mommy Sylvia. Those rare occasions when the four mothers are all together with AJ are special and we all toast iced tea to ourselves for having survived our old lives and slid happily and contentedly into our new ones.

I have *finally* learned to dance wearing high heels.

Harley is still as grumpy as ever so that hasn't changed. My story? No, it didn't win a Pulitzer for him, but it put him and me on all four morning TV news shows. I gained some notoriety and he gained a solidly respectful reporter. Dave and Merriam dated once and Dave saw his life needed go somewhere else and he never called her again, not as a date. His son, Nathaniel, is good and seems to respect both of his parents. John Newell calls occasionally but will never be a romantic interest. He looks a bit *too* much like Evan.

The oddest things that happened? Well, one December night just after a bad storm, the doorbell rang and I jumped up with AJ and we scampered to the door. She was at that stage. She scampers everywhere and wears us all out. I opened the door to LeRay Morrison. He was holding a small vase of roses in one hand and a bag of my favorite candy

Chapter Twenty-Six

in the other – Hershey Nuggets. "Everyone needs a friend, Morgahna," he said with a smile. "I need a date."

Yeah, LeRay Morrison is my boyfriend. Maybe that's a little extreme because Evan hadn't been gone for eight months when he knocked on my door. That night? We never did make it to dinner. We spent the night cooking one and called Debbie to come upstairs and join us. Kanita knows how to do barbecue and LeRay hired her as a part-time cook in his restaurant.

The best part though?

LeRay curled my toes when he kissed me goodnight.

God, I wanted to sleep with him right then and there.

He put his hand on my shoulder and said, "We have time, Morgahna. Not tonight."

Then he kissed me again and went home.

That was a tough night.

I smiled all night long and giggled every time Debbie sang that sing-song, "Morgahna has a boyfriend."

I always thought life was great and all mine, too. I was wrong. Life is great and belongs to all of us, not just to me. Now? Now, when I go to work, I sometimes carry a diaper bag and meet Kanita downtown in one of the squares. I went to LeRay's re-grand opening and ate a sandwich that Kanita cooked. Heaven in a bun. Mmm.

The business is doing better. That cook? Well, his name turned out to be DeWayne and he proposed to Alease and they're going to get married next June. Alease is a June bride. LeRay will be his best man and Kanita will be the matron of honor.

Tommy Underwood's trial is still ongoing, but at least he's in custody and off the street. Karin Hubbell took what was left of the business and moved it to a smaller location, but kept Shawna and Lisette. Bridget's marriage fell apart but she's stayed friendly and has another legal job in Historic Savannah. She became Aunt Bridget because AJ needed an aunt. Shawna is an occasional friend and we always find time for each other whenever life pushes us together. You can't have too many friends. She's dating Todd Gilmartin. Mom loves being Granny Evelyn and Mark came in and tossed AJ around like she was a doll. She laughed and giggled every time he tossed her and caught her. Uncle Mark is a lot better than my brother used to be.

Dave is dating *Debbie.* She is pretending to like his decorating.

Life has settled down and all of us are finding fun in it.

It sure beats the alternative.

Trust me on that one.

It *really* beats the alternative.

www.ingramcontent.com/pod-product-compliance
Lightning Source LLC
LaVergne TN
LVHW010147070526
838199LV00062B/4283